ECLIPSE

ECLIPSE

DIRK WITTENBORN

DODD, MEAD & COMPANY · NEW YORK

1 2 3 4 5 6 7 8 9 10

Library of Congress Cataloging in Publication Data

Wittenborn, Dirk.
  Eclipse.

  I. Title.
PZ4.W83Ec [PS3573.I924] 813'.5'4 77–24285
ISBN 0–396–07383–2

To Sarah

I would like to thank Allen Klots, Robert Peter Miller, and J.R. Wittenborn for their help and encouragement.

ECLIPSE

I

Spring had made a number of starts that year, but each time the crocuses and forsythia were ready to reveal their colors, winter would return. There had been a blizzard Easter morning, and spring continued to flirt with New York right into May.

But overnight all that changed. Winter was forgotten. A reluctant spring gave way to an eager summer. It got very warm, and sometime between midnight and dawn Steven Lerner kicked the blankets off the bed and began the most perfect day of his life.

He awoke very slowly on that second Friday in May. He wasn't yanked into reality by his wife's alarm clock or the baby or any of the other sounds that usually drove him out of bed. Instead he was roused by the touch of a heated wind on the small of his back. He felt as if he were being petted by a giant hand, and like the hairless beast he was, he shifted his position so he could feel it run the length of his back.

Like most people, Lerner and his wife rarely slept facing one another. He had always found it uncomfortable to dream so close to another person. But that morning when he opened his eyes, they lay front to front, their naked limbs tangled together. Her breasts were flattened against his chest, and her mouth was open and damp against the soft part of his neck. It was the way he had always thought lovers should sleep before he had ever spent the night with a woman.

Sarah was still asleep; her blond hair was spread out around her face like a golden fan. Without saying a word, Lerner pulled just far enough away from her so that he could touch her. He ran his finger down the inside of her neck, circled once around her left breast, and then moved toward her navel. The curve of her bosom and hip, the line of her stomach and neck fascinated him, but not in a sexual way.

This body that he had looked at and lived with for so long seemed

1

different. He knew it wasn't just that Sarah's shape was returning after having the baby. The contours of her form, the way her body rose and dipped against his own, reflected the feeling of that first day of summer. It had the same soothing rhythm as the breeze that had blown winter out to sea and awakened him so gently. The idea that she was part of the day, that as she slumbered by his side she was contributing to its magic, excited him. He felt himself grow hard against her thigh.

Without saying a word, without any grunts or pinched skin, they unfolded their limbs and rearranged themselves so that they filled each other's hollow spots. He kissed and fingered all the out-of-way places on her. As Sarah's body grew damp and opened for him, Lerner felt he was bringing her to life.

That Friday began with love as Lerner had always dreamt of it, but as it had never been. Sarah's mouth didn't taste of morning and his beard didn't chafe her flesh. As he slid himself into her, there were no hands pushing him away, no fingers reaching for the diaphragm in the bedside table, and no running off to the bathroom.

Penetrating deeper and deeper into her and himself, he drifted further and further away from the world that was beginning to take to the street and honk its horns outside their window. When the alarm went off, they didn't rush themselves or worry about Sarah's being late to work. None of that mattered. They let it ring. Riding each other faster and faster, its reminder faded into the background.

Blown on by a wind whose enthusiasm matched their own as it playfully scattered drawings and papers around the room, he forgot about where he was going or how he might be disappointed when he got there. There was only the now of the moment, nothing else. No thought, only feeling.

Clinging to one another, gasping for breath like two who had been washed overboard but miraculously awakened safe on shore, he knew they had traveled somewhere beyond their bedroom on Twenty-eighth Street. There he had seen something, felt something more basic and more immediate than anything he had ever known. It was beyond sex or love or passion. It might be called contentment but without the connotations of domesticity that the word normally conveys. He felt a primitive sense of satisfaction, a primeval lack of want.

Even after they separated themselves and began to dress, the day continued to charm Lerner. Sarah made crepes and they ate a whole jar of raspberry preserves with them. He never thought of the argument they had had a week before when he had told Sarah she was a "stupid little bourgeois goya" for squandering eighty cents on the preserves. As he licked off his fingers the same brand of jam that Rockefeller used, Lerner was able to laugh without any feeling of resentment or competition as Sarah recited in her Waspiest accent a rhyme for the day.

> Uncle Jim and Auntie Mabel fainted at the breakfast table;
> Listen, children, heed this warning. Never do it in the morning.

Then Lerner did a monkey imitation that sent mother and daughter Wendy into hysterics. He pretended to pick bugs off both of their heads and then eat them. After a first course of imaginary insects, Lerner went at a banana, scratching himself monkey style and making what he imagined to be chimp noises. When Wendy spit out the bite he offered her, Lerner picked up the half-masticated gob of fruit and then, to the amazement of all three of them, ate it with a great show of lip smacking and salivating.

Mrs. G (they called her that because no one could pronounce her last name), the Greek lady who ran the candy store downstairs, took care of the baby during the day while Lerner and Sarah worked. When Sarah picked up the infant and started toward the door, Lerner kissed them both several times. He tickled the baby with one hand and lifted up Sarah's sweater with the other, licking her breasts and doing anything else he could think of to delay their departure. Like every other aspect of the morning, their exit was exquisitely staged. Mother and daughter left with him telling them to stay. It wasn't until they were gone and Lerner licked away their raspberry kisses that he realized he was glad to be alone and was ready to work.

He expected the rhythm that had started his day so wonderfully to give way to his normal work routine. He was happy with the progress he had made that winter. He had planned to finish what he had been working on for the last two weeks. But the rhythm didn't fade; it was in him now, and it swept away his plans.

Instead of taking up where he left off, Lerner opened all the windows to get as much encouragement from the morning as he could and started something totally new. He didn't ease himself into

3

his work the way he normally did, with cigarettes, coffee, and several trips to the john. He started off at full speed and worked right through the morning, not stopping once to consider what he would do next. Lerner had no idea where he was taking himself.

He often talked to himself while he worked, but like the precocious child who asks his parent to feed him questions to which he has already memorized the answers, Lerner posed to himself only problems that he had already resolved. That day a voice that he sensed belonged to him, but that he had never heard before, whispered solutions to problems he had not even seen.

He worked that way until three o'clock, and then quite suddenly Lerner heard the voice of the first day of his summer hiss, "Get back," as if it were telling him to get out of the way of an oncoming car. He stopped, and when he stepped away and examined what he'd done, Lerner saw that any addition or alteration would only make it less. It was more complete, more finished than anything he had ever worked on. In a few hours he had gone further than he had all winter.

The weather, the way they had made love, his work—they were all too perfect to believe. He hadn't once been reminded of, or bothered by, the fact that he hadn't made a hundred dollars at his profession that year, that his own family was so ashamed of him that they told their rabbi he was dead, and his wife's parents told her every Christmas and Easter, "If you had to marry a Jew, Sarah, at least you could've married one that knew how to make money."

All this and the day wasn't even over yet.

Lerner was aware of how fragile perfect things are, how quickly they can be shattered by alarm clocks and babies' cries, by one's own doubts. But he couldn't resist the temptation, as he stood by the open window, of going over the events of the day, trying to break them down, to find some pattern, some explanation as to why he was filled with an optimism that was almost frightening. He searched his mind for the missing factor in the formula of this special day in May.

He compared it with the few other moments in his life he remembered as being perfect—the damp morning under the front porch steps when he was first touched by someone other than himself; the afternoon he learned he could transpose onto paper the light which mottled his family as they drank big glasses of seltzer water after eating too much lunch; the day he had amazed his bearded grandfa-

4

ther, who was a well-known amateur lepidopterist, by capturing a Diana butterfly in his bare hands, a species the old man insisted had never been sighted on the open plains of the continent.

Lerner knew the dates and details of these past flashes of fulfillment, but they all came and went so quickly he never got a chance to examine them fully. In the excitement of it all he forgot the split second when he knew they were peaking. He remembered vividly how these experiences had begun and ended, but the heart of them remained a mystery.

The spell of satisfaction that surrounded these past highs was brief, but that Friday the same feeling was still alive in him hours later. He wanted to capture the elusive quality of this day. Just the way he had caught that butterfly as it floated haphazardly over a field of black-eyed Susans, taken home that dark Diana, its black wings spotted with a blue borrowed from a robin's egg, preserved it with chloroform, and framed it behind glass, Lerner wanted to grab hold of the essence of the day. He wanted to extract its secret, bottle it up inside himself so it would always be there, so that at will he could transform the ordinary into the sublime. He wanted to mystify the world just the way he had his grandfather. Never had he been so close to it. He could feel it brushing him like the velvety wings of that butterfly fluttering against his sticky palms.

Steven Lerner was an explorer. If you called him that, he probably would have returned the compliment by telling you that you were an asshole. But that's what he was. He was built like a boxer and dressed like a laborer. He had the sort of muscled fleshiness that has to be exercised or it turns to fat. At thirty-five he was still hard.

Lerner's expedition didn't take him out of New York. He was able to purchase all the equipment he needed in a hardware store on First Avenue. His adventure took place in the north light that filled the front room of the railroad flat he lived in on Twenty-eighth Street. He shared the same passion as the men who searched for cities of gold or the Northwest Passage, but what Lerner pursued was more illusive. Steven Lerner was a man in search of feeling. He was exploring that last unmapped area whose topography is still vague, that unknown realm waiting to be explored by each of us—ourselves. It was this search, this exploration of himself and others, that made him an artist.

Lerner painted pictures of the feelings he pursued, but his paintings bore no resemblance, gave no hint of the scene where he had first sensed the feeling he would later paint. There was no reference in his work to the individual or incident through which he had discovered an emotion that he would eventually struggle to capture on canvas. To include that sort of information would limit his art.

The picture he had painted that Friday made his other paintings look muddled and stilted. It wasn't that this latest painting was more beautiful than the others. It was just less an imitation; it had a life of its own.

He hadn't been thinking of the sea when he painted it, but that was what he saw when he looked at it now. The colors floated on the canvas. They seemed to shift and rearrange themselves before his eyes. The blues and greens of the painting rolled and reached out to him.

Lerner discovered many things on that Friday in May, but he never recognized that it was his struggle, the adventure that went into the making of his art, that gave his canvases their real beauty and made them timeless. His search, the scale of his voyage, not what he found, testified to his brilliance.

But in 1952 there were few who would have called Lerner an artist. Not more than a hundred people had any idea of the struggle he was making on Twenty-eighth Street. He was in the tradition of the explorers who have made our most potent legends. The world at large didn't believe or understand the object of his quest. It wasn't ready to recognize his discoveries.

No one painted like Lerner, but there were a few other artists in New York at that time who shared his desire to do more with painting than reassure the world that a chair has four legs and that a person has only two. Lerner knew most of these men and women who wanted to change the way the world looked at art and artists, but he was friends with only two—Billy de Kalb and Jackson Pollack. They were the only ones who tested his eye, whose work and spirit held up to his examination.

He couldn't remember how they had met the others who sat with them in the sculpture garden of the Museum of Modern Art every Friday afternoon. These artists sought each other out in spite of glaring personality conflicts and discrepancies in talent. Their lack of success, their hunger attracted them to one another. Lerner, Pollack, and de Kalb were the heart of this group. Even then they left little room for the others in terms of both personality and art.

Normally Lerner looked forward to talking with these men who shared some of his problems. Usually he was eager to check his progress against theirs, to talk of revolution and art instead of how they would pay the rent and the grocery bill. But that Friday Lerner was not interested in the comfort and competition he found with the artists who met in the garden of the Museum of Modern Art.

Lerner stood in wonder of the painting he had just finished. The life in this sea of color was more real than his own. He felt himself being eclipsed. Then he heard the roar of a car engine and the smell of leaded exhaust. He looked out the window and saw Mrs. G's son, Jimmy, sitting in his brand-new Buick convertible. The top was down and the radio was blaring.

A crowd of old men and young boys was gathered around Jimmy. He sported a greasy jet-black pompadour of such substance that it looked more like a helmet than hair and a white satin Korean War jacket with an eagle embroidered on the back.

Jimmy was a celebrity on Twenty-eighth Street. He was a war hero, a mythic figure who hadn't obliged the fates by dying gloriously in the war or expiring quietly after the treaties were signed. His exploits in the private battle he continued to wage were legend—the night he outraced the police on the Belt Parkway, the time he was arrested for swimming nude before a dirty dawn in Central Park. Some said the $6,000 car was stolen. Others insisted that Jimmy worked for the mob. Those who were drawn to Jimmy and his car knew no more of the truth about Jimmy than the artists who gathered in the garden of the Museum of Modern Art knew about Lerner.

Jimmy's and Lerner's friendship was unlikely. They had nothing in common but an overriding fear that their real feelings were misperceived by everyone, even themselves. Late at night they cruised in Jimmy's convertible, drank beer, threw the empties out the window, and laughed when the other tried to be serious. Jimmy drove Lerner to the Museum of Modern Art every Friday. When Jimmy looked up and saw Lerner peering down on him from the third-floor window, he shouted, "Hey, quit playing with yourself and get down here . . . you're late."

Lerner looked at his watch. He should have been at the Museum ten minutes ago. He was tempted to forget it, to stay in the sanctuary of the world he had painted around himself that afternoon. But when he looked out the window at Jimmy, who was spellbinding those who only partially dreamed what he acted out in full, Lerner saw this prototype of James Dean as a blank canvas. Feeling the same sweet breeze that had helped him begin the day, Lerner was filled with the arrogant optimism that he might be able to order the range of emotion he sensed in Jimmy. Lerner believed that he might be able to bring a dormant part of Jimmy to life just the way he had infused energy into a few square feet of pigment on canvas.

Lerner grabbed his coat and descended the stairs three and four at a time. The engine roared, the tires squealed, and they were off. Jimmy started to tell Lerner about a girl who couldn't speak any English. He had picked her up the night before at Palisades Amusement Park.

Before he finished the story, Lerner suggested, "Why don't you write it all down?"

"What are you talking about? I ain't no writer—can't spell or nothin'."

"That doesn't matter. Just put it down as if you were talking to yourself."

"Only nuts talk to themselves."

"You know what I mean . . . getting it down is what is important . . . so you don't forget it."

Jimmy shifted the blue kitchen match that protruded from his lips like a fuse. "Bullshit! Forgetting them as soon as I tell them is what is important about my stories. That's why I tell 'em."

"Bullshit!"

Jimmy pressed the accelerator. "O.K., wise guy. There's a pencil in the glove compartment. I'll tell you the story of last night, and you write it down." Before Lerner could reach for the pencil, Jimmy began. "When we was on the rides and laughin', it didn't matter that she couldn't hardly speak any English, but when we woke up after I fucked her, I knew I was just screwin' myself. She didn't understand a thing, and I wanted to get rid of her 'cause I knew I'd feel less alone by myself than with her." Jimmy was angry at Lerner for pressuring him to reveal so much. "Go on. Why don't you write it down? . . . It's your story just as much as it's mine."

"No, it's not," Lerner insisted.

"Oh, yeah? . . . Then tell me why it is that you lock yourself in a room all day and paint . . . 'cause it helps you to forget that in the end you're always alone."

Jimmy shifted lanes recklessly, braked hard to avoid a taxi, then pushed the accelerator to the floor. Lerner pointed in the direction of the Museum and shouted at him to make a right on Fifty-fourth Street, but Jimmy didn't hear. He roared past the corner, ran the light at Fifty-ninth Street, and turned into the park.

It was then that Lerner realized how fast he was going. People, cars, the trees of the park were all a blur. The colors smeared together. The images became impossible to define. The sensation frightened Lerner—not because he thought they might have an accident, but because it reminded him of what he had been after all morning, of what he was chasing even as he was painting, the moment that becomes lost in the heat of life.

He yelled at Jimmy to stop. When he didn't, Lerner grabbed at the plastic knob with the four-leaf clover sealed in it that was fixed to the steering wheel. The car swerved, just missing a street lamp, then it bounced over the curb and skidded across a field where a large flock of pigeons was feeding. When the car came to a stop, there was only the sound of pigeon wings beating the air.

Lerner left Jimmy gripping the wheel so tightly his knuckles were white. As Lerner walked away, Jimmy began to laugh. The engine roared to life and Lerner wondered, *Is he laughing at me?* But when Lerner turned around to ask him what the joke was, the car and its driver had vanished. He could hear the Buick chirping and laying rubber as it skidded north through the park like a steel cricket.

The Museum of Modern Art had always been special to Lerner. As he walked toward it that afternoon he remembered how he had journeyed there the first day he had arrived in New York in 1946. Carrying an old blue suitcase with a rope tied around it and a cardboard box containing his paints and brushes, he had stepped off the bus from Chicago and had walked straight to the Museum.

He didn't quite believe that the Mondrians, Picassos, Matisses, Klees, and Brancusis that he had looked at in photographs really existed. The prospect of seeing them in person, of being able to stand close to them, gave Lerner the same thrill that viewing celebrities gives most of us. When no one was looking, he put down his possessions and ran his fingers over the surface of Picasso's "Les Mademoiselles d'Avignon." He stayed in the Museum until the guards made him leave.

9

It was more than a museum to Lerner. At first he went to study the art—to see what the artists had done, to see where he could go that they had never been, to clarify his own talents—but it quickly became something more than that. Looking at all the art that had triumphed over the limitations and short-sightedness of the age when it was made gave him hope. Lerner made so many pilgrimages there that he became friends with the club-footed Irishman who took the tickets, and he didn't have to pay to get in.

That Friday several long, black limousines were parked illegally in front of the Museum. Walking past them, watching the way their buffed fenders distorted his image, Lerner heard a chauffeur, wearing boots as brightly polished as the car, announce, "Had Ike in the back with him and his old man this morning. From the way they were talking, you'd think they was the ones that was running for President, not him."

The Irishman who let Lerner in for free pointed out the rich and powerful men who were on the board of trustees of the Museum. They walked in as if they were entering one of their homes and passed by Lerner as if he were invisible. Lerner had seen the faces of these men who were "yes sirred" by future Presidents, who for almost two hundred years had succeeded in giving the American people the illusion that they really had a choice when they voted. Lerner had always despised them, but somehow the fact that they had built this Museum, that it really was their house and their paintings, had never bothered him. This Museum that had given him so much had never been tainted by them until that afternoon.

Lerner was surprised the others weren't waiting for him. Normally he would have visited his favorite pictures, but the urge to see these paintings that had become like old friends over the years was gone. He decided to wait for the others in the sculpture garden. As he stepped outside, Lerner told himself that the estrangement he felt for this place was due to the chauffeur's comment, but it was more than that. Just as the rich ignored his person, this museum ignored his art. Lerner's paintings didn't hang in the Museum of Modern Art.

Standing in the stone courtyard that was just a touch lighter than the gray of Rockefeller's suits, Lerner looked up at the sky. He had the urge to run home and touch the picture he had made that day. He was sure he would find it more satisfying than running his fingers over the limbs and lips of Picasso's "Ladies from Avignon" as he had

10

on his first day in New York. Lerner no longer needed the Museum's art or even his friends. He was beyond that sort of dependency.

It began to rain as Lerner reveled in the new-found sense of independence that the day had delivered to him. It was a warm rain; it relaxed him, and he laughed as the others in the garden ran back into the Museum to escape the shower.

Pollack arrived eating an apple. When he stepped inside the glass doors to the Museum, he shook himself like a dog and looked at the people scurrying down the street to get out of the rain. He was reminded of the movie "The Wizard of Oz," of the Wicked Witch of the West melting. Holding his apple in his mouth, he shook his head once more, showering a nearby guard with a fine spray, and looked for his friends. He was usually the one who kept them waiting, and he didn't like it that they weren't there. When the guard he had sprayed told him, "You're not allowed to bring food into the Museum," he was ready to leave. But then he saw a girl wearing a bra that made her breasts so pointed they reminded him of the cone that was used to demonstrate problems in geometry class. Pollack swallowed the apple in two bites, eating it core and all the way horses do, and followed her. The girl's breasts were so pointed he imagined they could pierce his flesh.

As that image was being replaced by one of a tribe in Africa, where the women altered the shape of their bosoms just the way Maiden-form did, Pollack saw Lerner standing out in the rain.

Pollack stuck his head out the door and shouted, "What are you doing out there?"

Lerner raised his arms over his head, smiled and answered, "Growing."

Pollack joined him and within minutes the rain stopped. He coughed up one of the seeds from his apple and spat it into the reflecting pool that surrounded the Maillol statue of a distinctly different species of woman from the one he had seen inside. "I don't believe the assholes in there."

"Did they make you pay?" Lerner asked.

"No, I got in for free."

"What's wrong then?"

"The guard wouldn't let me bring the apple I was eating inside. I mean, what is the point of a fucking rule like that?" Pollack wondered aloud.

"Most people like rules like that."

"That's like saying most people are assholes."

"All right, then, why do we put up with them?" Lerner demanded.

"The rules or the assholes?"

They were all out of sorts with the Museum that day.

Their friend, Billy de Kalb, appeared with pieces of string tied around his pantlegs to keep his cuffs from getting caught in his bicycle chain. It made his trousers balloon, giving the frail man a lighter-than-air quality, as if at any moment he might float away. This blond, bespeckled painter's comical appearance made Lerner all the more conscious of how this man was forever squinting, trying to look beyond some terrible glare.

De Kalb sat down across from them, lit a cigarette, and announced, "After making a quick tour of this Museum, I have made an important discovery."

"What?" Lerner asked.

"That the biggest problem in my career is that my parents came to America. If they'd waited a year and I'd been born in Hamburg instead of Hoboken, I'd probably be famous."

Lerner pushed his wet hair behind his ears. "How's that?"

"I don't think they believe great art can be made by Americans." Billy gave special emphasis to the word "they."

Lerner looked at his feet. "We're a very insecure country."

Pollack didn't appear to be listening. He pushed droplets of water across the smooth surface of the bench as if his stubby forefinger were a brush. When Pollack realized his doodle was beginning to look like the girl with the dangerous breasts, he wiped the drawing away and joined their conversation. "They'd rather have the worst studio sweepings from Gertrude Stein's salon than our best painting."

When Robert Farthington, the tall thin painter in his late twenties, stepped into the garden, Lerner spit into the pool. Farthington borrowed heavily from all three of the painters, but there were others who did that. What Lerner couldn't ignore, what made him so angry that he refused to allow Farthington to see his pictures, was that Farthington took what was the weakest from all their work. Farthington didn't even have the vision to steal their best.

The others didn't mind Farthington as much as Lerner did. They admired him for admitting that he had rich relatives and refusing the money and position they offered him, but Lerner wasn't taken in by

12

that. He was certain that Farthington's hollow-eyed shabbiness was studied to match their own hungry look. Lerner had an image of Farthington sitting in his studio going at new clothes with razor blades and sandpaper to make them look worn out.

Farthington was accompanied by Luccio Cortesi, a nineteen-year-old Italian who had been hanging out with him that spring.

After handshakes and hellos, Farthington positioned himself between Pollack and de Kalb, pointed toward the glass-walled fortress of art, and asked a question they all raised privately. "Do you think we will ever be hung in there?" He used the plural "we" that always infuriated Lerner, as if by linking himself to them, by riding their creative coattails, he might increase the chances of his pictures' hanging alongside those of Europe's middle-aged modern masters.

De Kalb took out the bottle of bourbon that helped fill out a jacket two sizes too large for him. As they passed it around, the conversation rebounded off their fears like the silver ball in the "Strike It Rich" pinball game that Jimmy manipulated so skillfully in the back of the candy store.

Each answered Farthington's question affirmatively, but in the comments made after their initial affirmation of faith in themselves and each other, the pronoun "they" took on a more and more ominous meaning. "Eventually they will have to recognize us."

"If our art is popular with the masses, then they will have to include it."

"They will hang our pictures, but they won't really value them until one or two of us have died."

Lerner wondered how this "they" had obtained the power to pick the art in our museums as well as our Presidents.

As Farthington's question hung over them, the voice that had coached Lerner while he painted came alive saying, "Of course, your paintings will be in there." But when it was Lerner's turn to reassure them, he didn't relay this message. Instead, he turned his head to make the most of the sun and answered glibly, "What difference does it make?" Lerner had wondered as often as any of them if his paintings would hang in the Museum, but the fate of his art no longer seemed in doubt. "They," with all their power, could do nothing to stop it.

As the silver ball of doubt bounced back and forth between the men, Lerner wondered if this voice that spoke up so clearly in him had always been there. Why hadn't he heard it before? Was it a new addition to himself sprouted from a seed blown in on that warm breeze? Did the others have a voice? What did theirs say? Would they tell him even if he asked?

Luccio had contributed very little to the conversation. It was understandable that he found these older painters intimidating. Lerner watched Luccio gaze at his own reflection in the pool. Reassured by his own beauty, by a physical perfection in himself that his work would never have, Luccio proclaimed in his slightly sing-song Italian accent, "It's all so contrary to the spirit of art. . . . You work in solitude for years, but then there is the desire, the urge to call them in. . . . Why do we want them so? Even if they were interested, the questions they'd ask would be absurd. Why did you do this or that, what does it mean? . . ."

Pollack gagged for a moment, then coughed up another seed and spat it at Luccio's feet. "It's not that simple. I want to show my work . . . I need to show my work to see if it stands up."

De Kalb looked surprised. "To them?"

"No, to their bullshit, to see if my paintings can survive the exposure, rise above their crap."

Luccio looked back at his reflection. "What if your painting survives but you don't?"

Pollack looked beyond Luccio. "If my painting makes it, I can take that."

The bourbon went back to de Kalb's lips. "If that happens, you don't have any say in it. It takes you, you don't take it. Unless you take care of it like Gorky."

Lerner wondered if de Kalb was referring to life or death by "it," then asked himself, "Is this what their voices tell them?" When de Kalb looked up for his opinion, Lerner stated flatly, "That will never happen to me."

De Kalb finished the bottle and put it back in his pocket, proclaiming dramatically, "Art is long, but life is short."

"That could never happen to me." Lerner waited for the voice to support his faith.

But before it could, de Kalb went on, "If your work is to be really good, you have to put so much of yourself into it that there's no way you can avoid being left more vulnerable than you were before you began."

14

Pollack winced, more at what de Kalb said than at the memory of Gorky's suicide. "Didn't he leave a note?"

"Yes, it said 'Good-bye, my loved's.' "

Their statements annoyed Lerner. He wanted to hear from his voice. "Gorky killed himself because his painting arm was paralyzed, his wife deserted him, and his work was destroyed in a fire. Showing his painting didn't have anything to do with it. Lots of people would've ended it after going through that sort of shit. His being an artist, his painting, had nothing to do with it." Lerner was shouting by the time he had finished. Everyone in the garden was staring at him.

They sat in silence, unable to comfort or communicate with one another. Then Farthington stood up, slapped his hands together and said, "You know someday we should get a really big canvas, put it down, and all go to work on it together." Everyone but Lerner laughed at the idea. They were all relieved to talk about something that wasn't threatening.

"We could each take a different color."

"Or we could divide the canvas up into quadrants."

"Like a map."

"The way you throw paint around, Pollack, you'd never be able to keep to your own territory."

"And you'd be sticking those fucking mouths of yours every-place."

The idea was Farthington's ultimate fantasy, and he kept repeating, "I'll buy the canvas."

Lerner had never worked on the same canvas with another man, but he had painted in the same room with others. Just a few weeks before he had allowed Luccio to paint with him. It would never happen again. Lerner knew he could never paint the way he had that afternoon in front of another human being, and he had no intention of painting any other way. It had become too personal. Lerner couldn't even entertain the idea. Farthington's suggestion repulsed him.

It was then that Stan Rothkoph arrived. Not being a painter, Stan was only a charter member of their group. To feed himself Stan gave tours at the Museum and licked stamps for a curator. It kept his tongue in shape. He was always talking about starting an art magazine that would be a showcase for new artists, and occasionally he

15

sold a review or essay about painting to an already existing periodical. In spite of the fact that Stan reminded Lerner of a man in his home town who became rich promoting dance marathons in the thirties, Lerner believed it when Stan said he was a genius.

Stan didn't have much more money than the rest of them. It was too hot for the brown tweed suit he wore all year around. His armpits were dark with sweat. He slipped as he hurried down the stairs, tearing loose the sole of his left shoe. They all laughed as Stan got to his feet and made his way toward them, the would-be critic's sole flapping like a misplaced tongue.

Stan grabbed Lerner and de Kalb and Pollack sputtering out, "I've got fantastic news for you." Their dreams had been answered, they would have their show, their chance to see if they and their work would survive. Silvia Horst was putting on the show in her new gallery. It was a converted gymnasium. They didn't expect to sell any of their paintings, but at least she knew this "they" that had no room for them in their museums. De Kalb and Pollack did a little dance to the gods who had bestowed this blessing, however mixed, upon them. Lerner only smiled and shook his head in disbelief at the day.

Stan was as excited as they were. "I told Robert that the show was a possibility the other day. . . . I was going to tell you all, but he told me it would be better to wait."

Farthington laughed nervously. "I figured if it fell through why should all of us be disappointed."

Pollack and de Kalb were too busy dancing to hear what was being said, but Lerner took it all in. Stan patted Farthington on the back. "Oh . . . and I hung the painting. It looks even better than it did in your studio . . . thank you again."

It was Farthington's turn to pat Stan. He turned to Lerner. "It was an early birthday present." He pointed toward Rothkoph. "It was the least I could do for the man. This man who will be remembered as the most important critic of the century will enter his third decade next week."

Lerner was positive Farthington hadn't been part of the show when Stan had first discussed it with Silvia Horst. As Lerner listened, Farthington continued, "Oh, and I tried out that idea you had for cutting down the canvas . . . you're right. It does give the images a more trapped feeling."

Farthington had been included not just because he massaged

16

Stan's ego; Stan wouldn't have fallen for something that obvious. He had indulged Stan's dream of getting his hands into a painting before it was finished. Lerner was sure that without ever declaring it the two had made a pact to facilitate each other's most egocentric fantasies. Stan would be more than just a critic. He would be a contributor, cropping canvases and picking colors, a sweating muse with a receding hairline, and in return Farthington would be linked to Lerner, de Kalb, and Pollack forever.

The arrangement disgusted Lerner. He told himself he would never believe anything Stan said about his work.

They decided to leave the Museum and go downtown to the Cedar Bar to celebrate their show. De Kalb took his bicycle on the subway downtown. He and Pollack had a contest to see who could ride from one end of the car to the other faster. The celebration almost ended there when Pollack, his head down and peddling furiously, ran into a policeman who had just entered the car from the other end. They were thrown off at Twenty-eighth Street. De Kalb bought another pint of bourbon and rode circles around the others as they walked the rest of the way to the bar.

An out-of-work actor, two other painters, a sculptor, and a stoned jazz musician joined the party at the Cedar. Stan said they were going to call the exhibition "The New York School." Lerner drank with them until Pollack got so loaded that he began to challenge Farthington to a fight. He left as soon as he had the satisfaction of seeing Pollack bloody Farthington's nose. He couldn't wait to tell Sarah how the day had fulfilled its promise.

Stan had said the ceilings of Horst's new gallery were very high. Walking home, Lerner thought about the painting he would make for the exhibit. He had no idea what it would look like—he wanted it just to happen, to come to life the way his painting had that afternoon—but he was positive he wanted it to be very big. Lerner found the idea of a painting two-stories tall terribly exciting, a painting so large "they" couldn't put it in their museums even if they wanted to. There was so much he wanted to show and tell Sarah that on Twenty-fourth Street he couldn't wait any longer and he began to run.

When he turned down his street, the sun was just beginning to disappear behind New Jersey. It was the same angry red color as Jimmy's car. Its glare blinded Lerner. He couldn't make out the faces in the crowd gathered in front of Mrs. G's candy store. The audience was larger than usual, and Lerner wondered what new feat Jimmy was spellbinding them with. He looked for the Buick, but a police car was parked in its place. There was no music, only the sound of static from the patrol car radio.

When he looked inside the store, Lerner saw Mrs. G. pulling at the bun that was coiled on the crown of her head like a black snake. She was screaming and and slapping at two policemen. Sarah was in the crowd holding the baby. They were both crying. Lerner didn't have to ask. From the comments being exchanged in the crowd, he heard the story, or at least the parts they would remember.

"I heard he was going eighty."

"What are you talkin' about? He told me just yesterday he could crank her up to a hundred easy on that stretch of road."

"Had a blowout."

"After he swerved to miss a kid."

"Anybody would have lost control."

"Went right through the windshield."

"Nah, the steering wheel crushed his chest."

"There was blood everywhere."

"He was dead when they got there."

"No, he wasn't. . . . I heard that cop there say that Jimmy was laughin' when they found him."

A pock-marked teen dressed exactly like Jimmy, a youngster Lerner had seen sitting by the fender of that Buick, feeding on Jimmy's myths, was so impressed by the idea of Jimmy excitingly laughing at some private joke that he dropped the bottle of Orange Crush he was drinking. As the glass shattered on the sidewalk, Lerner's day began to splinter.

He took Sarah up to the apartment, half hoping that they might find some way to forget what had happened. He kissed her tears and took her to his studio. He wanted to show her the painting.

"I have a surprise for you." As he opened the door, Lerner had the terrible fear that it would be gone, that like Jimmy this painting he knew to be better than anything he had ever done might not have survived. But it was there, lying on its back, reaching up to them in the last light of the day. It was more complete than he remembered. It made him forget. Looking into it, he felt that breeze on his back;

18

its undulating rhythm comforted him just the way Sarah's body had that morning.

Lerner whispered to her the way he used to in temple. "Do you feel it?"

Sarah began to cry. At first he thought she was weeping because the painting was so beautiful, because it offered such relief, sanctuary from the horror story that was being told and retold on the street below. But then he saw that she wasn't even looking at the picture. "I can't look, Steven . . . all I can think about is that boy dead."

"He wasn't a boy." Lerner had opened himself up to Sarah, but she wasn't able to fill the place he had made for her. The fact that he resented Jimmy for spoiling this moment, for coming between them in death, made Lerner doubly depressed.

The baby cried throughout dinner. Lerner made a halfhearted attempt to cheer the child by putting on a repeat performance of his monkey act, but it didn't work. All that seemed to be left of the joy they had had with each other that morning were the dirty dishes in the sink. Lerner didn't even feel any satisfaction when he told Sarah about the show.

After the baby exhausted herself with her tears and fell asleep, Lerner sat in the kitchen and smoked cigarettes while Sarah washed the dishes. As the gray haze of cigarette smoke gathered around them, he thought of their conversation about the chances of survival for both art and artists, and he remembered de Kalb's pronouncement, "Art is long, but life is short."

Then Sarah, scratching a gob of dried preserves from one of the breakfast plates, said, "Why did he do it?"

"Do what?" Lerner thought of Gorky.

"Carry on the way he did . . . always taking chances . . . driving crazy . . . what was he trying to prove?"

"I'm not sure."

"It catches up with you sooner or later when you take those kinds of risks. Such a waste. . . . He never accomplished a thing."

"How can you say that?" Her attitude shocked him. Lerner felt that he was talking to a stranger.

"What did he do? He never worked at anything."

"He made an art out of living. . . . Don't you understand?" Having succeeded in making her cry, Lerner heard from the voice that had

19

remained silent throughout the tradgedy. "All great art is tragic and timeless." Lerner started to repeat its message to Sarah, but then stopped, realizing that piece of information would only make her feel more helpless.

He stood up, took the dish from her hand, and kissed her. Though their mouths were bitter with the taste of tension and cigarettes, the warmth of their bodies comforted each other. Lerner led her to the bedroom, knowing that Jimmy had killed himself. Maybe he had swerved to avoid a child or had had a blowout. That didn't matter. His life, his legend, and his vision had set him on a collision course just as surely as if he had driven the Buick into the concrete highway divider on purpose.

Eager to forget, wanting to start fresh the way they had that morning, they pulled at each other's clothes. Two milk-white buttons flew from Sarah's blouse as his mouth searched for her nipple. They might have recaptured some of what they had found so easily that morning if they had been gentler, if they had taken more time. Lerner didn't stop to admire the hollows and mounds of her body, and Sarah held him so tightly that he could do nothing else but grind blindly against her. Her arms and legs were wrapped around him as if she were trying to squeeze an apology from her husband for making her see how limited her vision was of Jimmy and of everything else.

There was an urgency to their movements as if they were racing the clock. Lerner didn't understand it. They were hurting each other in their desperation. They were touching the same places, mouthing the same parts of each other, going through all the same motions they had that morning, but it was a completely different act they were engaged in.

He felt her hand, her nails cutting into him as she jabbed him at herself again and again until her body opened in spite of itself. Lerner tried to alter the pace, to find the rhythm they had traveled with before, but it was hopeless. Fast or slow, their movements carried the same message.

Their bodies sweated from the labor of it all. In the end, just as Sarah had misunderstood Jimmy, she mistook Lerner's gasping effort to save something of the day for both of them as passion. She reached around behind him and squeezed his testicles as if milking him.

Sarah screamed as she came and then squeezed him again, but he

20

felt nothing. Lerner could have made himself have an orgasm, but he didn't want to. He was hard, but he had nothing for her. He jammed himself into her once more, grunted, and rolled off her. He put his arm over his eyes and nodded when she asked him if it was good.

It wasn't that Lerner didn't love Sarah, or that she didn't excite him. It was beyond that. Lerner wondered where he could go, where he might feel less alone.

He waited until Sarah was asleep before he left her. The temperature had climbed into the eighties. Their skins stuck together as he pulled himself free from her. Then, without hesitation, without stopping to put on trousers or a shirt, he went into his studio.

Lerner squatted by the painting he had done that day and peered into it to see what lay beneath the colors that glistened on the surface of this picture that spoke of the sea. The picture glowed blue-green in the darkened room as if illuminated from within. It reminded Lerner of the bits of life that he saw luminescing in the surf the night Sarah had coaxed him, this boy from the Midwest who could barely float, into the water over his head.

The rhythm of the picture caught him and washed him back over the day. Hunched over his still-damp creation, Lerner became lost in the memory of the way he and Sarah had made love that morning, and for an instant he caught sight of that moment when he had escaped time, when he was so completely involved that he forgot about how it would end.

His vision of perfection now flickered before him like that dark-winged Diana. It excited him, and as that part of him that Sarah had squeezed without result brushed against the canvas he saw what he had done.

Naked, Lerner jumped up and turned on the light. As he examined his other paintings, Lerner saw that this one was really no different, it was just more evolved. In making it, he had realized what he was pursuing, what part of experience he was after. It was those moments we don't seem equipped to remember, that are too intense for us to learn from, as if part of our brain isn't developed enough to correlate and store information about them.

Lerner saw what he'd been hinting at, flirting with, since he'd begun painting, since that afternoon he'd felt like Houdini after drawing a beam of light. Lerner knew that whatever magic he had created had occurred by chance, in spite of himself rather than because of himself. But at least now he knew where he was heading, in what direction to set his charts.

He would paint the picture for the show that night. Using up the whole of a roll of canvas he had expected to last a month, Lerner stretched the cloth from wall to wall. This painting that blocked his way to the door, that left him no way out, was eight feet wide and nearly twenty feet long.

The voice directed his hand and eye as he started in on the painting with great sweeps of yellow and orange. Lerner, now the captain of his own ship, felt that he was finally getting the winds he had been waiting for. It never occurred to him that he was being blown toward the eye of the storm.

The brushes and sponges Lerner normally painted with weren't big enough for this picture. There were places on the canvas he couldn't reach, so he tied his largest sponge to the end of a broom handle and worked with that.

He mixed dozens of colors, splattering himself with shades of yellow and orange that he laid one on top of the other. He wove together a hundred variations of these hues, so intricately that no one could perceive the order, the formula he and his voice had arrived at. He wanted the picture to be like the sun, and when this heavenly body he had created was ready to challenge the day, Lerner's voice told him it was done.

Standing before the painting, his naked body splashed with paint, holding the clublike brush he had fashioned to help him paint, Lerner looked primeval, like some ancient man staring at a monument that he had built with his own hands but did not fully comprehend. Under the lights Lerner's muscles stood out. His thighs and stomach were stained red as if he had just gorged himself on an offering to this creation. Lerner was wary of the painting. It frightened him. It was so bright he couldn't look at it. From where he stood, he couldn't see clearly what he had done.

The temperature was nearing ninety. Lines of sweat ran across the colored markings on his body. His limbs ached from his labor. Then he remembered that the stepladder he had used to paint the apartment was in the closet behind him. Maybe that would help him get a better perspective on what he had accomplished. It took the last of Lerner's energy to pull out the ladder, set it up, and climb to the

22

top. He hadn't realized how the day had drained him. He sat on the topmost step, held his head in his hands, and looked down into the painting. From there he could see everything he wanted to see. It had an energy, a warmth all its own. The painting was as the voice had said it would be.

Lerner waited for dawn. He wanted to see how this picture would stand up to the sun the rest of the world looked to. It was then Lerner thought he heard the sound of Jimmy laughing in the distance. Lerner turned to the open window and cocked his head to single out the ring of laughter from the night noises. When the voice began to whisper, "It will never die," Lerner forgot about Jimmy and looked back at this painting whose immortality the voice proclaimed.

II

On a cold but clear Friday afternoon in January 1969, more than ten thousand people gathered in New York City to protest the war in Vietnam by marching the wrong way down Madison Avenue. The air was so cold it made the back of one's throat feel as if it were bleeding, but the chill only made their penance seem more real. Their frosted breath and flared nostrils complemented the air of self-righteous indignation that was so in vogue during the last year of that decade. The long hair that swirled in the winter wind made some of the demonstrators look like Renaissance royalty and others look like gnomes. Some blue-jeaned and booted, others patched and colorfully mismatched, they all wore variations of the uniform that those men who sat in the garden of the Museum of Modern Art during the last nonwar war wore. What had been necessity had become fashion.

You could be cynical and say that most of the old and young who were marching had money in their pockets, were white, protected by their education, and had no real fear of going to Vietnam, but you would also be missing the point.

It was a lack of illusion that made the war in Vietnam so scarring to America. If those protestors could have believed, if life had given them an adventure, they wouldn't have marched in the streets. But it is obvious and easy to say this now.

There was a sense of kinship, an affinity, among the marchers that day in 1969. It went beyond age, lifestyle, or politics. It wasn't just outrage over a war which, like all wars, was stupid and obscene that tied them together. Wars end and are forgotten. That bond, that outrage, was one that would dissolve over the years. They weren't out in the cold just to protest a war. They had taken to the street to show their anger for a world that had made it impossible to believe in it or in themselves.

The sky was more than clear. It was empty. There were no clouds, no streams of jet exhaust or industrial haze from New Jersey. There was nothing to give any sense of depth or perspective. It was an odd day.

There was a vacuum between heaven and earth, and the light that rained out of this void was so bright and unrelenting that it tricked the eye. It made everything shimmer—the marchers, the mannequins that pouted behind glass, the barred bank fronts, the mounted police that were there to escort the marchers, even the derelict old woman who had gathered herself and her bulging shopping bags out of the stoop where she had spent the night to see the marchers off—they all glistened. They all seemed special and golden in that cold light.

Just as the march was about to begin, Steven Lerner, who had not aged well in the last seventeen years, climbed out of a Checker cab on Park Avenue and lumbered west toward Madison Avenue and the assembled protestors. A small man and a red-haired woman hurried after him. Lerner's new uniform was tailored by Dunhill, but his expensive clothes didn't disguise his bloated body. One would have hardly recognized him as the same man who had stood naked before his art in the darkness.

There were artists in that march. When Lerner had received a letter asking him to join the demonstration, he had laughed and thrown the request away.

Instead of stepping into the avenue and taking the place that was waiting for him at the head of the march, Lerner threw open the door of Chenonceaux, a French restaurant with tea roses, crystal, three forks, and the best *saumon en croûte* on the continent. On that Friday in May 1952, Lerner hadn't known this restaurant and the things for which it was famous. He could have painted and lived for a month for the price of dinner for four at Chenonceaux.

Now he could easily afford to eat there. But Lerner didn't have to pick up the check for luncheons and dinners in fancy restaurants. Artists who become famous, who become legends before they die, are always taken. Artists pay with something much more precious than money—they pay with their time.

The week before, Lerner had attended a party at Chenonceaux given by one of those men who never used to see him when they passed in the Museum of Modern Art. He was guest of honor. Several Lerners hung in the Museum now.

The aging painter stood in the doorway of the restaurant and glared at the crowd. Harold Barclay, the elegant little man who owned the Winston Gallery in New York, Paris, London, Rome, Zurich, Los Angeles, Tokyo, and Toronto, held the door open for Lerner. Barclay had backed Lerner's legend. He had made a fortune selling Lerner's art around the world.

Maggie Lawrence shook her red hair, turned down the collar of her sable jacket, and stepped inside. Lerner had written a check for the jacket the day after Sarah's funeral. It was the only thing of real value Maggie had obtained from Lerner. He hadn't given it to her because he cared so much for her, or so little about his wife. He did it to protect himself. The jacket was a weapon. He could point to the sable as proof of how exploitative he feared Maggie to be.

Lerner was quick to judge the marchers. He was ready to announce, "They're the ones who are getting fat off the war. They aren't risking a fucking thing. They've never taken a stand alone in their lives." But he saw something in the cold glare of the sun that stopped him.

Whistles blew. Unintelligible voices spoke gravely through bull horns, and the crowd surged forward. But they were not confronted by the war machine or elected officials, or that fabled hydra, "the system." It was the bag lady who stood in the empty avenue to face them. Carrying balls of string she would never unwind and old newspapers she would never read, the old woman screamed, "What do you want? Are you all crazy? There's no way you'll ever . . ." But before she could finish, the chanting crowd was upon her. It swallowed her up and drowned out her warning.

There was something about the old woman that was familiar. She caught Lerner's eye. Who was she? What did she remind him of? Then the memory of Jimmy's mother screaming in her candy store began to echo inside the hollow fat man named Steven Lerner.

Mrs. G has to be dead by now! Lerner told himself. It was the way the bag lady coiled her hair into a bun that made her look like Jimmy's mother. The snake of hair had turned white.

Lerner hadn't thought of Mrs. G or Jimmy for years. As he eyed the demonstration, he wondered whether Jimmy would have joined them. Or would he have stayed on the sidelines and watched, perched on the seat of whatever was the equal of that big Buick today? Would he have laughed?

26

Maggie was getting impatient. "I thought you were hungry."

Lerner had organized the luncheon. Barclay touched a gloved hand to the painter's shoulder. "Come on, Steven. Let's go in. I can't wait to hear this new plan of yours."

But Lerner didn't respond. He was overcome by a need to belong. He stepped toward the street. "Why the fuck didn't you tell me they were having the march today?" Lerner looked at the marchers longingly. "That's where I belong, not in some bullshit French restaurant."

Barclay and Maggie exchanged an exasperated look. "We can go wherever you want," Barclay told him with a forced smile.

"I want to go with them." Lerner pointed to the first line of marchers. He recognized Billy de Kalb. Lerner was embarrassed, then angry.

Maggie stepped out in the cold and took his hand. "But you said yourself that they are just protesting to make themselves feel less guilty. . . . Remember?" Lerner didn't remember, but he had said it. "You told me you were going to write an article about it. . . . I'm sure Harold knows a magazine that would publish it."

Barclay took Lerner's other hand. "Of course. All you have to do is write it." Barclay's smile mocked him. It reminded him of how many months it had been since he had touched brush to canvas.

As thousands marched down the glass and steel walled canyon of Madison Avenue, Lerner allowed himself to be led into the paneled and scented cave of Chenonceaux. Many of the men and women who were marching so optimistically downtown that day were just as desperate as Lerner, but his growing awareness of his depression and the futility of trying to escape it made him particularly pathetic.

There was one in that march who was different, at least then he was different. He had no interest in protesting, no desire to judge, no need to demonstrate his passion in such an obvious way. Andrew Crowley only wanted to watch. His only demand of himself and others was that his view not be obstructed.

From a distance this tall, thin, but slightly round-shouldered owlish painter with his white hair looked like an old man, as if the perspective he kept on life had aged him. But up close Andrew Crowley didn't seem at all old. His bleached platinum-blond hair, a shade lighter than Marilyn Monroe's, and his hot pink oversized horn-rimmed glasses accented the youthful spirit that he embodied.

He had a pointy nose and large green eyes. His face was always flushed, but it didn't have that just-slapped look that men who drink too much get. His cheeks were rosier, his coloring more childlike than that. Andrew's perpetual blush of innocence made him look even younger than his twenty-nine years.

Andrew stood out in that mass of individuality that filled the street. He wore a black satin jacket embroidered with the name of an Air Force base in Korea and an eagle clutching bombs in its talons. A pair of white flannel trousers, a shirt with vertical stripes, a tie with horizontal stripes, and a broad-brimmed cowboy hat with a sprig of mistletoe in its band completed the costume. As always, his socks didn't match.

Andrew and his art were full of irony and contradiction. He painted light-hearted subjects seriously and serious subjects comically. His pictures were realistic, and that factor alone separated him from most of the art world. He was the exception, not the rule.

His work didn't fit into any genre. It wasn't pop. It wasn't surreal. And it certainly didn't fit into the common definition of abstract art, though it was undeniably abstract in the truest sense of the word—in its effect on the viewer. He was different from the abstract expressionists like Lerner or Pollack—men who had rebelled against the whole concept of art, who started the New York School of painting and whose influence could be seen in a dozen different second-generation painters like Frankenthaler, Stella, Louis, Holland, and Nowland. Andrew wasn't burdened with that responsibility. His painting was too specialized, too peculiarly personal for others to follow. If he wasn't bound to any manifesto or movement, his revolution, his insights were private.

The scenes he painted were often easily recognizable—swimming pools, bedrooms, supermarkets—but there was a subtle way he altered the reality of things and places familiar to all of us that set the imagination free, that transformed them into a springboard for one's own fantasies. There was none of that what-you-see-is-what-you-see attitude in Andrew's art.

He filled many of his paintings with people, posed friends and acquaintances, some famous, some not, in such a way that far more of their story was told than they had ever intended. Andrew's paintings were like riddles.

The same qualities Andrew wanted in his art he looked for in his

28

friends. He was always more satisfied with what he found in his work than what he saw in people. In that way alone he was like Lerner.

Andrew had also been asked to take a place with the artists and politicians and poets and priests and movie stars and college presidents, those who earnestly showed their best sides to the TV camera that rolled before them as they led the march. But Andrew was quickly pulled into the heart of the crowd. He found the nobodies so much more interesting than the somebodies. He could invent stories and feelings to match the features on their faces or the cut of their clothes. Andrew would gather bits and pieces of life, images and ideas, from the nameless thousands that surrounded him. Then he would reassemble them in his studio in a way that told more of the everyday mysteries of life than the real people or the actual facts could have.

Everyone knew Andrew, but he had only three friends. When a woman nearby shouted, "That man stole my hat!" Andrew knew without looking up that one of them had found him.

A girlish enthusiasm bubbled beneath Tessa Merritt's words. She was accompanied by the other two, Bob Cross and Sidney Hauptman. "Better your hat than your heart," Bob Cross told her as he touched his chest.

Sidney put his hat over Tessa's crotch. "But we all know where her heart is."

Tessa looked as if she had just sauntered off the pages of *Vogue*. She was that rare woman who was comfortable in the poses, as well as the clothes, of haute couture. Tessa liked to slum it with the rich and the poor. She was a jewel lost in the gutter of her late twenties, a well-set beauty with onyx-black hair and aquamarine eyes. The way she wore clothes, the way she moved made her beauty seem harder and more frightening than it really was. She was pursued and let herself be caught regularly. She swore that Andrew and Sidney were the only men she could spend a whole day with. No one ever saw her husband, and no one ever would have guessed that she had two daughters, one in nursery school and one in kindergarten.

Sidney was the sleepy-voiced curator of twentieth-century art at the Metropolitan Museum of Art. He looked like a bearded fat boy playing dress-up in his embroidered cowboy shirt and bow tie (which Andrew had taught him how to knot properly). At first glance, Sidney seemed neat and self-conscious, but Andrew knew him to be

29

aggressive, shrewd, loyal, and, in spite of his physique, to have broken many a heart on Christopher Street. Sidney appeared to be anything but a curator of America's most staid and important museum.

Bob Cross was just as enigmatic. He was an Episcopalian in a primarily Jewish guild of art dealers. While he was at work, he appeared to be the embodiment of the "get loose," "anything goes" spirit of the sixties, the perfect man to sell Andrew's art. But each evening he went home to his college sweetheart with a sigh of relief.

Tessa kissed Andrew. Andrew kissed Sidney. Bob kissed Tessa. Sidney kissed Bob. By the time that was taken care of, Tessa had forgotten about the cowboy hat that Andrew had borrowed from her. "God, the funniest things have happened to Sidney this morning. He was showing me that Bacon I've been thinking about buying, and we finished just as the girls were getting out of school, so we decided to have a quick lunch with them. In the middle of her ice cream, Anabelle reached up and ran her finger over Sidney's face and beard and said, 'You're fat . . . you smell bad . . . you're funny-looking . . . you wear glasses, and I love you.' "

"I always wondered what your secret was," Andrew said.

"Usually it takes only one of my charms to get them," Sidney boasted.

Tessa took out a cigarette and waited for a light. "God, Andrew, don't you think you're pushing it a bit getting your picture in *Vogue, WWD,* and *Time* all in the same month?"

Andrew struck a match, "It was my mother's idea."

"Pretty soon you're going to be famous," Tessa warned him.

"Wouldn't it be awful if they loved you more than your art?" Bob speculated.

Andrew laughed. "I'd just write to Ann Landers."

It was true. Andrew was becoming a celebrity. He was the most sought-after young painter in New York or anywhere else. These three guarded their relationship with him. They were careful not to let others get too close to Andrew for fear they might lose the influence they imagined they had over the white-haired artist. Messages weren't relayed, guest lists were screened, and newcomers who were too clever were made to look foolish. Andrew didn't mind the Machiavellian manipulations that went on around him. This triumvirate, like Andrew's idiosyncrasies, helped keep the world at bay.

They marched down Madison through the Seventies and the Sixties, past the galleries that were stacked on top of each other on Fifty-seventh Street, the elegant showrooms where a single Crowley or Lerner was often sold for more money than most people earn in a year. As they walked out of the Forties and into the Thirties, Andrew, Tessa, Bob, and Sidney talked about organic food, super-realism, the heartbreak of psoriasis, Sidney's piles, Rembrandt, Tessa's crabs, Andrew's last opening, the new show at the Metropolitan Museum of Art, Bob's wife, Tessa's boy friend, Andrew's boy friend, Sidney's boy friend, the price of gold, the melting of the polar ice cap, and how paraplegic war veterans went to the bathroom. They talked about everything except the war. Their feelings about the war were obvious, and the obvious was the one thing they could never bring themselves to talk about.

The march was to end at Washington Square with speeches and a rally, but at five-thirty, still fifteen blocks shy of the finish, Tessa shouted, "My God, we're late! . . . We've got to go right now."

As she began to tug on his arm, Andrew called out, "Where are we going?"

"To a party," she said as she steered him toward the sidewalk.

"What sort of party?" Andrew felt himself being pulled against the human current he had been moving with.

"The usual last night on the planet sort of affair."

III

No one gave parties like Libba Winthrop. Who was there and what happened in her house were reported in papers and talked about for weeks. Everyone liked these parties because they seemed so spontaneous. But in truth Libba plotted every detail of these events with the utmost care. She created a lovely arena for her guests. She did more than just supply the usual drugs and drinks that allow us to give and receive wounds without feeling too much. She picked music that would add just the right element of tension and nervous energy, pink lights to make everyone's complexion rosier than it really was, and compiled her guest list as if she were matching gladiators for the games, games made all the more vicious by the amount of ego and the lack of bloodshed.

Libba was an elegant woman, and just as she knew all the subtle and hard-to-find ingredients that go into a coquilles St. Jacques or a good steak tartare, she knew just how to put together a perfect party. She had a genius for it. She always used the best raw materials.

The party was for her new boy friend, Ben Holland. He was part of that second generation of abstract artists that followed Lerner. His show had opened that afternoon at the Winston Gallery. All the names from the art world were there—artists, dealers, curators, collectors. For seasoning, she had also invited Black Panthers, ambassadors, fashion designers, luminaries of the rock and movie worlds, and the headmaster of her son's prep school. There were equal parts beautiful people flown in for the evening and downtown types who took the subway to Seventy-seventh and trucked over to Fifth. There were dirty T-shirts, bare bosoms, and black ties.

Ben Holland would base a whole show, paint twenty or thirty pictures, on just one of the colored ideas that rippled across the surface of a single Lerner. Lerner's struggle and international success made it possible for the thirty-three-year-old Holland to earn well over $100,000 a year from his art. What Lerner resented most was not Holland's money and fame, but his ability to enjoy them.

"I've finished five pictures in the last month. Painting better than I ever have . . . ever. I'm working on one now that's fifty feet long. Had to knock down a wall in the studio to put it up. You have to see it. . . . I'm gonna have a big show in the spring," Lerner told those who crowded around him hungrily flashing their teeth in smiles.

The party that Friday night wasn't for Lerner, but by baiting those around him with references to new pictures and shows that would never be, the big man who had become fat succeeded in making it his party. Yet he wasn't happy; he felt trapped.

As the elevator doors opened and they stepped into the hallway outside Libba's penthouse, Andrew was still protesting, "But I don't want to go to this party for Holland."

"It will be fun," Tessa told him as she led the way toward the roar of the party.

Andrew picked at his teeth with the gold toothpick he wore around his neck. "But I didn't go to Holland's show . . . I don't even know what his new paintings look like."

"Does it matter?" Sidney added dryly as he lit a fresh Cuban cigar.

"Holland still paints stripes, only now they're like the ones on your tie instead of like the ones on your shirt," Bob told him with a smile.

Andrew looked down at his horizontally striped cravat. "I knew I shouldn't have given him one for Christmas."

Tessa kicked open the door with the toe of her red snakeskin boot. There was Ben Holland, puffing on a joint, contorting his face as he described the moment he discovered the artistic implications of the horizon. Holland looked up. Andrew patted him on the back and announced, "It was to die, Ben . . . to die. That's all I can say." Before Andrew had to explain, he disappeared into the party.

Holland didn't understand, but a few minutes later he was heard using the expression, "It was to die," when referring to the strain of the transition from the vertical to the horizontal stripe.

Tessa, Bob, and Sidney found Andrew sitting in the corner hiding behind the *New York Times* reading an article about endangered species. He was wondering how he might include one in a painting.

"You can't take him anywhere," Sidney whispered to Bob.

Tessa snatched the newspaper out of Andrew's hand just as he was reading about the plight of that first cousin to the unicorn, the narwhale. "You just don't want to have a good time tonight, do you?"

Andrew peered through his glasses at the room full of people. "It looks like a lot of fun. I wouldn't like it."

As soon as Tessa exposed Andrew, several people in the room began to gravitate in his direction. Men and women looked, pointed, and whispered. Conversations were cut short and hors d'oeuvres swallowed in one gulp. The first to make a move was a large-lipped curly-haired young man who had alternately sulked and looked for Andrew for the last hour.

His name was Jamie Katz. He was twenty-three years old. He was the son of a nouveau riche furrier in Scarsdale. When Jamie was naked and silent, he reminded Andrew of one of Caravaggio's boys. Andrew had lived with Jamie for almost a year. They were lovers but not friends. Andrew found it easier that way.

Jamie was always looking for some crack in this jewel in whose glow he loved to bask. But he could never see a way to bite into Andrew. He had tried to hurt him, to distract him, to make him jealous, but because of Andrew's attitude of emotional laissez faire, he always ended up looking foolish. Jamie was left with no alternative but to worship Andrew.

Jamie put his hand on Andrew's thigh and leaned forward to kiss his lips, but all that Andrew offered was his left cheek. "Where have you been?" Jamie demanded.

"Protesting," Andrew said sweetly.

"Tessa, why did you tell me to come so early?"

"She wanted you to see democracy in action." Andrew winked at Sidney.

"And what does this have to do with democracy?" Jamie asked as he gestured toward the crowd.

"Being able to rub shoulders with those you envy is what democracy is all about."

Everyone laughed except Jamie. They quickly settled into their favorite game, commenting on the people that were drawn toward Andrew. Stan Rothkoph was the most important modern art critic in the world. He had named movements and schools of painting. Those who used his colors were always in the running and usually won in the ongoing art sweepstakes of the sixties. When Rothkoph appeared, Andrew whispered to Sidney, "The thing I can't under-

34

stand is if Stan tells Holland and the rest what to paint—how wide the stripes should be and what colors to use—then crops the pictures, why doesn't he just paint them himself?"

As Sidney stood up to embrace Stan, he answered matter-of-factly, "He's allergic to paint."

The next to join them was Alden Thayer, the Lindsay look-alike who was director of the Metropolitan Museum of Art. He gestured toward Holland and the party and asked, "Well, Andrew, what do you think?"

Andrew shocked them all by answering, "Modern art bores my ass off. That's why I like that place of yours."

Then Bob pointed to a white-haired society matron with a cane and a diamond tiara. She had parked herself near the caviar. "She's a Chrysler or a Studebaker . . . one of those car people. She comes into the gallery twice a month, looks at everything, writes down the prices, asks for a discount, then takes me to lunch, but never buys."

Before anyone else could comment, the old woman looked at them and called out, "That's right . . . and I tell you, one doesn't have to possess something to appreciate it."

Andrew liked the idea. The old woman stared at him, then pointed at his hair with her cane. "Young man, why do you dye your hair?"

Everyone smirked and waited. Andrew had been asked the question thousands of times. He had many good answers. Andrew smiled impishly. "Blonds have more fun."

The old woman wasn't taken in. "Rubbish!" she told him and left the room.

Her response made Andrew think twice about why he really did bleach it. He ran his fingers through his platinum hair and remembered that when he'd left home nine years ago it had been dark brown. He had bleached it the day after he arrived in New York. He did it the first time for the shock value—to make it clear to himself and his family that he was different, that he was an artist. But he kept it that way for another reason.

Andrew lit a cigar. When he looked up, Tessa was staring at him. "Why do you dye it?" she asked.

Andrew smiled, and, mimicking the dowager's Boston Brahmin accent, answered slowly, "To remind myself that my adventure is special."

"Look! Andy's got a dachshund." Jamie waved to Andy Warhol

and his gang. They all looked wonderfully white, as if they'd spent the first ten years of their lives in a closet with nothing to eat but mothballs.

As Jamie blew kisses, Sidney told the others, "Yesterday I went down to the Factory and saw the portrait Andy did of me."

"Is it a very wide portrait?" Tessa innocently asked the overweight curator.

"Don't tease. Anyway, it wasn't very good so I said, 'Listen, Andy, it's O.K., but I'd like you to do it again and put the art in.' "

"You didn't!" Bob shook with laughter.

"What did he say?" Andrew asked.

"He slapped his forehead—" Sidney did the same "—and told me . . . 'Oh, that's it! I knew I forgot something.' "

Warhol and his entourage were going to another party. "It'd be a howl! Let's go with them," Jamie begged.

"I don't think so." Andrew yawned.

"You're such a pill today."

"Does that mean I don't go down easy?"

Tessa goosed Andrew. "No, it means you go down hard."

The room was crowded with people and egos. Peering out at the world through his thick, hot-pink spectacles, Andrew felt as if he were looking into an aquarium filled with a species of fish that luminesced most brilliantly when feeding. He saw it everywhere. It was taking place all around him.

Thayer motioned for Harold Barclay to join them. Barclay had tried several times to induce Andrew to leave Bob Cross's firm and join the stable of artists at the Winston Gallery. Andrew wanted more than money. Libba Winthrop, radiant with her new face lift, smiling as if she had a coat hanger in her mouth, charged toward Andrew. Bob's wife had just arrived, and Andrew knew she was nervous and would feel snubbed unless he talked to her alone for several minutes. Jamie was holding up Warhol's squealing dachshund for examination, and Sidney wanted to introduce Andrew to the Californian who had just paid $54,000, the highest price on record, for a Crowley.

Andrew was surrounded, but unlike most of us who have an eye, who see what's happening in the aquarium, Andrew never felt trapped. He never let his feelings about the spectacle of life paralyze him. He had a thousand tricks to elude them, to keep them from cornering him.

Smiling to himself, Andrew pulled out the little Minox camera that he carried with him everywhere and announced, "I think I'll take a picture."

They loved it. Instantly the little group that had formed around him began to arrange itself. Andrew walked away from them and put in a flashbulb. There was a great jockeying for position and posing. But Andrew had no intention of photographing them.

He turned his back on them and focused the camera on a red-nailed hand braceleted in gold. The person belonging to the hand was putting out a cigarette in a plate of food that had been left unguarded. The flash made Lerner pause in his monologue. He shook his head, rubbed his eyes, then went on aggressively, "What are you talking about? Anytime you use a figure in a painting it's a crutch! . . . Of course, you can tell if a guy's a fag by his work. It shows every time. . . . Asparagus . . . asparagus makes my piss stink. . . . I never cared about the money. . . . Barclay and all the rest, they're all merchants. The joke is they're not even good merchants. In this last deal I made, I got all of 'em by the balls."

Lerner stuffed a handful of macadamia nuts in his mouth, chewed noisily, and asked the young painter whose work was reminiscent in spirit, but not style, of some of Lerner's own early paintings, "I saw you at Cortesi's, didn't I? . . . You were talking to Billy de Kalb's wife. You fucking her? . . . You fucking him?" Before the painter could answer, Lerner asked another question. "You still painting?"

"I'm a painter."

Lerner put his arm around him comfortingly. "Forget it; it's already been done. Go into insurance; that's where the real money is. People are frightened to death of losing what they have."

Lerner grabbed another drink and lumbered into the library. He looked around the room for someone either too intimidated or too dependent upon him to challenge what he said or did. He was just zeroing in on a number of likely victims when he noticed a man sitting at a chess board in the corner.

He was the headmaster. He sat there so confident and sure of himself in his tweeds. Libba had told him about Lerner, and as he waited by the chess board he hoped Lerner would come by. The

37

headmaster prided himself on his game. He honestly believed that the fact that fat ugly men like Lerner made art and were famous was one of the great injustices of the world. He felt that those like himself, those who looked right and sounded right, whom he liked to call civilized, should play that role. He made his move. "Would you like to play?"

From the way the chess men were positioned Lerner knew the man was better than he. Lerner smiled condescendingly.

"I think I'm out of your league. I was chess champion three years in a row at Harvard."

The headmaster gave Lerner the same smile he used with the child he knew was cheating but couldn't prove it. Anyone who had ever glanced at one of his catalogs or read the endless stream of articles about him knew Lerner had never gone to college.

Lerner still couldn't figure out why he felt trapped, why he felt as if he were being watched. As he finished his fourth vodka, he realized that in every room he'd been confronted by one of his own paintings. In the dining room there was the square blue one he had finished just after his son Peter had been born. In the library there was a little red one called "Heat," which Libba had sandwiched between a Warhol silkscreen of Jackie Kennedy and a bronze beer can. Lerner would have preferred that his were the only paintings in the room, but it really wasn't the way they were hung or the company kept that bothered him.

He so wanted to be comforted, to be distracted from this feeling that pushed him into the night, that he didn't mind when Luccio Cortesi embraced him and kissed him on the cheek. "How are you, my friend? You have been so busy with those lawyers that you have no time for me." Luccio still painted. He was known, but not famous.

"It's all settled now."

Luccio had been talking to Libba's cousin, Sally Byrd. She was on the board of a museum her family had founded in Cincinnati. Lerner was pleased that Luccio was so quick to turn away from her. "You know I spent all morning gazing into that first picture you gave me. You remember, the yellow one, "Midday." It was amazing the way it held me." Luccio squeezed Lerner's fat arm. "I wanted to take my shirt off and lie in front of it. It was like I was by the sea."

It was just what Lerner wanted to hear. He smiled at the memory of it. "It was a strong picture, wasn't it?"

38

"Of course, you know Sally Byrd." It was obvious that she found the prospect of Luccio's taking off his shirt far more exciting than the picture. Luccio put his arms around both of them. "You must come to my house and see the picture."

He beamed at Lerner and hugged him again. "We painted back to back in the old days, and because there was so very little money we had to steal to eat. And of course, because I looked so innocent, he made me take the things." The woman barked out a shrill laugh.

They had painted together only once, and he had no memory of Luccio's ever stealing anything for him. But Lerner found Luccio's nostalgia soothing. Sally Byrd screamed, "You didn't!"

"Of course! I would do anything for this man. Sally thinks the museum in Cincinnati might want my big painting you like so much. The blue one . . ."

Suddenly Lerner saw what Luccio was up to. He thought to himself, "That bastard never stole for me! He thinks he can trade on my name."

But then Luccio put his face to Lerner's ear and whispered, "Simon told me about your wanting me to be an executor and everything. Of course, I'm flattered, but I'm not very good at that sort of thing. . . . You really ought to think about someone else, you know."

"Simon will talk you into it." Lerner wondered if he were wrong, if he had judged this man he had known for seventeen years too harshly. He always wished that there was some way to test things, to be certain of his art, of himself, of his friends, those who said they liked him and his work. He longed for some way to cut to the bone of the truth. It had become an obsession and colored everything he did.

As Lerner lumbered into the next room, Luccio called out to him, "We have much to talk about. I'm going to come down to your studio at dawn and surprise you. Maybe tonight. We'll drink and argue the way we used to."

If Lerner hadn't seen Andrew, or, more accurately, the eagle embroidered in gold, silver, and scarlet thread on the back of his jacket, he probably would have started a fight at the party. He had done it before. But that jacket made him think of Jimmy. When the figure turned around and he saw that it was Andrew Crowley, the two characters became linked in Lerner's mind. Except for the jacket, Jimmy and Andrew had nothing in common. Their hair, their clothing, their features were all different, but that didn't matter to Lerner. He had had eight vodkas, most of a bottle of wine, and two Valiums since lunch. He wanted to think that there was hope.

"Jimmy's dead, Andrew's alive, and I'm . . ." Lerner thought. He watched Andrew laugh as he put the camera back into his pocket. Lerner asked himself, "How has this one survived . . . how did he get away with it?"

If Andrew had painted like Lerner, if he had in any way infringed on or challenged Lerner's position, if his art weren't so rarefied, Lerner wouldn't have been able to appreciate it. His ego would not have allowed him to call out, "Hey, Crowley, I want you to do a drawing of my kid . . . my son." Like the cannibals of New Guinea who believe that they will attain the skills of those whom they devour, Lerner actually believed that he might find the answer in another man's art.

Andrew looked up. He and Lerner knew of each other, but they had never talked. A grunt from Lerner and a nod from Andrew were all that they had ever exchanged. Andrew was startled by the request. "What?"

"I'll pay you whatever you want." For a moment Andrew thought Lerner was challenging him, trying to embarrass him in public. He'd seen Lerner do that to other painters. But when Lerner continued, "You're the only one I can trust to do it right. You're the only one left with an eye," he realized Lerner was serious.

Maggie put her arm around Lerner. "Now aren't you glad you came to the party?" She spoke as if she were addressing a child. Lerner ignored her.

She kissed Andrew. "I was just thinking about you today."

The older man's eyes were glazed. He wasn't focusing on Andrew. He seemed to be looking at something in the distance, something beyond Andrew's horizon, something that was moving toward them. Lerner seemed spellbound.

The answer would have to be "No." Andrew could not waste his talent on that sort of sentiment. But before Andrew could make up an excuse, Lerner's thirteen-year-old son appeared.

Lerner had promised Peter that just the two of them would go out to dinner and then to a movie. But lunch with Barclay had gone worse and taken longer than he had expected. He had to go to his

40

new lawyer's office, then see Simon Pyne, and, of course, there was Maggie, and so Peter Lerner was added to the guest list at Libba Winthrop's party.

Peter reached up and fondled the pearls that dangled between Maggie's breasts and interrupted his father, "Hey, those are neat!" Then he added innocently, "Are they real?"

Lerner pushed his son's hand away from Maggie's bosom and, forgetting about his old struggle, announced, "Of course, they're real. I gave them to her."

Andrew wondered if Peter really knew what he was doing.

Trying to change the subject, Maggie pointed to a Holland on the wall and asked Peter, "What do you think of Mr. Holland's painting?"

Peter yawned. "Quite original, but a bit too decorative for my taste."

Lerner wasn't listening to them. He grabbed Andrew's arm. "Will you do the drawing?"

The boy was gone now. Andrew watched Peter dart in and out of the crowd that had become so oppressively boring. Because he was the child of this living legend, this man whose work hung in every major museum in the world, his antics were tolerated. Andrew found the recklessness of Peter's movements refreshing in contrast with the insane and stylized art chatter that was being spewed out around him. The boy was delightfully original. He pranced from group to group, butting in and stealing the conversation so skillfully that no one minded except the person who had been holding court.

One minute Peter would be very much the artist's son, speaking with surprising sophistication about the latest exhibitions and openings. The next minute he'd be rattling on about Joe Namath's passing statistics. Peter kept people off-guard by alternating his performance in this way. When they attempted to deal with him as an adult, he became a child, and when they tried to dismiss him as a child, he became an adult.

Then Jamie appeared. Lerner pointed at him. "What's she want?"

Jamie blushed. "Well, Andrew, I'm leaving." Andrew didn't care. He stared at Peter and answered, "Fine."

"Aren't you coming?"

"No."

Andrew hated it when Jamie whined. He liked his friend most

when he was being as bitchy and as manipulative as he knew how to be, not because he found that style so amusing, but because then he didn't feel guilty about how little he gave him. As Jamie sulked out of the building, Andrew noticed that he was wearing not only a suit of his, but his gold Cartier watch, and he thought, "God damn it, you leech, stay out of my things!" Andrew was surprised at how much it annoyed him. Lerner's anger was contagious. Usually Andrew didn't care in the least when people took those sorts of things from him. It was then that he decided to do the drawing of Peter.

"What do you say, Crowley? Will you help me out?" Lerner rasped.

"Send him down to my loft."

It was decided that Peter would go to Andrew's studio the next morning. Peter shook Andrew's hand and nodded as his father told him the plan. Andrew wrote his address on the back of a blank check and handed it to the boy.

As soon as they said good-bye, Andrew heard Barclay whisper soothingly to Lerner, "Simon showed me the papers, and I must say I think choosing him to be executor was an excellent idea. After all, who could be a more responsible and dedicated guardian?"

Lerner glared at Barclay. "If you want that show of mine this spring, you're going to have to tear out those fucking spotlights in your gallery."

A smile passed across the diminutive art dealer's face. "We installed them for the Picasso show. They were his choice, you know. It was a brilliant show. His work held up wonderfully against them, but, Steven, if you think your work requires something else, I will, of course, help you in any way that I can."

Lerner looked spooked. His head reared back and his dark eyes rolled mistrustfully. Like an old horse who had been tricked so many times that he shied away from both the good and the bad, uncertain of what each new encounter would bring, a slap, a pat, a bit, a rod, Lerner never knew what to expect. As Andrew watched, he marveled at the way Barclay dealt with Lerner. It was done in such a subtle manner he couldn't be sure whether Barclay was just trying to deal gracefully with a madman or whether he was really manipulating Lerner.

Andrew pushed those thoughts aside. It was the boy who intrigued him. He took one last look at Peter Lerner. He hadn't realized how bored he was. He blew a very large smoke ring, and, whistling "Zip-A-Dee-Doo-Dah," stepped through it and out of the party.

Peter Lerner was also bored. He called a school friend, was invited to a basketball game at the Garden, looked for his father, couldn't find him, and left without saying good-bye.

Lerner was staring at the picture he had painted late that night in 1952, "First Light." It comforted him to see that in spite of its new owner, the canvas still glowed from within.

When Lerner turned away from his old painting, he saw one of the paintings from his last show, the one Carter Remington, the *Times* art critic, had called "an expedition into worlds of color and tone not yet explored by any of the other color field painters." Lerner couldn't even remember the name of the painting. It represented a journey he wished he had never taken. It was so dark and drained of life that it frightened him.

Lerner didn't want to see any more. He looked for Maggie. She wasn't in the room. He jumped up and grabbed Bob Cross's wife around the waist, pushed himself against her, and announced coarsely, "I can't stand it anymore." Everyone looked up. "I'm running off with you right now. You'd never regret it," Lerner panted.

Lerner ground himself against her. "Is it true you goyas never do it doggie style? I'll show you what it's all about." She felt the outline of his belt buckle against her.

"One night, that's all it would take, and you'd never go back to him."

She and Lerner had gone through that scene before. He chose her because he knew that she was happily married, that she would never take him up on his offer, because he would never have to perform. This mating dance, this sexual proposal by the greatest living abstract expressionist, brought a half-dozen art groupies of all sexes and ages to his side. They fluttered out of the woodwork like gypsy moths. They circled around him, giggling and pawing his fat fifty-two-year-old stomach.

Lerner muttered obscenities and tried to lose them in the crowd, but before he could make good his escape, the man at the chess board stepped forward. He gestured toward the Lerner paintings at either end of the room, the old one that was still so alive and the new one that seemed so dead. "You see it all in those two pictures—before

43

and after . . ." Lerner was all set to say "Before and after what, asshole," but before he could, the headmaster said, "Fame." And Lerner was caught.

The painter's head snapped back. As he looked out of his great dark eyes at this stranger who had come too close, he began to tremble. The comments in the room grew louder. He saw his adviser, Simon Pyne, gesturing toward that new painting Lerner loathed, and he heard him say, "Technically as well as intellectually it is a far more challenging painting. It demands a great deal from the viewer, but in return one gets so much more."

He heard Tessa Merritt shriek, "Love it to death!" as Sidney did his Carmen Miranda imitation.

A lady a few feet from Lerner pointed and whispered to her friend, "Oh, this is nothing; you should have been here the night he urinated in the fireplace."

Hers and a dozen other comments crescendoed around this legend who stood lost in the center of the crowded room.

"Have you heard about his daughter? She's crazy, too."

"The little boy is cute."

"I guess that's the price you pay for genius."

"What are you talking about? Picasso's the only painter alive who's really a genius."

"At first I didn't wanna get a dark one like that one there because it didn't go with the rest of the furniture. . . . But Harry says it's such a good investment. . . . We just keep it for a year or two, and we'll be able to turn around and sell it and have enough to get what we really like."

When Maggie Lawrence, the woman who brought Lerner to the party, stepped into the room, he threw his drink at her and began to scream.

"You fucking cunt, you whore! What are you trying to do to me!?"

The Black Panthers turned around. Lerner shouted at them all.

"You think being able to write a check makes you special?"

Maggie walked toward him, smiling, reaching out her hand to him as if approaching a frightened animal. He pushed her hand away.

"Don't touch me! You're worse than any of them."

Simon and Libba rushed to the aid of the abused Maggie. As he left the room, Lerner heard Maggie call out, "Steven, please don't! We're your friends. Please, let's talk about it."

44

Because Maggie never turned on him in public, because she appeared to take his insults and abuses like the kind-hearted good sport she wasn't, no one ever listened to what Lerner said about her.

Lerner and Maggie had fought in public before. She didn't understand what set him off, but he was never gone for long. Usually he'd just go outside—buy a pack of cigarettes or a paper, scream at the traffic, and then go back to her more dependent, another step closer to giving in.

But that night Lerner surprised himself. He felt like a fighter, who'd won the first round. The adrenalin surged through him. He jumped in a cab and announced, "I'm going home." He was so keyed up it took him a few minutes to decide just where that was.

IV

"I'm sorry, Daddy, but I can't."

"Why not?"

"I have a date."

"It's almost eleven. Who goes out on a date then? Come on. You and me. We'll get something to eat."

"We've already had dinner. We just stopped off at the house for a drink. We're going to a concert."

"What's his name?"

"Teddy."

"Who is this kid?"

"He goes to the Columbia School of Journalism."

Lerner's eighteen-year-old daughter, Wendy, put down the phone and called out, "I'll be there in a minute, Teddy . . . don't forget my cigarettes. They're on the kitchen table." Wendy put the receiver back to her ear. "Listen, Daddy, we're going to be late. . . . I'm going to have to hang up."

With that, the surly skepticism of Lerner's voice fell away. An angry plea came across the line. "Listen, break your fuckin' date! There's something I've got to talk to you about. It's important. I want . . . I mean I need . . ."

She'd been tricked by that voice before. "It'll have to wait, goodbye!" As she slammed down the receiver, Wendy thought to herself, "God, he always thinks I have nothing to do. He's not the only one who's popular. People want me, too." For a moment she almost believed it. But there was no Teddy, there had been no dinner for two, and there would be no concert. While her father had been at Libba's party making a fool of himself under Maggie's watchful eye, she had been sitting in the kitchen of their brownstone smoking dope, watching TV with the sound off, and eating turkey left over from New Year's day.

Wendy hated Friday nights. Her dateless state was testimony to just how fat and pathetic she feared herself to be. Reality had a way of cornering Wendy. It made her do and say things she later regretted. Sometimes a lie was the only way out for her. It didn't matter if the person to whom she told it suspected or not. If it helped her through the night, that was enough.

Except for being overweight, Wendy didn't look anything like her father. When people talked about her, they said all the trite things they always say about fat girls, "She could be so pretty if only she lost some weight." But with Wendy it was true. Beneath her double chin, chipmunk cheeks, and unwashed blond hair, a beauty lurked. She had an aquiline nose, high cheekbones, and beautiful soft skin. She hid behind a mask of fat. There was someone else inside her that no one ever saw, someone striking and seductive.

When she was little, Wendy had been cute. But when she was twelve, when her breasts began to bud and she started to menstruate, something happened to her appetite. She gained thirty pounds in four months. She didn't want to be pulled into the world of grownups, into her parents' madness.

Her parents put her on all sorts of diets, but she thwarted any attempts to alter her shape. She hid family-size bags of M & M's and Good and Plentys beneath her bed, and a dozen doughnuts were always stashed under her bathroom sink. By the time she was thirteen, she was a regular at Lane Bryant and other shops catering to "big-boned" girls.

Wendy was bright—she could see right into the heart of things outside herself. She was instinctively aware of the lies and inadequacies of others. But when it came to examining her own emotions and feelings, Wendy at nineteen was often no more perceptive or realistic than the twelve-year-old who had used her weight to shield herself from the world that awaited her.

She had been the smartest girl in her class, scored 800 on two of her college board achievement tests, and had been accepted at Radcliffe. All summer Wendy had been looking forward to getting away from her family. She couldn't wait to go to college. She told herself, "Everything will be different. My feelings will fall into place once I get away from Daddy. The lies and the hysteria will stop." But as the day of her departure drew near, she became more and more apprehensive. She kept thinking, "What if it's still the same?" The night before she was to be in Boston for freshman orientation, Wendy's temperature shot up to 103°. The doctor said it was mononucleosis. Wendy never went to college.

Wendy felt guilty for having lied, but she was far more concerned with keeping her father from seeing through her story. She knew he'd call again, so she took the phone off the hook. But she still couldn't be sure he wouldn't come by. Wendy remembered all the times he'd come back to the house like a ghost, screaming that he'd been locked out and pounding on the door, insisting that he couldn't get in even though his keys were in his pocket. She thought of all the nights when he'd called her "a fat pig" and a "whore," when she'd ignored his drunken insults and put him to bed. Then she pushed another handful of potato chips in her mouth.

Going somewhere would make it seem like less of a lie. Wendy considered a movie, but seeing a film by herself would only make her feel more lonely than she already was.

Mixing up another glass of chocolate milk, she hit upon the solution to her dilemma, "Max's. Max's Kansas City. I'll go there."

Wendy knew all the tricks to make herself look five pounds slimmer, but in her case five pounds didn't make much difference. She tried on several outfits and threw them on the floor when they failed to give her the look she longed for. She finally settled on a loose-fitting shirt over her blue jeans. She thought that this combination camouflaged her girth; but in reality it made her look not only fat but also pregnant. On top of all that Wendy wore a long black belted trenchcoat. She wore it everywhere. She thought it made her look thinner.

She got to Max's just before midnight. It was packed. As soon as she stepped inside, she regretted having come. Everyone at the crowded bar seemed to stare at her. Self-consciously she tightened her belt and ordered a vodka and tonic. She disliked the taste of liquor, but at bars she had to drink. Each time someone looked in her direction she was sure they were thinking, "What a pig!" Anytime someone laughed, Wendy would cringe, certain that she was the butt of his joke.

There was a typical Friday-night crowd, lots of lonely straight people in the front, and lots of gays and drag queens in the back. Wendy liked them. They never seemed lonely, and they didn't make her feel so nervous. Sometimes when the loneliness of the crowded bar became too much, she helped them put on makeup in the ladies' room.

Then she saw him. At first she thought he was a rock star. They came to Max's after shows all the time. He seemed to be looking for someone. He was very skinny. He had on tight blue velvet pants and a brown leather jacket. He looked like Keith Richard. Wendy loved that type.

"Can I borrow a cigarette?"

"Only if you promise to give it back." She cursed herself for saying something so stupid, yet he seemed to be amused.

"I promise. . . . Crowded tonight, isn't it?" As he lit up her cigarette, Wendy motioned toward the couple who were making out next to them.

"Yeah, I think they're going to spawn soon." As he laughed she thought to herself, "My God, he seems to like me." Wendy couldn't believe it. It was too much like one of her daydreams.

"Where are you from?"

"Los Angeles."

"What do you do?" she asked.

"I'm a musician."

It was even better than the lie she had told her father.

"Are you in a band?"

"No, I'm . . . a . . . studio musician. I play with lots of groups. Back them up on records and shit like that."

He spoke hesitantly. Wendy loved it. He seemed more nervous than she.

They got a table in the back room. When he asked her what she did, Wendy announced, "I am a painter." The lie was out before she knew it. "He's from L.A., he'll never know," she thought.

"What sort of things do you paint?"

"I'm into superrealism. I can't stand abstract art, just smearing colors around. I mean, anybody can do that sort of shit." Wendy said that just because she knew that it would have driven her father crazy.

The waitress brought lobsters and artichokes to the couple next to them. He reached under the table and squeezed her thigh. Wendy was so excited and so nervous that she was tempted to order something to eat, but she couldn't do that. She thought, "Maybe a cigarette would help." She was out and he didn't have any. She opened her bag, took out some change for the cigarette machine, and got up from the table. She didn't stop to talk to the drag queens who were hanging out in the back; she had no need for them that night.

As she walked back to her table, Wendy thought about how good it felt to have someone. Then she saw him leaving. He was hurrying through the crowd at the bar. When she called out, he began to run. As he dashed out the door she saw her purse in his hands.

She thought about chasing him, but that would only have drawn attention to her. She stood in the middle of Max's feeling fatter and uglier than ever. A waitress carrying a tray loaded with dirty dishes nearly tripped over her. "Could ya get outta the aisle?"

All the eyes in the room, all the laughter seemed to be directed at her. The noise was deafening. She wanted to scream, to shake them, to make them stop.

Wendy hadn't really expected all that much. She had been used by men she had met in bars. They had taken her back to their apartments, drunk and sloppy. They had mauled and mounted her. It was always the same. When finished, they pushed her away and told her to leave. But at least they made her damp. For a moment, she had the illusion she might be satisfied. Wendy could live with that, but this was worse.

She put on her coat and cursed that slim-hipped fellow. "How could I have been stupid enough to think he liked me? That bastard. I hate him." By the time she reached the end of the bar, she was crying openly. When an innocent little man asked her what was wrong, she pushed him so hard he fell.

Wendy was comforted slightly when she found some change and a Hershey bar in her pocket. Crying and eating her candy, she started toward the subway. Each of the carefree couples that passed her on their way to Max's reminded Wendy of what had happened to her, of the situation she was in. She resented them all. Then she felt the locket around her neck slap cold against her breasts. Her father had given it to her mother. A long time ago she'd thrown away the picture of them that had been in it. She had replaced it with two hits of blotter acid. In the interest of romance, she always brought enough drugs for two. Wendy finished her candy bar, wiped away her tears, and, without any hesitation, took the acid.

She never made it to the subway. Somehow she had gotten turned around. Wendy walked very quickly, as if she were about to break into a run at any moment. She guessed the LSD was cut with speed.

She felt the drug sweeping over her in waves. It washed away the memory of the purse and the boy who had stolen it. The streets glistened and the street lamps shone so brightly there seemed to be no shadows.

It began to snow. She stuck out her tongue to catch the flakes. Everything was going to turn out all right. It wasn't until she was halfway across Washington Square, the place where the march had ended, that Wendy realized that she was heading downtown. She was moving swiftly toward a destination that had not yet been revealed to her by the drug.

The platform where the leaders of the march, the college presidents, priests, and poets had shouted out in the cold stood empty. The scattered leaflets that told of madmen and massacres were quickly covered by the snow. Within moments, Wendy's world was white. It was as if God were sprinkling it with powdered sugar, just for her.

Wendy began to run. It was very slippery. She held out her arms and slid for nearly fifteen feet, then she lost her balance and fell. She cut her knee on a bench. It bled, but she didn't feel it. The sensation that registered in her brain wasn't physical pain. When she got up, Wendy found herself thinking of her father, mumbling, "It's all his fault it happened . . . it's his fault. He made me this way." He wasn't responsible just for that night. She held him accountable for her fat and her neuroses. She saw her miseries as being genetic, as a birthright, an inheritance she would never escape. As Wendy marched uptown, as she staged her private protest, each acid rush exposed a bit more of the anger and pain that lay within her.

V

As soon as Lerner stepped into the apartment, he knew something was wrong. When he saw the boxes he hadn't unpacked, the clothes he hadn't had the energy to take out of their suitcases, the cigarette butts, food wrappers, and half-finished pints of potato salad scattered across the floor, he knew it was going to be a bad night. He went straight to the kitchen, opened a fresh bottle of vodka, and sat in the center of the living room in one of the new chairs he hadn't yet unwrapped. He didn't turn on the lights. He didn't want to be confronted by any more signs of this strange malaise that for more than a year had kept him from moving into this duplex in the Dakota.

Although the walls were bare, Lerner had the same feeling he had had at the party. He felt as though someone were watching him. As he reached into his pocket and took out two of the antidepressants Dr. Fine had prescribed, he thought to himself, "Why can't I move in? This is the best fucking place I've had in my life." When he leaned back, the chair beneath him cried out in pain. "What a piece of shit. Why did I buy these chairs? I can't even sit in them." Lerner continued to twist back until he heard the arm of the chair crack. "Jesus Christ, I never wanted any of this crap. These stupid chairs, this fag apartment are all part of the bullshit Maggie and the rest of them tricked me into going for."

The chair groaned as he stood up, and Lerner knocked it down. "This whole fucking night stinks of everything I hate most . . . all those pretentious assholes who think that when they buy one of my pictures they get part of me."

He stood there, sweating, red-faced in the darkness, bottle in hand, ready to take on all comers. But there were none, except a voice within Lerner himself, a voice he hadn't listened to for almost ten years, a spirit Lerner had abused and betrayed.

The words snapped through Lerner's subconscious before the vodka or antidepressants could catch them. "That's a lie, that's not who you hate the most."

The voice came and went before he knew what hit him. Lerner shook his head and hurried to the phone in the hall. He dialed the number of the house on east Eighty-eighth Street—that place Lerner had called home. He had moved out just two months before his wife died. His children still lived there with Dora, the housekeeper. Before he was halfway finished with the call, the voice reminded him, "Peter and Wendy aren't home, and you don't have a wife." Lerner slammed the receiver down before the voice finished. He tried to reach Simon, but the service picked up for him on the first ring, and they wouldn't wake him.

"Jesus Christ, if I can't sleep, why should he?"

Lerner was angry and frightened. He began to dial his sister's number in Chicago; as he picked out the exchange, the voice coldly reminded him, "She's been dead for two years. . . ." The next call was a reflex. Lerner always made it when he'd run out of numbers, when he was alone. Before it rang the voice mocked him, "If you hate Maggie so much, why do you always call her?"

Lerner threw down the receiver and ran to the bathroom. He rummaged through the medicine cabinet and grabbed three sleeping pills, and one of the mood elevators that the psychiatrist he had seen in '67 had given him. He washed them down with vodka. He drank until he began to gag, then dropped the bottle, sputtered down the hall, and threw himself on his unmade bed. He waited for the dreamless sleep he longed for, but it wasn't coming. The image of those two pictures at either end of Libba's living room didn't fade. His head ached and his body sweated. The stimulants and depressants that he had taken battled each other, not the voice. Lerner lay helpless while it boomed out, "Whose fault is that, Steven?"

Lerner hid his face in his pillow and screamed, "I didn't know!" With that the voice grew angry. It grabbed hold of Lerner and jerked him through the past. The voice made him see his life as it was, not as he liked to recall it. "I told you from the start that your vision was as good as any inside. It wasn't your wife, Sarah, who taught art so you could paint, or your children, or anyone else whom you claimed to love who helped you make art. It was me. I made you face the canvases when you were ready to run."

Everything the voice said was true. It had helped him lay color on color so carefully that the eye became lost in the hues. "I was the one who kept you from being too precious with yourself, too satisfied with your art. It was I who made you use your ancient eye."

Lerner tried to rub away the memory of how a fresh canvas used to challenge him, but he remembered all too well how frantic he would become once he'd started a new painting, frightened that his vision would vanish before it was realized. He remembered how he would race around the canvas, cursing and scrambling for the right color, struggling to make his own rainbow.

"I was the one who raised you from sleep to paint that night. I made you work while the rest of the world dreamt with its eyes closed."

Lerner remembered the painting that had been the finale to that remarkable day in May seventeen years before. He saw himself naked and alive, perched above "First Light" and squatting on the last step of his ladder, watching his kingdom of color stand up to the dawn. The voice reminded him, "I showed you its secret . . . your magic that night."

The voice pulled him toward the present. It reminded him that he had taken that ladder to the new studio he had built on Thirtieth Street off Fifth in 1960. "I was with you even then. You still hadn't lost it."

The voice jerked Lerner helter-skelter over the last few years, through parties, paintings, awards, and analysis, reminding him of what he had lost and what he had hoped to gain.

"Is that what you've become? Is that why you've done this to yourself, because you can't create, because you can't do it anymore? Why have you stopped listening? Why can't you mount the ladder?" The voice was openly interrogating him, and it wouldn't accept any of the excuses he gave the psychiatrist or the art critics. It wanted him to admit what had happened.

Lerner could take no more. He screamed and sat up. He grabbed at the clock by the bed. It was 4:00 A.M. He was ready to try another round of sleeping pills, but then he had an idea. Maybe it would help, maybe he could silence the voice, if he went to his studio. Maybe if he poured his colors on the canvas the way he used to, he might escape the spell that held him captive. He picked up his coat and ran from the apartment, from all the things that reminded him of what he had become.

When the cab came out of the park, turned down Fifth, and stopped at the traffic light in front of Dr. Fine's office, Lerner shuddered, "I'm going out of control," and that was just what Dr. Fine had been hired to prevent. The voice was stripping away all the elaborate emotional checks and balances which had kept Lerner in place. He heard Dr. Fine's fatherly counsel, "Everyone has certain feelings of paranoia from time to time. But the people you mention to me seem to be the ones who love you most, who have been most loyal, who only want to safeguard and see that you enjoy your success."

Then the voice screamed out, "You aren't crazy, don't listen to him. He's paid to tell you what you want to hear, to corroborate their lies. Fine is their henchman, hired to sedate you twice a week with lithium to remove your passion as if it were a gallbladder acting up."

Lerner had no more second thoughts. He staggered out of the cab in a rage. He was dazed by the drugs and liquor, by the jet stream of hostility the voice had cast him into. "Maggie, Wendy, Simon, Peter, Barclay, Luccio, Sarah." The voice threw up the names of his family and oldest friends, and Lerner pronounced them all guilty.

"They're always talking about me, stealing from me behind my back, coming around the studio telling me what to do, telling me what paintings are strongest. What the fuck do they know? They all want something."

Lerner hadn't gone to his studio for several weeks. He had been midtown seeing lawyers. He had finally decided what he wanted to do with all his pictures, what would bring him the most pleasure. All those people whom he now saw responsible for his plight knew something about the plans or were involved in them. Simon had helped with much of the paper work for the new foundation, but the voice had kept some aspects of the plan secret from everyone, including Lerner.

His studio was more than a hundred feet deep, taking up the whole third floor of the building. There was a twenty-foot high-arched window facing north. Lerner painted on a raised platform in front of that window. The way light poured in that morning the room looked like a church. The long, low wooden stage where Lerner worked was stained and splattered with the colors of hundreds of canvases and a square of light was superimposed on the space, so that it was illuminated like an altar.

There were pictures everywhere, lined three and four deep against the walls. In the back of the studio five rows of picture racks were stuffed with finished canvases. Lerner had held on to hundreds of them. Barclay and Simon were always telling him to put them in gallery warehouses.

Lerner raced around his studio with an intensity, a sense of urgency, he hadn't felt in years. He unrolled a big piece of canvas in the center of the painting platform, gathered up a dozen jars of acrylics and some brushes, then went to the closet in the back of his studio and pulled out that old ladder. He wanted it to be there when he was ready. Lerner thought of the night, the hope, the memory he was trying to bring back to life on canvas. He remembered that he had gone to his art naked that night, and he took off his clothes.

Naked he stood before the snow-white canvas. The open space challenged and flirted with him while more than five hundred paintings watched. His creations, those pieces of cloth he had brought to life, lined the walls and filled the darkness behind him. They watched over him as he looked into the nothingness he would have to fill. He accepted their challenge. He looked at the canvas for a long while without picking up a brush or touching a jar of paint. He wasn't sure. As he glanced at the canvases that were propped against the wall, he could see how his work had changed over the years. His yellows had first turned to orange, then red and now were dark, dark brown. The lush blues and greens, the garden colors that Lerner had once used so lavishly, had given way to gray. Simon and Barclay and all the rest couldn't tell the difference, but he could. There was no real magic in them. Anytime he tried to paint with passion, anytime his art wasn't contrived, it grew dark.

He reached down and gripped that part of him that had become soft and useless, he tugged on it as if he wanted to pull it off.

"Show them, Steven, show them what you really are." Slowly Lerner dipped his long brush in a yellow as bright as the sun. As he placed it firmly in the center of the naked canvas, he told himself that this picture would be more vibrant than any he had ever done.

He painted by instinct. He was exhausted, but the voice pushed him on. He worked until he barely had the strength to hold up his

56

head. That voice told him when he was finished.

Then, without even looking, without resting for a moment, he turned his back on the canvas that he had made damp, on the picture that glistened in the morning sun, and he mounted the ladder. Lerner was so nervous, so keyed up, that he trembled. But as he climbed the ladder, he felt as if he had succeeded.

When he got to the top of the ladder and looked down, Lerner cried out. The picture was darker and more somber than any he had ever done. Just as Lerner had been betrayed by those around him, he had betrayed himself. He had lost his ability to convey his feelings in his art and life.

But as Lerner looked into the darkness he had created, he slowly came to realize it wasn't that he had failed, it wasn't that at all. He had hidden his light, his color, his magic on purpose. He had grown tired of wasting it, of having it stolen by a world that wasn't appreciative. And because part of him, most of him, was so easily manipulated by that world, he had even hidden it from himself. He knew now what the voice had wanted him to admit. "I'm no worthier of it than the rest." Over the years the elaborate haze of color that he spread around himself had become harder and harder to penetrate. For a while only his eye could pierce the opacity. Now he had succeeded in tricking even himself.

Lerner sat alone atop his perch faced with the lonely awful fact that he didn't trust or believe in anyone, not even himself. Once faith had accompanied his gift. But that was no longer the case.

He began to weep. "What can I do? How can I climb down? How can I go back to the world knowing this?" He waited for the voice that had once told him when and what to paint, the voice that had finally forced him to face the fact of his self-betrayal. It would tell him what to do.

VI

Andrew had loaned a back room to a friend who was a clothing designer from England. He was putting together a new collection for a fashion show at the Plaza. Two models were trying on dresses that had just been finished. The song "Heat Wave" was blaring in the background. Andrew spent the morning sipping tea and watching the girls strut out into the living room, make three-quarter turns, squeal and pose dramatically. As the little blonde model threw her hands up à la Marilyn Monroe, one of the buttons on the front of her cream-colored dress popped off, exposing her left breast. Andrew giggled and said, "I think that's the way you ought to wear it all the time."

When he heard the doorbell, he knew it was Peter Lerner. Purposely he left open the door to the room in which the girls were trying on Aubrey's clothes. The first thing Peter saw was a tall, thin black model with red nipples like the erasers on the ends of brand-new pencils and almost no breasts wriggling into an emerald green-sequinned dress. He pretended not to notice and thought to himself, "This might not be so bad after all."

When Peter had started down to Andrew Crowley's place in Soho, he was prepared to be bored. He was reconciled to spending his day with Andrew watching the clock, but it wasn't that way at all.

Andrew lived and worked in an immense loft on Prince Street. It was so large you could ride a bicycle around it, and Andrew kept one by the front door just for that purpose. Peter had expected it to be a studio like his father's, a barren, cold, raw space cut off from everything else. But Andrew didn't work that way. He painted at one end of an all-white living room filled with plants. There were flowers everywhere, big cut-glass vases filled with yellow roses and tulips. Even the floors were white.

"Hello, Peter, good to see you." He put down his empty teacup.

58

"Can I get you anything? . . . Something to eat? . . . A drink? . . . A beer?"

Andrew smiled at his last suggestion. When Peter answered, "No, thanks, I never imbibe before three," he laughed.

Without saying a word, Andrew closed the door on the designer and the two models, then took "Heat Wave" off the stereo. He replaced it with a recording of Wagner's "Die Meistersinger" and lowered the volume. Walking back to the Art Nouveau cabinet at the working end of his living room to get what he needed for the drawing, he noticed Peter staring at the fold-up bike by the door.

"Go ahead, take a spin."

"Really?"

"Be my guest." He studied Peter for a moment as he pedaled once around the big beige Deco couch in the center of the room and turned into the kitchen. Andrew didn't seem the least bit concerned when Peter nearly knocked over a blue Chinese bowl with a dozen white tulips in it. He tuned it out just the way he disregarded everything that took him away from his art, that distracted his eye.

Andrew gathered up his pencils. "I don't think I can do you on the bike. How about in that chair?" He placed Peter in a high-backed wing chair. Then he put the bowl of tulips on a little table to the boy's left. That was better, but Andrew hadn't got it quite right yet.

As Andrew walked around the room biting his thumbnail trying to decide what was lacking in the scene he'd set, Peter stared at the closed door to the room where he had seen the nipples and thought to himself, "I wonder if they have any underpants on."

Andrew didn't like the color of the shirt Peter was wearing. He went to his bedroom and got the green silk bathrobe which he had given Jamie for his birthday. It was just the right touch.

"Here, let's try this. It'll be a bit big on you, but that won't matter." As Peter put the bathrobe on over his shirt, Andrew started to ask him to take his shirt off, but then he thought, "I don't want to make him nervous . . . it doesn't really matter. I can draw him as if he were naked underneath. I only need to see his neck." Andrew was surprised at his reaction. It was open to so many sexual interpretations he didn't have time to think about it just then, but he knew he'd come back to it later.

"Do you still want me to sit in that chair?"

"Yeah, that's it. I think that will be quite good actually. Could

59

you undo another button?"

"Why don't I just take my shirt off?"

Andrew looked away, wondering, "Does he know? Is he just being helpful or testing me?"

Once Peter was positioned the way he wanted him, leaning back with the light streaking over him, looking away from the flowers, one hand in his lap, the other dangling over the arm of the chair, Andrew organized his things. He laid out two trays of colored pencils on a low table in front of him and pinned a large sheet of heavy paper to a drawing board. He plugged in his electric pencil sharpener and put it on the floor between his feet.

Just when Andrew had everything ready, Jamie arrived. He looked at Andrew, then at Peter. He didn't say hello. Andrew had done lots of paintings and drawings of Jamie; he was good at posing. Andrew turned round, "You had a couple of calls this morning, Jamie."

"Oh, really, who from?"

"I don't remember their names, but one was a girl."

"God, Andrew, you could take a message."

He turned back to Peter, "Oh, yes, now I remember who the woman was. It was Joanne Woodward. She says she'll leave Paul if you'll still have her. She left a number—it's on the kitchen table." Though Andrew was quite amused by his little joke, Jamie didn't think it very funny. He stormed into the back room and slammed the door closed.

Andrew scrutinized Peter for a long time before picking up his pencil. His features were sharp and well defined, much finer than his father's. It was easy to see what Peter would look like when he was a man. But Andrew wondered about this clever child. "So many people who are precocious, who shine when they are young, lose it along the way. Is it a natural process that those who have seen too much must go through from butterfly back to caterpillar? Or does a jealous world steal it from them?"

While Peter waited for Andrew to begin, he thought about the times he had watched his father work in his studio. It scared Peter the way he'd struggle and sweat, the way he ran around the canvas on the floor. Painting seemed so painful for his father. He didn't understand why it had to be that way. Andrew didn't paint on the floor. He worked at an easel. There was nothing frantic or strained

60

about the way he made his art. But the biggest difference between Andrew's and his father's studios was that there were so many distractions in Andrew's. Peter was impressed that Andrew was able to work while other people were in the room. It didn't annoy him if they talked or even walked around while he was working. He didn't seem to notice.

Peter's father rarely let people outside his family watch him paint. If someone walked into the room while he was working, he cursed them and told them to leave. Andrew didn't have to work himself into a rage to make art. He didn't have to cut himself off from the world to create. Andrew didn't look up when Jamie, and the models left.

After twenty minutes, Peter began to get impatient. "When are you going to start?"

"When I'm ready."

"How do you know when you're ready?"

"My nose begins to twitch."

When Andrew drew something, he wasn't just interested in producing a likeness. Anyone could do that. For Andrew to be satisfied, he had to give an interpretation that would say as much about him as about the subject.

Andrew hunched over his drawing board and squinted at Peter. He held the board close to him as if he didn't want anyone to see what he was doing. He reminded Peter of a boy in his class at school who twisted himself around his work shielding it with his body so no one could copy from him.

Andrew worked in bursts, concentrating on tiny portions of the picture at a time. In some spots his drawings were incredibly specific, filled with minute details, while other passages were vague. Andrew sought a delicate balance between the finite and the infinite. His style of drawing required a very fine point. He stopped every few minutes to stick his colored pencil into the electric sharpener.

After about an hour and fifteen minutes, Andrew began to get a headache, and so he took a break. He had done everything except Peter's eyes and mouth. Those were the hardest parts. He put down the drawings and stretched. "Well, you really nailed your father over the pearls he gave his friend."

"Who?"

"That red-haired woman—you know—what's her name?"

61

"Maggie. Yeah . . . maybe I did."

"What's she like?"

"Like most people," Peter told him flatly.

"And how is she like most people?"

Without the slightest hesitation Peter said, "She wants my father to give her a painting for free."

It wasn't really funny, but it was so painfully true that Andrew couldn't help laughing. "That's good . . . you're right on that one."

"Do people try to get pictures from you for free? Have you ever given one to that friend of yours?"

Andrew smiled and changed the subject. "Do you play backgammon?"

VII

There were already four people at the corner looking for a taxi when Maggie arrived. She never liked to wait. When a cab pulled up and the people ahead of her began to discuss who was there first and thereby entitled to the taxi, Maggie saw her chance. She pushed aside the skinny boy with the bad skin and the cello as he gallantly offered the taxi to a pregnant woman with a pair of children. Maggie always got away with tricks like this because she never hesitated. She leaped into the waiting taxi, slammed the door in the woman's face, and announced innocently, "Forty-two East Thirtieth Street, please." Maggie and the cab driver were gone before anyone knew what had happened. As the big yellow Checker accelerated down Central Park West, Maggie looked back at the four outraged New Yorkers she had left at the corner and giggled. The little victories of the day were just as important as the big ones to Maggie.

Maggie had a unique combination of innocence and chutzpah, a rare mix of the shrew and the ingenue that enabled her to wiggle past people's defenses. She leaped into their lives and pursued what she wanted in just the same way that she jumped into that cab.

Maggie Lawrence was a ferocious little woman with short curly red hair. Her eyes were too small and her chin much too large. But because Maggie was always jockeying for position, one never focused on her features. Although she wasn't pretty, this energy, this drive of Maggie's kept her very fit for a woman who would be forty-four the following week.

It had been a hard morning for Maggie, too. She had been up since nine trying to track Steven down. She had tried the house, but Wendy wasn't any help. "She never is." Then Maggie had called Simon, but the last time he had seen Lerner was at the party. Finally in desperation she had called the doorman at the Dakota. "Is Mr. Lerner in?"

"No, he left early. I wasn't even on yet, but the night man said he ran out at about five."

Although there was no answer at the studio, Maggie was sure he was there. "He never answers the phone when he gets upset."

Maggie hadn't been distressed the night before when Lerner had thrown his drink at her and called her a fucking cunt in front of everyone.

When he had stormed out of the party at Libba's, Maggie had been positive that he'd be back in an hour, begging to be forgiven, frightened to death that he might have broken free and been on his own. She had expected to find him in another room, drunker and more pompous than ever, pontificating to a group of nobodies who didn't know this abstract expressionist myth was burned out.

It annoyed Maggie that Lerner had gone through with that old threat of his. She had to stay at the party longer than she liked just to make sure everyone understood that nothing had changed, that she was still in command. She was almost the last one to leave. She made a great show of being taken home by a wealthy young German dealer. "Oh, Max, you're such a dear. Of course, I'd love to come up for a quick bite. . . . I bet you are a fantastic cook." She would torture Lerner with that later.

As she remembered it all, Maggie thought to herself, "I didn't think the ball-less bastard had it in him to walk out on me like that."

Maggie wiggled around sideways in the back of the cab, put her feet up on the seat and thought to herself how difficult Steven was. She guessed that was part of the bargain with artists. Maggie's ex-husband had been a painter. He was handsomer than, but not nearly as important as, Lerner. Maggie never had trouble worming her way into painters' lives. The problem was once she had them she never knew what to do with them. She had always been in it for the challenge, but with Lerner it was something else.

She studied her reflection in the divider as she practiced that face she made when Steven Lerner screamed at her in public. She wondered how much longer it would be before she could get him to marry her.

When Maggie caught the cabbie looking at her in the rear-view mirror, she first thought he was going to tell her to take her feet off the seat. But it wasn't that. He was just staring at her legs. She pretended not to notice and squirmed down further in the seat. As

64

the cab lurched downtown, Maggie let her dress ride further and further up her thigh and thought about her birthday. She knew just what she wanted. She wanted that big brown painting Steven had sent to the art fair in Cologne last year, but had refused to sell to a Swiss banker. Lerner had driven Simon and Barclay crazy when he wouldn't sell that painting. That was the one Maggie wanted, and on the back of the canvas she wanted Lerner to write in red, "To Maggie, with all my love."

Steven was always promising Maggie paintings, but, when she came to get them, he changed his mind. He didn't even like her to be in his studio.

The taxi pulled up by Lerner's building, and Maggie let the young cabbie take one long last look at her legs before she pulled her skirt down. The fare was $3.90. She quickly stuffed $4.00 in the change slot and jumped out of the cab. He'd had his tip.

Maggie was already irked about the evening as she rang the bell. When there was no answer, she began to get angrier. She was positive that he was in there. "Where else could he be?" Maggie could always find people. She was like a bloodhound. Even though she knew he couldn't hear her, she banged on the iron door and screamed up at his window. Finally she rang all the buzzers in the building, and one of the other tenants let her in.

As she bounded up the stairs, Maggie thought to herself, "Boy, am I going to give it to him!" But by the time she was halfway up the last flight, Maggie had calmed down. She abandoned any ideas that she might have entertained about turning on him openly. Maggie knew the way to get what you wanted out of Steven was through guilt. "I'll make him feel very bad, and then I'll frighten him."

She knocked, but there was still no answer. When she tried the door, she discovered it was unlocked. "God! Anybody could have walked in. . . . I wonder if everything is all right." She didn't worry long. As she stepped inside, Maggie looked longingly at the picture rack in the back of the studio. "I deserve that picture after all the crap I've put up with. Maybe if I play on his paranoia in just the right way, he might give it to me today. Who knows, he might even propose." They were girlish fantasies, but she loved them. There were so few artists like Lerner; this would probably be the last chance Maggie would have before her bosom began to fall and her bottom to drop.

There was a little kitchen at the back of the studio. Maggie guessed that he was there. "Steven, may I come in? . . . Come on, everything is all right. I understand." She could just see him sulking. He was probably drunk, too. "Steven, I don't want anything except for you to be happy . . . that's the only reason I'm down here."

Every time Maggie walked by those picture racks stuffed with canvases, she had the urge to take one or two. "He'd never miss them." When Maggie saw the pool of wet paint and the footprints, she knew that he was there. "Steven, you can't go on like this . . . you need help." She followed his footprints to the front of the studio. Then she saw it—that brown painting she wanted so much was leaning up against the wall.

"It wasn't out before. Maybe he's going to give it to me." Maggie thought. It wasn't until she opened her purse and put on her glasses that she saw Steven lying at the foot of his ladder, surrounded by paints, brushes, and a razor.

Lerner was sprawled naked beside the canvas. There was blood everywhere. The crooks of his arms were cut. His right hand was stretched out on the canvas and that wrist was also slashed. The pool of blood beneath his arm was the only color in that last dark painting. It looked as though he were reaching for something. Maggie cried—not because she was horrified or sad, but because she didn't know what else to do. She prided herself on her poise, on knowing just how to act, just what face to put on in any situation. But this was one scene Maggie Lawrence had never rehearsed. This wasn't part of her plan. Suddenly all the minor victories she had scored in her courtship of Lerner didn't matter. He had defeated her.

Maggie's eyes wandered over the details of his death—the blood-stained razor he had used to cut that last canvas free, the gashes in the small of his arms, the way the left arm looked as if it had been gnawed by a beast, the blood splattered across his bloated stomach just beginning to dry and turn dark. She couldn't look away.

A dozen different looks flashed across her face, but none of them adequately expressed what she felt. Steven's death changed everything. She was suddenly faint. She sat down in a chair a few feet from the body. Her first impulse was to go get a towel and clean up the mess that Lerner had made in taking his life. She couldn't believe how much blood there was. But that was too grisly. He was even uglier, more naked and repulsive in death than he had been in life.

Maggie lit a cigarette, stared at all those pictures that could have been hers, and began to think. "What can I do now that he is dead?"

VIII

Simon Pyne was like a snake. After he ate, he wanted to sleep. He got back to his office at about two-thirty. He was tempted to curl up on his couch and take a nap, but he told himself he had too much work.

Simon was sixty-three and looked even older. Wrinkled flesh ticked with age spots hung from his face. His eyes were continuously bloodshot from the paper work he did. His loose skin dripped down from his tired eyes into double chins that shook when he talked. But with Simon's white bushy hair the overall effect was quite pleasant. He looked like a sophisticated Santa Claus. You didn't notice his angry red eyes.

Simon took off his shoes, unbuttoned his trousers, and went over all the things that were on his agenda that afternoon. He had put off looking at the slides Mrs. Werner had dropped off the week before. Her son was an art student and the slides were of his work. She was going to call that afternoon so he had to look at them. Simon loathed doing it, but advisers often had to do things they didn't like.

He was connected with all sorts of people. His clients ranged from rich frumpy ladies like Mrs. Werner to artist friends like Lerner. Each had to be handled differently. They all wanted to be told that they were special, that Simon was more concerned about their wants and needs than anyone else's, that he put their desires above even his own. Mediocre art was depressing, but the thought of Mrs. Werner's nine Monets and that wonderful little Van Gogh cheered him. "If I keep impressing her with how much trouble they are, the dangers of theft and fire, she'll turn them over to me. I won't have any trouble working out a deal with Barclay on those." Simon burped and told himself, "Oh, well, I only have to look at his work long enough to say something. They don't really listen anyway."

Within five minutes Simon had dozed off. He sat slumped in his chair, one hand in his pants, softly snoring.

When his private line rang, Simon was tempted not to answer. He rubbed his stomach and yawned. He knew if he let it ring five times his secretary would pick it up and say that he was in a meeting. But then he remembered Mrs. Werner. He rubbed his eyes, sat up, and glanced at one of the slides.

Simon was expecting to hear Mrs. Werner's delightful Texas twang, but the voice on the other end of the line was hoarse and strained.

"He's dead!"

"What!"

"Steven . . . Steven's dead. He killed himself."

"Oh, my God. . . . What happened? Where are you?"

"I don't know. I went down to the studio, and there he was. He slashed his arms. There's all this blood. It's horrible!"

"How terrible! You didn't call the police?"

"No."

"Good. Just stay there. Leave everything as you found it. I know it must be hard for you to talk. I'll come down right now, and we'll do it together."

Talking with Simon made Maggie feel more comfortable with her role. She sobbed, "Oh, God, Simon! It's awful. I don't believe it!"

"I know how you must feel. Having it end this way is hard on all of us."

Harold Barclay was a wiry little man who always had a bemused look on his face. He rarely smiled. He looked at everything in life with that same smirk. Barclay wasn't his real name. It was Berkowitz. He had changed it when he went to London after the war. He named his gallery after the prime minister and himself after the bank. His clothes were always so conservative, so elegantly understated, and his manner so unobtrusive that he blended into any setting. Barclay spoke and moved slowly. He didn't like unnecessary attention, to reveal any more of himself than was absolutely necessary. His gallery, Winston, with its slate floors and stark white walls, was run the same way.

Barclay never ate much. Food bored him. He had skipped lunch and spent the afternoon at his gallery, checking the arrangements for a Pollack show scheduled for the next fall.

When Simon called, Barclay was dictating notes to a new secretary at the gallery, Christina Hansen. "We'll get Lee Childers to write an essay for *Art News* on the show."

"Steven has killed himself."

Barclay motioned for her to leave the room.

"Oh, dear. Did you find him?"

"No. Maggie Lawrence did. At his studio."

Barclay knew instantly what it meant. "Has she alerted the authorities?"

"No. I'm going down now. I'll call them."

"Good. I'm sure you know how to handle this sort of thing better than I. I'll take care of things at this end."

"Poor Steven . . ."

Barclay touched the wallet in his breast pocket. "Yes, it's such a loss. He was only beginning to get the recognition that we had hoped for . . . that his art deserved."

"Yes, it is terrible it had to happen, but he wasn't well. At least everything is squared away. We can still proceed as we had planned."

When he hung up, a bemused look was on Harold Barclay's face. He viewed it as a business phenomenon. He followed his natural impulse. He made a long-distance call to William Beatty at his ranch in Venezuela.

Barclay never had any problem selling Lerners. A medium-sized blue one had gone out of the gallery that morning for $50,000. Lee Thedorcopolis had bought it for her daughter. Now that Lerner was gone, now that the supply was limited, the pictures would be even more desirable. But Barclay wasn't sure that things might not have been easier with Lerner alive.

"Hello, Billy, how are you?"

"Fine." Billy had taken the call by the pool.

"And your wife?" Barclay asked as he wondered what had been found. He wished it hadn't happened in the studio.

"Everyone's fine."

"I'm sorry to bother you, but something's come up. I thought you'd want to know about it."

"Really? What?" Beatty rubbed a bit more coconut oil on himself.

"Steven Lerner died this morning. . . . I'm sure you are as shocked and surprised as I was."

"Yes, that is distressing news."

70

"I don't need to tell you the effect this will have on his work, and since when we talked last month in Zurich you expressed an interest in that early series of pictures, I thought you might want to act now . . . before his death becomes public."

Simon wanted it done with dignity. Before he told anyone else, he would call Stan Rothkoph and report that the greatest painter of the age was dead. Stan would write the obituary. Simon spoke of Lerner reverently. He let his sorrow, his grief flow freely. Every pause, every inflection conveyed and reemphasized his sense of loss. "The greatest tragedy is that Steven was just maturing as an artist. His vision was just beginning to expand. It's an incredible loss."

Rothkoph was equally somber and sincere. "He will emerge as the most influential painter of the second half of the century." He stole a line from Faulkner's Nobel Prize speech. "His art will not only endure, it will prevail."

Simon chose his words carefully. He was on record, and he wanted his praise, his evaluation, his devotion to Steven Lerner, the man and the artist, to be remembered correctly.

Simon tried Luccio, but he wasn't in. There were others to call, but he wanted to take care of everything at the studio first. It wasn't a good idea to leave Maggie there alone any longer than was necessary.

Maggie had been surprised by her reaction to the sight of Lerner's dead body. She had an urge to clean up the mess, to pull Lerner's carcass off the picture and wipe up the blood. Simon seemed to possess the same need to impose his order on the situation. He kissed her quickly, then inspected the studio. He straightened a picture on the wall, righted a chair, picked up two cigarette butts, a piece of paper, and three yellow pills. He put a dirty dish in the sink and closed several cabinet doors. It was minutes before Simon even looked at the body.

He asked a long series of questions, when she had arrived, what she had seen, and what she had done. It seemed rather pointless to Maggie, but Simon was always very thorough. When the police came, he did all the talking. The detective in charge said the case seemed pretty routine. Simon and Maggie simultaneously took exception, telling him what a genius the dead man on the painting was —of his importance to art, to civilization—but the detective wrote none of that down in his report book.

Two Irish cops alternately picked their noses and fingered their files as they looked at the paintings scattered around the studio. They had stepped into another world. Neither the art nor what Maggie and Simon said made any sense to them.

The tall cop pointed to the crowded picture racks behind him and asked Simon, "What's he got all those for?" Simon didn't answer. "Couldn't he sell 'em?" This point interested the detective. He stopped drawing the diagram of where the body lay and waited for an answer.

The question was so ridiculous it made Simon angry, but he wanted everything to go smoothly. Simon patiently began to explain, "His work was always in demand, every museum in the—"

It was too much for Maggie to bear. She blurted out, "He could've sold a hundred of them in an afternoon and made more than all three of you put together will ever earn in your miserable little lives."

Her insults slid off the policemen's backs. They were used to the beratings of those associated with the deceased. The shorter of the two patrolmen elbowed his friend and whispered, "What a racket."

Simon looked away when the men from the morgue arrived and pushed Lerner's body into a brown plastic body bag as if they were stuffing a synthetic sausage. Though the blood had dried and turned dark, the floor was splattered with damp paint. When one of the men carrying the body slipped on a gob of burnt sienna and put his elbow through a canvas, Simon shouted and Maggie began to cry.

It wasn't until they had taken away the body and the police were sealing up the studio that Simon remembered Lerner's children. The detective let him go back in to call them. He would be relieved to be able to track Wendy and Peter down. It was important that he be the one to tell them. "After all," he thought, "I was close to their father. . . . I'd hate for them to have to hear it on the news or something like that."

The line was busy. In the darkness with the body gone, the studio suddenly seemed eerie. As Simon waited to try the number again, he was overcome with the fear that he was being locked in, that he wouldn't be able to escape. The feeling was so strong he decided to make the call from Maggie's. The canvases Lerner had brought to life watched silently as Simon's shadow moved across the last of their kind. It was a silly thing to think, but as he hurried to the door, he felt as if he were running from a temple that had been desecrated.

IX

The phone rang. Andrew made no move to answer it. He sharpened his blue pencil and touched the left eye of the drawing. It rang more than twenty times before stopping. In a minute it started up again. Andrew tried to block it out, but he couldn't. He stomped over to the phone thinking, "That Jamie is really getting to be a pain in the ass."

Andrew made no effort to disguise his annoyance. "Hello!"

"Is this Andrew Crowley?"

"Yes." Andrew didn't recognize the voice.

"This is the Apocalyptic Church of the Second Coming. Are you familiar with our work?"

"No." He whispered to Peter, "Listen to this guy," and held the phone out to the boy.

"Well, we believe that Moses, Jesus, Confucious, Buddha, Mohammed, along with our own leader, Father Chi Vivikenandass, are divine messengers on a holy mission to save man from his own destruction." Andrew rolled his eyes. "We were wondering if you or any of your loved ones might be interested in coming to our prayer meeting tonight."

"I see . . . do you make blood sacrifices?"

There was a long pause on the other end of the line. "No . . . but we burn incense and light camphor."

"I'm terribly sorry, but I only believe in blood sacrifices. If you were going to bleed a lamb or perhaps a small child, I might have been interested."

They laughed and Peter resumed his pose. He enjoyed the attention he was getting. He had never had so much fun doing nothing before. He was curious to see how his white-haired friend saw him, but Andrew was careful when he answered the phone to lean the drawing board against the chair so Peter couldn't see it.

74

Andrew had made him very beautiful. Peter's skin was so white it was almost transparent. Faint blue veins streamed down his neck and fanned out across his open chest. There was something hermaphroditic about the body that was wrapped in the silk bathrobe. "Do you believe that?"

"What?" Andrew wasn't really listening.

"What you said to the weirdo on the phone."

Andrew was just finishing Peter's right eye. He was staring so intently at the boy that he hardly looked at what the pencil in his hand was doing. He made the lashes unnaturally long and the irises unbelievably blue. He reached for a deeper shade of blue. It had a touch more purple to it. The point came down in the center of the pupil. It moved, then paused, then moved again. He changed pencils. Andrew picked a green one that matched his own eyes. The drawing seemed to be finishing itself. Peter's eye caught and penetrated you no matter what angle you viewed him from. The word—the idea— of an oracle was in Andrew's mind as he shaded the boy's eye.

He took Peter's question quite seriously. In a way he did believe in sacrifices. As he stuck the red pencil he was now working with into the sharpener, he answered, "Sort of. . . . I guess I do believe in sacrifices," and then asked over the electric hum of the sharpener, "What do you believe in, Peter?"

"It depends who I'm looking at. It changes. Different people make me believe different things." Peter wasn't quite sure what he meant himself.

"And what do you think I believe in?" Andrew was squinting at him.

"What you see."

"And your father?" Andrew was pushing him.

"He and my sister only believe in what they can eat."

Andrew stopped drawing. "Well, they're both fat." Peter giggled nervously, and Andrew laughed in wonder.

Andrew looked at this one-eyed drawing—the face he wanted the viewer to feel held a secret—and then looked at the figure seated before him. Andrew wondered how much of a likeness he had created. Then the phone rang again.

"Hello, Andrew, this is Simon Pyne." Andrew couldn't imagine why he would be calling. "Is Peter Lerner there?"

"Yes."

"Well there's been a family . . . emergency. Would you send him home?"

"Something's come up. We'll have to finish later. I have to go uptown to the Nose Gallery." Andrew guessed what had happened. He was involved, somehow committed to the figure in the drawing. He felt he had to see it through. He couldn't just put Peter in a cab and send him home alone. "I'll drop you off."

"But I live on Eighty-eighth. You're going to Fifty-seventh."

"That's O.K., I'll drop you off anyway."

Andrew was uncomfortable on the cab ride uptown. He suddenly didn't know what to say to this thirteen-year-old with whom he had chatted so freely all afternoon. "What sports do you play at school?"

"Soccer, hockey, and tennis. . . . Hockey's my favorite."

"Hockey's quite rough. . . . Do you . . . do you like . . . school?"

When Andrew began to ask him about subjects he knew Andrew had no interest in, Peter became suspicious. He wondered if Andrew had received some bad news on the phone.

As the cab pulled up to Peter's house, Andrew thought to himself, "Should I just drop him off or go in with him?" The feeling of responsibility was new to him. He didn't know the right thing to do. "Why did I ever come up here with him?"

He was tempted to leave Peter at the door and be done with it. "It's not my place to be here anyway," Andrew told himself, but instead he said, "I don't have to be at the gallery for thirty minutes. Will you make me one of those stingers you said you used to whip up for your . . ." Andrew started to say the word but then stopped.

Simon wasn't prepared to see Andrew. At first he didn't like the idea that an outsider was there, but then he decided it might make things easier after all.

The two men exchanged a knowing glance. They didn't shake hands. Andrew braced himself for what was to come. Simon looked at Wendy. "It's difficult to say this, but your . . ."

Wendy threw down the newspaper and interrupted him. "My behavior is what, Simon?" she snarled.

Simon quickly walked across the room, sat down beside her on the couch, and put his hand on her shoulder. Peter had his back to all of them. He tasted the stinger he had just made Andrew, smacked his lips, and announced in a French accent, "Monsieur, the stinger, she will be ready *dans un moment.*"

76

Simon cleared his throat and Andrew winced. "Your father died this morning."

The news snapped Wendy out of the funk she had been in all day. She pulled away from her father's adviser and friend, then screamed and hit Simon so hard in the face that his glasses flew across the room. "I don't believe you."

Peter put down the drink. He didn't turn around or say a thing. He ran out of the room without showing any of them the expression on his face.

Watching grief and sadness sweep over Lerner's children, Andrew thought, "I never should have come here." Standing there in his red cape and elf shoes, he suddenly felt like a freak, like some aging Puck who excited himself with his own hand as he watched life from the shadows. Andrew had chosen the role. But why?

Andrew looked at Simon, then at Wendy. "I'm terribly sorry." It was such a stupid, inadequate thing to say. When someone died, Andrew always felt particularly guilty for living.

As Simon walked him to the door, Andrew saw that Wendy had scratched Simon's nose when she struck him. A large tear rolled out of the accountant's eye and across the cut, trickling pink down his wrinkled cheek. Andrew asked if there was anything he could do, but Simon assured him, "I think I'll be able to take care of everything."

Andrew had no idea where he was going. He just started walking. After about twenty blocks, he remembered that Jamie had mentioned a party on Beacon Place. Andrew didn't feel like a party, but he didn't know where else to go. He didn't want to think about what he had seen that day.

Andrew got very drunk at the party that night and had a terrible time. Everyone kept asking him what was wrong, but he didn't tell them. He couldn't put his finger on exactly why he felt so peculiar, so disturbed. He knew it wasn't just Lerner's suicide.

Jamie stroked and kissed Andrew, but Andrew didn't find this attention very comforting. As the couples danced around him in the style of the times, together but alone, their movements made all the more ungainly and confusing by the strobe light that flashed overhead, Andrew reviewed the unexpected progression of that Saturday and wondered, "Do I want to get into it?" By "it" Andrew told himself he meant finishing the drawing of Peter.

X

Simon's house was like a museum. He'd bricked over most of the windows facing the street to create more wall space for his pictures. The only natural light allowed in the house came from long, narrow panes of glass across the top of each room. From the outside Simon's townhouse looked like a gigantic safe.

It was a house built for art, not for people. The temperature and humidity were kept at a level which was excellent for paint, but bad for Simon's wife's asthma. Her high-pitched cough echoed through the galleries, but Simon never heard it. There was little furniture, and the only lights were tiny hidden ceiling spotlights. They illuminated the paintings as if by magic.

Simon could twirl the knobs on the control panels in each room and single out one picture, bring it to life with light, then put it back into darkness and bestow the same favor on another painting. He never tired of the game.

Simon collected the treasures of the twentieth century along with those of ancient Greece and Rome. Art had always been his passion; he knew a great deal about the things of beauty man had fashioned between these two eras, but he did not feel the need to own them. He liked to think his collection commemorated two golden ages for man.

Unlike most of the vieux and nouveau riche who collect art, Simon had been born with an eye that could spot beauty and truth that the rest of the world remained blind to for years. Sometimes the work in which Simon invested his time and money was not profitable, but he never bought bad art. Simon misjudged artists but never their art.

Simon began his collection when he was a young man. In 1930, when he was only twenty-four-years old and lucky to be making $2,000 a year, he spent all of his savings and borrowed $2,700 to buy a Matisse from a shipping magnate who had gone under in the Crash.

It wasn't a light or carefree Matisse like those already in vogue. The Matisse for which he took this risk was dark and of the same substance as a Rembrandt.

His fiancée's parents thought him a fool for squandering his money on the painting. They postponed the wedding for a year, warning her, "Being married to a man who takes risks like that, you might as well be wife to a card shark, a mountain climber. . . . He's not bad, he just can't help himself . . ." Simon hadn't even considered the $750,-000 that the Japanese motorcycle manufacturer had offered him for the Matisse in December of 1968.

Simon did sell his art from time to time, usually for ten or twenty times what he had paid for it. But unlike most men who make a business of art—or, if they're shrewd, a fortune—Simon had the wisdom never to sell the best.

Though he enjoyed the money and social status his collection brought him, Simon didn't acquire the art for either of these reasons. Unlike the Lehmanns or Guggenheims or Rockefellers of the world, he didn't collect in the hope of obtaining some kind of cultural immortality.

When asked why he took so much art in under his roof, Simon would say simply and seriously, "Because I love it." He did not worship the masterpieces in his collection. He respected and cared for them the way men looked after women in the last century. Though Simon never admitted it, he believed great art too fine for most eyes. Sometimes, he even went so far as to indulge the fantasy that the men who brought these ladies of beauty to life had no more right to have them than the barbarians.

There were other collections of modern art that were larger and much more famous, that contained many more Matisses, Picassos, Cézannes, and Mondrians than his. But no one—not in America, not in the world—had more masterpieces by those abstract painters that blossomed after the war. Where Simon looked at his Picassos and Matisses as wives, he loved the Pollacks, de Kalbs, Rothkos, and Lerners as children. In turn, he looked on the painters that followed in the sixties—the Louises, Frankenthalers, Nolands, Stellas, Hollands, and Olitskys—as grandchildren. He had watched these two generations mature; he had helped them through their changes in the fifties and sixties.

Simon had been given most of these postwar pictures by artists in return for his advice. Officially Simon was an accountant. Usually the first type of counsel he gave was financial, but the longer Simon was involved with a painter the more fatherly his advice became.

He did what he believed was best for their art. If he thought an affair or a reconciliation would keep the artist's work on the track he thought best for it, he would do everything within his power to encourage and facilitate it. Divorces, adoptions, acquisitions of new studios—Simon could draw up the papers and make the arrangements for all. By helping artists with personal problems, by relieving certain pressures, Simon liked to think that he allowed them to move more freely as artists. In return, Simon would drop by their studios once or twice a year and pick up a painting or two for himself.

It pleased Simon more than anything else in the world when an artist's work reflected the influence he had hoped to have over them. Simon took the first painting Lerner completed after he started going to Dr. Fine. It was a large one that seemed to have a black hole in the heart of it. Simon liked to think of it as a doorway he had opened for Lerner. He saw the effect he had had on Lerner's work as his greatest triumph.

The pictures in the Pyne house moved. Simon never mentioned the shifts that were constantly taking place. He acted as if the paintings rearranged themselves. Very young artists, whose careers hadn't yet begun but who had promise, along with older painters whose careers had begun but had gone nowhere, stayed on the fourth floor of the house.

Pictures placed in the living room were more important than those in the dining room, paintings in the front hall more significant than those in the music room. As a painter's career improved, so did the position of his paintings in Simon Pyne's house.

Being placed in Pyne's bedroom was a mixed omen. It meant he wasn't sure just how your career was going and wanted to think about it. For some making the fifty-foot descent from the fourth floor to the living room took only a year, for others a lifetime.

The greatest works were always hung in his library, a big room with few books. There Simon kept his collection of classical art, as well as the best pictures of the postwar period. Placing his abstract masterpieces alongside his headless statue of Dionysus and his bust of Alexander the Great seemed to confirm the role in civilization that he believed this art would someday play. Simon thought these undefinably brilliant abstract paintings in his library possessed the same magical qualities as the figures of Apollo and Artemis that walked across his orange and black urn from the island of Rhodes.

Simon liked to say that "the great abstract art of the fifties and sixties, like the art of ancient Greece and Rome, does not idealize the real. It realizes the ideal."

Simon removed a contemporary painting from that room only if the painter had deserted him. Painters had given up his services before. When that happened Simon, playing the role of betrayed lover and father, felt hurt, bewildered, and angry. Simon had hung that gray Lerner, that triumph of his will, above the mantel as soon as he'd picked it up at the studio. After Lerner's death it was a comfort to know that he would never have to move it.

The one person whom Simon needed to talk to after Lerner had been found had vanished. Simon called Luccio's loft all day Sunday and finally went down there himself, but no one in the building had seen him that day. He had tried all Luccio's friends since then, he'd even called Luccio's mother in New Jersey, but no one had seen him or heard from him for the last three days. Simon was alternately frantically worried, then frantically angry about Luccio's disappearance.

Simon sat down to his poached egg Tuesday morning, picked up the paper, and tried not to think about Luccio. He found it comforting to lose himself in the news of the day, to read of troop arrivals in Vietnam, the famine in India, and the trial of James Earl Ray. As he read of the world struggles, Simon thought how clear-cut, how simple they seemed when typed up in neat columns. They all were far more convoluted situations than the one he was involved in; it was silly to agonize over everything.

An article in the lower lefthand corner of the front page brought him back to the problems the body at the morgue created for him and everyone else who knew Lerner. A gravedigger's strike had been declared the night before. No one could be buried until it was settled. The article discussed the emotional strain it would put on New Yorkers, as well as the potential health hazard it posed.

Simon told himself that there would certainly be exceptions and that Lerner would be one. He knew how to fix things like that. But still, the idea of having the corpse in limbo gave him a chill. Simon knew it was best for everyone to have Lerner buried quickly.

His chill turned to nausea when he threw down the *Times* and sorted through the mail. On the very top of the stack of letters beside his breakfast plate was one from Lerner. Simon recognized the scrawl. As he licked the yolk from his lips, he tore it open. It was a new copy of the will with a note attached from Lerner. It read, "Had some second thoughts about everything."

Simon knocked over his tomato juice as he pushed himself away from the table. Its stain moved slowly toward him. All Simon could think of was, "What is he doing to me?" He thought of Lerner as if he were still alive. Simon was angry and frightened.

He relaxed as he read the will. The basic provisions were unchanged. Lerner had had Harrington, Dupont, and Blaine specify that Wendy, rather than Simon, be Peter's guardian and that she receive control of her half of the estate immediately.

It didn't make sense. Lerner was always worrying about Wendy, saying how incompetent she was. At first the idea annoyed Simon. It was as if Lerner had had second thoughts about him, doubts that he had waited until he was dead to voice. But perhaps this last rash act of Lerner's would make things easier. He was sure Wendy would listen to him. It would be better for Wendy to take some responsibility for the decisions he would make. But still the changes in the will, coming the way they did, disconcerted him more than he would admit.

XI

They slept like spoons, one slightly longer than the other, placed on opposite sides of a large white round Deco dinner plate of a bed. Andrew had his back to Jamie. He was curled up naked and warm beneath a white comforter. The inside of his thighs and pubic hair were still slightly damp from their gluttony a few hours earlier. Andrew always dreamed like a white-haired fetus, shoulders hunched, knees to his chest, and arms tight to his sides as if he were hiding something.

Suddenly Andrew was wide awake. He didn't slowly drift into consciousness. It was as if someone had flicked a switch inside him. Something was wrong, out of place. Holding that same position, he opened his eyes. Was someone there? A burglar? The week before a chiropractor in the Village had been stabbed in the eye by a junkie. Had someone come to get him?

Andrew slowly turned his head and surveyed the room. There was only Jamie.

Andrew felt like an ass for being so paranoid. "What time is it? Two? Three? Four?" He looked at the digital clock by the bed: 3:07 —1—19—69. The moment glowed in the darkness. He tried to shut his eyes to his disconcerting sensation of intrusion, but it wouldn't go away. The curtains rhythmically billowed out toward him, and then were sucked back against the open window as if this presence were breathing.

He was sure something was wrong. Andrew got out of bed, put on his glasses, and went out into the loft to investigate the source of this feeling. He sniffed at the air. "Is the gas on?" Even though the only scent he could discern was from a bunch of freesias, he checked the stove. It was off.

"Maybe I've forgotten something?" He thought of the water, and as he ran to the bathroom, he remembered the time he, Jamie,

Sidney, and Tessa had smoked dope and drunk champagne all afternoon in his six-foot-square copper tub. They were so loaded that they had run off half dressed to eat oysters at Gage & Tollner in Brooklyn and left the water running. It had begun to leak through to the floor below just as Tessa dug into her second dozen bluepoints announcing, "I'm going to hurt someone if I eat any more of these." But when Andrew checked the bathroom, he found the faucets screwed tight.

"What could it be?" As he stepped into the main room of the loft, Andrew remembered that Tessa had picked up a black man with a diamond in his tooth at a party and had brought him back to the loft. Andrew peered into the back room. He guessed Tessa and her new friend were gone. Half of the collection was off the hangers and scattered across the floor. A pair of underpants that he guessed were Tessa's crowned the head of the mannequin. "Maybe they left the front door open. . . . That's probably it . . . that would account for the draft and the curtain." He was disappointed to see that Tessa had closed and locked the door.

Andrew hadn't turned on any lights. The main room of the loft was dark except for a line of light from a street lamp outside. It cut across the couch, the backgammon board, and the prayer rug, pointing to the corner of the room where he worked. As Andrew walked down the beam of light toward his easel and paints, the feeling that something in his world was amiss hovered over him. It reminded Andrew of that vague fear all children have, that undefinable emotional claustrophobia there seems no escaping from. It is a nameless fear that comes over you in sleep as if you were being smothered by an immense pillow. As Andrew tried to figure out why at twenty-nine it had come back to haunt him, he saw himself as a child waking with the terrifying sensation that if he slept a minute longer he'd be lost. Running from his bed, crying to his mother, unable to tell her what the matter was, unable to give a name to what was wrong, Andrew remembered nodding dumbly, his throat choked with tears when asked, "Did the dark frighten you?"

Andrew looked at the painting on the easel. It was of a man at a cocktail party, peering intently into a large aquarium. It was a good example of the Crowley style that had developed over the sixties. Some passages in the painting were executed in Düreresque detail and others were deliberately vague and slapdash. Andrew put no more into his abstract rendering of the cocktail party than you ever

84

get from those frantic stand-up affairs where it is impossible to eat, drink, or promote yourself comfortably.

The figures in the background were just half-finished outlines, partially filled with colors approximating flesh and cloth. But the specifics of the event that Andrew did supply—the cut of a lapel and the pink rose in its hole, an empty glass at a pair of voluptuous lips, a shell-shaped ashtray, a flip of hennaed hair, a pleat, and a piece of cheese—all tied together with a ribbon of dove-gray cigarette smoke that made your eyes sting—so clearly conveyed the spirit of these events that the viewer began to perspire, halfway expecting to be asked, "And what do you do?"

The man and the aquarium, serene and surreal, were set against this backdrop of hysteria. The aquarium was painted very flatly. Andrew deliberately tried to make it and the sand, plants, and porcelain castle in it look fake. The man was depicted in the same manner.

The only things that had beauty, that had life, were a pair of fish in the aquarium. They were more subtly colored than any you could buy in a pet store. Their scales, flecked with gold, shimmered orange and blue, and their elongated fins and tails were variegated with stripes of violet, green, and yellow. Before painting the fish, Andrew had looked through several books, combining the most intriguing features from a number of different types. Using sable brushes, he had created a species more brilliant than any in the waters of the Barrier Reef or the Bermuda Triangle.

The glass of the aquarium seemed to be right up against the canvas. One of the fish peered out at the real world, while the other looked up to the surface as the man offered it fish food with one hand while reaching for a pack of Eagle Claw fishhooks in his jacket pocket.

Andrew had started "The One That Got Away" three or four weeks before Lerner's death. It was almost finished. He examined it carefully to see if there was something off in the color or composition of the picture. Maybe that was what he was worried about. He had awakened in the middle of the night before and spotted flaws he hadn't been able to see in daylight. But Andrew saw nothing in the cocktail party or the aquarium that could account for his state of mind.

Andrew didn't hoard his paintings the way Lerner did. He let them collect for a year or so, permitted ideas to surface, intermarry, and breed. Then he would have a show and send them out into the world. He refused to take on the responsibility of parent. He had brought them to life. He did not feel bound to live with or by his art. The questions the paintings posed became the problems of their new owners. Andrew used his painting the way most of us use analysis. The only difference was that he was paid for unloading his feelings on the world. Pursued by collectors, sold and resold by those shrewd enough to invest in other's dreams, Andrew's work continued to compound the enigma of Andrew and his art.

The only Crowley that wasn't for sale, that never left home to join the small army of art that protected Andrew, was a self-portrait he had painted while still in college. A nineteenth-century bronze tiger by Cartier stood guard beneath the painting. Andrew's technique, his genius, had been apparent even then. It just wasn't as carefully focused.

Andrew had painted himself ascending a huge beaux arts staircase lined with busts. Andrew was near the top. The statues below him were unidentifiable, but all had a classical quality that spoke of gods and greatness. The last three busts were unmistakably Leonardo da Vinci, Rembrandt, and Picasso. In comparison to them, Andrew had depicted himself comically. His hair stood on end. He wore a black leather motorcycle jacket and an expression of disbelief. Andrew stared at himself for fifteen minutes before looking at the cloven hooves he had given this figure with his face.

Andrew could see things wrong with the picture, places where vagueness was an excuse, not a device. If he were to paint it now, he would make himself naked. The motorcycle jacket suddenly seemed a cheap trick. It distracted the viewer from the point of the painting. That was how Andrew had seen himself at nineteen. But had his vision changed?

He turned to the big oak chest where he stored his drawings. It had very wide shallow drawers. It had been used by a cartographer in the last century to store his maps. Andrew didn't know exactly what he was looking for, but he was sure he would recognize it if and when he saw it.

His sweaty fingers marked the drawings as he shuffled through them. Several fell to the floor. He didn't stop to pick them up. Andrew didn't even notice when he tore the stem of a blue tulip a friend of Sidney's had offered to buy for $4,000 the day before.

It was in the last drawer, the one the cartographer had stored his star charts in. It grabbed him just as surely as if a junkie had crept up and put his hands around Andrew's throat. He dropped the other drawings he was holding and looked into the gaze of this incomplete picture of Peter Lerner. Andrew remembered wanting to render Peter like an oracle. He saw things in the drawing that he had no recollection of including.

Only one eye of the face was finished, but in Peter's blue iris Andrew saw his own reflection. He saw an image of himself that was so tiny, so elusively subtle, that at first Andrew thought that he was imagining it. He told himself that it was a slip of the hand, an accidental variation in the color and line of the fibers of the iris.

But when he shined a 200-watt light on the drawing, the skeptic in Andrew saw that the image was no accident. The drawing had a maturity Andrew didn't see in the work scattered at his feet. He was no longer just flirting with classical problems of color, line, and light, using his gift to kick up his heels and poke fun. But the fact that this drawing was so much more ambitious than the others was only a very small part of what was bothering him. It was just the tip of the iceberg. It was the way in which he had committed himself emotionally, not technically, in the drawing that was bothering Andrew. This fear, this sense of danger, to which Andrew had awakened was reflected in Peter's gaze.

Andrew studied the drawing for a very long time. He ran his fingers over the boy's face as if to brush away the strands of hair that curled over Peter's forehead. Then he saw it.

Andrew often included himself in his work in self-deprecating ways. No one could accuse Andrew of being precious in that respect. He had painted and drawn amusing as well as grotesque caricatures of himself. He had rendered himself boyish, endearing, and pink-cheeked as well as jaded, sallow skinned, and lifeless. Andrew had drawn himself as both the dinner and the diner. He had played many parts in his art, but he had never fantasized himself in this role. He had never considered the possibility that the drawing presented. Andrew understood why he was so frightened. He had drawn himself blind. Though his eyes were open, Andrew was sure that the white-haired figure in Peter's eye saw nothing.

Andrew turned out the light.

Standing there white skinned and white haired in the darkness, looking not quite human, as if the life had been bleached out of him, but glowing, luminescing nonetheless, Andrew saw that those vague fears that yanked him out of sleep lay within himself. He saw signs, reflections of this danger from within—not just in his drawing of Peter, but in Lerner's bloodletting, in his reactions to the children's grief, and most especially in his own boredom. They were all part of this immense pillow of fear that he felt coming down on him.

Andrew wondered how he had let it come so close, how he had slept so long. How could he make himself safe? Andrew wasn't sure. Maybe Peter could help? He would finish the drawing, then begin a painting of this boy who had alerted him to a dissatisfaction with himself and his world.

Andrew felt relieved and refreshed by his discovery. The fear was gone. He had no urge to join Jamie back in bed. He sat down, opened a lapis cigarette box, and rolled a long narrow joint. He licked it so it would burn evenly. Andrew made a little sucking noise as he took the sweet smoke in. He held it for a moment, then set it swirling out his nose. He looked like a dragon. As he put the joint to his lips for the second time, he heard a glass shatter. There was someone after all.

Andrew turned around and saw Tessa step out of the kitchen. She was naked. "What happened to your friend?"

"Who?"

"The man you met at the party."

"He left. I must have passed out. Were you frightened?" Tessa's body was all darkness and shadow—only her face was in the light.

"No," Andrew lied.

Tessa stepped into the light. She was very thin. Her breasts were small with almost no nipple. She was built straight up and down. Like a boy. She did not look so different from the way Andrew imagined Peter would look naked.

"Are you frightened now?" she asked with a half smile.

"No." Andrew lied again.

Tessa looked at the drawings scattered across the floor, "What were you doing?"

"Thinking about how I got here."

She sat cross-legged next to him and took the joint from his lips. "Why did you come to New York . . . in the beginning, I mean?"

"I felt like I was being smothered by my family . . . college . . . the usual things."

"They didn't want you to paint?" She asked.

"No, if they had really been against me, if they could have provided me with something to fight against . . . to be different from . . . it wouldn't have been so bad, but they were indifferent to me, to themselves. . . . Christ! to life. They had no idea what I was trying to do."

"What were you trying to do?"

"Believe," he said hoarsely.

"In what?"

"Then? . . . Anything."

"Now?"

"I don't know."

"Did you come alone?" Tessa wondered aloud.

"No. . . . Yes."

Tessa looked at him quizzically. "What do you mean?"

"I came with a man but . . ." Andrew stopped to think about his flight. He remembered walking out of the quad at nineteen, carrying that picture of himself on the staircase in one hand and a wicker picnic basket that he used for a suitcase in the other, getting in George's car and driving to New York. George had been at school for the week lecturing about abstract art. Andrew tried to remember George's last name, but couldn't. He had believed in Andrew and his art, but that wasn't why Andrew had picked him. The pawing and the patting, the stickiness of being so close with him in the dark, were just the first installments toward the price of Andrew's one-way ticket.

He looked at Tessa and wondered if it had had to be that way for him—was that the only way he could have broken free, had his chance? "But I just spent the first night with him. The next day I moved into a Y.M.C.A. I found a bottle of peroxide under the sink."

Tessa smiled at him and ran her fingers through his white hair. For a moment he forgot they were naked, that she was a woman. "How did you come to New York?" Andrew asked.

"Pretty much the same way as you did—with a man . . ."

"Did you leave him the next day?"

"No, I married him."

It was quite light by then. The sun sat atop the spire of the Chrysler Building as if it were getting a fix. Tessa touched her stomach, "I'm hungry."

"I know."

They dressed quickly. "We'll go to the all-night diner over by the river." Andrew told her as he pulled on his pants.

By the time they were on the street they were talking about what they were going to eat. "I'm dying for some French fries." Tessa sighed.

"For breakfast?" Andrew asked incredulously.

"With lots of ketchup" she licked her lips.

They were lucky. They got a cab right away. Tessa snuggled close to him. "What do you want?"

"Eggs."

"With ketchup?"

Andrew laughed. He was glad he wasn't alone. "No . . . I want poached eggs on English muffins and a side order of bacon. . . . No, I think I feel more like sausage and pancakes with lots of maple syrup . . ."

"You can't."

"Wait and see."

Tessa laughed and hugged him. For a moment the world seemed no more awesome than a big breakfast—anything seemed possible. But as the cab cruised through the trucking district a memory made Andrew sit up and take his hand from Tessa's. He thought of the night he had taken on a leather boy wearing studded wristlets and a tattoo of a snake around his waist in the back of an unlocked truck trailer. With his leather and his chains the man was like an executioner. Andrew could hear the sound of the stranger's keys jingling in the night and he remembered even as he was being brutalized how he was able to marvel at how this deadly lover had no idea how really to hurt him. He came no closer than the others to cracking the shell that allowed Andrew to look at life so closely.

Andrew had done it for the thrill, out of a desperate urge to risk something. He wondered what had happened to the adventure he thought awaited him when he painted himself ascending the staircase of genius.

The cab stopped at a traffic light by an A & P warehouse. Tessa

90

was still hungry. "Maybe French toast would be better than pan-cakes?"

Andrew watched slaughtered sides of beef, red flesh wrapped in white blankets of fat, being rolled off a truck and suddenly thought of Lerner. "I wonder how they did it to him?" Andrew asked himself aloud.

"Did what, to who?" She didn't understand.

"To Lerner." Andrew was alone again.

XII

"Hello."

It was Luccio. Simon resisted a temptation to shout into the receiver, "Where the fuck have you been for the last two days?" From the tone of Luccio's voice he knew that any of the speeches he had prepared while he had waited for Luccio to get in touch with him would only complicate matters. Luccio must have had a reason for staying away so long. But why? "Where are you?" His words were as tight and knotted as his stomach.

"I'm home now."

Luccio knew Simon was angry, but he didn't care. All he could think of was what he had been through since Lerner's death. "It was not so hard for him . . . he was not so close." The memory of that day he had painted with Lerner—when he had felt he was in the presence of some incredibly rare and wonderful natural phenomenon —came over him. It was quickly followed by his vision of what the body must have looked like when they found it. What made it so hard was that the blood did not wash away the first image. The Lerner of the fifties who had his hand on more of the alchemy of life than one man really has a right to glowed neon in Luccio's consciousness simultaneously with the Lerner who had been bled to death years before his heart stopped beating Saturday morning. Luccio began to weep.

"We have to talk."

Simon had to know what had happened, what Luccio was thinking, what he was feeling. Simon's strength had always rested in knowing other's secrets, in being the only one to have all the pieces of the puzzle.

"I know."

Luccio looked at his reflection in the glass of the phone booth he was calling from. He didn't like what he saw. His hair was matted and streaked with dried paint. His clothes were stained and his jacket ripped. His face was covered with several days' beard, and his eyes were red.

Locked in that phone booth, Luccio had the bewildered look of a caged animal—exhausted, but still frantic. It wasn't so much his physical appearance that bothered Luccio. It was the odd sensation that he was losing something of himself.

Like the bits and pieces of stray trash that blew down the avenue —candy wrappers, a paper bag, and now a gray fedora with a tire track across its crown—Luccio felt as if part of him were being swept away. He knew it would be pointless to turn back and try to recapture what he had already lost. It was too late for that. Luccio could only hope to get out of the wind before he lost more of the collage titled "Luccio Cortesi, Painter" that he had carefully compiled over the years.

"I'll be at my house this afternoon at five." Simon was making neither a request nor a command. The two men knew they needed each other.

"I'll be there." As he looked away from his reflection, Luccio knew Simon would never really know how hard it had been for him, how much he had lost. How could he explain what he did not understand himself?

"Good-bye." Simon hung up the phone and began going over the possible explanations for Luccio's behavior. Was it something Lerner had said to Luccio at the party? Did Steven call him later? From the studio? What did Luccio know that he didn't?

Before Luccio and Simon would attempt to interpret or explain Lerner's death, before either would commit himself in any way, each wanted to find out where the other stood. They had questions to ask, positions to discuss that could not be dealt with over the phone. Some would not be verbalized even when they met in person. These two men who had lived off their eyes knew that they would get the clearest reading of each other, learn more of the truth, from what they saw in each other's faces and actions than by the words they would string together in Simon's library.

When Luccio arrived at Simon's house, there were still a few bits of yellow paint in his hair, but he had shaved and was in clean clothes. He had thrown the dirty ones away. He didn't look at all bad. In fact, the effect of the weight he had lost because of

93

his trauma was rather becoming.

But as Luccio entered the house, he was acutely aware that the bounce in his step, the spring that had been so much a part of the entrances and exits he had made his whole life, was gone.

He glanced into the dining room on his way to the library and was surprised to see that the last picture he had given Simon, a red one flecked with blue called "Sicilian Summer," had been moved downstairs. It had not only been promoted, but it had usurped the position that Farthington had held for years above the sideboard. Luccio liked seeing himself there. But why now? He hadn't been to Simon's for more than a month, and he wondered if it had been moved before or after Lerner died.

As soon as Luccio sat down, Simon began his lecture. He would try to bully what he wanted out of Luccio. His anger was on the verge of breaking through each word. "Do you know how many decisions have to be made now that Steven is . . ." He let Luccio's imagination fill in that part. "Things aren't going to get easier. . . . We have a responsibility . . . a commitment. . . . It's done and we can't change how it happened." Simon studied Luccio's face. He hoped to catch sight of some sign that might tell him whether Luccio did know something more of how "it" had happened.

Luccio wouldn't look at him. He kept his eyes on a headless statue of a god no longer worshiped for his divinity but believed in for its beauty.

"There's no way you can forget what Lerner did . . . to himself." Simon gave special emphasis to the last two words.

"I wasn't trying to forget," Luccio mumbled.

"Then why did you run off? Did you go on a bender?" Luccio had disappeared for days before, stayed drunk, and fucked anything with any warmth to it. But Simon knew that Luccio's disappearance could not be explained so simply.

"I had to find something first."

"What? . . . What could have been so important to keep you away at a time like this? . . . What in God's name were you looking for?" As Simon barked out these questions, others took their place in his mind. Was Luccio looking for something of Lerner's? . . . A note— was there a note that they hadn't found? Had Lerner had the time or the strength to leave a message, a letter? Where was it? What did it say?

94

Luccio had never seen Simon so tense. He was trembling. Was it with rage, or fear, or . . . ? Before Luccio could think of any other alternative, Simon asked him eagerly, "Did you go to the studio? Did you find it there?"

Luccio just shook his head. He had gone to Lerner's studio, but not the new one just off Fifth Avenue. Luccio would never go back there. Instead he had gone to Lerner's old studio, the one above the candy store on Twenty-eighth Street. Things had begun so peacefully there. Luccio looked for the building for more than two hours, but never found it. At first he thought he had remembered the wrong address. He walked back and forth between First and Fifth on every street in the Twenties, but what he was looking for had vanished years before. It wasn't until he repeated his processional through those streets that he realized that the building he was looking for had been razed, and the ground it had rested on had been blacked over with asphalt for a parking lot.

Simon was impatient for an answer. "Did you find it?"

"What?"

"Whatever it was you were looking for."

"It wasn't something I could touch. It was a memory—something I had to remember before I could return to . . ." He gestured with both hands at Simon and the art around them in that classic Italian manner that answers one question with another.

"Where did you go? I called you fifty times. I even went down to your place myself."

Luccio remembered letting the phone ring and hiding in the bathroom when Simon knocked on his door Monday afternoon. Luccio had felt paralyzed. He had left his mail unopened. He hadn't even read a letter from Libba's cousin Birdie, although he knew it contained an invitation to visit her in Vermont so that they could decide about the paintings for her uncle's museum in Cincinnati. If she took two, he would get $15,000 at the very least. If the week went particularly well and he told her stories about the old days in the garden of the Museum of Modern Art, he might do even better. He could say that Lerner had chosen the two paintings for himself before she had seen them and that Lerner's children really had a claim on them. If he juggled the truth in just the right way, he might get $25,000 out of the weekend.

But Luccio was curiously incapable of addressing such intrigues.

He sensed that he would not be able to embrace the life he had made for himself until he settled his memory of Lerner.

Simon was positive it was something more concrete than a memory. "Did he call you?"

"No. Did he say he was going to?" Luccio asked nervously.

. "Did you call him that night?" Simon demanded.

"Was he still bleeding when you found him?"

"I didn't find him. Maggie did. Do you know how many excuses I've had to make for you?"

"Was he still alive?"

"No. Are you listening?" Neither man really was. "Are you sure that he didn't say something that upset you or made you . . ."

"Oh, God, and the blood. . . . Steven vomited when he saw me kill a chicken." Luccio thought of Lerner's retching at the sight of his own blood. "He always hated the sight of blood."

Each was certain that the other was holding something back. It made them feel more vulnerable than they already were. When the two men stared into each other, they didn't discover what they had hoped to find. All they saw was a reflection of their own vision of Lerner's death, the blood gushing out of him as he reached across the canvas.

"Oh, Christ! Luccio, do you know what it was like going through it all with Maggie and the police at the studio? Then having to tell the children. Wendy hit me."

Simon pointed to the scab on his nose, and Luccio remembered that after he had failed to find what he was looking for on Twenty-eighth Street, he had gone uptown to Lerner's house on Eighty-eighth Street, hoping there he might find and face the spirit, the memory that haunted him. He had watched from the corner. He didn't know what he expected to see or feel, but when Wendy appeared at the window of the house and looked in his direction, he ran.

"The police. . . . I couldn't have talked to them. Oh, God, I'll never set foot in that studio again . . . not after. . . . I couldn't!"

Simon was reminded of his own fear of Lerner's loft. When he stood alone in the space he felt trapped in the dark tomblike studio. "And now we're going to have trouble with the burial."

"Why? What's wrong? In the paper I read that he was going to be buried tomorrow." Luccio had been looking forward to the sense of relief that he hoped the funeral would bring him.

"There's a gravediggers' strike. Do you think I like having to take care of all this by myself?"

Luccio was whimpering, "What else could I do? . . . It took so much out of me. . . . He took part of me with him."

"So that's it," Simon thought. He hadn't realized that Luccio had been in love with Lerner. "I wonder if they ever . . ." The image of the two men linked together like that fascinated him. He would never know, but if he had even suspected such a thing, such a bond, he would not have brought Luccio into this. Simon would admit his own attachment—an emotional vulnerability to Lerner's art, but not to the man.

"We are all guilty," Luccio mumbled.

"What are you talking about?" Simon would not accept that. "He did it to himself."

Luccio shook his head and looked at Simon's collection of ancient daggers. There was a Roman one, so heavy and symmetrical, Luccio had always coveted it. It was like a piece of sculpture. Now he saw it as a blade used to murder ancient martyrs.

"It was like the killing of a saint," Luccio whispered.

"Saints don't kill themselves." Simon's voice was as hard and cold as the blade. "You have to keep your perspective on this . . . separate the art from the artist, the man Lerner from the genius. There were always two Lerners." Simon's words cut Luccio free from the maelstrom of guilt and grief that he was caught in.

Luccio sensed Simon was right. He used his gift to color the past, to supply himself with an image of Lerner that he could live with. Luccio would not remember the Lerner who obtained patrons and shows for him, things that he didn't deserve. He would focus on the Lerner who made him feel he was a con man, not an artist. He thought of all the times Lerner had rejected him and others. "He would not accept what we offered. . . . He would not let us believe in him or ourselves. . . . He never shared any part of himself. He gloated over his brilliance by himself in his studio. For years he lived with the blade to his vein. . . . It was a selfish threat."

These thoughts relaxed him, and he looked up at Simon and declared, "If there was a saint in Lerner, Steven executed him long ago. I can never forgive him for that." As he spoke, the Catholic in Luccio remembered that successful self-destruction is the greatest

97

sin. Worse than murder.

"You're right. In many ways he was a selfish man. It was always easier to believe in—to have faith in—his art than him."

Sitting in the shadow of that gray Lerner over the mantel, the two men now felt confident enough of one another to be able to embrace and weep openly. The impenetrable darkness in the center of the painting made it appear to float. It seemed to reach out like a veil over the two men who believed that the worst part of their ordeal was over.

Within a few minutes they had assumed their old roles, Simon sorting papers behind his desk and Luccio posing next to the head of Alexander. They comforted themselves by talking about "the world's loss" and how "Lerner was just beginning to tackle the major questions in his work."

Though he wasn't a lawyer, Simon had drawn up Lerner's will just two days before he had died. Lerner had been in a rush to get it done. The will left all his cash and stocks along with the brownstone and everything in it to the children. The paintings were all to go to a foundation to help older artists, who as Lerner liked to say "didn't have the misfortune to become famous."

Lerner had been desperate to get the will signed and witnessed. Whenever Simon raised a question or pointed out wording that was vague or unclear, Lerner had sneered, shaken his head, and jabbed at the draft they were working on, saying, "The wording doesn't matter. You and Luccio know what I want. It doesn't even matter what I say here. You'll take care of it."

Luccio and Simon were executors of the will, as well as trustees of the foundation, for life. More than eight hundred paintings Lerner had hoarded over the years were in their hands.

Simon had expected that he and Lerner would draft the papers for the foundation just as they had written up the will. But instead, Lerner had arrived Friday afternoon with an envelope full of documents drawn up by Harrington, Dupont, and Blaine, a stuffy firm of lawyers that had nothing to do with the art world. It seemed a bit more elaborate than it had to be. Simon was surprised that Lerner had had the good sense to bear with the lawyers through all that legal jargon. Every clause was spelled out in great detail. Simon didn't like to be hurried, but he gave in to Lerner and had signed the papers and had them notarized the day of the march. He knew that it was essential that the foundation rest on very firm legal grounds.

As trustees, he and Luccio would be in charge of the sale of the paintings. The income from the work they chose to sell would be used for "unspecified charitable grants." They were to appoint three other trustees who, along with themselves, would decide which artists were deserving and how much each should get.

Simon looked upon them as his paintings now. He would be able to oversee their fate, to impose his order over a body of art in a way that he had never been allowed before. With Luccio, one of the original disciples, at his side, he would distribute the relics Lerner had left behind. They would be the keepers of the faith.

Simon read the documents to Luccio carefully. He wanted to make sure Luccio understood which clauses he was emphasizing, how he was reading the guidelines for the will and foundation.

When Simon was finished, he took off his glasses and smiled. "As you see, it's really in our hands."

Luccio hadn't wanted it to be this way, to have so much responsibility. Neither man could refuse the role Lerner had offered with his death.

Quite naturally they came to the decision that they deserved what Lerner had left them. Simon listed all the doctors he had taken Steven to see, and Luccio reminisced about the times he had come to Steven's studio late at night and talked him through his depressions. By six o'clock they were both feeling quite confident.

When the phone on the desk rang, Simon didn't answer it. "I've never been able to do that until now—not without worrying. Sometimes Steven would call me thirty times in a day."

Luccio smiled. "Even if you hung up on him, he would call back."

"It was hard to know what he really wanted."

Luccio shook his head. "He didn't want anything in particular. He didn't want what he asked for, I know that. He just wanted to know there was someone there on the end of the line, that he had your attention. The minute Steven thought he had you interested in him, in his problem, he'd call someone else and see if he could get them."

The phone stopped ringing. "Who knows? Two weeks ago he called at three o'clock in the morning. Betsy answered the phone . . . frightened her to death. He said it was urgent and when he got me on the phone all he wanted to know was where I got my overcoat." The two men laughed; they felt good.

"Oh, one last thing, Steven told me on Friday that you signed a trustee's agreement that morning. . . . I'd appreciate it if you could drop it by sometime tomorrow."

"What do you mean?"

Simon held up several sheets of paper. "It looks like this."

"We did not talk that morning. I signed nothing."

The realization that Lerner had misled them on this small point broke the aura of altruism they had spun around themselves. Simon looked bewildered. "You know, he really wasn't well. It's awful to say, but, well, he's probably happier now that . . ."

"He's out of his misery." Luccio finished the thought for him.

"He told me specifically you signed it, Luccio. He went on about how you said he should pick someone else, but that it wasn't hard to convince you. I remember those were his exact words, 'You can talk Luccio into anything.' "

"We spoke about it at Libba's but I signed nothing. He said you'd talk me into it."

The fact that Luccio had not yet signed the agreement was not insurmountable. The will was signed and witnessed, and it mentioned Luccio as trustee of the foundation. Luccio could sign it now, and they could back-date it. Simon reassured himself aloud. "He wasn't well. He didn't know what he was doing."

The truth each was trying to hide from himself and from the other showed clearly on their startled faces. This man whose mind they had made up for years, who was so weak and dependent on them while he was breathing, was now taking charge of their lives.

As Simon wondered how many other things Lerner had kept secret from them, what other surprises awaited them, Luccio announced, loudly, "He didn't have any idea what was going on. He didn't know what he was doing—all that crap about aging artists. It's all horseshit. All he cared about was himself." Though they would not admit it, each was wondering how he could have been so naive as to so underestimate Lerner's power. They were every bit as dependent on him as he was on them. Just as Luccio and Simon were feeling most vulnerable, Maggie burst into the library. She was crying, holding a fresh handkerchief to her nose which still showed red beneath the coating of Erase she had just painted on.

Maggie had been on the phone constantly since Sunday, reminding

100

everyone she could think of just how close she had been to Lerner. She didn't just discuss the subject with the influential and important, those whose stand might be helpful to her cause. She found herself spilling out the tragedy to the clerk at the grocery store and the delivery boy from the dry cleaners. She was frantically trying to remind the world of the relationship she had had with Lerner and the right she felt it entitled her to. Like Luccio and Simon, she was only beginning to become aware of what she had lost.

More than the man, they mourned the passing of the control they had had over him. His will, his decision could not be tempered by threat or pressure from Dr. Fine. Death gave Lerner a power, an influence, that he had never had in life—one that was unchallengeable.

First the maid and then Simon's wife had tried to keep Maggie from barging into the library. "Mr. Pyne's in conference."

"I'm sure Simon will be with you as soon as he finishes with Luccio. Would you like a cup of tea?" When Maggie found out Simon was talking to Luccio, she became all the more adamant. She glared at Betsy Pyne.

"There are things we have to talk about. They can't wait."

Maggie knew that Simon no longer needed her. She got no reward for stumbling on the body. Simon almost seemed angry it was she who had discovered the body and not Lerner's helper or one of the collectors Alfred Dutton (the director of the Winston Gallery in New York) had planned to bring to the studio that Saturday afternoon.

He said it would have been "easier . . . not as awkward" if someone else had found Lerner. His attitude made her furious. As Maggie stepped into the library, she thought to herself, "Next he'll tell me it'll look better if I don't go to the funeral. I was part of his life. I deserve something."

She was just leaning toward Luccio to accept the peck on the cheek she demanded upon greeting when she saw the will on Simon's desk. "I thought you said you wouldn't have a copy of the will until after the funeral."

Simon had lied because he had wanted to settle things with Luccio and take care of the funeral before he told Maggie that she was no longer a part of the play. She would not be forgotten, but she would not have the billing Simon had encouraged her to bank on when she had first started sleeping in the same bed with Lerner. "It just arrived yesterday. Steven mailed it himself. He must have done it that night," Simon explained quickly.

Instantly Maggie envisioned Lerner unable to return to her that night, filled with remorse, writing her name in a dozen different places in the will, and mailing it at dawn just before he took the razor to himself. She thought of that somber brown painting Lerner had refused to give her. She wanted it more than ever. Its value had changed now. She would never sell it. She needed it to point to as evidence of how close she had come to having it all. She told herself she'd been silly to worry. "Of course, he remembered me. I was in his mind at the end, that's why he mailed it at the last minute like that."

Maggie didn't want to seem eager, but she couldn't resist asking, "You don't have to tell me all the details now . . . unless, of course, you want to. But did he mention the painting, the one he promised me for my birthday?"

"We all know how he changed his mind. It's hard to know what he really wanted, especially in regard to his art. But the fact remains that in this will he—"

Maggie didn't let Simon finish. The sudden uncertainty of her position was unbearable. She dug her long red nails into the flesh of her palm. She had to act quickly. She knew her position would be even more precarious once Simon had said the words. "He promised me that painting!" She said it like a threat. She couldn't let them know how desperate she was. "There are lots of people who heard him promise it to me. I'm sure that he put it in writing. There's probably a note that hasn't surfaced that mentions the painting. All the junk and papers he had scattered around—how do you know what he was thinking that night?"

Simultaneously Luccio and Simon insisted, "There was no note."

"How do you know? It was obvious he knew this was coming, running around to all those lawyers." She sensed that she was on the right track. "He knew that this was coming, that it would end like this. You know that he told me everything."

They talked for several hours, but they no longer pushed and

102

challenged one another. Without ever coming out and saying anything that would be difficult to live with or that they might later
regret, they reached an understanding. Among other things, the
threesome agreed to respect each other's illusions about Lerner and
their relationships with him.

XIII

Death has a way of shaking truths loose in us. Some we embrace; others we insist don't mean a thing. A few are flushed out instantly by the sight of the body or by a strange voice telling us the news over the phone. Others are like thorns that we can't see well enough to remove, so we let them heal over. These truths are foreign particles that leave the flesh inflamed and sensitive, but don't work themselves to the surface for years. We discover secrets about ourselves, about the way we really love, about the lies with which we comforted ourselves, as well as secrets about the person who was close to us but now is dead. Searching through the bottoms of their drawers and the backs of their closets, we find private things. We look at letters that weren't addressed to us and diaries we were never meant to read. Sometimes in the course of this process which death initiates in the living we discover that we not only never knew the one who has died, but we never knew ourselves. When a life close to ours ends, it doesn't change our life so much as it makes us see it more clearly.

The process is one of disillusionment rather than one of disappointment. What we thought we had lost we see we never possessed, and the things we never valued we see are gone forever. As the bodies of Lerner's children shook with their tears, this process began to take place in them.

Like all of us, Wendy tried to fight it. Lerner had failed her in so many ways as a father. Now she had the understandable impulse to want to focus on those rare moments she had had with him when she believed he forgot about his art and his exhibitions, when she commanded his thoughts and his love seemed so real she could reach right out and grab it.

The time that came to mind, that was closest to fulfilling Wendy's need, occurred during the summer her family had spent on Martha's Vineyard. It had been the last summer she hadn't been embarrassed to wear a bathing suit.

The house they had rented was on a large saltwater pond that was connected with the ocean. All the children who lived near them had sailboats and took sailing lessons. Naturally Wendy wanted to try, but her father refused. "I don't want you to have anything to do with that rich kid bullshit." It wasn't expensive to have the blond senior from Yale take you out for an hour, but Lerner said that the idea was extravagant and ridiculous. He refused to talk about it. But a few days after Wendy had asked him, she discovered a brand-new bright green Skipjack with a yellow cockpit tied up to the dock in front of their house. Lerner insisted he didn't know how it got there. "Some rich kid probably tied it up and rather than come back and get it had his father buy him a new one."

Wendy knew the truth. She didn't mind the way he gave it to her, but what she didn't understand was that even though the boat cost a thousand dollars her father refused to pay for lessons. She watched the others with their boats and read all the books on sailing in the public library before she tried her sailboat. After capsizing several times and nearly drowning once when she got caught under the sail, Wendy mastered that little green and yellow boat and became a proficient sailor.

Her father spent almost the whole summer indoors painting. He appeared at the beach only at the end of the day when the sun was on the run. Even then he didn't put on a bathing suit.

The people remaining on the beach at that time of the day were real sun worshipers. They sat in striped beach chairs and stared up at the sun with closed eyes as if they could will it to stay aloft a little longer. When Lerner appeared, the men, women, and children of this cult turned their taut and tanned bodies around to stare at this pale fat man who didn't dress like them, talk like them, earn his money like them—who didn't look at any of the objects of their obsession as they did. They didn't like Lerner on their beach. He made them nervous. Why wasn't he out there with them where they could see what he was doing? Children pointed and parents whispered.

Lerner would hold his boots in one hand, let the waves lap at his soft white feet, and compare New England sunsets that looked like the inside of a shell with those he created in the pine-paneled guest room he used as a studio. During the following fall Lerner's paintings began to lose their color.

He painted a great deal in June and July, but in August his work began to go very slowly. He said it was the heat. Wendy would pass the studio in the morning, look through the window, and see him sitting on a stool holding his head in his hands scowling at a painting. When she returned at the end of her day, she'd see him sitting in exactly the same position, his expression and the painting unchanged as if he hadn't moved all day, painter and painting judging one another.

On a breezy day at the tail end of that summer Wendy's father appeared on the porch, pointed to the boat he refused to admit he had bought, and announced, "Show me what you've taught yourself."

There was a crispness to the air that spoke of fall, a chill that raised goosebumps on the back of her arms whenever a cloud drifted across the sun. Lerner sat in the bow of the boat. Wendy raised the sail, took the rudder, pulled in the sheets, and steered the boat out across the blue-black water of the pond.

There was a steady breeze. The boat moved quickly. Lerner peered into the water, saying, "These ponds were all cut out by the glacier when it came south."

Wendy knew he wasn't talking to her, but she responded anyway. "I know. There are holes in this pond more than fifteen hundred feet deep. That's why the water's so cold."

Lerner touched his hand to the water. "You know, you can't see a glacier moving, but they do all the time. Imagine a sea of ice coming at you like that! You wouldn't even know you were in its way until it was too late . . . caught like a mastodon."

"You know, at the Explorer's Club they ate the meat of a mastodon they found in the ice," she told him.

Lerner didn't hear. ". . . dark ice moving with such force nothing could stop it. They could cut right into the earth." He took his fingers out of the water when he realized they were growing numb.

They were in the center of the pond, and the wind was coming up. Lerner looked at the dark clouds that were crowding the corner of a baby-blue sky and turned to Wendy, "You learned to sail that kid's boat pretty good. . . . Let's go in now."

"Oh, we can't! You've hardly seen a thing." Without warning, Wendy brought the Skipjack about and headed toward the opening

106

to the sea. The stays creaked as the boat began to plane.

Wendy watched her father grip the rail of the boat. Then he turned to her. "You can't let things frighten you."

Wendy knew her father could barely swim. "What things?"

"Like this boat. I watched you almost drown, but you stayed with it even though it scared you."

A bit of chop began to pick up, and the boat bucked beneath them. It was then she realized that the faster and more recklessly she maneuvered the boat, the more her father was talking to her, the less he was directing his comments to himself.

The water sprayed up on them. Their clothes were soaked through. Wendy turned the boat closer to the wind, and her father stared at her. "Once you set a course you can't turn back. It's O.K. to give something up, to change, but never because you are afraid. You're lost if you do that."

Wendy had never left the shelter of that dark and deep pond and sailed out in the ocean. She had never seen anyone take a Skipjack through the creek that connected the pond with the sea. But Wendy headed right for the open water. Her father hadn't ever spoken to her like this before, and she wanted to hear more. His dark eyes were on her. It excited her so much she barely heard him. "Oh, God, Wendy, it's a risk, and I can't promise that life won't trap you, that if you head out and take the chance, you'll be able to get back. You can lose more than you thought you ever had."

The tide was coming into the pond. The water raced through the opening to the sea. The wind took them one way and the current another. They were caught. The water splashed up over the bow. The sheet cut her hand, and it was all she could do to hold the rudder. But Wendy didn't care. She wasn't thinking about the boat. Her father was crying. She'd seen him weep before, but this time he was crying for her as much as for himself. "Oh, God, baby, I love you, but I can't promise you anything."

The boat was totally out of control. The wind roared around them, and whitecaps whipping across the Atlantic threatened to swamp them. But Wendy was curiously content. She was sure that she occupied all his thoughts. In the course of their sail she had drawn something precious from him. As disaster threatened them both, he had confessed and proved his love. For a moment, he was no longer

107

a mystery. It was then that the boat jibed. The boom just missed Lerner's head. With a crash, the mast snapped and the white sail fell on them.

For days Wendy savored the memory of that afternoon when she had been so sure of her father's feelings. But when she had tried to think of another encounter that left her feeling that way, she couldn't. That was the only time Wendy was really positive that her father was talking to her and not merely addressing himself and anyone else who happened to be present. Wendy refused to believe that all she had gotten from him was one stormy afternoon at the end of an eleven-year-old summer.

Tuesday she went through her mother's photo albums hoping to find a snapshot of her and her father, one that might bring to mind some intimacy, some moment of satisfaction that she had forgotten. She looked into more than twenty years of photographs, some cracked and yellowed like dirty windows, but Wendy saw only lies.

Just as Wendy closed the last of her mother's dream catalogs, the phone rang. It was Simon. He called several times each day to see how they were doing, and he had taken them out to dinner twice. When Simon told her the funeral would have to be postponed at least until the weekend, Wendy knew she wouldn't be able to hold out that long.

Pushing the last photo album up on the top shelf of the bookcase, she knocked over a stack of old *National Geographics.* As the magazines fell past her, a handful of torn blue note paper fluttered down. The rest of the letter was buried between an article on Japanese puffer fish and a story about a middle-aged man who lived to tell about sailing to the top of the world with his cat. Normally Wendy would have left the magazines and the scraps of paper on the floor for Dora to pick up, but when she recognized her mother's handwriting, Wendy got down on her hands and knees and began to gather up the pieces of paper. It was like putting together a puzzle. In the background she could hear her brother crying upstairs.

Peter sat on his bed staring at a papier-mâché mask of a penguin. He had made it for Halloween. His father had liked it so much that he insisted on bringing it to a picnic to show Luccio. Between mouthfuls of roast beef and pumpkin pie, Lerner held the mask up for the people at the party. "What do you think?"

108

"It's really an extraordinary object!"

"Has some of the feel of totems in British Columbia."

"Reminds me of the little sculptures you made once."

"Would you make me one?"

As Lerner passed it around, bits of paint began to flake off the mask, revealing the combination of news- and toilet paper it was made of. Having satisfied himself of their interest, Lerner emptied his Dixie cup of vodka down his throat, belched, and took the mask away from them. He handled it roughly. His greasy fingers left their mark on the white of the mask. Peter could see several cracks in its beak. When Maggie called out, "How did you make it?" Lerner laughed and tossed the mask to Peter.

"Ask him."

They asked, but the conversation moved on quickly. He knew that an object fashioned by his father had quite a different effect from one made by him. It was clear that Lerner was playing a joke on them, but there was more to the scene. Peter saw it in his father's eye, and heard it in his voice when he answered Maggie's question. Lerner was boasting, not for Peter, but for himself. The mask and their approval of it was testimony, living proof, of his creative talent, both as a man and as an artist. Lerner really did feel that because he had fathered Peter he was directly responsible for the creation of the mask.

He watched Maggie turn down a piece of pumpkin pie, shaking her head and smirking as she patted Lerner's stomach, "One moment of bliss, a lifetime of regret!"

His father grabbed at the spare tire around his middle as if he could pull off the unwanted flesh and throw it away. "I'm going to start working out at the gym. Go down there tomorrow." As soon as he had committed himself, Lerner began to think of excuses. He turned to Maggie. "You know where my sneakers are? And my shorts?"

Peter poured himself a glass of cider that was just ready to turn and entered the conversation. "You ought to buy some sweat pants."

"How come?"

"You work up more of a sweat."

Lerner turned to Maggie to pass on the directive that a pair of sweat pants must be purchased before he could start. It would give him a little longer before he would have to admit that he had no intention of going to the gym. Then Peter looked at his mask and added, "Besides, when you wear shorts, you look like an egg on stilts."

It was quite true. The only part of Lerner that ever got skinny was his legs. Everyone laughed except Lerner. He was ready to slap his son. Peter could see it in his face. The boy held his head up for the blow. But Lerner was still sober enough to know that doing or saying anything before an audience would only make it worse. He belched again and went into the bedroom with Maggie.

When they came out, it was time to go home. Lerner pulled up his pants and proclaimed, "I'm not in such bad shape after all."

Maggie yawned and added, "We did have a good nap . . . that's one of the things Steven's taught me . . . it's not good to work yourself up after eating."

So often when Peter followed adult conversation, he felt that everything was being said in code, but it was a code neither party really knew how to transmit or receive. He found their actions, even when accidental, far easier to interpret.

When they got into the car, Lerner closed the door on Peter's hand. He blamed it on Maggie, but Peter was positive that his father had done it on purpose. He did it with just enough force to tear the skin and cause Peter to lose a fingernail, just hard enough to get even.

Peter wiped his nose with the hand that had been crushed in the car door. You could see the scar. Peter put the mask in the drawer. He cried for himself, and then for his father. Other memories took its place. Some were good. Some were bad. Peter lay on his bed and rubbed his eyes so hard he saw colors. His mind hopscotched and leapfrogged from year to year. Peter jumped from one memory to another across the flow of his life as if he were leaping from stone to stone across a stream.

Peter felt a huge puzzle lay before him, infinitely more complex and frustrating than the ones he used to struggle with—that of Peter Pan flying over Captain Hook's boat or Snow White eating the poison apple. He was caught between the urge to stop everything and try to put it all together or to scatter the pieces and run.

He didn't want to cry. He jumped up and opened the window hoping the cold air might retard his tears. But that only conjured

110

up thoughts of his mother looking out of the window for him as he came home from school. He could see her waving from behind the pane of glass. Then his nose began to tingle and his eyes to sting. Sobbing, he fell back into his bed, "But with Daddy it was different. He planned it . . . he did it to himself . . . he knew I would feel like this."

When his mother had died, Peter had tried to describe this feeling to his father. He had tried to talk about the puzzle, but Lerner was too drunk to listen. All he could say was, "It's no good, take it out on your art . . . try to impose your order there and not in your life. You won't be so disappointed that way because there is only one thing you can really believe in and that's death." His father's response made no more sense now than it did then. Peter flushed with anger. All he could think was, "The liar, how could he expect me to believe . . . dying like that."

In an hour Peter's active rage toward his father had passed, but it was not forgotten. As he splashed cold water on his face, he thought of Andrew and told himself, "The trick is not to let it show."

Peter sat at the top of the stairs and watched Wendy as she stared at the letter she had pieced together. She had found all the pieces and assembled them correctly, but the message gave her no satisfaction. It told her just how trapped she was. It wasn't a letter to an old friend or a secret farewell to a lover or any of the other things Wendy had imagined it to be as she was piecing it together. It was a suicide note Sarah Lerner had written to her husband on the morning of her death.

Her mother's heart had stopped, but it wasn't by accident. Wendy was left with no other conclusion than that the same fate would await her. She could no longer tell herself that she might have the good fortune to develop the less destructive characteristics of both her parents. They were a part of her inheritance, as real as the house, or the paintings, or anything else.

Wendy felt so angry, so cheated and shortchanged, that she couldn't cry. When she saw Peter staring at her, she screamed, "What are you sneaking around spying on me for?"

"I wasn't spying. I was just wondering why . . ." He was wondering so many things, he didn't know where to start.

"Why what?"

111

"Why Daddy didn't leave a note."

As Peter walked toward her, Wendy rearranged the pieces of her puzzle. It would be her secret. "People who kill themselves don't always leave notes."

"Yeah, but you know how Daddy always sort of had to have the last word." Peter thought about the car door closing on his hand, but he felt no pain.

"And you think his last words would be about you?"

"No."

"Well, what do you think you'd find out from a note?" Wendy demanded.

"Why he did it, I guess."

"He did it because you . . . me . . . Mother—all of us—betrayed him."

"What do you mean? . . . I . . . we all loved him, we all tried."

"It's easy to love. It wasn't because of love that we betrayed him . . . it was because he couldn't believe in us that we betrayed him." It was true, but it was such an ugly truth to hit him with. Wendy wondered why she chose it, why she always drove him away. She wanted to hold and be held. She wanted to reach out and cry with him . . . yes, and even though he was her brother and only thirteen years old, she would have liked to kiss and touch him and forget. But she couldn't—not because she didn't like him or because it was wrong. It was none of those things. She was frightened of herself, not him.

Standing there knowing that she could reassemble the pieces of her puzzle, show him the truth and make him cry, Wendy realized that she was saying these things, trying to drive him from the room to protect him. She was trying to shield him, not just from the truth of their mother's suicide, but from the larger and far more bewildering truths that lay within herself. "Peter just leave me alone, you wouldn't understand anyway."

"He could believe in me . . . if . . ."

"If what?"

"If he didn't believe in death."

"Why do you think he believed in that?"

"He told me so . . . but I was there for him."

"You weren't there that night he died. You were at a stupid basketball game." Wendy wanted to warn him, to tell him to get

112

away from her, but she couldn't. "If you had been there when he needed you . . . who knows?"

"If he'd asked me, I would have."

"How could he believe in a self-centered thirteen-year-old? You're so fucking fickle. You think you're such a darling—always performing . . . how could he believe in anything as hollow as you?"

Wendy couldn't stop herself. "You know why he believed in death? Because it doesn't lie. He could see it." She turned to a mirror. "When you get older, Peter, you'll realize that you see death every time you look at yourself." Wendy thought of what her father had said about glaciers. "It's others . . . it's the life around us that's hard to get a good look at, that flashes by before you see it clearly. If you could slow life down, feelings down, get hold of people, freeze them in the middle of what they were doing . . . you might learn something before it is too late. Then you might be able to believe."

Wendy studied her own face. She saw the death, the aging already taking place. She could see where the wrinkles and crow's feet would appear. What she couldn't see, what was unknown and frightening, was the life beneath the fat.

When Peter answered softly, "But you kill things when you freeze them." Wendy thought he was making fun of her.

"How can you make a joke when your father isn't even buried? You don't care about anyone but yourself. You know what his suicide means? He did it for the same reason our mother . . ." Wendy spun around ready to cut Peter down with her secret, but he was gone.

Instead she saw Simon Pyne standing in the open door holding a cake from Greenberg's bakery in one hand and his briefcase in the other. In Simon, Wendy could see the slow death she was talking about, and she didn't want it to happen to her. The light in the open doorway caught him in such a way that it highlighted his wrinkles. His face looked like a white raisin. He seemed smaller than he had the day before, as if someone had turned up the heat inside him and the life he had left was evaporating at an accelerated rate. "Why didn't you tell me my mother killed herself? What right do you have to keep secrets like that?"

Simon looked bewildered. He put down his briefcase and the cake. "What do you mean?"

"Mother did it, too. You knew that!"

"No, I didn't. What makes you say that now?"

Wendy pointed to the note. Simon reassembled the pieces of paper, read them, gathered them up, and put them in his pocket.

XIV

Simon hired a limousine and a driver to take Wendy, Peter, and himself to the funeral. As the Cadillac cruised up Third Avenue to get the children, Simon congratulated himself on how well he had arranged things.

Simon, Luccio, Wendy, Maggie, Barclay, Peter—they all had their reasons for wanting to get Lerner out of the morgue and buried. None of them could afford to wait for the gravedigger's strike to be settled. Lerner and the questions his life and death raised needed to be buried. Simon's idea of taking advantage of local laws and burying Lerner on Luccio's farm in Wainscott, Long Island, was a stroke of genius. Simon should have thought of it in the beginning.

Luccio didn't want the grave on his land. In fact, he had refused to have anything to do with the funeral. As Simon searched for a classical station on the radio he remembered Luccio pulling at his mustache and shouting, "How much do you want from me? . . . This, too, I have to give. . . . No, I will not! You have no right to demand this."

His suggestion had made Luccio tremble with what Simon first interpreted as anger, but later recognized as superstition. Luccio's response was so violent that most men would have stopped right there, or if they were to continue the argument, they would have challenged Luccio on the grounds that he was being childish and selfish. But Simon knew that you never get people to change their minds by challenging them directly. He always allowed them the illusion that they had come around to his point of view on their own.

Once Luccio said "no" to his plan for the funeral, Simon changed the subject. He talked of Luccio's paintings, telling him that though he was nearing fifty his career was just beginning. He calmed Luccio by envisioning a future for him and his art that was as sublime and as enduring as the Mozart concerto he had found on the radio. "I have complete faith in you, Luccio. You were wise to let the others grasp for newness and novelty, to stand back and re-evaluate your influences. Now I think you have the technical skill, as well as the maturity, to answer the questions your early work raised. Your time is coming, I can promise you that."

Simon talked with Luccio about his work for quite a while, asking all the right questions, ones that Luccio could find the answers for in his own art. All the while he spoke, Simon made Luccio feel that this greatness he had always longed for, envied in those close to him, but for some reason had never been able to believe existed in himself, was now there for the taking. Simon made it seem that this spiritual vanity that was not reflected in Luccio's art would suddenly blossom if only . . . But before telling him what incantation and sweep of the hand would transform him, Simon without pausing for breath went back to the subject of the funeral. "Remember Brenner? He was keen on your early work. He is going to speak at the funeral, regardless of where we have it."

"I thought he was retired and living in France."

"Yes, but he's agreed to come back. . . . You know when he had that New York School show at the Modern . . . back in . . . when was it, fifty-seven or fifty-eight?"

"Fifty-eight."

"That's right. It was fifty-eight. Anyway, Steven walked right into his office. Didn't knock, just said he had to show you with the rest of them. He didn't ask Brenner to do it. He told him to. I don't think Steven would have put his work in the exhibition if Brenner had said no. He needed the money then, too . . . but getting by, living, really never was the most important thing to Steven, was it?"

Simon chose his words carefully. Each had two edges so that no matter how Luccio tried to turn it over in his mind there was no way he could get away from the cutting edge of what Simon was saying. Within a matter of minutes the connection between the rosy future Simon had painted for him and the Lerner who was waiting to be laid to rest, though never spoken in words, was spelled out so clearly that Luccio would never be able to erase it from his mind.

Luccio had to protest a bit more. "I don't want a shrine. . . . What the fuck are you trying to turn this into? The next thing you'll have me selling relics."

"It's an honor."

116

To protect Lerner's art, to safeguard his own role as its guardian, Simon would have sacrificed Luccio, but he knew he wouldn't have to do that.

From Lerner, Simon had learned that the quickest and easiest way to convince an artist of anything is not to threaten to hold back funds, but to tell him that the proposed course of action will help him be remembered as he hopes to be, to bribe him with the promise of a place in the art history books of the twenty-first century. "It would only testify to the bond between the two of you, your position as the younger painter carrying on, expanding, adding to what Lerner began. Don't do it because he was your friend or out of responsibility as a trustee, or, God forbid, because I'm asking you to. . . . Do it for yourself as an artist." It was decided that Lerner would be buried behind Luccio's herb garden.

Just as Simon's thoughts shifted to the Winston Gallery and the success he was having in getting Barclay to come around to his long-range plans for the paintings, the car lurched to a halt. Neither he nor the driver could imagine what could be the cause of the flashing lights and the long line of cars ahead of them. It was too early for bridge traffic, but Simon wasn't worried. Remembering the last-minute delays before Sarah's funeral, he had left twenty minutes early.

When, a half hour later, Simon still found himself trapped between Forty-eighth and Forty-ninth Streets, he became concerned. Then one vehicle at a time the traffic began to move to the left. A sewer main had broken, and a small pond of brown water stocked with shit had formed at the intersection of Forty-ninth and Third.

In spite of the pumps and the efforts of the workmen, the water continued to rise, and by the time it was the big Cadillac's turn to cross this Slough of Despond the sewage was almost up to the tops of the tires. Halfway across the cab in front of him stalled. As the Caddy's five hundred horses began to gag, Simon tossed a twenty into the front seat and ordered the driver to disregard the policeman in hip boots and gun the car to the right. He hoped their momentum would take them through the deep water. A six-foot V of brown water sprayed the police and workmen as the black limousine, now mottled brown, fishtailed and skidded to the other side.

Once he had collected Wendy and Peter and they had gotten onto the highway, the speedometer stayed at ninety-five. By the time they reached the exit for Luccio's house, they had made up for most of the time that had been lost on Third Avenue. As the car braked and turned up the ramp, Simon thought of the order he was bringing to Lerner's world. It had been so frantic right after Lerner's death that it was hard to see things clearly. Just as the frozen landscape that had been a silver gray blur at ninety-five was now breaking down into a recognizable series of empty potato fields, leafless trees, and boarded-up fast food stands, the prospect of dealing with the paintings and the principals no longer seemed as frightening as it had in those first few days.

They appeared to be the last ones to arrive at the funeral. As soon as the car stopped, Wendy jumped out of the back like Athena from Zeus's head, ready to do battle with her tormentors. The fringe of a white leather jacket with a Zuñi eagle beaded on the back flashed up and down as she walked. She wore a red velvet gown from the thirties which she had bought at a secondhand store in the Village. She could get it over her hips, but the bodice was too tight. She left it unbuttoned from her neck to her navel, and, more for warmth than for modesty, she had opted to cover her front with a tie-dyed T-shirt.

Her outfit flaunted her fat, and that was just the effect she wanted. She, like so many young, used herself to shock her father's world. Her flesh was no longer armor, but a weapon, a way to demonstrate that she was different. She skipped across the field, fringe flying, seemingly unfazed by the weight her father had found such a burden. Breasts bouncing, she stopped, held her hands up to the sun, stretched, then hugged herself.

There was a little space at the front of the crowd right by the coffin. Peter knew that they were meant to fill it. He took his place next to Wendy, and Simon stood behind them. Then without warning, Wendy stepped forward, plucked a rose off the bronze casket, stuck it into the waist of her dress, and turned to face this audience filled with the powerful and famous faces Simon had told them about in the car. Their sniffles and tears stopped when Wendy announced, "I guess I should thank you for coming today. Knowing how my father felt about money—" Simon's and several other faces flinched at the word—"I don't think he really would have gotten off on his fancy coffin. I mean, there are a lot of hungry babies who could have been fed for what this cost, aren't there?" The one or two representatives from the Left, from Lerner's old political days when he had written,

118

"To be free, the artist must burn his bank book," nodded in agreement.

Wendy gestured toward herself, smiling, "But then I guess we all forgot about the hungry." As she spoke, she thought, "I can take this, can you?" She finished by saying, "Anyway, funerals comfort the living, not the dead. I hope this helps all of us. But let's remember who he really was and not leave here with an air-brushed image of my father . . . an image designed to make us feel better about ourselves."

Wendy felt good about her extemporaneous demonstration. Simon was relieved that it hadn't been longer. Peter didn't care. He was thinking of his mother's funeral, wondering why it and now his father's was as unreal as any of the funeral scenes he had seen in movies or on TV. The only difference was that it rained in the movies. The sun always seemed to be shining at the funerals he attended in real life.

As Simon cleared his throat to introduce the first of those he had asked to say a few words about Lerner, another limousine pulled up. The chauffeur opened the door and very slowly, as if in pain, Maggie stepped out of the back and walked toward them. The mini-skirts and push-up bras that she had used so successfully in the past were gone. She wore a very conservative, almost matronly black suit and a pillbox hat with a veil. The wind assisted her performance by blowing aside the veil to reveal a face made up to emphasize the circles under her eyes, the hollowness of her cheeks, the strain of her grief. Simon stepped forward to usher her into a hollow spot in the crowd, but she dismissed him with her best Katherine Hepburn smile, wedged herself between the two children, and placed a gloved hand on the shoulder of each child.

Instinctively Wendy's shoulders began to twitch, and as Simon began his address, Maggie struggled to maintain her pose. Finally, Wendy reached around and knocked Maggie's arm away, hitting her hard with the point of her knuckle. Peter knew from experience that those punches left a bruise.

Farthington was the next person to speak. He took more than thirty minutes to spit out his "few words about Lerner." He mentioned his own name and Lerner's so many times in each of his run-on sentences that it was impossible to tell whether Farthington was referring to himself or to Lerner when he proclaimed, "He will

119

be remembered not just as a great American abstract expressionist or a great twentieth-century painter. His work speaks eloquently and succinctly not just to his own age, but to the whole history of art and of man."

Somewhere in the middle of Farthington's speech, a little boy in the heart of the crowd dropped a red ball he was holding and, as he watched it roll between several pairs of legs toward the open grave, he began to cry. Everyone assumed he was weeping for the man his mother had told him was "sleeping" in the coffin. Wendy giggled when she saw the real object of his distress roll between her legs. She grabbed the ball just before it fell into the grave, turned, and whispered to the child loudly enough so that everyone could hear, "We almost lost it. . . . Come on. I'll play with you."

Before anyone could stop either of them, Wendy and the four-year-old boy were running across the field next to the grave site. With each speaker, Wendy's athletics became more vigorous. When Pazzolini, the Italian movie director, stepped forward and said, "Many of you know that Steven helped me with the sets for one of my films, but his influence began the first time I saw one of his magic pictures, and his colors, his images will be in every film I make. He taught me new ways to use my eyes," Wendy kicked the red ball so high that it disappeared for a moment in the glare of the sun.

A man from Amnesty International surprised everyone when he announced that Steven had given fifty thousand dollars the year before to aid political prisoners, but the figure didn't reach Wendy, who was chasing the red ball as it bounced over the stone row and into the wood lot. She didn't want to hear.

Alden Thayer, the director of the Metropolitan, spoke next. Peter could see that this art impresario was adjusting his jockey shorts with the hand in his pocket as he spoke so eloquently about the artist's struggle and society's debt to him.

Peter studied the crowd and wondered how many of them were really thinking about how they needed to go to the bathroom or where they itched or how they wanted a drink. The man behind him was cleaning his nails with a little silver knife, and out of the corner of his eye, Peter could see Maggie taking note of how well her gloved hand looked on her almost-stepson's shoulder. Peter was sure that even the ones like Barclay or Simon who stood perfectly still in their charcoal-gray suits and kept their eyes respectfully downcast were really thinking about the shine of their shoes or if they should buy gold—anything but what was really going on before them. Peter looked at Wendy as she kicked the ball higher and higher into the air. All those serious faces were really doing the same thing as she. They just weren't so obvious in the ways they tuned out. Peter's most disconcerting realization was that he was no different from any of them. He was no more able to accept the reality of the funeral than they.

De Kalb was the last one scheduled to speak. His white hair was matted to one side of his head. He looked as if he had just awakened from a nap. His hands shook ever so slightly as he fingered the bottle of bourbon that still helped him fill out his jacket. He had become as famous and as rich as Lerner. He rarely ventured out of the glass and steel airplane hangar of a house he had built in East Hampton. He wiped away the little bits of spit from the corners of his mouth and began, "Once when we were both young, I made Steven very upset when I said cavalierly, 'Art is long, but life is short.' . . . But he was not angry at the obvious cynicism of the remark. What upset him was my view of both art and life as forces with an end. I don't think he ever really believed in death." The words meant more to Peter than they did to de Kalb.

"Could it be true," Peter wondered. "Had his father lied? How could a man change so much?"

The men from O'Brien's funeral home lowered the coffin into the grave by hand. Wendy rejoined the crowd and returned the child and the ball to its mother. Wendy took one last look at the coffin as the crowd moved toward Luccio's house, and the men began to fill the hole with dirt. She had the urge to toss something into the grave, to leave something with him. She started to unpin the little turquoise and silver flower she had attached to her headband, but then reconsidered the gesture.

De Kalb was ready to go home. Peter hurried after him as he walked toward his 1962 Plymouth station wagon. Peter called to him, but he didn't hear. He wouldn't have had the courage to ask him if the old man hadn't dropped his car keys. Peter picked them up and handed them to him. "Thank you."

"You're welcome."

De Kalb squinted at Peter. "You are his, aren't you?"

"Yes." Peter could tell that de Kalb didn't like to look at him. He was getting ready to dismiss Peter in one way or another. He had to ask right then. He wouldn't have another chance. "What did you mean?"

"By what?"

"When you said my father didn't believe in death . . . in things ending."

De Kalb was embarrassed by his own sentiments. "I just said what I wanted to hear."

"What did my father believe in?"

De Kalb felt the bottle in his pocket. He didn't like to be pushed. "You know the big gold watch he used to wear?" Peter remembered. It covered almost the whole back of his father's wrist. "Well, that's what he believed in."

Though there were just a few wispy clouds in the sky, the rain Peter had thought the ceremony needed to make it as unreal as the funerals in the movies came just as Simon took Luccio aside to introduce him to Herbert Elderstein, the lawyer he had picked to handle the affairs of the estate and the foundation. Simon took their arms and escorted them to his limousine. "My briefcase is in the car. Why don't we talk there? It'll just take a moment." Simon opened a brown attaché case no thicker than a box of chocolates and said, "I thought this would be as good a time as any for the two of you to meet and for us to sign the papers necessary to probate the will."

Elderstein nodded, but his hearing aid was a bit off that day and he didn't quite understand what Simon was saying. He peered through his trifocals, his cataracts making his eyes look milky, signed the papers an inch above the line alloted for his signature, and blinked in Luccio's general direction. "I'm sorry. I didn't quite get your last name, Larry."

At first Luccio thought it was peculiar that Simon had chosen a lawyer well into his seventies who not only knew nothing about art, but could barely see it. "I have the first piece of what I am confident will be continuing good news about the paintings we will be watching over. Barclay wants to mount a major retrospective of Steven's work that would coincide with the Biennale in Venice this summer. What do you think?"

Before the old man could say a thing, Luccio snapped, "That's a stupid question! Of course, we agree. An exhibition like that only makes all the pictures more valuable." When Elderstein did not

122

check or qualify his answer as most lawyers who get involved in art would, Luccio decided that Simon had chosen well after all.

Elderstein nodded in agreement, "It looks like a logical way to begin."

Luccio enjoyed flexing his new muscle in the back of the car. "We should have only the very best pictures displayed there. It should be an exhibition that will never be forgotten. Don't let Barclay or that horseshit Dutton pick the paintings we will send. Do it yourself . . . and I will help. They have no idea which are the best."

Elderstein tapped his hearing aid with his fountain pen, "It's a point well made."

"I was hoping you'd both see it this way." Simon smiled and waved as Barclay's long gray Daimler limousine slithered down the wet driveway.

Wendy hadn't run into the house like the others. She squatted below an elm tree not far from the grave and rolled a joint. As she watched the three men flipping pages in the back of the limousine, she shook her head and thought to herself, "They just can't resist . . . talking about money . . . about those fucking pictures." If her father were alive or if he were a ghost, Wendy was sure he'd be right back there with them now.

Simon told the driver to mind the speed limit on the way home. There was no hurry now. Just as they crossed the Triborough Bridge, Peter turned to Simon and asked, "Do you know where Daddy's gold watch is?"

"In the studio with the rest of his things, I imagine. Or maybe in the apartment."

"May I have it?"

Simon smiled. "Of course, you may. You can have whatever you want." He touched both children. "You both must feel free to come to me anytime you want. I can't give you what your father could, but I do care about you both very much and will help you in any way I can."

As Wendy changed the radio station replacing Chopin with Sly Stone, Simon turned to Peter and, as if he were telling him a bedtime story, said, "You know your father bought that watch when you were a very little boy. Got it in Switzerland. It was his first trip to Europe. He took your mother with him for the opening of his first one-man show there. Mr. Bruno, a Swiss banker, bought half the show the moment he stepped into the gallery. It was sold out by three o'clock. A great success. In one day your father made more money than he had in his last ten years of painting. I gave a dinner party for him at a wonderful restaurant where they have all the famous people who eat there—writers, presidents, princes, artists, actors— sign their names and leave their message in a big book.

"They asked your father to sign it that night. I don't remember what he wrote. You will have to go there and see it sometime. Anyway, after the party on the way back to the hotel your father saw that watch in the window of a jewelry store and announced he had to have it . . . to celebrate. He wanted to break the window, take it right then, and leave a check in its place." Simon laughed at the story, then looked back at Peter, who was trying to digest all that had been said about the watch. There were tears in Simon's eyes not for the memory of Lerner but for the paintings. He whispered very softly, "It was a beautiful show."

XV

On Ground Hog Day, Wendy appeared at Elderstein's office thirty minutes late for an eleven o'clock appointment. Her glad rags were gone. Now she was wearing overalls and boots, workclothes. Wendy had just been hired for her first job. Before she would listen to anything Luccio, Elderstein, Simon, or the two pin-striped lawyers from the firm of Harrington, Dupont, and Blaine had to say, she insisted on telling them all about it. "I work in a day-care center in the basement of a church up on One Hundred Twenty-eighth Street. It's another world up there. I don't imagine any of you have seen it. This little girl I explained conjugation to yesterday told me, 'I uses da *Times* for ma blanket and da *Daily News* for ma pillow.' I won't be working just with children. Some of them are as old as I am and still can't read or write . . . that's how we keep them poor."

Because Wendy was late, one of the lawyers would miss his squash game. As he crossed the match out of his appointment book, he asked dryly, "Do they pay you for this?"

"No, but does that make it any less of a job?"

Before Wendy could turn the lawyer's comment into an issue, Simon congratulated her. "I think the job sounds fantastic. It's just the sort of thing I think you should be doing, widening your horizons." His endorsement took something from her enthusiasm.

Elderstein read the will. Like a child, he ran his finger under each line he read. He didn't want to lose his place. Simon watched Wendy. He had been observing her carefully since the funeral. He had stopped in at the house or called every day. Once he had even spotted her asking people for spare change outside Bloomingdale's. When he asked her if she needed money, she just laughed. In fact, every time Simon saw Wendy she seemed to be laughing at what he said and did.

Even now, as she heard her father's last wishes, she was smirking and shaking her head, but Simon didn't care. People had laughed at him before. He remembered how his wife's father, whom he was now supporting in an old-age home in Naples, Florida, had laughed when he had bought his first Matisse. Anyway, Simon would rather have her laughing at him than calling up all the time, screaming or, worse, silent at the other end of the line. Those had been her father's ways of asking for help. Wendy's amused indifference only made his job easier.

Simon didn't know if it was romance, or the times, or drugs that was responsible for this new-found confidence and optimism that she continued to radiate, but regardless of its source, he knew that it would pass. When Elderstein finished the reading Simon took advantage of the situation. He knew that she didn't want to be there, that she wanted to be free of him and of her father's memory. Simon volunteered, "Of course, if you aren't pleased with any of this, you can change it." The comment startled the other men. Luccio was ready to protest, but Simon continued, "Under New York State law, anytime a man leaves the bulk of his estate to charity, the heirs have a right to challenge the will and claim half the estate. Since you are Peter's guardian it's your decision. Mr. Elderstein or myself or any lawyer could file petition against your father's will in behalf of you and Peter."

"You mean sue my father, the estate he set up?"

"Basically, yes."

Simon wanted the situation to remain as it was, but he had to give Wendy the opportunity to challenge the will. When she began to laugh, Simon knew that she wouldn't take up the offer. Wendy turned to Simon, "You must really think I'm as fucked up as he was. Jesus, that's what he was always threatening to do! He sued my mother. I remember once he even said he was going to sue you, Simon. . . . I don't care about the money or the pictures. They are your responsibility. It all sounds O.K. to me."

It was a busy day for Simon. After the meeting at Elderstein's he had to meet Alfred Dutton downtown to pick the Lerners that would go in the special exhibit Winston was organizing to coincide with the Venice Biennale. Luccio had made an issue of being there when they chose the paintings, but at the last minute, Sally Byrd called and asked him to come up to Vermont. He couldn't pass up the opportu-

126

nity to place those two paintings of his in her uncle's museum in Cincinnati.

Dutton was accompanied by Christina Hansen, the executive secretary at Winston, and a black man who would move the paintings around for them. Christina had spent the last few days organizing the papers on Lerner, double-checking not just the records of those paintings in Winston warehouses, but those Lerner had squirreled away in his studio, on the top floor of the house on Eighty-eighth Street, and in private warehouses around the city. She didn't understand a lot of what she was told to do. It didn't make sense that Winston Gallery was paying the rent on Lerner's studio and the bills for the warehouse space he used to store his paintings. She filed letters from Mr. Pyne describing Mr. Dutton as the "official appraiser of" and "under bond to" the estate. When she asked Dutton what "under bond" meant, he had no idea. But so many things were always going on at Winston that no one except Mr. Barclay really knew.

At each of the three warehouses they visited, Simon stood back and let Dutton choose the first fifteen or twenty Lerners. Christina put a red sticker on each and recorded the names and sizes in her notebook. Simon made a point of complimenting Dutton's choices, then stepped forward and made a few selections of his own. Simon chose quickly as if he had the paintings memorized. When Dutton commented on the speed with which he chose, Simon blushed self-consciously. "I love them all so much that if I stopped to flirt with each one, I'd be here all day."

It was obvious to Christina that the paintings Mr. Pyne chose were much stronger than Dutton's selections. She wondered why Simon didn't pick them all. He refused to select more than five or six even when Dutton asked for his help. She guessed they were playing some ego game that she wasn't aware of.

The last group of Lerners they were scheduled to see was the lot in Lerner's studio. The room had been cleaned, the cigarette butts swept up, the dirty dishes washed, the chalk outline of the body erased, but there was still a stain on the floor from the blood. It showed beneath the sheen of the freshly waxed and buffed floor. There had been so much blood that it had leaked through to the floor below. Christina had sent a check to the tenant who lived there for the inconvenience Lerner's death had caused him.

While Dutton made his choices, she could hear Simon in the back of Lerner's studio opening and closing drawers and cabinets. When he appeared, looking worried and holding Lerner's trousers in his hand, Christina said, "I never thought Lerner would be the type to catalog his pictures so carefully." She pointed to the white stickers Lerner had placed on the frame of each picture. They looked just like price tags. "He never struck me as being so meticulous. It's so much more organized than the back room uptown."

Dutton tried to make a small joke. "Are you suggesting that we're not neat? Whatever happened to loyalty to the firm?" Simon looked around the studio as if he had lost something.

Christina wondered what he was searching for. "It's like a museum the way he organized it."

"Supermarket might be a better word," Simon thought as she turned out the pockets of a pair of Lerner's pants. He hated the way Lerner sometimes handled his paintings. He didn't mind when Lerner was precious with them. He could understand that. But the way Steven sometimes seemed to delight in abusing them made Simon angry. Once when Barclay brought a pair of Texans to the studio, Lerner flicked his cigarette ashes on the paintings and talked about money as if he were a pimp.

Dutton turned to Christina. "How many paintings are there altogether?"

She looked in her notebook, "Eight hundred twenty-three."

Without thinking, Simon corrected her, "Eight hundred twenty-one."

"I just went through the slides. I'm positive there are eight hundred twenty-three."

"I know, but two are missing, a small one—not very unusual—and a very good brown one . . . the one Lerner refused to sell that Swiss dealer last year."

Both Christina and Dutton were shocked at how blasé Simon was about the missing paintings. He had always taken such a personal interest in Lerner and his work. The woman Christina had replaced at Winston's had been fired the day after Simon saw her drop a cup of coffee not on, but near, a Lerner.

Dutton was outraged, "You should have told me."

"Barclay knows."

"What happened to them?"

"I don't know. Either Steven gave them away—he did things like that sometimes, though usually he asked for them back—or someone stole them. The door was unlocked when Maggie found him that morning."

They all jumped when the door behind them opened and Peter appeared in the doorway. The shadows half-hid his face, making it appear as if he were wearing a mask. Christina and Dutton laughed when they recognized him, but Simon didn't like to be surprised. "How did you get in?"

"I found a key at home."

"What are you here for?"

"I came to look for the watch," Peter told them shyly.

"I told you I'd look for it."

"Did you find it?"

"No."

"But you said I could have it."

"I don't know where it is."

Peter was on the verge of tears. Dutton tried to sound cheerful. "What's the matter?"

"I want my father's watch."

Simon threw down Lerner's pants. "I've looked everywhere, Peter. Don't you understand? I just don't know where it is." Simon was angry at his own feelings of fear and frustration.

Peter looked at the dark stain in the center of the floor. He knew that was where his father had died. "Wasn't he wearing it when you found him?"

"I don't remember. . . . I mean, Maggie doesn't remember. She's the one who found him. . . . We'll get you one just like it."

"It wouldn't be the same."

"They all tell time," Dutton said.

Christina winced at Dutton's remark. "It'll probably turn up." She didn't understand why Simon was more concerned about a misplaced watch than about $75,000 worth of paintings.

Being in Lerner's studio had a strange effect on Simon. He lost control, not only of others, but of himself. He was disturbed by memories that could do him no good. As a tear broke from Peter's eyes, Simon realized how harsh and inappropriate his choice of words had been. He wished he'd had a copy of the watch made and had lied to Peter about it. They both would have felt better. He started to apologize, but before he could finish, Peter ran out of the studio, knowing but unable to admit that even if he had found the watch it probably wouldn't have told him any more than the time.

Peter didn't want to go home. Wendy was at work, and all Dora would do would be to make him a cup of hot chocolate. As he ran down the stairs, he knew just what Dora would say to him, "You can cry your life away, and your tears will still have salt in them." She said that when anyone cried. He still didn't know what she meant.

Somewhere in the Village Peter stopped crying, and as he walked down West Broadway, he looked at his reflection in the glass storefronts to see if it was apparent that he had been crying. It wasn't.

He ran up the stairs of the loft building hoping to find an explanation. But when he opened the door, a spotlight hit him in the eye. The face that he had memorized, that he had wanted to focus on and laugh with, was just a dark shape against the blinding light. Peter burst into tears. His lip trembled and his body shook as he sputtered out, "They won't let me have the watch."

Andrew had tried to call Peter on four or five different occasions to set up a date to finish the drawing, to talk about starting a painting. Each time Wendy answered. His messages were never relayed. Wendy flustered him on the phone. Normally Andrew could be more of a bitch than anyone. He could say exactly what he wanted, but there was something in Wendy's tone, in the way she said, "I'll be sure to tell my brother what you had in mind," that intimidated him.

The spotlights were there for the movie camera. The BBC was doing a special on Andrew, not just as an artist, but as a man whose eccentricities, whose lifestyle spoke for the decade. Jamie, Tessa, Bob Cross, and Sidney were posed around the main room of the loft. A cameraman and a sound man, coached by a goateed man named Ian McCarg, who had no specific talent but called himself a director, aimed their equipment at Jackson Whole and his pet pug dog, Nero.

Jackson Whole was much better known to the general public than Andrew or anyone else in the room. He was a writer, but he did not write about art. He had written a number of best sellers, the last one on a mass murder in New Orleans. The book had been made into a very successful movie. He was a chubby pink little man whose flesh from head to toe was like that of a baby's bottom. When Peter burst

130

into tears, Jackson's hairlip whined, "Tell me, Mr. Crowley, are androgynous young orphans always weeping on your doorstep?"

No one but Jamie laughed. He flicked his ash at the camera which was recording the whole scene and squealed, "He staged this all for you, Jackson. Next week we have Little Nell coming." Before Jackson could think up a sexual quip about coming, Sidney told them both to shut up.

Peter was leaning against Andrew's chest crying, "I'll never find it." Andrew could feel Peter's tears damp against his skin. He looked at this audience he had allowed to assemble and at the camera poised on the man's shoulder like a gun. The shutter of its glass eye opened wide, not missing any of his uncertainty about putting his arms around Peter to comfort him.

Sidney had known Andrew, watched Andrew longer than anyone in New York. He had seen Andrew pull his escape act—that miraculous way he was able to withdraw from people and their demands so many times. He still didn't see how Andrew got away with it. Andrew's poise, his cool in dealing with people or his intelligence in not dealing with them, was frightening. But now it was Andrew, the Houdini of the art world, who was frightened. Sidney guessed that Andrew's fear, his uncertainty, was because no one had ever asked or offered anything so real as this child crying in front of him.

More out of sympathy for Andrew than for Peter, Sidney told the cameraman to stop. When the man ignored the request, Sidney didn't argue about cinema verité or cause a scene. He blocked the camera with his girth. Deftly Sidney unplugged the spotlight with his foot, took Peter and Andrew by the hand, and led them into the back room. Having done this, he told Jamie to plug the spotlight back in, refilled everyone's champagne glass, and made himself a little sandwich of Beluga caviar, unsalted butter, and rye toast.

Jackson did the same, and as he crushed a whole school of fish against the roof of his mouth with his tongue, he said, "To quote someone whom I have never known to be wrong—myself—'it's so much more rewarding talking about people than talking to them.'" Snowcapping a second Fujiyama of unhatched sturgeon with minced onions, Jackson turned to Bob Cross and asked, "What do you think the best approach is?"

"To what?"

"To the truth, of course." Jackson winked at the camera.

"About Andrew?" Bob yawned, trying to appear bored.

Hamming up the role of the reporter, Jackson posed with pencil and pad.

"Just because this film is about Andrew doesn't mean we have to talk about him. What's the best way to see the truth?"

"Look into a mirror." Bob sounded just like Andrew.

"Don't mirrors ever lie?"

"Yes, but their lies are easier to believe than those we can't see."

Though Andrew's face would not appear on the film exposed while he was in the other room with Peter, his presence, his influence, could be seen. Andrew was their mirror.

Peter collapsed in a corner of the room in a pile of bits and pieces of cloth left over from the fashion show. Sobbing about something that was lost, something that he had pinned the word "watch" to, Peter rubbed his cheek against the white wall, finding no more or less comfort than he had when he pressed his face to Andrew's hard and slightly hollow chest.

Between bursts of tears, moans, strings of obscenities, and gasps for breath, Peter told his story. It was the first time he had cried in front of anyone since his father died. He spoke haltingly, starting then stopping, repeating the last few words he had just sputtered out before going on, as if he had to build up momentum. Peter was struggling to get the story out. Looking at the boy's contorted face, his trembling body, Andrew remembered a film he had seen once on natural childbirth.

Andrew understood that a watch was missing, but he didn't understand the rest of what was being said, not because Peter was crying or the facts of his unsuccessful quest were being retold in a confusing manner. Andrew couldn't listen, couldn't concentrate because the scene was too human. He had to look away when Peter began to hit his head against the wall, choking on his curse, "Goddamn fucking shit! It's not there. I tried, I tried, but I couldn't find it. I should have looked sooner. Nobody will help."

Andrew turned his back on Peter, but he saw the same scene in a long narrow mirror on the wall opposite Peter. Because of its placement and size, the mirror looked like a window. The effect reminded Andrew of trompe l'oeil. The mirror and the image on it did not trick his eye, but rather his sentiments. The discipline of the

132

rectangle removed Andrew from the drama of Peter and his pain. The boy's problems and his need no longer frightened Andrew. He did not concentrate on what Peter was crying about, but on how the mucus from his red nose glistened as it smeared against the wall. Andrew was fascinated to discover that from certain angles it was impossible to tell whether Peter's face was controted with laughter or with tears.

Andrew's eye noted the violet jumble of taffeta, the little snips of pink silk, the long green strips of linen, stems for the bunches of red chiffon on which Peter had collapsed. When Andrew had first stepped into the room, he hadn't noticed that the mannequin was still there, Tessa's now dry and slightly stiff panties crowning its head as it looked down on the boy.

Andrew smirked when he saw the rosary hanging in its left hand and the heart-shaped valentine candy wrapped in red tinfoil pinned to her chest. He wondered if Sidney had put them on this nippleless Madonna before he had left.

Andrew had to paint them both. He would use that shade of salmon pink he had admired in the sweater a receptionist at the Met used to hide her hairy arms. He had been saving that color for something special. He would add it to the scraps of fabric in which Peter had collapsed. He would paint the heart as if it were drawn with lipstick. Just as he made up his mind to do the painting as a reflection in the mirror, Andrew was struck by what he was doing. He had turned his back on life. He, not this weeping red-faced boy, was grotesque.

Andrew knew now that he kept his distance, that he turned his back, not because he was afraid to show his emotions, but because he was terrified that there would be none if he tried to draw on them. The realization shook Andrew and made him turn and face the child just in time to hear Peter cry, "And there's no way I'll ever know what he believed in now."

"What do you mean?" Andrew had to fight the temptation to look and listen to the reflections on that mirror in his mind instead of what was actually happening before him.

"The watch. Mr. de Kalb said if I wanted to know what my father believed in I'd have to look at his watch."

Andrew vaguely remembered the gaudy gold chronometer that

weighted down Lerner's brush hand.

"But I looked and looked and I couldn't find it, and without it I'll never know."

"Know what?"

"What de Kalb meant—what my father believed in."

"But it's quite clear what he meant." Andrew had offered an answer before he'd even thought of one.

"You've seen the watch?"

Andrew nodded, searching for an adequate explanation, for an offering more real and less compromising than the hug and the caress that he was too suspicious to give.

"Why did my father believe in a watch?" Peter was ready to throw out the possibilities he had considered for Andrew to confirm or deny.

But before Peter could speak, Andrew blurted out, "He believed in the watch because . . . because art is about time, and, when it's great, it triumphs over time. That's the only thing we can ever really hope for. That's what your father did in his paintings."

Andrew hadn't expected to stumble onto something so true. "Something beautiful is like a perpetual motion machine. It defies all the laws of God and man . . . it's the only real magic there is for us."

There were still red spots on the side of Peter's forehead where he had hit it against the wall, but he had stopped crying. It gave Andrew an odd sense of satisfaction to watch the boy untangle his body and his emotions. Andrew enjoyed the effect of the unexpected truth he had uttered. He had entertained and abused people with his words. This was the first time he was conscious of healing someone. He felt like a magician who discovers he doesn't have to hide a rabbit in his hat to produce one.

Peter turned Andrew's words over in his head like polished stones in a tumbler, hoping that they would shine for him. He looked in the mirror now; he saw a scene different from the one Andrew had seen. He stared at Andrew, seemingly so serene, so content and controlled, and then he looked at himself, collapsed on a bed of elegant trash, his face covered with blotches. Peter was embarrassed by what his feelings had done to him. He envied Andrew his cool.

Andrew didn't turn back to the mirror. He longed for the spontaneity, the lack of control, that he saw in Peter and that he knew

134

he lacked. Andrew wanted to restore the flow of emotion, of life, in himself. He didn't care if it was painful. He just wanted to smash this device, this thing in him that kept him from being swept away, that gave him perspective, vision at the price of feeling. Peter envied the mechanism that Andrew wanted to destroy.

Perhaps if each of them had had a third eye, an eye that could look into the mirror as they stared into each other, they would see that each wanted what the other was finding impossible to live with. Both Peter and Andrew mistook the other's awe and envy for pity.

Peter made the first move. He stood up. Ignoring the tears on his cheek and his runny nose, he plucked the chocolate heart from the mannequin's left breast, took a big bite, and announced, "Well, if beating time is what it's all about, I better not waste any more like this." Peter bowed to the mannequin and, putting on his best smile, moved toward the door.

"Are you sure you're ready to go back in there? I could send them away and we could work on the drawing."

"I'm O.K."

Andrew would still make that painting he had just envisioned. He would still use that shade of pink he'd been saving, the mannequin, and Peter. But the point of the painting would be completely different. The viewer would still not know whether the boy was laughing or crying, but it would no longer make any difference. All that would matter was that the boy was feeling, alive, and that the mannequin with hair just a shade darker than his own was not.

They came back into the main room of the loft just as Tessa looked out of the corner of her almond-shaped eyes and said, "Andrew's the sexiest man in the world."

"And why is that?" Jackson asked.

"Because you have absolutely no idea what he's thinking about. You're always in the dark with Andrew."

Climbing onto the fold-up bicycle by the door, Peter pedaled into the conversation. "Maybe you should wear one of those hats miners use with little lights on the front."

Tessa pushed aside a swirl of hair as dark and lustrous as the ebony sharps on a keyboard, flashed her ivories, and asked Andrew, "Would you find that more romantic?" She knew just how to play herself.

135

Jamie had been trying to think up something to say. He took a big swig of his Tab and asked Peter, "Feeling better? What was the matter?"

"Nothing." Peter pretended to be concentrating on negotiating the bike around the camera, lights, and people.

"Well, it was an awfully big nothing. It must have been something. Tell Jackson about it. He'll understand."

Jamie's antagonism toward Peter was too obvious to amuse any of them. Jackson took the conversation and aimed it at Tessa. "Do you find most things sexier in the dark?"

"Not sexier, just more romantic."

Jackson turned to Andrew, who was filling his pen with ink. "And what do you find sexy, Andrew?"

Andrew was going to say "Fountain pens," but before he could, Jamie shrieked, "That should be obvious." At first Andrew thought Jamie was going to announce, "Me," but when he saw Jamie eying Peter, he knew what the answer was going to be. Peter sensed it, too, and just missed running into one of the lights.

Refusing to be the conscience for the group, Jackson turned to Jamie and yapped, "Well, don't keep us waiting . . . tell all."

Andrew was going to stop the film right there and throw them all out, but before he could, before Jamie could "tell all," Peter deliberately drove the bike across Jamie's bare foot. Jamie shouted, "You little shit!" and kicked at the boy. He missed Peter, but he connected with the bike, knocking off a toenail and sending Peter sailing into Tessa's lap.

"Jesus Christ! Look what he did!" The camera moved in for a close-up of Jamie's foot and its bloody big toe, but no one else bothered to look. They were too busy laughing.

When the laughter died down enough so that he could be heard, Peter pointed at Jamie's foot and said, "If you'd kept it in your mouth, that wouldn't have happened."

Jackson howled, "I wish I'd said that!"

As Jamie limped off to the bathroom, Tessa shouted to Andrew, "Where have you been hiding this little monster? He's divine." Without warning, she kissed Peter on the lips. He had never been kissed that way before, and in spite of the fact that he pulled away, he liked the way her tongue felt as it moved across the silver bar of his retainer.

136

Tessa felt it too. She stuck out her tongue, touched it with the tip of her forefinger, and giggled, "What have you got in there?"

Normally Peter would have been embarrassed. The only reason he'd worn the retainer that day was because he'd been thinking about his father, who always complained about the orthodontist's bills. But Peter refused to be rattled. He took the pink plastic plate out of his mouth and held the glistening device in his hand for her and the camera to examine. Tessa picked it up, turned it over slowly as if she were admiring a Fabergé egg, then popped it in her mouth, and smiled at the camera.

She turned and winked at Peter. "Can I borrow it for special occasions?"

"You can have it."

"Really?"

Peter knew he would never go back to the orthodontist. "It's yours."

Tessa kissed him a second time. Her lips touched his, but he was disappointed not to feel her tongue now that he was prepared for it. She sat down, opened a silver cigarette case, lighted a joint rolled in paper the color of her lips, offered it to the camera and the man holding it, and asked Peter, "I think you're wonderful, but who are you?"

Andrew had a pad in his lap. He was sketching Peter, working at combining the agony he had seen on the boy's face with the expression of surprise and glee he had observed just after Tessa had kissed him.

Tessa repeated the question, "Who are you?"

Andrew's pen moved across the paper, "He's my muse." When he lifted the pen, there was a lip where there had been nothing.

"When you fill out your income tax, do you write artist or modern artist?" Jackson asked.

"Artist."

"What do you think of most modern art?"

"It bores my ass off." Andrew paused to let Jackson come up for the bait. "It's not original."

"Modern art or the comment?"

"I meant the comment. I say it whenever I think the conversation needs picking up, but I can't say I disagree with your opinion that modern art isn't original."

137

Sidney glanced at the camera that was saving all this madness for history. It was his duty as curator of contemporary art to protest even though he agreed with Andrew. "You don't really mean that."

"Yes, I do."

"You don't find some of it beautiful?"

"Sure, some of it's beautiful. Some of it gives my eye pleasure, but not my mind . . . and that can be boring."

Jackson licked a lone fish egg from the corner of his lip. He was on to something. "Do beautiful things bore you?"

"Sometimes." He was just turning down the corners of Peter's mouth. "I mean, Frankenthalers are pretty to look at, but so what?"

"Now, now, now. Let's not be catty," Jackson chided Andrew. "You're just giving it to her because she's a woman."

"It's her painting that is limited, not her sex."

Sidney looked to Bob for help, but the young dealer was getting a vicarious thrill out of Andrew's comments. Sidney faced the camera as he rushed to the defense of abstract art, but the cameraman was too busy positioning himself so that Tessa could massage the inside of his crotch with her foot. "But you have to admire it intellectually in terms of its effect on the history of art."

Jackson couldn't have cared less about the history of art. "You don't like Frankenthaler's work?"

Andrew scratched his nose. "It's not the art so much that offends me. It's her as an artist. She has no spiritual—no emotional—generosity." Andrew stopped drawing, suddenly aware that he was talking about himself.

"What do you mean by 'emotional generosity'?"

"Just what I said."

"What do you think of yourself as an artist?"

Andrew knew the next question would be, "Do you have spiritual generosity?" He looked at Peter's eyes, then at the camera. He didn't want to answer that question. If he was lying, if he did lack it, the human eye would see it even if the mechanical one missed it. He had to think of something that would throw Jackson off the track. "I think . . ." He covered the drawing of Peter's face and quickly sketched a ragged and rather predatory outline of Jackson's. "I think I'm overrated, maybe the most overrated, overpaid artist in the world." What he also thought, but didn't say was, "But I'm still better than any abstract painter."

138

"Why are you overrated?"

Looking quite innocent as he smeared a few drops of ink into a dirty gray mouth, Andrew answered, "Because I'm paid an awful lot of money for really very narrow, very private paintings . . . pictures that aren't about big ideas or part of revolutions."

Jackson pointed to a copy of *Time.* "But there's a man in here who says you're a genius, that your paintings capture the essence of our time."

Tessa looked up. "Jackson . . . you of all people should know. You can't believe what you read these days."

Andrew dropped the drawing he had made of Jackson. It was irresistibly ugly. One had the feeling that Jackson, like some bloated toad, would open his mouth and grab you with his sticky tongue. "What I do . . . in my painting is a trick, really. I make up a story with lines." Andrew opened an oversized book of his work and pointed to a painting of the Great Pyramid. It made the Seventh Wonder of the World look like a toy in a sandbox. "I did this from a photograph I took when I went to Egypt, but the pyramids didn't look anything like that. I invented that pyramid . . . designed it to fit a feeling I had about the pyramids. I painted that to support a feeling. It supports . . . it represents me, not life."

For years Bob had watched Sidney pick up the sketches Andrew tossed away like unfinished sentences in a conversation. He had the best collection of Crowleys in the world. This curator who looked like Humpty Dumpty picked up Andrew's work, not so much out of greed, but out of respect for Andrew and his art. Andrew never seemed to mind, but this time as Sidney bent over with a little grunt to save the drawing from the cameraman's feet, Andrew deliberately ground his foot into Jackson's face, tearing the paper.

"It is easy to find truth and order in a world of your own design. But to solve real mysteries, to find truth in the world as it is, is the real challenge. My best paintings—at least the ones I find most satisfying—are the ones of swimming pools and windows, not because they contain any intellectual commentary on modern life of the human condition, but because they explore, and I think in most cases resolve, rather straightforward technical mysteries or problems, such as water and glass, both of which are rather mysterious things . . . things you really can't describe in words, not the way you can a chair or a rose.

139

"You see, if I could solve a real mystery, not one of my own invention—if I could reveal the mystery behind just the simplest emotion or feeling, not as I want it to be, but as it really is—then I think I would deserve all that I've gotten. What I do is really very safe, but not nearly as safe as the abstract art that's being made today —the New York School potboilers walking over the same ground again and again. Motherwell painted the same picture for twenty years. He spends more time on his signature than on his painting. I've always said that life must be an adventure, but it took me a long time to realize what that means for an artist. It's not an adventure unless you risk something. Even though the public is so undiscriminating and easily satisfied, I won't be. I'm starting a whole new series of paintings. They'll be portraits, very realistic and very oldfashioned some might say. They'll be of people I don't know very well, too, because I think I'll have to look at life differently in order to get out of it—out of them—what I need to make the pictures successful."

"Differently how?" They all wanted to know the answer to Jackson's question.

"More honest." There was a touch of a dare in the way Andrew made his new pronouncement.

"Sounds like you're trying to make a fresh start."

"Isn't that what all dreams are about?"

Everyone in the room was listening, even Tessa. His seriousness frightened them. He tried to make a joke out of his confession and turned to Jackson, who wasn't sure what he had discovered. "You see, I couldn't paint my friends the way I intend to do these paintings because they wouldn't be my friends afterward."

Peter knew Andrew was going to paint him. It hurt him to think that this rendering of himself that he so wanted would mark both the beginning and the end of their friendship. He got back on the bike and began to pedal around the room.

Tessa protested, "Oh, Andrew, don't be silly. There's no way anyone can keep from falling in love with you after you do them."

Sidney added his own endorsement, "I probably shouldn't say this with Andrew in the room, and it does sound corny, but there is a lot of love in Andrew's work. The drawings he has made of me over the last eight years have helped me far more than any psychiatrist. His drawings have helped me figure out who I am."

140

"Just the fact that we're talking about drawing tells us what is so special about Andrew's work. There's almost no drawing in abstract art." Bob had a way of making the obvious sound profound.

Andrew stood in the corner cleaning his teeth with his gold toothpick, watching his friends and the camera examine his drawings. He wished he could believe what they said, believe in these pictures that helped them believe in themselves.

He said nothing until that first drawing of Peter was passed around for inspection. Sidney and Bob both thought it was wonderful and prodded him to finish it. Tessa said she'd never noticed how sexy Peter's eyes were.

Peter liked the drawing, not because of its artistic merits or because it was flattering, but because it somehow made him feel more complete. Andrew was hurt when Peter quickly handed the drawing on to Jackson without comment. He didn't understand that Peter felt that if he looked at it too carefully, if he showed too much interest, his ignorance about himself would be obvious. If he touched it, stared at it the way the others had, the cool wisdom Andrew had given him would vanish, and the drawing would begin to tremble and cry.

Jackson, like the others, recognized the brilliance of the drawing. He smiled at Peter lasciviously, "This drawing will make you famous. It will always bring joy to the rest of the world, but it won't be long before it brings you something more. It will remind you . . ."

Andrew jabbed the gold toothpick so hard into his gums that he tasted blood. "Remind him of what?"

Jackson touched the cheek of the face on the paper with his middle finger. Andrew wanted to slap his hand away. "It's something in the eye." Jackson put on his glasses, "There's a light, a reflection that I've seen only in the eyes of very precocious children and men who have never been in love."

Tessa's hand was now casually resting on the cameraman's ass. He and the camera jumped when she pinched him. She did it just hard enough so that he couldn't decide whether he wanted her to do it again. "Men who have never been in love, though often charming, are only precocious children."

With the exception of a few drawings of Bob and his wife and those of Tessa, who was always shown alone, reclining with a slightly expectant expression on her face, all the drawings were of men, men

141

lying nude on plastic rafts in blue swimming pools, men walking together, men washing each other in the shower, men lying together in bed.

Peter had never seen men lying together like that. He thought of the time he had walked in on his father and mother when they were doing it, of the nights he'd sneaked downstairs and watched Wendy struggling behind the couch with boys slightly smaller than herself, her dress hiked up and her brassiere cutting across the top of her breasts. In both cases he was not quite sure whether they were struggling to get close or to get away from each other.

The pictures didn't excite Peter, but he was drawn to them because there wasn't that feeling of struggle between the men. Sometimes from the expression on their faces Peter could see that they didn't like each other, or that they didn't trust each other, but the one thing they seemed certain of was that they knew what they wanted from each other. There was none of the push–pull confusion that he had seen in the darkness between men and women.

As Andrew began to tell the story behind a drawing of Cocteau, Tessa whispered in his ear, "I've got to talk to you," and pulled him into the bedroom.

"I hate to do this, Andrew, but I just can't help myself. He's so cute and after looking at myself all alone in those drawings, I just have to have him."

"What?" Could she mean Peter?

"The cameraman. I've just got to make it with him. I can't wait."

Relieved, Andrew laughed and pointed to his big white round bed. "Well, do it here."

"I couldn't."

"Why not?"

Tessa wrinkled up her nose. "It's too, too, too . . ."

"Too what?"

"Too much like a hospital! Christ, I'd feel like I was having an operation making it on this bed." Tessa lay back in Andrew's bed. She was no longer thinking about the cameraman.

Andrew had never noticed it, but there was an antiseptic, sterile quality to the room he chose to make love in.

"Darling, I know it's frightfully chic, white and all, but it doesn't do anything for me. I look at that bed and I think 'operating table.' " She pointed to the chrome bedside table. "I feel like there should be

142

scalpel and forceps there. Be a dear and think of something."

"Why don't you use the spare room?"

"They'll hear everything. You know how shy I am . . ." She was flirting openly and harshly.

Andrew was too preoccupied with the idea of his bed's being like an operating table to argue with Tessa about her shyness. He winced at the thought of all the surgery he had undergone in that room. Andrew turned away and told her, "I can't help you."

It was dark outside when Peter left Andrew's. Everyone offered to drop him home, but he made up a very convincing story about meeting his sister two blocks away. It had fooled them all, even Andrew. Peter wanted to be by himself. As he walked up through the Village, he saw the same sights and sounds that his sister had such faith in. But Peter wasn't old enough to take part, and he knew it. He had grown his hair, and he did his best to dress like a hippie, but he knew that this trend, like flattops and surfboards, would pass before he could really do anything with it. Peter wondered what there would be for him when he was ready.

As he walked down into the subway on Astor Place, Peter began to think about all those drawings of naked men. The express train rattled north and he remembered what had been said before the camera about decadence and the sixties and free love. He got off at Eighty-sixth Street and climbed back to the surface. It was then that Peter decided the next rage, the Hula Hoop of the seventies, would be sex, but not the free, easy variety of the sixties.

Standing there under the street light, Peter thought to himself, "If it isn't free, then it has to be paid for." And as he contemplated the price of this new craze he foresaw, he caught sight of his sister on the other side of the avenue getting off a crosstown bus.

He waved, but she didn't see him. Dodging a gypsy cab, he ran across the street to her. "Why didn't you get off on Madison?" They lived on Eighty-eighth Street between Madison and Fifth.

Wendy giggled, "I forgot where I was going."

"Well, where were you coming from?" He didn't want to tell her where he had been.

"The Planetarium."

"What were you doing there?"

"Making love . . . it was beautiful."

"But how?"

143

"How what?"

"How did you do it?" They couldn't have done it standing up, and Peter didn't think there was room for his sister to lie down between the rows of seats.

"We didn't actually do 'it,' but we made love."

"How?"

Wendy was amazed that she was telling him all this. She looked at the blood sausage hanging in the window of one of the German pork stores on the street and told herself she was doing it for his own good, to liberate him. "Well . . . I gave him a blow job."

Peter didn't say a thing. She guessed that he didn't know what it meant. "I kissed his penis."

Peter looked at her lips, wondering how it tasted, if she swallowed it. "What did he do for you?" He was learning the facts of life quickly.

"Nothing."

Wendy remembered that he wouldn't kiss her on the lips when she was done. "I didn't want anything out of it except to make him happy. Coco's been in jail four times. He's one of the black guys I've been tutoring. You wouldn't believe how awful his life has been. I got something out of it just by giving. It made me feel better just to . . ."

"Then you got something out of it after all."

"You're as fucked as Daddy."

Her words did not hurt him. They merely told Peter he was right.

As they walked home, Wendy thought about the two different types of satisfaction going down on that black man-child, who spelled cat with a "k," had given her. The first kind stemmed from his dependence upon her, the way he moaned and pushed himself against her in the darkness while the Big Dipper glistened above them. If she had left him, or stopped, there would have been no one else, at least not in the Planetarium, and Coco would have had to turn to his own hands for comfort. But the greater satisfaction she got from this educational outing on West Eighty-first Street came when Coco wouldn't kiss her. When she placed his hand on herself, he pulled away and said, "You got any more of dem Juicy Fruits?"

XVI

"The French would go wild if they had this fish."

Harold Barclay looked the long gray fish in the eye. "What type is it?"

"Shad . . . the same fish they get the roe from, but I don't care what anyone says, the roe is nothing compared to the flesh." Simon's mouth was moistening at the thought of the wild and slightly oily flavor of the meat.

"Are you sure the French don't have this fish?" In spite of the fact that Winston Gallery made most of their money off American art, Barclay still believed the French had the best of everything. "Where do they come from?"

Simon pointed west. "Right over there, in the Hudson."

Barclay drew back from the fish. "But the river is polluted."

"No, it's not . . . not where they net these it's not. And be sure to take some of that sauce. It was cooked with Sancerre and fresh tarragon."

Harold Barclay took a much smaller piece of fish than he originally had planned to.

Simon slid the belly portion of one of the shad onto his plate. He took a bite, chewed once, was tempted to swallow, then thought better of the idea and pulled a bone as long as a needle from between his lips. "I have to apologize for the bones, but you can be sure that you are getting a really fresh fish when you buy it unboned.

Betsy Pyne pointed to the tureen to Barclay's right. "Harold, you must try the potatoes. They are whipped with steamed garlic." Spitting a transparent fishbone into her napkin, she turned to Barclay's new wife, Margot. "Why do you suppose it is that the very best things always have one problem that makes them so annoying . . . like the bones in this fish or the leaves on an artichoke or the shell of a lobster?"

145

"You could say the same of people." Margot wasn't nearly as beautiful or as rich as the Italian jewess Barclay had been married to before, but her family had signed the Magna Carta.

Simon took a bite of fish, then one of the whipped garlic potatoes, and then a sip of Sancerre. He savored the flavors in his mouth, then swallowed. "But we sometimes learn to love those unbearable things in people."

Barclay pushed his fish to the corner of his plate. "You have far more patience in that respect than I."

Betsy Pyne smiled at her husband. "That's why Simon gets along so well with artists."

Her comment made him think of Lerner. The memory so absorbed Simon he didn't notice when the bite he had prepared so carefully fell from his fork and tumbled across his tie. When he bit down on the prongs of his empty fork he smiled across the table at Barclay. "You know, I knew from the start this is what you were leading up to with the paintings." Simon hadn't gotten angry when Barclay had told him he would not show any of the Lerners at the Biennale unless he could buy the hundred outright. Barclay didn't know how Simon really felt. All he had said was, "I'll have to speak to Luccio about it. . . . He is the other executor."

"Did you really know my plan for the paintings?"

"That's why I let Dutton pick so many paintings." Simon could tell by the half-smile on Barclay's face that he had seen the slides and understood how the Lerners had been selected. He let the Winston have just enough of the really strong paintings to mount a good exhibition. "You have to remember, Harold, I'm only your accountant, and accountants work with figures, not paintings."

"Executors take care of that, don't they?" Simon didn't answer, but Barclay was so impressed by the way Simon had handled things that he decided to take his advice and eat the shad after all. "And what did Luccio have to say?"

Looking at Margot, so like the Gainsborough her family had sold to Barclay just after the war, chin too small and nose too large but wonderful hair, Simon thought twice about telling the truth. "He told me you were just like every other Jewish merchant and that we should let you satisfy yourself in a rather intimate way and let another gallery handle the Lerner estate."

"And what did you say?"

146

"I told him that if I were a principal of Winston's, regardless of my Jewishness, I would have insisted on being allowed to buy the hundred paintings."

"Does Luccio really think that a Wasp businessman like Tiffany would have behaved differently?"

"Tiffany was Jewish," Simon corrected him.

"No."

"Of course."

"Oh, stop it! Why is it the most anti-Semitic people are always Jewish?" Betsy Pyne always took charge when the conversation began to go astray.

Margot took a sip of iced water and, cracking a cube between her teeth, announced, "I don't understand."

But they did. As Betsy rang the bell for the dinner plates to be cleared away, Simon was already describing the dessert. It was chocolate cake made with twenty-four eggs and ground nuts instead of flour.

Simon was most at ease negotiating over food, perhaps only because he didn't feel guilty about exploiting people after feeding them so well. The best artists of the century had been poor. Simon had entertained many of them. Most were genuinely so impressed or intimidated by the five courses and fine wines, the Spode china, Georgian silver, and Waterford crystal, that they became easier to manipulate. Barclay was far too shrewd and worldly for that; besides, he didn't really like food. But the atmosphere Simon created did relax even the Barclays of the world just enough to get them to listen to, to try things, like the shad, that they normally would have had nothing to do with.

After dessert Simon took Barclay into the library. The wives went into the living room to wait. As they walked down the hall, Simon thought of a dinner he had given years ago.

It was in 1961. The supply of Old Masters Barclay had bought so discreetly from the English, French, and Germans after the war was beginning to dry up, and he was sure that the run on American abstract art hadn't even begun. "Do you remember the first time you came here to dinner?" Simon asked.

Barclay adjusted the handkerchief in his breast pocket and smiled conspiratorially at Simon. "I will never forget Lerner cracking the shells his snails were served in as if he were eating a lobster . . . and

147

you telling him when he got embarrassed, 'It's quite all right. Everyone eats them that way in the south of France.' "

It was quite true. Simon had set up an elaborate and intimidating dinner as the stage for Lerner to meet Barclay, the European dealer who had bought and sold Rembrandts and Rubenses and who promised to make him rich and famous in his new gallery. After the snails there had been black truffle soup, pheasant under glass, asparagus as thin as tulip stems, profiteroles, brandy, and Cuban cigars. Before any of them had recovered from the feast, Lerner had agreed to show at Barclay's new gallery, and Simon's firm would be the accountants for Winston.

Beginning with Lerner, then de Kalb, Simon led more than a dozen artists into the Winston stable. The postwar painters with all their politics and principles were quick to desert the art dealers who had started them, who had given them their first taste of money. They were eager to join the corporate structure of big galleries like Winston. They wanted security. They became merchandise.

"And do you remember what Steven called you?"

"A parasite . . . but that didn't stop him from selling me fifteen paintings for nearly a hundred and fifty thousand dollars, insisting that I mark each one up at least forty percent, too. He had more than a bit of the Jewish merchant in him." Simon didn't seem to hear his words. He just stared at the Lerner over the mantel. "You know, you are so close to the art of so many of them that it seems foolish for us not to work more closely. You have an amazing eye . . . a gallery would offer you a stage from which you may be able to do far more."

Barclay's offer broke the spell of that gray Lerner. Simon turned his back on the painting. They shook hands and agreed that he would take a position at and for the Winston Gallery. There was no need to talk money. They knew each other's price.

"What will my title be?"

"Secretary . . . treasurer. . . . Whatever you like."

Simon offered him one of the same Cuban cigars he had given Lerner at that dinner almost ten years ago. He had to smuggle them in from Switzerland now. Simon tried out the titles. Secretary . . . treasurer . . . why not both?

Simon looked forward to telling Betsy the news. She was still enough of her father's daughter to appreciate the security he would have as secretary-treasurer of Winston. It was the first time in more than thirty years that Simon had worked for anyone else. As they passed the door to the dining room, Barclay stopped and asked, "What about Luccio? Do you think he will understand?"

Simon hadn't expected him to push the point so quickly. "He has his own mind and as executor must approve sales . . . but I think he'll see the wisdom of what we have decided."

Barclay walked up to the bright-red painting of Luccio's that was hung above the sideboard. He pointed at it with his cigar, coming so close to the surface of the canvas with the glowing ash Simon thought he was going to brand it. He wasn't aware that Barclay was familiar with Luccio's work—he hadn't ever commented on it before. Barclay looked at Simon out of the corner of his eye. "His work never has gotten the proper push . . . a man his age must find that very frustrating." Simon understood that Barclay was interested in Luccio, not his art.

When the men returned, Betsy Pyne poured espresso and passed around the plate of amaretti. Simon was feeling so confident, so sure of his position, that he threw away the colored wrapper of his almond cookie. He took the time to comment on how much the wrapper looked like a piece of currency but did not bother to light it to test his luck.

A few blocks away from the Pyne house, at a dinner Tessa had organized around Andrew, those same cookies were just about to be served up but in a far less conventional manner.

The dinner was at Raffles, a private club on the second floor of the Sherry-Netherland. Andrew had ordered his lamb "as pink as Ms. Merritt's tongue." He had heard the abbreviation for the first time that afternoon and thought it so awful that he insisted upon using it anytime he could, pronouncing it as though there were a bumblebee in his mouth. But the waiter must have disliked the abbreviation because the lamb chops that arrived in their white ruffle were gray inside.

Though the meal at Raffles was far less appetizing than the dinner at Simon's, the conversation between Tessa, Andrew, Jamie and Ian was just as heavily seasoned with innuendo and offers. But Andrew was too busy thinking about the secret in his pocket to pay very much attention to what was being asked of him and offered to him by Ian with Tessa's backing.

"Come on, Andrew, it would be fun." Jamie's dreams of co-star status were on the verge of coming through.

Andrew fingered the secret thing in his pocket and answered, "Yeah, it probably would be fun," then turned to Tessa, "but what if it didn't work out . . . going to see something at a movie theatre and watching it on TV are two different things. What if no one wanted to see it? I would feel awful, you losing all that money."

Tessa sensed he was weakening. She swallowed quickly. "First, seventy-five thousand dollars isn't that much money, and my husband has his boat, so he owes me this. Besides, even if it is a flop, he needs a tax write-off this year, but none of that's important. Andrew, if you saw the rushes of what was shot last week you wouldn't have any doubts." Andrew smiled at the bit of film lingo Tessa had picked up.

"Why won't you look at it? My God, I'm the one that comes off looking like a cross between . . ."

Jamie was going to make a movie analogy, but before he could speak, Tessa supplied an anatomical metaphor. "Asshole and cunt are the words I think you are searching for."

They all laughed, but no one found the idea of merging the two sets of muscles more amusing than Jamie. "Can you imagine the combination of an asshole and a cunt—that would demand more attention than me. . . . But really, Andrew, why don't you want to see what Ian shot the other day? You looked wonderful. What are you embarrassed about?"

"Nothing . . . nothing in the film at least."

Tessa wanted an answer. "Ian says that you can have final say about what he includes in the film."

"What's it going to tell me? What am I going to learn? Or for that matter, what would anybody learn if I pick and choose the parts of my life to go in the film?"

Andrew wondered what a third eye would see in him. "It would remember things I forget. Words, actions that wouldn't seem important at the time would take on a greater meaning when they were projected larger than life on an empty space one, two, ten years from now. But would the importance the camera assigns these bits of my life be any more accurate? Would . . . could it be any more objective than my own eye?"

From the way Ian tore the meat from the bone on his plate, Andrew knew that this film was terribly important to him. "What

150

I meant when I said that to Tessa was I don't want the film to be in any way sensationalist. I wouldn't include a scene just because it was titillating. That's why I don't want Jackson to be part of this. The film I am proposing with Tessa's help would be a very different sort of project from the one we just did for the B.B.C."

Andrew knew the reason Jackson wouldn't be included in the film was because he wouldn't do it, but that didn't matter. "I don't understand exactly how this film you are talking about will be any different from the one you just finished."

"First of all, it will be three times as long, and it will cover several months instead of just a few days in your life. You won't be interviewed. There will be no script, no prearranged questions for you to answer, at least. You said yourself you were starting something new, not just a new series, but a new approach to your paintings . . . so it offers us an incredible opportunity to capture on film the creative process." Ian made it sound as if it were an endangered species.

Tessa reached across the table and touched Andrew's cheek. "You should have seen the expression on your face when you talked about starting these new paintings. When you said it, I thought you were just saying it because you liked the way it sounded, like the time you told that woman from the *Times* that you were going to draw the Dalai Lama."

"I still might."

Tessa was serious. "But it wasn't like that. It excited me. I got that same feeling I had those one or two times I watched a really brilliant actor. . . . God, I don't know, it was as if you were in a play . . . as if it had all been rehearsed."

It was just what Andrew didn't want to hear. "You said yourself that the cameraman had an incredible touch." The answer would be "no." Andrew would tell them that he didn't have the time, that the film would get in the way of his work.

Ian sensed what was coming, and before Andrew could begin the excuse he blurted out, "But you are not just a painter . . . there is more to learn from you than what's in your paintings."

Andrew found Ian's statement both offensive and flattering. He was ready to answer pompously, "If you are any kind of filmmaker, you should know that there is nothing more than being an artist." But then Andrew looked up at the photographs of the "in" members of Raffles that were hung around the room. There was one of the

151

birthday party Tessa had given him the year before. It was placed just above the dessert tray. The guests ranged from Candy Darling to W. H. Auden, from Mick Jagger to Kay Graham. They were all wearing crepe-paper hats. They came because of Andrew, not because Tessa invited them. There were few other people in the world who could have drawn so many different and brilliant variations of the species to feed.

Ian was right. Andrew was more than just a painter, but was that something extra Ian felt merited a film just his celebrity status, or did he mean that there was more to Andrew as a human . . . as a man?

Cecil Beaton left the table where he had been feeding as if at a trough and pranced over to their table like a slightly arthritic fawn. He was the man who had picked the colors of the room, who had struggled to create as conducive an atmosphere as possible for the digestion of the rich.

"Tessa . . . Andrew . . . Jamie . . ." He looked at Ian. "I don't know you. What are you horrors scheming over here?"

Tessa hit him with two quick kisses. "We're trying to talk Andrew into letting Ian make a documentary about him."

"What a marvelous idea."

"I'm not sure." Andrew wasn't.

Cecil patted Ian's shoulder, "Well, I hope you are kinder to Andrew than he was with me." He slapped the underside of his jaw with the back of his hand. "He made my wattle worse than it is, and every time I peeked at the drawing and asked if he could perform a little plastic surgery, he'd smile and then exaggerate it all the more. You made me look like a chicken . . . I can't thank you enough."

It was true Andrew had exaggerated his chin, but not by drawing in more flesh than was already there. Cecil was the most dapper man Andrew had ever known. He had lived his life by fashion. He was fashion. It seemed only right that Andrew should put life into those parts of Cecil's person that reflected this—the texture of a chocolate-brown felt fedora, perched so rakishly it looked as though it were pinned on; the starched white of his collar set on the azure body of his sea-isle cotton shirt. Cecil's mouth and eyes, the features that normally convey emotion, were drawn so faintly that they were almost invisible.

The folds of flesh under the chin gained weight and importance through visual osmosis because they rippled above one of Cecil's

152

incredible bow ties. It was cut more generously and tied more fop-pishly than the normal bow tie; Andrew had drawn its fold luxuri-ously. He rendered its red polka dots, each with a little black dot flecked with yellow in its center, like a hundred eyes shimmering so brilliantly against the blue background that this knotted strip of cloth became the key to the drawing, to Cecil. His double chin was exposed and distorted only because it was near this tie that had caught Andrew's fancy.

Wondering what the eye of Ian's camera might draw attention to, what might be exposed inadvertently in the film he was proposing, Andrew felt for the secret he had drawn pleasure from all day. But his hand went to the wrong pocket, and he found an amaretto instead. He had bought a dozen for himself at Balducci's that morn-ing. It was the last one left. When he took it out and unwrapped it, Tessa said, "I wondered what you had been fooling with down there. I was beginning to think you had developed a new habit."

Jamie wanted one. "Don't you have one for me?"

"No."

"Don't you believe in sharing?" Tessa chided.

"You're asking me to share my life . . . don't be greedy."

"So you'll do it." Ian wanted it settled.

Andrew pushed his plate away and rolled up the wrapper of the cookie into a long thin tube. Then he turned his butter dish upside down on top of his water glass and placed the rolled wrapper on the little altar he had made, "Does anyone have a match?"

Tessa handed him a gold lighter as thin as a tea biscuit and demanded, "What are you going to do?"

"An Englishman told me they do this in Italy to test their luck." He lit the top of the wrapper, "If this wrapper gets off the ground, I'll do it. You can film anything you want, but if it does not defy the laws of gravity, the deal is off . . . agreed?"

"But . . ." It seemed unbelievable, but Ian was sure that Andrew was serious.

"No 'buts' . . . quick, now or never. It's almost burned down low enough to go."

"Agreed . . . but how is it supposed to get off the ground?" Ian was shouting.

"Have faith! It happens sometimes."

By now their corner of the dining room was watching and waiting to see whether the wrapper would rise. Cecil clucked, "You're such a tease . . ."

Tessa giggled. "I can't stand it. This is a serious decision."

"That's why I am leaving it up to the gods." Andrew didn't know why he was doing it this way, but as he stared at the burning cookie wrapper, he knew he would abide by its decision.

The wrapper rose ever so slowly. Ian—angry, but relieved that he had won—kissed Tessa. As the ash rose, the diners clapped, not knowing or caring what was at stake.

Cecil shouted at the waiter to bring a magnum of Dom Perignon to the table and said, "I expect front-row seats at the premiere."

Jamie reached under the table and squeezed Andrew's thigh. "Can I put a star on the bedroom door?"

As Andrew watched the cinder hover overhead, he reached back into his jacket pocket and felt the object he had suddenly attached such importance to. It was a gold Cartier watch. He fingered the inscription on the back. He couldn't actually feel the words. The engraving was too shallow, but he knew what he had had inscribed: "To love the game beyond the prize."

Andrew had spent all morning trying to decide what to have engraved on the back of the watch. He had thought of Scott Fitzgerald's line "The victor belongs to the spoils," but he decided that it should be something of his own. He had considered, "All the world loves to eat," but he thought the message should be more than merely true. He had had second thoughts about the gift and the inscription even after he had arrived at the jeweler's, but in the end he went with his first instinct. "To love the game beyond the prize" was the only unqualified piece of advice he could offer.

As the charred wrapper descended toward him, Tessa shouted, "God, I love you, Andrew." The exuberance of the sentiment as much as its breathy delivery disintegrated the ash in Andrew's face, powdering the lenses of his oversized glasses with a film of soot that made all the smiling faces in that elegant dining room of Raffles look slightly dirty as they toasted him.

154

XVII

The classes Wendy taught met in an old storage room in the basement of Our Lady of Perpetual Help Church on 128th Street. She sat behind a card table that had a broken leg. Coco had fixed it for her, making a splint out of a broom and adhesive tape. He hadn't gotten around to cutting off the three feet of broom handle that stuck up above the top of the table. It reminded Wendy of a mast. It made her think of that boat in which she and her father had sailed out into the open water years before. She felt as if she were going on an adventure each time she sat down to teach.

One of the priests, Father Wallace, had a sister who worked in a travel agency. When he offered to get some posters to brighten up the room, Wendy suggested, "Try to find some of Africa, Egypt, Morocco . . . Kenya . . . tigers, zebras. . . ." But she was presented with a half-dozen Swiss travel posters showing blue-eyed blonds in lederhosen playing alphorns, the mountains, and carefree skiers sailing through deep powder. The priest told her, "I thought it might help keep them cool. . . . It gets awfully hot down there, you know."

Wendy wasn't at all surprised when her black students turned on the posters. The day after she hung them up they were covered with phalluses drawn in black Magic Marker. Immense black cocks penetrated every orifice of the pink-cheeked Swiss as they licked the fondue from their lips and blew their alphorns.

Originally she had volunteered to work at the church only two afternoons a week; now she came in every morning. She found Coco and the Savage Nomads much more satisfying than the suburban nomads in the Village. The Savage Nomads she taught were even more alien to her father's world, to her past, than the hippies she had sought sanctuary with before.

It was Coco's turn to give an oral composition and the subject Wendy had chosen to test him on was the 1969 version of

155

"What I did on my summer vacation."

"Coco, I'd like you to tell us about the most meaningful experience of your life."

"Which one you want me to tell you about first?" Coco asked as he cracked his knuckles.

"Not which one. . . . I want to know about just one time, the single experience, that when you look back over your life means more than all the others."

"Can't."

"Why?"

"Man, you start sayin' dats it . . . I done it . . . I got it . . . you leave yourself nowhere to go. But I tell you the baddest thing I did yesterday."

Wendy nodded, realizing it was her question, not his.

Coco rubbed the pony fur inserts on the front of his black leather jacket. "Got dis."

"How'd you get it?"

Coco winked at Taki. "Stole it from Wilson's House of Suede . . . cost over a hundred bucks." He reached into his pocket and tossed the price tag to the rest of the Nomads.

"I was so slick, the way I walked in there, you never seen anything like it . . . least not at Wilson's House of Suede. Like I was invisible." Wendy knew Coco was right. She leaned forward as she watched him, in his red sharkskin high-rise trousers, act out this small miracle he had engineered between five-thirty and six o'clock on a rainy Wednesday afternoon in March of 1969.

His white teeth snapped the air as he told the tale. He was hungry, but his appetite was different from hers.

As Coco pulled at his crotch and announced, "I always drove the girls crazy, but when I wear dis jacket der pussies weep," Wendy thought how, even in sex, she was so eager to come, to tremble, to be paralyzed by emotion, that she really wasn't able to enjoy any of the foreplay. Even when Coco was between her legs prodding her with himself, Wendy was saving herself, getting ready for some devastating orgasm that never came.

If Wendy could have settled, if she could have sustained some nourishment from the journey emotion takes us on, rather than always longing for some spiritual Never-never Land, she might not have been so ravenous. The child in Wendy kept asking the grown-

156

up, already weary from a trip she knew would never end, "Are we there yet?"

Coco finished his story. Taki took a hit of wine and shouted, "That ain't nothin' compared to what I pulled off yesterday."

"Bullshit, Taki. You never hit the man for more than a candy bar."

"Oh, yeah? Well yesterday I cost somebody a candy bar worth about a grand."

It was the excitement, the danger of going up to 125th Street, of stepping into another world, that had excited Wendy and drawn her to Coco and the Nomads. Perhaps the very violence they lived with every day enabled them to take this attitude, to feast so freely. When Taki revealed how he had cost "Whitey" a grand, Wendy shouted, "That's what I want to do."

Wendy and the Savage Nomads took a Number 5 train to East 180th Street in the Bronx, climbed a chain fence, and they were there. Taki, whose skill with Magic Marker and spray paint were legend in all three boroughs, led the way, pointing to the third rail, "You dead, baby, you touch that."

Each time she stepped over the charged rail, Wendy got a thrill. The danger—the idea that she could slip or fall or be pushed onto it, that if she chose she could just reach down and touch it and be finished—did make this childish and destructive assertion of herself more "meaningful."

It was dark by then. The subway cars lined up in the yard looked like sleeping animals. Wendy chose the cleanest one she could find to put her brand on. As Taki tried to compute how many thousands of dollars the City of New York had spent removing his name from the sides of subway cars, Wendy went to work. It took her nearly an hour to cover both sides of the car. When she was finished, when she had joined the ranks of Taki 169s, Small Time Leroys and King Split 60 Goodfoots that adorned the other cars with her own pink and white, candy-caned WENDY 12 E. 88 ST. in letters taller than herself, the Nomads clapped.

Wendy wanted to see her car move. But a guard spotted them and they ran again.

Part of the satisfaction and fascination she had for Coco and the rest of the Savage Nomads came out of a genuine desire to help and part out of the feeling of superiority she got when she was with them.

157

But what really drew her into their world was the mystery, not of their blackness or their poverty, but the mystery of their ability to satisfy themselves under the most adverse circumstances. In an effort to gain their confidence, to get close enough so that she could see what enabled Coco's eyes to twinkle in spite of the darkness of his world, she did them favors.

If they had all asked for sex, Wendy would have found some way of rationalizing it, but the sexual revolution had hit Harlem a hundred years before it pulled down the drawers of the rest of Manhattan. Wendy provided them with the names and addresses of the parents of rich East Siders she had gone to school with. She didn't feel guilty about masterminding the rash of robberies that plagued the parents of Dalton School alumni. She told herself, "I always make sure no one's home . . . so they can't be hurt. Besides, if they can afford Dalton, they can afford to contribute a few stereos and TV sets to the poor. It's the least they can do to help." But it was her cause they were helping, not the Nomads'.

Wendy found a note under the door of her classroom on the last day of March. The handwriting belonged to Father Castor, the pastor of the parish. For a moment she panicked, "What if he knows?" But it was quite a friendly note, asking her just to stop by his office for a "chat." Wendy had never really talked to the pastor before; she guessed he wanted to ask her about teaching another course. She was unusually aware of a hunger that morning, her desire for something that would still have mystery, that would still confound and excite her even after she had lost herself in it.

Father Castor and Father Wallace were both waiting when she arrived. There was not only coffee, but also Sara Lee strudel. Wendy liked cake. She took two bites of strudel—eating helped her forget about this other hunger that was gnawing at her—but she swallowed hard when Father Castor noticeably fingered the magazine on his desk and announced, "I had a long talk with Coco yesterday. . . . He's still a bit rough on the outside, but you've taught him a great deal. He really seems to be learning how to be able to work within the system . . . and of course you're the one responsible for all that."

Father Wallace stepped forward. "That's right. I was just telling Father Castor how much you've done for the older boys. How many changes—good changes—you've made. It's almost your program already."

158

Wendy had to bite the inside of her cheek to keep from laughing out loud. As the two fathers went on about all the good deeds she had done at Our Lady of Perpetual Help, Wendy wondered what Coco had said to inspire their faith in her.

"What we wanted to know is . . . would you be interested in heading a whole new program that would operate out of the church —one designed to appeal to other gangs like Coco's as well as the adult community, with night courses and things like that? We can go into the details later. . . . I know it's a lot to ask, but would you be interested in taking on . . . in helping us?"

Wendy didn't believe it. Had they really understood and appreciated what she was trying to do? "You want me to run it?"

"Would you consider it?"

"Consider it . . . of course, I'll do it."

"I'm sure you're aware that the sort of program we're envisioning —with you in a directorial post, of course—will be expensive and . . ." Father Castor began to fidget with the magazine again. When he turned it over, Wendy recognized it as *The New York Times Sunday Magazine* from two weeks before that had a picture of her father on the cover. Peter had read the article on him several times, but Wendy hadn't been interested.

The second priest took over. "And our budget for that sort of thing is already stretched to the limit." Wendy took another piece of strudel. She couldn't wait to tell Coco. "And we were hoping you could help us . . ."

"Sure. . . . I already said I'd love to take on the job."

"We would have spoken to you about the project sooner, but we didn't realize how committed you were."

Father Castor handed her a sheet of paper. "We've worked out a budget, and we think we could get this new program on its feet for about $25,000."

Wendy licked her fingers, "Sounds good . . . but I'm not very good at the business end of things. I have some ideas for new courses, though."

The two men seemed to be impatient. She looked at the budget again to see if she had missed something. "Where are you going to get the money?"

"Coco told us we should ask . . ."

"Ask who?"

Father Castor held up the magazine, then put it down on top of his Bible. "Well, I read here that your father did establish a foundation, and though this isn't directly related to the arts or artists, we thought—Coco thought actually—that an exception might be made in the case of Our Lady of Perpetual Help. It isn't a lot of money . . ."

Wendy was out in the street before Father Castor had finished the sentence. Her father had found her, touched her, colored her life even above 125th Street. She had made a point of not telling anyone at the church who she was. She had said her father had sold insurance. Coco certainly had learned how to work within the system.

The junkies and the hookers, the people on the street who had seemed so foreign that morning as she had walked to work, no longer looked any different from Simon and all the rest. They were just in blackface. Wendy thought of those two mercenary priests looking at her with dollar signs in their eyes, wanting her to make an exception, and she turned back to Our Lady of Perpetual Help and screamed, "Fuck God in the mouth."

The sidewalk tilted, and the pimps in their chartreuse Cadillacs blurred. The Sara Lee strudel splattered on the sidewalk and Wendy clung onto a broken parking meter as much to keep from being swept away by her own emotions as to keep from falling down.

When it was out of her system, Wendy walked straight over to the abandoned building where Coco and the Nomads had stored the things she had helped them steal over the last few weeks.

Wendy kicked the door open. Coco, Taki, and two Puerto Rican girls lay tangled together under a baby blue quilt that had been stolen from a house across the street from Wendy's. Stereos were stacked one on top of another. There were a dozen TV sets. The room looked like an appliance store. The lyrics of "Baby Love" were pouring out of one of the speakers. Wendy tried to turn off the music, but when she couldn't find the machine it was coming from she pushed over a whole stack of stereos and screamed, "You fucking son of a bitch . . . you ignorant piece of shit . . . you told them."

"Told what, bitch?" Coco pulled on his trousers.

"Who I was . . . well I'll tell them all about you, too."

Wendy hadn't meant she was going to call the police. She was ready to tell him that he was just a dick like the ones they drew on the posters. She was going to tell the rest of the Savages what a

160

disappointment he was in bed, which wasn't true, and how he had cried in her arms one night after telling her how when he was little he used to fall asleep listening to his mother turning tricks at the other end of the room, which was true.

He hit her on the side of her head with his fist so hard that she fell down. For the first time since she had entered Coco's world she felt in danger, but it was not the physical sort. "You tell the cops on me, girl, you're dead."

Wendy had stopped crying. "I don't care." It was Coco who was now frightened. He had observed enough people who were cornered and who had a weapon to know when they were no longer bluffing.

Wendy didn't just mean she didn't care about his threat. She meant she didn't care about him. He had betrayed her without realizing it. The mystery she had seen in him had vanished. She knew that the only thing he would miss when she left was the help she had given him in setting up the robberies, but before she could leave 125th Street, she had to shatter her image of him so completely that she would never be tempted to come back.

Taki stood there naked except for an overcoat and an erection, and screamed, "I told you the bitch was crazy."

Coco slapped him, then turned back to Wendy. "Listen, if you haven't told the cops we should be able to work something out. Now I know cuz a . . . your old man, an' all—" He spoke of Lerner as if he were still alive. "You think they'll believe you and not us . . . but you're what they call an accessory . . ." Wendy didn't have to turn on him, he shattered himself right there before her eyes. He was as scared, as intimidated, as the rest by her father's power.

We can be hurt, wounded by others—things, even ideas, can be stolen, but our passion can be plundered, our feelings vandalized, only when we allow them to be. That is what the expression "consenting adult" is really all about. Wendy lost something of herself that day. It was that outer skin that builds up when you become very involved with new people quickly. But it was not ripped off like Coco's stereos and TV sets.

Alone, on the crowded express train downtown, Wendy picked at Coco and the Nomads, at the times she had spent above 125th Street, as if they were a callous, dead skin. She didn't have to make things up. She knew enough ugly truths to destroy any fondness or loyalty that remained. She used the truth like a knife, and by the time she

161

reached Eighty-sixth Street she had cut and picked apart so much that she was down to the raw part of herself, that last opaque layer of skin that shielded the Wendy that had gone into hiding at twelve. As she walked toward her house, Wendy knew that if she didn't turn herself, her mind, on someone, something else, she would begin to claw at that, too.

She had a key, but she didn't look for it. She didn't even ring. Instead she kicked and pounded on the door, screaming, "It's my house too. Why the fuck do you always lock me out? Let me in . . . let me in." The words echoed in her mind. It wasn't until Peter opened the door that Wendy realized that the voice echoing her cry was her father's. She couldn't remember how many times he had come home and pounded on the door like that.

The front hall was dark. The sapphire on the stem of Peter's new watch glistened. The hour glowed on his wrist.

"Why do you wear that thing? Take it off. I never should have let you keep it."

"It wasn't given to you."

"He's a fag, Peter. Do you know why he gave it to you?" She followed him into the living room. The way he moved around the room turning on the stereo, opening the window, made it hard to zero in on him. "He gave it to you because he wants to fuck you. He's famous for it, for being perverted." As she said the words, a voice in Wendy whispered to herself and to God, "Forgive me, I have to."

"Do you know what it's like to be fucked by a man?"

"No, but you do."

"They do it up your ass. Do you want to blow him? Because that's what he wants you to do. . . . and where did you get that shirt?" It was a white silk one of Andrew's. They had begun the painting that day. Andrew had said he wanted Peter's body to disappear against the white walls and white-lacquered floors of the room. Peter had forgotten to give it back on purpose. "And button it up. . . . What are you doing to yourself?" Peter glanced in the mirror over the mantel and touched himself. He liked the way it looked and felt. "Why do you go down there all the time?"

"I like it."

"Why?"

"They have a better stereo than we do." He was already learning Andrew's art of answering questions. Peter batted away Wendy's

162

questions and insults for more than ten minutes. He sat down and opened a copy of *Wind in the Willows*. He had heard Andrew and Sidney talking about it. Andrew had said it was his favorite book. Peter had taken it out of the library that afternoon.

"What are you reading a children's book for?"

"I'm a child." He was glad she hadn't noticed he was holding it upside down.

If her initial attempt to hurt him had been more effective, Wendy wouldn't have had to go so far, but she couldn't stand being so alone with her pain. It was all she knew how to share. "You're fucking him, aren't you?" The idea, the image of himself and Andrew that he knew was in his sister's mind was so repulsive and made him so nervous that he felt sick. It was as if her saying it made it true. For a moment the protective mechanism, that machine he had just assembled in himself, jammed. He felt he had to turn on her, on Andrew, on the whole world to be safe—to keep from being tainted.

But as Wendy screamed, "I know what you are . . . I know . . . I know," Peter saw that she didn't. That was why she was so angry. He realized that if he could turn Wendy's doubts back on her, if he became a mirror, what she said or what Andrew thought or wanted would no longer matter. When she or anyone else reached out for him, they would feel themselves. When they tried to touch or scratch or grab him, they would only get themselves. Peter began to search through the drawers of his mother's desk, knowing that if he could learn to reflect fear, if he could polish himself so brightly that when others looked into him they saw themselves, he would be safe.

He found what he wanted in the bottom drawer of the desk. As Wendy screamed, "Are you listening . . . do you understand what I'm saying?" he made sure the settings were correct, then he turned around quickly and flashed the Polaroid in her face. He had watched Andrew use a camera the day before.

He counted to five and then pulled the film from the back of the camera. Looking at his watch, he waited for it to develop. Wendy was shouting, but he didn't hear what she was saying. After sixty seconds he peeled off the cover of the photograph and handed it to his sister. "I just wanted you to see for yourself how pathetic you are."

It worked. Wendy crumpled the picture up in her fist and ran upstairs. She shouted, "You'll be sorry," then slammed her bedroom door. Peter was too pleased with the way he had disarmed and dismissed her to think about whether she was threatening him or warning.

Wendy threw the photograph in the corner, then collapsed on her bed and began to cry. Like eating, crying had become a habit. In a few minutes she became curious about the picture. Wendy rolled off the bed and began to search for it among the soiled clothes, old newspapers, and dirty dishes scattered across the floor. She found it behind a stack of *Vogues*. The photo wasn't pathetic. Peter had been wrong, but it was no comfort either. She didn't know if it were under- or overdeveloped. Her face was a black circle rimmed in an angry shade of red. The image reminded Wendy of an eclipse.

Wendy dropped the photo and picked up the April issue of *Vogue*. A chocolate kiss had melted in the heart of the Health and Beauty Section. The pages seemed to have a will of their own, flopping back to a section on the "new look in bathing suits" each time she tried to get past it. Girls in bikinis with hair not as golden as her own and eyes not nearly so blue smiled up from the pages mockingly. "Why is it so easy for them . . . why didn't they have to get fat?"

Wendy didn't understand that if her hair had not been that shade of blond that hairdressers never succeed in copying—white on the outside and gold beneath—if her eyes had not been so dark and deeply blue that when you looked into them you felt you were looking into heaven on a cloudless night, if the curve of her lips had not been so irresistible, if the power of her gifts had not been so frightening, Wendy would not have had to hide. Life would not have been so difficult.

She threw the magazine across the room, knocked over a half-finished quart of Diet Rite Cola, and began to cry again. She had to have something. Wendy picked up a jumbled *Village Voice*. She was thinking about going through the "Personals," of calling a stranger. She had read one once that started out "I like them big," but she was crying too hard to read. Wendy was frightened. She knew that if she didn't find someone, something soon, she'd have to turn on herself, and she knew what she would find there. She thought of Simon.

He was having dinner with Luccio and Elderstein. Wendy told the maid it was an emergency. She felt better immediately. Wiping away her tears, she got ready to scream at Simon, but then her eye caught

164

sight of an article on radicals. There were photographs of Abbie Hoffman, Tom Hayden, and Jerry Rubin, quotes from Stokely Carmichael and Eldridge Cleaver, and a poem by Leroi Jones. She scanned their indictments of the system, of the "powers that be." They wanted to tear it down, to bring it to its knees, to start fresh. When Simon picked up the phone, she was just reading about Mark Rudd, one of the founders of Students for a Democratic Society. He had led the sit-in at Columbia the year before.

"Wendy, what's wrong?"

"Everything."

"I thought you were happy working at the school for the underprivileged."

"I had to leave. We were just teaching them how to rip off people legally . . . how to be good capitalist pigs. I called to tell you I've joined S.D.S."

Simon thought of all the times Lerner had interrupted his dinner with a phone call.

Wendy made it seem as if she were already an active member in the organization, sort of Mark Rudd's left-hand girl. In answering Simon's questions, she read straight from the article in the *Voice*. Wendy didn't look on it as lying. She would join tomorrow.

Wendy was glad Simon didn't like the idea, that he found it threatening. "Wendy, everyone has a right to his own political views. I don't agree with most of what you've been saying, but that is your right. But don't . . . you must promise not to do anything violent . . . never to break the law. Society is based on order, and it's the thinking man's or woman's responsibility, not just to government, but to civilization, to maintain order. Without law . . . without order, we're lost." Simon sounded like a politician, as if he were reciting a speech he had memorized.

"We each do what we have to." Wendy hung up without saying good-bye.

XVIII

A white Frisbee cut through the darkness, then ricocheted off Alexander Hamilton's head. The first blades of grass crumpled and the mud oozed beneath their feet. The wind blew in fits, and Mark Rudd shivered as he led them across Columbia's south field. He had forgotten his coat. Wendy offered to go back and get it, but he said that it didn't matter.

She was with him, but not in the same way she had been with Coco. That position was held by Shelley, the Jewish girl from Great Neck with no ass and large hard bullet-shaped breasts. Wendy's talents were suited for a different type of service.

Rudd stopped and looked up at the president's office. "I still don't believe it."

Shelley pointed her breasts at him. "That they were in on Lumumba's assassination?"

"Fuck, what are you talking about? I've been saying that for two years. They're capable of anything. No one's safe. What I fucking can't believe is how Wendy got those files."

Wendy smiled. "I told you how I got them."

Rudd scratched his beard and looked at her. "Yeah, but the crazy thing about you is I can't tell any better than Cordia's secretary or that asshole who believed you were from the Historical Society and gave you a set of plans for the biological sciences building. If you're telling the truth. . . . Man, there's just no telling with you."

It had quickly become apparent to Rudd and the rest of the underground that Wendy could lie better than any of them. The more outrageous the lie—the greater the risk—the more she enjoyed it.

Rudd turned and pointed at the light glistening in the second floor of Schermerhorn, the biological sciences building. "The fucking CIA is probably up there right now, working on a new nerve gas. Man,

166

that's what college . . . that's what all the ivory towers have become —just places to invent more efficient ways to murder, to plot how to gain power. But with those files Wendy stole for us today, we know how far they've gone. We've got facts and figures. There'll be no more sit-ins. The time for demonstrating is past. It's time to shut it down forever. When they hear Schermerhorn, then the bank, then Dow Chemical all explode at once, they'll know the time for change has come, and there'll be nothing they can say, 'cause we have proof. No more . . . it's our time now."

Rudd turned his hand into a gun, pointed it toward Schermerhorn, and shouted, "Boom!" Then he turned around and aimed at their invisible targets downtown. "Boom! Gotcha! . . . Boom! Gotcha!" His voice echoed in the empty field, and, as Wendy looked into the darkness, it seemed as if he were taking aim at far more than three buildings on the island of Manhattan.

It was a lush and heady spring, where the world seemed to be a great many people's oyster. The risks involved and the power required to crack it were being calculated by a great many. "The time has come . . . we can, we must take the risk . . . it's our right and our responsibility" were words spoken not just by the Mark Rudds and the Richard Nixons of 1969. It was a naive and willful spring, an easy time to rationalize the ends as well as the means of passion.

Simon and Luccio stood at the top of the spiraling walkway of the Guggenheim. The Guggenheim is not well designed for displaying pictures, but it does inspire one. Luccio pointed down into the heart of the shell-shaped building. "You know, I always have the urge to jump when I come here."

"I never thought of you as being suicidal, Luccio."

"That's just it! There's something about this place that makes me think I could survive such a leap!"

"Beautiful things have that effect on some people." Simon switched from that idea to the subject he really wanted to discuss. "I was offered a position at Winston."

Luccio waited to hear how Simon had refused.

"And I accepted." Simon pushed on before Luccio could protest. "Because with me working there, we will not only be able to obtain more advantageous terms for the sale of this first group of his paintings, but it will allow us to take care of the rest of them just the way

167

we discussed. Don't you see, with me there—with Winston behind us—we will be able to do everything Steven asked and more, years before we originally expected. I had to accept the job—we will never have another opportunity like this." Looking down the dizzying spiral of the Guggenheim, Simon was almost able to believe it all.

The view had quite another effect on Luccio. He was ready to shout, "You liar . . . you cheat . . . you expect me to believe this? You cannot be on both sides. Either you are with us, or with them." But then he realized that there was another side to be played. As his eye followed the tightening curve of the wall, he told himself to be silent, to wait. His position would only become more secure. The longer he waited before he took the demanding leap he had in mind, the more rewarding it would be.

It is much easier going down than coming up. Simon and Luccio hardly looked at the paintings that lined their corkscrewing descent.

"Because of my professional connection with Winston, Elderstein will sit in for me during the actual negotiations, but, of course, it is right and proper that I assist and approve any contract. You and I will have to sit down and come up with a price, but, you know, Barclay can be a very tough bargainer, and it might help if we had an outside appraisal of the value of the hundred paintings. I thought Richard Fence might help us out. I've done business with him before and. . . . Yes, it would make sense to go to other galleries and get competitive bids, and, of course, if that had been a viable option for us, I wouldn't have accepted the post at Winston, but because of the exclusivity clause in Steven's contract, we have no choice but to deal with Barclay for the next nine years. Steven didn't want us to wait. He wanted it established before he was forgotten. . . . Don't worry. I assure you the fact that New York State is involved in the foundation doesn't mean we have to have court or any other outside approval. We only brought the State in on it so that we don't have to pay taxes on the profit from the paintings. . . . Regardless of whom either of us works for, this is our decision. We can sell the Lerners to whomever we want for whatever we want."

As they walked around and around and down, it became easier and easier to explain. Exchanging questions and answers, both Simon and Luccio believed the courses they were plotting were quite direct. Their future seemed certain and secure, so unlike this whimsical exhibition hall they were moving through with no straight lines, only curves.

Elderstein read Richard Fence's appraisal once with his trifocals on and once with them off on the morning of May 16. It read the same way both times. "The unfortunate thing, Simon, is that he waited so long to send us this appraisal. I know he's a friend of yours, but it certainly seems to me as if he did it deliberately. We must postpone the negotiations with Barclay. We'd be foolish to go in to Winston to bargain with this."

"We can't wait!" Simon insisted.

"Why?" Luccio and Elderstein asked simultaneously.

"Because if we delay, Barclay won't have time to get ready for the exhibition. He wants it to coincide with the Biennale. He'll barely have enough time as it is. I had no idea that this was the attitude toward Steven's market value, but I can't stress the importance of this sale and the exhibition that hinges on it."

"But $800,000 for a hundred Lerners is ridiculously low!"

"Fence has got his head up his ass. Barclay is getting them cheap at the $3,500,000 we're asking."

"What shall we do?" Elderstein fiddled with his hearing aid to be sure he heard Simon's answer.

Simon neatly folded the appraisal, put it in his pocket, and announced, "We will ask for exactly what we had first decided—three and a half million dollars—but we have to remember that the art boom is just that. People are wary about buying large numbers of paintings at one time. The market can be flooded easily . . . "

Luccio picked up an obsidian Mayan blade, tested its weight, then held it to his wrist. "I thought his death fixed that. . . . Now that he's gone, the supply is limited."

Simon went on as if he hadn't heard what Luccio had said. "If Fence's appraisal is any indication of the general feeling about Lerner, we will have to prepare ourselves to accept less. It's a simple matter of supply and demand."

It began to rain as soon as Simon, Elderstein, and Luccio stepped outside. They couldn't get a cab in front of Simon's house, so the three of them, huddled under one umbrella, walked to the avenue. But there were no taxis there either, and after waiting under a leaky awning for ten minutes, they moved on. They walked half a block, then waited for a cab, walked half a block, then walked all the way down to Fifty-seventh Street. By the time they arrived at the Winston Gallery, they were thirty minutes late and quite wet.

Simon took their raincoats. Luccio and Elderstein started to follow him as he stepped behind the receptionist's desk and hurried down the hallway, back into the inner offices of Winston. But there was something in the way Simon called back, "I'll tell Harold we're here," that told them that they were not to follow—that they were on their own.

Luccio looked around at the paintings on display. He knew just how he would hang a show of his at Winston.

Elderstein leaned over and whispered loudly in his ear, "Don't hesitate to tell me what you think, but let me do the talking. . . . The important thing is not to get personally involved. Strictly business. . . . I know how to handle these things."

Luccio smiled at the show he was putting together in his head. His eyes twinkled at the thought of the party he knew Winston would give to celebrate his opening with them. He patted the deaf and blind lawyer on the back. "We'll come out of this all right."

Simon bickered with Barclay in his office. They weren't arguing over price, but over how long the transaction would take.

Christina Hansen fed the appraisal into the Xerox machine. Usually she made a point of not reading the letters and contracts that she handled, but there was something about the way Simon signed his name, the way he looped around the top of his "S" and put a slash through it to make it serve as the "P" for Pyne that caught her eye. She had seen it on several Winston checks that Simon had written to Richard Fence.

In a few minutes Simon returned to his friends and led them into the largest of the Winston showing rooms. The room was dark except for a spotlight on an empty easel. He seated Luccio and Elderstein in a pair of Breuer chairs covered in beige glove leather. The seats were so soft and comfortable that they were hard to get out of. The soft lighting, the padded walls, the plush chairs—the whole room was designed to make the client feel so comfortable that he or she forgot the time, the price, the world—everything except the art. It was a room designed to make one say "yes."

Barclay entered the room by the door through which the art was

170

usually carried. He took his place before the empty easel. There was no preliminary conversation. Elderstein hadn't even opened his briefcase when Barclay asked, "So what do you think they're worth?" As Elderstein fumbled with the latches, Barclay smiled. "Surely you haven't forgotten your price."

Elderstein looked for Simon to come to his aid, but he was no longer with them. "Our price is three and a half million dollars."

"And mine is nine hundred thousand dollars." Barclay was prepared for this moment. He stepped to the window, drew the drapery, and pointed to the Dow Jones sign atop a neighboring building. "The market's been going down for several months. Today it's at a new low. Think about the risk involved in such a large purchase. Nine hundred thousand dollars seems more in line with that figure." He gestured again to the sign. The Dow Jones dropped another point. Then Christina Hansen slipped into the room and whispered in Barclay's ear. "Think about it. I'll be back in a moment," Barclay said.

The wind shifted. The rain became more intense. It hit the window, blurring this magic number that determined the price of art. Luccio and Elderstein became angry, not because Barclay offered so little for so much art. They expected that—they were prepared to compromise, but as equals.

Elderstein broke the pencil in his hand. "Does he think we don't know?"

Luccio stared at the empty easel. "We ought to fuck the whole deal, call it all off."

For a minute they really did think of making a stand, of stopping it before it went any further. But then Barclay reappeared. He made the first of several final offers. "One million two hundred fifty thousand dollars." As he announced the figure, he waved a copy of Fence's appraisal at Luccio and Elderstein, scattering any serious thought they might have had about rebellion. That piece of paper reminded each of all the pieces of paper and promises that rested in this bargain. They were still angry enough to make Barclay pay a few hundred thousand dollars for his arrogance, but the two men knew that they would never get another chance like this again. Elderstein thought of his grandchildren, and Luccio of his painting on the display easel in the Winston showroom.

There were three other final offers. The fourth, a price of

$1,995,000, was accepted. As soon as Elderstein agreed, Barclay left. Simon burst into the room like a trainer consoling a fighter after he had just taken a dive. "Congratulations! You've made a very good deal for us."

Then Barclay returned, opened his Hermes appointment book, and dictated the terms. "This transaction will be with Winston A. G. of Liechtenstein. We have thirteen years to pay without interest . . ."

One million nine hundred ninety-five thousand dollars seems like a very large sum of money. With inflation, Winston was paying a little over thirteen thousand dollars for each painting. This is still a great deal of money. But these figures become far less impressive when one considers that while Barclay waited between his second and third final offer, Herbert Krankiet, the young Herschorn of the art and business world, bought two large Lerners from this group for which Barclay was negotiating. Krankiet paid $178,000 in cash, for paintings Winston Gallery didn't even own yet. As Krankiet wrote the check, Barclay said, "It's quite a reasonable price for Lerners of this size and quality."

To Barclay, Simon, Krankiet, even Elderstein, $1,995,000 was not a mind-boggling sum of money. They all recognized that it was a bargain, a steal. But Luccio, like most artists, like most people, was impressed by such a figure. He tried to think of it in terms of stacks of twenty-dollar bills. His resentment mounted as he computed the interest on such a figure each year. It wasn't fair that Lerner could command so much even in death. As he signed the contract, Luccio thought to himself, "Jesus Christ, it's a damned good deal!"

Christina Hansen gathered up the copies of the contract. She filed a copy with the contracts Lerner had signed while he was living. Again her eye was caught by Simon's elaborate signature. She, like Luccio, was impressed with the numbers on the contract that had been signed that day. As she considered how such a sum could alter her life, she thought of the last Lerner contract she had filed. She remembered something called a "put clause" in it whereby Winston guaranteed to buy four paintings each year for the next eight years at ninety percent of the market value. She knew that Lerners left the gallery every month for $70,000 and $80,000.

As she brought Simon, Luccio, and Elderstein their raincoats, she realized that the estate would have received more money over a shorter period of time if they had just sold four paintings a year for the next eight years. As she remultiplied the figures in her head, she thought she must have misread the contract. Christina Hansen, like Luccio, didn't understand money.

The flirtation, the preparation leading up to big business deals often takes months or even years, but once the actual negotiations begin, once the principals are in the same room facing each other, things are usually settled quickly if they are ever going to be settled. The negotiations and sale of these one hundred Lerners took place in a little less than an hour. The contracts were flown that night to Liechtenstein, where they would be signed and flown back the next day.

It was still raining when they went outside. The three men said good-bye quickly. Simon kept the umbrella. He laughed to himself as he walked along the crowded sidewalk.

Simon had made an arrangement to take Peter out to dinner. He had invited Wendy, too, but she hadn't wanted to go. Taking care of Lerner's child after taking care of the paintings made the day complete. He had made a reservation at Pearl's, and as he waited inside the door for the boy, he pondered Peter's future. "Wendy is so like her father. It's probably best to separate the children now. It would be good for Peter to get out of the city and go to boarding school. Choate or St. Mark's. I wonder if it's too late to apply for the fall term. He'd be a sophomore."

As Simon thought of whom he knew on the board of each of the schools, who would overstep a few rules and push an application through, Peter rode Andrew's fold-up bicycle down the steps of St. Patrick's Cathedral. His head snapped as the bike bounced over each step. He splashed through a large puddle, sprayed a Japanese businessman taking a picture, circled back to apologize, then pedaled furiously downtown.

Simon watched several cars stop short to avoid the boy on the bike. "He really should go away to school. I'll call about it tomorrow," he told himself. In his usual fashion Simon would introduce the idea to Peter in such a way that the boy could claim it as his own. "I won't tell him I'll have to pull strings to get him in . . . there's no reason for him to know."

There were a great many things Simon thought no one else had any reason or right to know about.

Simon stepped outside. Peter skidded to a stop in front of him. He looked up at the violet-gray cloud that canopied the sky, then at Simon's face. Simon's eyes were red and the rain on his cheeks looked like tears.

"Nasty weather," Simon said.

Peter locked the bike to a "No Parking" sign. "I know. You never get rainy days when you want them."

They stepped into Pearl's. Simon shivered as he took off his wet raincoat. "And when do you ever want weather like this?"

Peter thought for a moment. "At funerals."

"What do you mean by that?"

"Oh, nothing . . . can I have Mou Shou Pork?" Peter also had secrets, thoughts he didn't feel obliged to share.

XIX

"How did it go?" Sidney rolled his Havana between his lips suggestively, then winked at Andrew.

"How did what go?"

"Peter's first time." Sidney paused to see if there was any truth to his fantasy, but Andrew's expression betrayed only boredom. Sidney winked again and played with the hairs of his beard. "You can't blame me for wondering. . . . You were gone an awfully long time."

"It's a long walk."

"Did Peter like his first black-tie opening? What did he say when you two left?"

"He told me he could take care of himself and got in a cab."

"Sounds like he was upset."

"What would he have to be upset about?"

"I don't know. You're the one that talked to him all night. . . . Are you upset?"

Andrew's actions answered the question. He poured himself a glass of Mer, but didn't drink it. He pointed toward an armchair Sidney had just had upholstered in zebra skin and said, "That's certainly better sculpture than the rusty iron and crushed fenders you had out at the Met tonight." Then he looked at an etching he had done of Sidney. He examined it so closely that his breath fogged the glass, and he announced that he was going to find a new printer. He sat down to read the next day's paper, but tossed it aside before he had finished the headlines. "You know, Simon Pyne ate fourteen shrimp in less than ten minutes . . . we counted them."

Andrew got up, sat down, paced, picked up things, and put them down. He wasn't upset; he was unsettled. Andrew was strangely uncomfortable with the thoughts and things that he and his old friends normally discussed with such relish and ritual.

Sidney liked to think of his art as the ability to understand and

175

interpret the work and actions of artists, not just for the spectators who passed through the exhibitions he organized at the Met, but to the artists themselves. Andrew was the only man Sidney knew who might, in a hundred years, be called a genius. Sidney was dependent on him.

He did not mind Andrew's restlessness as much as he wanted to understand it, and so he returned to the subject of the boy. "The kid did look incredibly cute in that wing collar. . . . Did you dress him yourself?"

"Stop it, Sidney."

"I was just teasing." Andrew was genuinely angry. It was an aggressive anger Sidney had never seen in him before.

"I don't tease you about your work." Andrew warned him.

"I would hardly call taking Peter Lerner everywhere you go work."

"And that's why you can't make art. . . . That's why you arrange it on walls. Including and excluding . . . putting what you no longer have any use for in a corner the way you did with Pop Art tonight."

"I put it there for a reason. I don't see Pop as a truly significant trend in American art since the war, and neither do you." Sidney could have lashed back, but to have turned on Andrew would have been to turn on himself. Andrew, the white-haired fawn in his forest-green velvet dinner suit, the creature who always seemed to be above this sort of viciousness, had become a man.

"You tell the world what pictures to hang. . . . You make art, Sidney, but you have no idea how it is made."

It was true, but it was a truth Andrew threw at Sidney out of a frustration with the evening, not out of any real dissatisfaction with his friend. There were several Crowleys in the room. Most were drawings and etchings of Sidney. They spanned almost ten years. In their midst was a sketch of a very handsome man sleeping in Andrew's bed. He was a model. The only reason Andrew remembered him was because his face was in a popular cigarette commercial. Andrew couldn't remember whether they had lived together in '66 or in '67. Sidney was the only constant figure in Andrew's art or in his life. The distance his words had put between them suddenly frightened Andrew.

Andrew sat down, put his arms around his friend, and kissed his bearded cheek. Andrew was not comfortable with the gesture, but

176

he felt lonely. An apology was not offered or expected. We can never apologize for the truth. We can only try to forget it.

Sidney spoke first. "I think this thing between you and Peter is fine. For years I've watched you involve yourself with Jamie . . . with boys who were pretty, but so limited, so insensitive that you were never tempted to invest anything of yourself in them, to really care. And if in spite of their limitations they began to care and demand more of you, you felt no qualms about ending it." They heard footsteps overhead. Sidney pointed upstairs. "I met Ted when he was seventeen, and the excitement . . ."

"It's not the same, Sidney."

Sidney didn't believe him. "The excitement came as much from turning him on to art and to reading Flaubert instead of *Rolling Stone* magazine as it did from any sexual turn-on. . . . That's the thrill of real friendship."

Andrew wondered why Sidney didn't use the word "love." Sidney spoke as if friendship were something men and women weren't capable of.

Because of his talent and his arrogance, Andrew had always thought himself unique, but he felt more akin to Sidney than to anyone else. They looked at life from the same angle. They shared the same tastes and sensibilities. But that night there was a stranger in the room. It was not Sidney whom Andrew didn't know, whose actions didn't make sense. It was Andrew.

"Peter's young, but if you're honest about what you're doing—not to me, but to yourself—you can both benefit."

"That's not what it's all about . . . I don't want to teach him my tricks."

"Andrew, look at me. I'm your best friend. We don't need this bullshit."

"I'm being honest."

"You're not just painting him because he sits still."

"Don't you see? He's teaching me."

"What?"

Andrew thought of the day Peter had arrived at the loft in tears. "To weep . . ." It was the best answer he could give.

Jamie was watching TV when Andrew finally got home from Sidney's. He had made the opening at the Metropolitan sound so stuffy and boring that Jamie hadn't wanted to go. He wouldn't have known that Andrew had taken Peter if Andrew hadn't deliberately mentioned it while they were brushing their teeth.

It always hurt when Jamie pushed himself too deeply into Andrew. He knew Jamie was doing it deliberately, but it didn't seem to matter. As Andrew lay there, pinned to the bed, he winced, gasped, winced, gasped, and thought of what Tessa had said about his bedroom—that it was like an operating room. With each stroke, with each grunt, Jamie hurt him more and more until Jamie came and then Andrew went numb. It was like a shot of novocain. It enabled him to let go, to forget.

It was his turn now. In out, in out—with each plunge he felt less and less. With each thrust he drifted further and further from Jamie, from this need which made him grunt and sweat and cling to a form that mirrored his own. They were so similar in shape and size that in the darkness it almost seemed as if he were fucking himself.

Andrew became more and more removed from the operation until finally when he closed his eyes and came, it didn't seem as if he, the Andrew he talked to when he painted, was taking part in the orgasm. It was someone who looked like him, an imposter whom the world mistook for Andrew Crowley.

For Andrew, the real thrill came in that instant he was so detached that he was as untouchable and as impenetrable as the darkness that surrounded them. Jamie fell asleep right away, but Andrew lay awake for a long time. He wondered if the desire to forget, to black out your partner and yourself, was at the heart of all sex. He thought of what Sidney had said about his choosing lovers he couldn't really care about. Maybe it was true, but maybe he did it because he understood what passion was really all about.

Andrew remembered that when he was eleven or twelve, before he had had sex with anyone, the thrill had not come from his own hand or any vision of man or woman. Feelings, sensations were important only because they enabled him to drown out everything and everyone else until all there was of Andrew Crowley was that part of him he had no image of or name for, that part he talked to silently the way some people do when they pray.

It frightened Andrew to think that it was all within, that he would always be so self-contained, that he would always be so alone. He leaned over and put his arms around Jamie as if he were hugging a large doll.

XX

"It's real life. . . there is no script. . . . We're just filming what happens." It was written in the articles that were already starting to appear about the cameras that followed Andrew Crowley around town. It was said again and again by everyone connected with the film. Conversations weren't rehearsed, and the filming was filled with surprises, but much of real life is scripted. We work out elaborate scenarios to keep ourselves and the rest of the cast from guessing the ending. Parts are assigned and roles played just as if the cameras were rolling twenty-four hours a day.

Ian insisted that the film would be true cinema verité. "I am basically just an organizer. I'll try to photograph it well, but Andrew, not I, will determine where the cameras aim. My job is to keep it from becoming staged . . . to keep us or Andrew from trying to set up situations just to prove a point or to jibe with what we filmed the day before." Ian referred to himself as everything but a director, but as soon as he chose the title, *The One That Got Away,* for his documentary on Andrew, he had begun to direct.

There was no set shooting schedule. Sometimes Andrew wouldn't let Ian and his camera into his home for four or five days. Then he'd open up and allow them to film everything—Andrew going to the bathroom, Andrew showering, Andrew being petted, Andrew being kissed, Andrew painting, Andrew eating, Andrew cleaning his brushes. Ian filmed Andrew going to bed, and then he and his camera crew slept in the living room so that they could show Andrew getting up.

The camera observed him rough-housing with Peter and making fettuccini. It came along on trips to the supermarket, to the tailor, to the florist, to the Metropolitan Museum of Art, and to the doctor. It got into cabs and rode the subways. It escorted Andrew to cocktail parties and dinners where the hosts and hostesses were asked whether they had three-pronged adapters for their light cords and macrobiotic food for the film crew.

This small army that accompanied Andrew soiled carpets, broke things even when they tried not to, and used far more of the drugs and liquor than etiquette allowed wherever they were. They took over. They stole the center of attention, and yet they were always asked to come again. The more outlandishly they behaved, the more in demand they were. Everyone in New York wanted Andrew and the movie.

Ego, the thought of seeing themselves on the silver screen, was involved in everyone's appearance in the film. But there were other motivations. The film allowed some people to present themselves exactly as they wished the world to perceive them. It provided others with a stage to say things they were unable or afraid to voice in real life. Andrew was the recipient of several tirades on the war in Vietnam, abortion, gay rights, and abstract versus representational art. He was told by four men and two women that they wanted to sleep with him. Affairs were announced. Divorces and marriages were planned, and a murder was threatened in front of Andrew and the camera.

The supporting cast, the regulars—Jamie, Peter, Sidney, Tessa, and Bob Cross—quickly got beyond the point of dressing up or down for the camera. But the sort of demands they made on Andrew in the film were far more taxing than those of the outsiders. The inner circle that had sat for Andrew wanted to be in his art because the drawings and paintings he did of them helped them to define themselves. The film became an extension of that. They did not merely want Andrew to put them into perspective on paper—they wanted him to color in their lives, to take what he had begun with pencil and paint and finish it off in real life.

Cheek . . . eyes . . . hair . . . nose . . . teeth—it wasn't until Andrew signed the drawing of Tessa that he realized to whom the features really belonged. Tessa pulled herself out of the dreamy pose in which Andrew had placed her and looked over his shoulder at the drawing. She saw how he had used her to mask his study of Peter. She picked up the drawing before Ian could focus the camera on it. She wouldn't let them see it. "It's not fair . . . I'm not finished yet."

Both Andrew and the camera missed the tear that slipped out of the corner of Tessa's right eye. Andrew appreciated her silence about

180

the drawing, but as she hid it in among the other sketches in the chart chest, she assumed a maternal role that was totally out of character. "Andrew has to get out and get some fresh air. I know he won't take any exercise, but maybe it will do him some good to watch some."

"What . . . where are you taking me?"

"It's a surprise. . . . Come on . . . I know what's best."

Andrew, Tessa, Ian, and the rest of the film crew squeezed into a Checker, and as they bounced uptown to a still undisclosed destination, Tessa tried to decide whether she was doing something nice.

The cab let them off at 91st Street and Central Park West. They arrived at the tennis courts during the finals of the Independent Schools Sixteen and Under Tennis Championship. The contest was close. A husky boy with hairy legs had won the first set easily. Peter had won the second with a bit more of a struggle. He hadn't told Andrew about the tennis tournament, thinking the painter would find it boring. In fact, the attitude he supposed Andrew would take toward the game almost kept Peter from entering the tournament. But he had placed the year before and the look of tennis whites and the smell of balls fresh out of the tin and the way he imagined the trophy would feel in his hand if he won were too much for the thirteen-year-old in him.

He hadn't told Tessa about the match either. When she was hanging up his coat at Andrew's loft, the mimeographed list of tournament rules and match times had fallen out of his pocket.

Long . . . short . . . long . . . short. He kept it up until his opponent hit the ball into the net. Then Peter turned and waved. His parents had rarely come to school activities or athletic events, and on those few occasions when they did venture into the world of normal parents with normal jobs, he and they were both obviously uncomfortable. The memory distracted him, and the ball ricocheted off the wood of his racket. Peter was so nervous about the possibility that Andrew would be bored or, worse, exhibit his parents' awkwardness and insecurities that the score reached ad-in four times before Peter was able to put the ball away and tie up the score of this deciding set. The loudspeaker announced, "Four all," and Andrew clapped.

The conservative spectators and parents of the other participants pointed and stared more openly at Andrew than they ever had at Lerner. But Andrew was not intimidated by this. He didn't feel at all awkward. In fact, he rather enjoyed the rhythm and order of

Peter's world, of the heads that turned in time to the thunk of gut on ball. He found it a delicious and soothing change from the flash and crash of his life.

When Peter saw this, he was able to relax, to follow through with his strokes and enjoy the sensation of being watched. He was more graceful than the other boy, but not as strong. He made several beautiful and effortless shots, but Peter's opponent's serve was so hard that it turned the racquet in his hand.

Long . . . short . . . soft . . . hard. . . . Peter lost that game, but won the next. The lead shifted back and forth, and Peter began to find this rhythm annoying. At "Six all" they began a nine-point tiebreaker to decide the winner. Peter's hand hurt, the sweat stung his eyes, and he realized that he enjoyed the sensation of being watched far more than this game, far more than the prize that glistened silver a few feet away from Andrew.

The older boy served. Peter swung and missed. It was in, but the referee called it out. Earlier in the match Peter would have smiled and thought himself lucky, but now he looked at Andrew and the camera, shook his head, and shouted, "It was in."

The referee glared at him and repeated his decision over the loud-speaker. "Advantage Lerner." Peter did not attempt to hit the next serve. The crowd and his opponent clapped at his gentlemanly be-havior. A moment later the situation was reversed. A shot of Peter's that was clearly in was called out, but his opponent made no protest. He took it gladly and hit the ball at Peter harder than ever.

For an instant Peter was ready to take up the challenge—to play and win by those rules, but then he felt the watch on his wrist. He was not above cheating, but not for this. He deliberately hit the next four balls out of the court. It felt good. He laughed when the specta-tors pointed at him, when he heard them say, "Childish behavior! . . . No wonder, look who he's with . . . bad sportsmanship . . . he gave up!" Both Peter and Andrew left feeling that they had won.

Tessa took Andrew, Jamie, Peter, and Sidney out to dinner that night to celebrate Peter's act of conscience. The evening went well until Andrew dared Tessa to throw a roll at the head of a bald man sitting a few tables away. The roll was thrown, protest lodged, they all laughed, and Tessa turned back to Andrew. "What's my reward?"

"Name it and it's yours."

182

"A kiss." Tessa closed her eyes, leaned forward, and parted her lips.

When Andrew placed one on her cheek, Tessa pulled away and glared at the men at the table. "Jesus Christ! Don't any of you know how to kiss?" She turned to Peter, put her lips to his, and dipped her tongue into his mouth. Andrew laughed nervously. Peter tried to see if he could taste the saliva. Tessa looked at them both and cried, "Oh, my babies!" and ran to the ladies room to call her own.

When Tessa came back to the table, she smiled and announced, "I called. Everyone's fine. I do worry."

Andrew saw more and more of Peter as it got hotter that summer. The people and confusion of the film made it easier for them to share experiences, to see and learn from each other's worlds.

From time to time there would be new additions to the supporting cast of *The One That Got Away*. Andrew or Tessa or Sidney would meet someone, be amused, and introduce them into the madness of the film for a day or two. Andrew usually tired of them first.

No one was surprised when Andrew invited Steve, a young actor from the Theater of the Ridiculous to come back to the loft. Even Peter thought Andrew did it because he found the nineteen-year-old thespian attractive. But what was unusual was that even though Andrew ignored him, he insisted that Steve join Jamie and him for lunch the next day. Steve had little to say, but Andrew pronounced him "perfect." Andrew invited him to dinner the day after that. Within a week Steve had joined the unofficial cast of *The One That Got Away*.

While this was going on, Andrew had the bedroom repainted and his bed replaced. The operations ceased, and he did everything he could to push Jamie and Steve together. "I'm too tired. Jamie, you and Steve go. . . . Steve, tell Jamie. . . . Can't you see I'm working, Jamie? Steve will play with you." Jamie found Steve attractive, but because he thought it was what Andrew wanted, he didn't do anything about it.

On a cloudless night in the last week of June when the cameras were rolling and Peter was safely away in New England looking at boarding schools with Simon, Andrew amazed them all by becoming jealous. First he sulked, but no one realized what his silence meant.

Steve helped himself to a third slice of Tessa's pineapple upside-

183

down cake, and Jamie patted him on the ass, saying, "Every sip to the lips goes to the hips."

"Goddamn it, Jamie, cut it out." Andrew blurted.

"What?"

"Get your hands off him."

Jamie thought Andrew was joking. "I'm a sucker for blonds. You ought to know that."

Andrew scowled and announced, "I'm sick of you two pawing each other in front of me."

Delighted with Andrew's show of emotion, Jamie began the courtship in earnest. As he and Steve left the loft to go out "dancing," Jamie had every intention of coming back—the next morning. Now he would be able to enjoy the relationship with Andrew.

"I've had it with that asshole," Andrew shouted as he went into the bedroom.

It had gone just the way Andrew had planned. He wanted Jamie to leave, he wanted to start fresh, but he didn't want to be encumbered by the guilt he knew he would feel if he openly asked Jamie to get out of his life now that he no longer needed him. It was on film that Jamie had betrayed him.

Jamie didn't have a suitcase big enough to hold all the crap Andrew had bought him. As Andrew threw Jamie's things into his own Vuitton trunk, he muttered, "It can be his fucking going-away present." Shirts, socks, shoes—with each item Andrew told himself, "He did it!"

An hour later Tessa walked into the bedroom. The trunk was half-packed. Andrew was sitting on his new bed anxiously picking his teeth with his gold toothpick. He looked small, frightened, and out of place on the king-sized bed.

Tessa sat beside him and pointed to the green walls that had replaced the hospital white. "I like the color."

"Thanks."

"What's wrong? . . . You wanted him to leave."

"Yes, but . . . but I can't go through with it." Andrew bent down, took one of Jamie's loafers out of the trunk, and tossed it back into his closet.

"Why not?"

"Because . . . I don't know . . . I'm not sure it's right for me."

"I am." Tessa wanted to make him feel comfortable. She wanted

184

to kiss him on the mouth and pull him down on that bed. But though she was more reckless, she was as uncertain as Andrew about how to comfort and be comforted. She kissed him as she knew he liked to be kissed and began to pack up Jamie's things.

Andrew said, "Don't," several times, but she didn't stop. She was much neater about this operation than Andrew. She folded the clothes, dragged the trunk out into the hall, and arranged for the locks to be changed that night. She stayed at Andrew's for the next two days to make sure Jamie took his things and Andrew didn't change his mind. The energy and ruthlessness she exhibited as she embraced his problems made Andrew all the more frightened and uneasy.

XXI

A week later Andrew sat alone in his empty loft. He had already tried two of the three types of preserves he had bought for himself that morning. He put a Wagner record on the stereo, thought about calling Ian and telling him it was all right to bring the camera over, but decided to try out the third preserve instead.

As he watched his English muffin turn brown, Andrew thought to himself, "I'm on my own . . . there's nothing to stop me . . . I'm free . . . but to do what?" Andrew had always just let things happen in his life. He had gotten more of what he wanted from it by not committing himself to anything or anyone except that extension of ego we call art. The energy most people put into making or meeting demands, into trying to change themselves or others, he directed into his work. But now Andrew had put himself into a new position.

The phone rang, the muffin burned, and in an hour Andrew was sitting in Simon Pyne's library trying to play a part he was not accustomed to—the responsible adult.

"So the main reason you want Peter to go to boarding school is because you think the city will corrupt him?"

Simon looked at Andrew's red clogs. Peter was wearing an identical pair. "I just think that it would be good for him to have other influences as well . . . to be around boys his own age." At first Simon had looked at boarding school as a way to separate Peter from Wendy, but after listening to Peter's constant references to Andrew on their trip to Choate and St. Marks, Simon had decided that Andrew might complicate the situation in a different way.

Andrew became defensive. "Life at a boys' school is just as corrupting and degenerate as life anywhere—it just seems to be less so because it is so brutal."

"I think you're making it out to be a bit more severe than it really is. I don't want him to grow up too quickly."

186

"But he doesn't want to go away to boarding school."

"But someone at his stage of life doesn't always know what's best for them, do they . . . for their long-range development?" Andrew wondered how many painters Simon had said that to. "Andrew, I appreciate, and I know Peter appreciates, your coming here to talk about the subject, but I've been to these schools and I don't think you understand what they offer."

Andrew was angry. He was no longer arguing because Peter had called him and he wanted the boy to be near. He was speaking out against arbitrary decisions, about choices being forced on one. Without realizing it, Andrew was angry about the position he was now in. "You can't force Peter to go. In the end, people do what they want to do."

"But the boy is thirteen and it is not the end."

Andrew was ready to shout, "No one has the right . . ." But then he looked at the art around the room and remembered who he was talking to. "Simon, I'm here because I think Peter has a special gift, one that can be best developed in New York. This is where art is made—you know that better than anyone. I think Peter's talents will mature faster here than anywhere else."

The idea that Peter might have inherited his father's gift had never occurred to Simon. Suddenly the boy came alive in Simon's imagination. "I had no idea you painted, Peter." It was the first remark Simon had directed to the boy.

"I don't." Simon was disappointed. Andrew was about to say that he was speaking generally, but then Peter added, "I write."

Peter was more surprised than anyone. He had never told Andrew of the desire—in fact, he had not been aware of it until Andrew had spoken of his "gift."

Andrew believed what he went on to say about Peter's specialness, but he said it for himself, not for Peter. He asked Peter a few questions about what he wanted to write but he didn't take it seriously. He thought Peter was merely playing along in his efforts to convince Simon not to send him to boarding school. Andrew was interested in what Peter could do for him, not what Peter could do for himself.

Andrew flattered Simon.

"You've made a life out of advising and helping talent. Do you think Peter's going to get that kind of guidance at boarding school?"

As Peter listened to Andrew he thought to himself, "I could write . . . I could write. . . ." Each time he said the words to himself it seemed more and more possible. Andrew enabled him to believe that he was special.

The discussion of Peter's gift reminded both Andrew and Simon of what was important to them. The conversation became more cordial and complimentary. It was decided that Peter would stay in New York and continue at Dalton, at least for another year.

As they left the library, Simon put his hand on Andrew's shoulder. "You know, you've been so kind to all of us that when the governor's wife asked me about your work, I felt almost as if I were talking about one of the family."

Family. It was a word Andrew did not feel comfortable with. He looked at the boy he had spoken for and muttered, "Oh, really?"

"The governor's wife is in love with that painting of yours she bought at the last show you had, she was interested in looking at some of your drawings."

"I just sent some up to Bob Cross."

"I'll stop by Noser Gallery and look at them . . . but if it wouldn't be too much trouble, I know she'd love to come down to your studio." Then the doorbell rang several times. "I'll call you about it."

Wendy had her fist raised to strike the door when Simon opened it. For a minute it seemed as if she were going to hit him. She didn't say hello to Andrew or Peter. "Simon, I want five hundred dollars." Though the sky was clear she had on a raincoat. She was dressed in shades of gray and brown. Her skin, her hair, everything about her was so lacking in color, so deliberately unobtrusive, that she disappeared against the green of the sycamore tree outside Simon's house. To Andrew, she seemed empty, lifeless, a blank slate against the summer colors and sounds that surrounded her.

"What do you want the money for?"

"It's none of your business. I need it."

"But I just gave you your allowance for the month."

"It's my money, Simon, and I want it."

"I'll be more than happy to give it to you, Wendy. Just tell me what you want it for."

"I can't."

"Then I can't give it you."

"Fuck you . . . you'll see."

188

Wendy slammed the door and Simon turned back to Andrew and Peter. "The money's not the issue. It would be so easy for someone to take advantage of her—she's a vulnerable girl."

Andrew and Peter left with Simon still explaining. When they closed the door behind them they saw Wendy picking a Coke bottle up out of the gutter. Andrew watched her turn and take aim at one of the narrow windows of Simon's house. He could see the hollow girl fill with rage. It colored her cheek and darkened her eye, and without any idea of what he could or should do, he shouted, "Wait, I'll help you."

She lowered her arm and turned her eyes on him. It was the first time he had noticed a resemblance between her and Peter.

"What can you do?" Wendy had to have the money or their plans would be ruined.

Andrew walked toward her. He could see her muscles tighten. He could hear her breathing. In her stare, beneath that gray flesh, he felt the same energy, the same power he sensed in Peter. But it was turned around in her. Peter radiated the life within him. She was being consumed by it. She bit her lip, then her nail. She was feeding on herself. Opposite life forces were at work. Andrew felt the pull.

"I'll give you the money" It wasn't so unusual for Andrew to give away five hundred dollars. He gave things away not so much because he was generous but because it kept him from placing too much importance on money and the things it could do. But Andrew wanted something. "I'll give it to you if you do me a favor."

"What?"

"Let me take your picture with Peter so I can do a painting of the two of you." Andrew took out his camera and his check book.

Wendy saw where Peter had learned the trick. She wanted to scream "Faggots!" and throw the bottle at them. But the photograph was a small humiliation to go through for the pleasure she would get from the demonstration the money would allow her to make. It was worth the sacrifice.

Andrew had to take two pictures. Wendy's eyes were shut in the first. She took the check and left without saying thank you. The money was to buy chemicals for bombs.

As Wendy hurried to the bank, Simon spread a dollop of ripe Brie on a water biscuit and savored the idea of bringing Andrew to Winston. He swallowed it in one bite then. Overcome by greed, he stuck his finger into the runny wheel of cheese. As he sucked on it he thought to himself, "I think I understand what Andrew wants." Peter was an unexpected asset of the estate.

Andrew shot the rest of the roll of film in his camera as he and Peter walked to the photo lab where he developed his pictures. Squinting at the world through his camera, he wondered if people were emptied by the kind of rage he saw in Wendy, or whether that rage comes when there is nothing else inside one to fill the void. That was the mystery he would pursue in this painting of brother and sister.

Like the rest of them, Peter had a plan. His was not as immediate as theirs but it was important to him. He thought of a story in which he could include all the funny-sad things he saw and felt that didn't make sense. Peter didn't know how the tale would begin or end, but as he posed for Andrew along the street he imagined how wonderful it would feel to write a story that would tie together all the pieces of life which one was certain were precious but could not explain.

XXII

When Andrew began the portrait of Wendy and Peter, he pinned a copy of the photograph he had taken of them outside Simon's house to the top of his easel. The photo exposed only a shadow of the innate difference between the brother and sister which Andrew saw and sensed. He did not need to be reminded of their expressions or the clothes they were wearing that day. Andrew was interested in what was within them. He attached the photo to the easel to reassure himself that the answer to the mystery they posed was really there.

Andrew painted the front of Simon's house, the spiked fence that guarded it, the tree behind the fence, and the empty pack of Lucky Strikes by their feet all very realistically. The perspective and colors were true to life, but the way Andrew glazed them with light, the way he cast his unseen sun, made this backdrop sparkle. Though it was a city scene there was an unreal, almost fairytale quality to the way he painted it. It was Peter and Wendy, the incomplete figures on the canvas, that transformed the setting. The effect of their presence, of the magic that linked them and yet made them different, could be seen.

Andrew was surprised at how quickly this first part of the painting had gone. It had taken him only three days to set the stage. Next he went to work brushing in the two white spaces he had left for the antagonists in this drama he was setting up.

Wearing white tennis shorts, a T-shirt, and red clogs, Peter stood to the right of Wendy. Though the figure of the boy was quite stationary, "stood" was not really the right way to describe his pose. His weight was on one leg, the other was bent and slightly forward. His tanned arms were raised in gesture and the fold of his clothes and the wave of his hair told of a breeze. There was a sense of motion to the figure. At any moment you expected the boy to shift his position.

Andrew exaggerated the length and thinness of Peter's limbs. The way he hung the shorts and the shirt on him exposed far more of Peter's physical radiance than if he had been drawn naked. Supple, elastic, the boy glowed.

Wendy stood stiff-legged, clutching a Coke bottle, braced for a blow. No breeze played with her hair, it lay close to her head. The photograph showed her to be pale, but Andrew had painted her flesh the off-white of stained porcelain in a urinal. She looked bruised and bloated, wrapped in a leaden gray dress. But she too glowed.

Andrew spent two days applying layer after layer of color on that dress. Veiling purples and turquoises with blacks and grays, colors swirled beneath the surface. The effect was like a whirlpool. The eye was drawn into the heart of the darkness that surrounded Wendy. Whereas Peter gave off light, she absorbed it.

In a photographic sense Wendy was the negative image of Peter. But there was life in them both. The energy in Wendy took from her and from the viewer. The force in Peter endowed the long-legged boy on the canvas and his audience with something special.

Together a sort of visual combustion took place between the two figures. The aura they produced caught the viewer. The painting pushed and pulled at you in two different directions. You were drawn and repulsed simultaneously—trapped. The figures seemed to pulse as your eye flashed back and forth between them. The power Andrew saw in them was frightening.

Andrew had always had an uncanny ability to shut out the rest of the world while he worked. In the past it had been a conscious act. He chose not to answer, not to look up when he heard people walking to the door. But in this painting the images of Wendy and Peter which he was struggling with blocked out other voices.

It was a week before Andrew even tried to put color to Wendy and Peter's cheeks. He scraped the oil off before it began to dry. He painted and wiped away new mouths, eyes, chins, and noses each day. In the past Andrew would have dealt with his uncertainty by making the features vague, but hinting at or alluding to answers was not enough. He no longer wanted his paintings to be question marks.

Andrew picked up a knife, raised it toward Wendy's heartshaped lip, then tossed it into his paint box. The mouth wasn't right, but he was too tired to scrape it away right then. He turned his back on the painting, took off his glasses, rubbed his tired eyes, and squinted at

192

the fuzzy figures sitting at the other end of the room.

Tessa closed the book she was reading. "You're really getting to be perverse . . . the face is wonderful. You certainly made her far more interesting than she is in real life."

Andrew had spent so many hours studying the photo of Wendy, he had painted her face so many times, that he felt as if he were related to her. He could close his eyes and see the way her lips curved. He knew the line of her body like a lover, yet he could not put the face on canvas. "I don't want her face just to be interesting."

The round blur across the room from Tessa rustled its newspaper. Sidney knew Andrew never listened to what was said about work in progress and almost never listened to what was said about it when it was finished. He tried to change the subject. "Did you read the article on the Lerner show at the Biennale? It was smaller than everyone expected . . . got very good reviews and . . . God, there's a picture of Maggie Lawrence standing in front of one of the paintings. I was wondering where she'd gone. . . . They refer to her as Lerner's 'companion.' "

Andrew put his glasses back on and reached for the paper. "Let me see it."

But Tessa wasn't finished. "Well, if you don't want their faces just to be interesting, what do you want?"

Andrew looked back at the painting. "I want you or anyone else who looks at it to know them. . . . I want looking at the painting to be a more intimate and telling interaction than any meeting you could have with either in real life."

Tessa looked at him in disbelief. "But you don't really know them. . . . Jesus, you've only talked to the girl four times in your whole life. You can't make that sort of painting about people you haven't . . ."

"Haven't what?"

"Haven't made any commitment to. We all know it's not your style to tie yourself up with people. You don't like to be intimate." There was a hard edge to her voice.

"What's that supposed to mean?"

"Just that. . . . God, what makes you a genius is that, unlike the rest of us mere mortals, you know that you never really can know . . . you understand that things, people, can't be resolved—that they're always in flux. . . . You're lucky."

193

When Sidney saw that Andrew wasn't listening, he joined in the conversation. "She's right. When you paint someone you're saying this is how you were or this is how you might be at a particular moment. Your talent lies in your ability to resist the temptation to insist that this is what you are now, were, and always will be."

No longer satisfied with this trick they took for genius, Andrew picked up the knife and with a flick of his wrist removed Wendy's mouth. It was Peter's mouth, anyway.

As Andrew methodically scraped off the faces of the two figures, he saw he was confusing the features of not only the brother and sister—he was jumbling in bits and pieces of Tessa, Sidney, Bob, Jamie, even the Italian woman who ran the grocery store on the corner of Spring Street and West Broadway. Andrew resented the intrusion.

Unsure as to how he could sort out the puzzle, how he could separate brother from sister, frustrated by his inability to keep this painting from being colored by the rest of the world, Andrew went to work on the background.

As he made the tips of the spiked fence that guarded Simon's house more pointed, Sidney put down the paper, opened the leather shoulder bag he carried, and took out a copy of *Moby Dick.* He was always reading and rereading.

Tessa went into the kitchen and called her husband at his office. He wasn't there. She left a message with the secretary. Then she called her children. They weren't in either. When she came back into the room, she looked at Andrew, arched her back, stretched, and sighed. "God, I'd like to take off."

Sidney looked up from *Moby Dick.* "You mean take a vacation or really take off?"

"Really take off, make a break . . . cut myself off."

"That's what *Moby Dick*'s all about. It's what Melville did in real life—left everything, went to the South Seas."

"I don't think the South Seas would be far enough for me. I wonder where you can go now and really get away."

As he listened to Sidney say, "That sort of trip, the long sea voyage that people like Melville were able to take, was really a substitute for suicide," the spike that divided the two figures which had begun to torment Andrew grew higher and higher. Andrew was shocked when his brush broke free at the top of the canvas. A black line separated

194

brother and sister. This arbitrary division only emphasized the explosive quality of the painting. The fission going on between the two figures seemed to split the canvas.

Sidney and Tessa were so engrossed in their conversation they didn't notice as Andrew silently put down his brush and walked toward the door.

Sydney rapped the cover of *Moby Dick* with his knuckle. "That's the tragic thing about our time . . . there are no distant places left."

The door closed. Andrew hurried down the stairs, and Tessa half-smiled at Sidney. "There never were any."

Peter had come home to find the front door ajar and the TV blaring. He listened to the tail end of a special news report on an explosion that had destroyed a townhouse in Greenwich Village that afternoon.

"One of the victims has been positively identified as Arthur Colson, who was wanted for questioning in the bombing of an ROTC building at UCLA. Firemen found three other victims, but they were too badly burned to be immediately identified." As the commentator spoke, scenes of firefighters and smoke and bodies under blankets flashed across the screen.

"According to several witnesses, a man and a woman were seen running from the smoking house minutes after the explosion took place. Police believe that the explosion occurred when one of the incendiary devices the victims were making was accidentally detonated, but it is still not clear where or when the devices were to be used."

Andrew arrived just in time to hear the commentator announce, "It was forty minutes before firemen brought the blaze under control, and for a while it seemed as if the fire would spread to the adjoining buildings.

Andrew lit a cigar and pointed at the smoking buildings, the actor struggling to save his possessions, the bodies being carted into ambulances, and the crowds gaping behind police barricades. "The trouble with summer TV is it's all reruns."

Andrew appeared to be as poised, as cool as ever. Peter had no idea that when Andrew had knocked on his door, he had been every bit as frantic and lost as Peter had been when he had arrived at Andrew's house in tears.

They talked for a few minutes. Peter asked how the painting was going. Andrew came to the point. "I know you and Wendy don't get along well now, but you were close once, weren't you?"

Peter nodded. "How did you know?"

"Just a feeling I got from the photograph. What happened? . . . How did you two grow up to be so different? Was it your parents?"

"No, it wasn't Mummy or Daddy who did it . . . it just happened."

"What do you mean?"

"One day we stopped being . . . close. . . . She stopped . . ."

"What?"

"She stopped playing. We used to play up in the top floor of the house for hours. That was before Daddy tore down the walls so that he could store his paintings there. The paintings are still up there."

"But it didn't happen all at once. Things never change all at once."

"We did."

"What games did you play?"

"It was always the same game. She called it 'Let's Pretend.' We'd make up stories and act them out. But with Wendy it wasn't just a game . . ."

"What do you mean exactly?"

"She really made you believe."

"How?"

Peter shook his head. "I can't explain it. I guess the same way you make people believe in paint and color. She had a gift . . . a gift for making people believe in her."

"Doesn't she have that gift anymore?"

"I don't know. She's still good at making people believe things. She's an amazing liar. But that's not the same as making people believe in you." Peter was surprised at how the memory of those afternoons moved him. His throat was dry, and he felt like crying. He missed those quiet times with Wendy.

Even though Peter told him the little rooms in which he and Wendy used to play "Let's Pretend" were gone, that the walls were torn down to make room for Lerner's paintings, Andrew wanted to see the space. He wanted to look out the narrow windows they used to play beside and to gaze on their horizons.

He had never climbed the stairs of the Lerner house. Following Peter up the zigzagging staircase, Andrew saw boxes piled in the

196

halls, guest rooms filled with possessions Lerner could not live with, but could not bear to give away. Andrew saw garbage that had never been carried out as well as skis, tennis racquets, and golf clubs that had never hit a ball, that had never even been unwrapped. Andrew was shocked by the sense of time, the memories that lingered with all these battered and broken things, unused and unwanted things Lerner had left behind.

There were so many questions to ask, so much Andrew had to know if he was to finish the painting of Wendy and Peter.

There was a steel door at the top of the stairs. Peter opened it. Andrew followed. As soon as Andrew stepped into the room, he felt dizzy. He had never known anything like it. The largest and most brilliantly colored Lerners he had ever seen were systematically stacked in long narrow picture racks and propped up against the walls of the barren white room. These Lerners were not in any of the art books. Andrew wondered why Lerner had hidden them there and how many people knew about them.

Peter gestured toward his father's art. "The paintings really do it to you, don't they?"

"What?"

"They do what you said great art can do . . . beat time."

All Andrew's doubts about Lerner's brilliance were swept away by the paintings he saw. The colors swirled around him. Blues, greens, aquamarines reached out to him. Andrew's eye was pulled into masses of color so deep he had to shut his eyes and shake his head to keep from falling. Andrew fixed his gaze on Peter to fight off the vertigo.

To finish his painting of Wendy and Peter he would have to look into this miasma of color they lived in. He would have to know Lerner too. The vision, the truth he was after, that he wanted to capture between brother and sister, was so vast that he did not have words for it. Trying not to be sucked into the violet heart of a blue Lerner that loomed before him, Andrew sputtered, "How . . . why did Wendy feel she had to turn away from you?" What he wanted to know was beyond Wendy and Peter, their similarities and differences, but Andrew did not know where else to begin. It was the only question that he could ask that would make any sense at all.

Peter looked at his feet. "I guess we stopped being close because she didn't know what to do with me. She didn't know how to

197

continue the game . . . of 'Let's Pretend,' I mean."

Andrew looked at the watch he had given Peter. Peter put his hand behind his back. Then the tall blue and violet wave crashed forward. It slapped loudly against the floor. Wendy glared at them. She had been hiding behind her father's wall of color for more than an hour. The gray dress Andrew had labored over was ripped. Her hair and face were smeared with soot. She had been crying. The dirt made her eyes look even sadder than they were. Her left hand was burned and blistered.

"It was me I didn't know what to do with . . . it's always been me." She cried.

The responsibility of what Andrew saw was too much. Wendy, Peter, the painting of them—it was all too much, too vast for Andrew. They became part of the pillow Andrew feared would come down on him and smother him in the darkness.

Andrew left Wendy, Peter, and the cachet of Lerners which they lived beneath with the too calm, too unhurried step of a man who is truly panicked.

He didn't tell anyone what he was doing. He went straight to the loft. He washed a dirty dish, emptied the garbage, packed an overnight bag, picked up his passport and his American Express card, and double-locked the door.

Andrew's ears popped. The jet leveled off on its flight across the Atlantic, and Andrew looked back. The sun was on the edge of the horizon and New York was shrouded by a heavy and poisonous cloud. The dirty sky was the same color gray Andrew had painted Wendy's dress. He would call Bob Cross from London and tell him to give the unfinished painting to Peter.

XXIII

They expected him. They waited. They looked for him. Disappointed, they went on without him. But even though they did not see him, Andrew was there.

Andrew sat on the edge of the fountain across the street from the Plaza Hotel. He was waiting for the show to begin. He had been waiting for almost four years. He was tired.

Hat pulled down low, Andrew peered over the wings of a stone ram and watched the people arriving for the premiere of *The One That Got Away.* He had come back to America twice before, and of course people had come to visit him in Europe. But the friends and acquaintances he saw filing into the Paris Theater on that last Friday in April of 1973 seemed to have changed. He wondered why he hadn't seen the difference before. It wasn't just the fashions, the hair cut short and held in place, the people's clothes tailored to glitter decadently, the men and women looking so alike. It was the way they walked, the way they held themselves and each other. He had noticed it when he had first stepped off the plane. America seemed settled. After all the stops and starts, the reversals of the beginning of the decade, they seemed finally to have fallen into a style they were comfortable with.

Andrew looked at himself in the pool around the fountain. He had misjudged the weather. Expecting a warmer homecoming, he had worn an off-white summer suit. He shivered as he studied his reflection. His hair was still white. He had worn the same clothes the summer he had left. He wondered why he hadn't changed. What was he waiting for?

When the last of the people arrived, just as the ushers were closing the doors of the theater, Andrew ran across the street. He had a return ticket to France in his pocket, but as he slipped into the darkness of the theater, he knew he would not be using it. He would

199

stay in New York. He had come home for good. He sat by himself on the aisle. No one saw him. The only explanation for his decision to stay was that he felt sufficiently foreign, that he was enough of a stranger to be comfortable there again.

Andrew had not really expected the film Ian had made about him ever to be finished. There were many reasons it had taken so long to be shown—Andrew had left the country, Tessa's husband had been hurt in the market, money got tight—but it was more than that. It was harder to generate enthusiasm, to work up momentum now. *The One That Got Away* was two-thirds finished when Andrew had left. But what took three months to accomplish in the sixties sometimes took three years in the seventies.

Andrew had not seen any of the film. It brought back memories of work started, finished, and left undone. He saw tennis matches, Quaalude parties, and all manner of games replayed. He watched people fall in and out of his life. He saw adventures he remembered, as well as those he had forgotten. It was interesting to see himself develop as a person and as a painter. He felt very good about the latter. Technically he had come a long way. There was a weight to his brush strokes; the thinness of the way he used to use paint was gone. As he watched himself finishing up the last of a group of paintings that had been shown at the Louvre in the fall of '72, the word "virtuoso" came into Andrew's mind.

Interwoven with these scenes of Andrew going about the business of being Andrew were interviews Ian conducted with those who had been close to him. The conversations all took place after Andrew had left.

Sidney sat on an ottoman. Surrounded by green ferns, hands clasped around his bulging stomach, he looked quite like the caterpiller in *Alice in Wonderland.* He blew out a cloud of smoke and announced, "Andrew sees himself as the fair-haired boy walking down the boardwalk of life kicking a can with an American Express card in his pocket . . . when people or situations demand more of him, he vanishes."

Tessa lounged on her bed, absent-mindedly playing with a rose as she spoke of Andrew. At first she was hard on him.

"He's not quite human. I mean, he doesn't want the things most people want, and, of course, he can be cruel . . . not in that calculating way adults are cruel, but in an honest and ruthless manner children

200

can be. But we can't resist making ourselves vulnerable to children, can we?" She pricked herself on the thorn of her rose, and her tone changed. She laughed. "But sometimes he can be perfect, really absolutely perfect, more perfect than his drawings or anything you can imagine. He can make a moment so complete—so utterly satisfying—that, God, you forget what time it is, where you're going—everything."

Bob Cross stood by the desk in his office. There was a photograph of his wife on one wall and a Crowley on the other. "To a painter who specializes in the human figure, aloofness can be dangerous. . . . I sometimes worry that Andrew is too alone . . . too self-sufficient."

Andrew was moved by these words.

He had had a few brief and unsatisfactory affairs right after he had left New York. But it had been more than two years since Andrew had been touched. He was surprised to hear Jamie talk about his "sex appeal." Andrew somehow thought he had left sex behind like a pet that had refused to become housebroken. But surprise turned to shock as the film took on a more and more sexual slant, with Tessa saying, "What makes him so intriguing is that he is emotionally androgynous . . . he is really the new man." And Sidney, speaking as an art historian about "emotional elasticity" and "the male figure" and "homosexuality" and "Caravaggio" and "Michelangelo" and Jackson Whole and Jacques St. Michel, the designer, and a half-dozen other queens whom Andrew had laughed at, never with, screaming about him as a gay hero celebrity trend setter for the seventies.

Ian's editing implied Andrew was running from a bad affair with Jamie. None of them knew, none of them understood what they were seeing—what Andrew was running from or to.

The film ended with Andrew looking out the window of L'Hotel, the little hotel on Rue de Beaux Arts where Oscar Wilde had died. A blank sheet of drawing paper, a fountain pen, and a January issue of the *New Yorker* lay on an unmade bed. Though there was snow on the rooftops of Paris, the window was open. The gauze curtains swirled back in his face. The camera froze him looking back toward his bed, then it slowly and deliberately dissolved this final image. Softening it at first to make it look like a Manet, then blurring it so completely that Andrew, dressed in blue against a blue sky framed

201

by the dark woodwork of the window, looked not unlike a Rothko. Finally, without warning, the camera focused in on him so sharply that Andrew could see the blush creeping across his cheek.

But Andrew was not distracted or interested in any of the symbolism of this finale. His eyes traveled to the *New Yorker* magazine on the bed. It was the January issue. It contained a short story by a seventeen-year-old boy. The story had caused quite a stir. An article had appeared about its author in the *Village Voice*, calling him a young Fitzgerald. It was a story of unfinished people and feelings in which the sex and age of the two main characters are unclear and unimportant.

Ian had not even thought to ask Peter Lerner, the author of that story, what he had thought of Andrew.

The audience clapped. Andrew slid down in his seat and put on his hat. The house lights came on, and Ian stepped to the front of the theater and began to answer questions. Flashbulbs clicked.

People whispered and heads turned as the crowd began to realize "he" was right there with them. Ian waved. Tessa, Sidney, and Bob Cross stood up and began to clap. As the audience joined in with the applause, Andrew noticed how similarly polished the crowd was. There was something oddly familiar about this style they had embraced. Andrew did not realize what they reminded him of until he caught sight of a man two aisles away with hair dyed white, wearing a pair of eyeglasses with fire engine-red frames exactly like the ones Andrew had left behind at L'Hotel. It was he they were imitating. It was almost funny. But then Andrew was caught by a stare that had singled him out before. Two eyes looked out at him from the consciously trashy, glittering, Deco, black lip and nail audience. Peter was being elbowed and petted by the same ones that had tried to get close to Andrew. Peter's hennaed hair stood up on his head like a rooster's and came to a sharp V on his neck as if he had a tail.

The crowd came in on him. In a few minutes Peter and Andrew were being pushed against one another. There wasn't room to shake hands. Peter wore a black tight-fitting suit with red satin lapels and no shirt. He looked like a thirties space cadet. Peter had grown. He was as tall as Andrew but thinner. Andrew wasn't sure whether Peter had on makeup or if there were circles under his eyes.

"You read my story?"

It was a question and a challenge. Andrew nodded. "I read it."

"I'm sorry about this."

Andrew wasn't sure whether the antecedent of "this" was the film, the crowd, or Peter's appearance.

"It's not your fault."

The rest of the cast joined them. Tessa kissed them both and shouted, "My God, it's a reunion."

Sensing but not understanding his anxiety, Sidney whispered in his ear, "You know, you could still stop the film from being released."

Peter was uncertain what to say, but wanting more from the meeting than just a good-bye, he blurted out, "I have the painting."

"I came back to get it . . . to finish it."

"Really? I thought you left it that way on purpose."

Before Andrew could decipher the remark, Peter took his elbow. "It's at the house. You might as well take it now."

Still hungry, the crowd followed Andrew and Peter out of the theater. This audience that had picked up what Andrew had tried to lose swarmed and shouted around them like gulls squawking and diving for the garbage a ship leaves behind in its wake.

Andrew found Peter attractive, but that was only natural since Peter had grown so like himself. Andrew didn't know how to finish the Peter in that painting he'd left behind, but he did not like the way Peter had colored himself in. Andrew looked out the window as the cab moved uptown wondering about the other face he had not yet completed. "How's your sister?"

"She spit on Simon Pyne this afternoon."

"How come?"

"He wanted to take my father's paintings out of the top floor of the house, and she told him he couldn't have them."

"Well, there's not much he can do about it, can he?"

"Not much except put her in Payne Whitney for four years."

"What?"

"She didn't go to college, you know."

Andrew winced. He heard himself. "They're your paintings, aren't they?"

"No, my father left them to a foundation to help painters who don't make it."

"Doesn't your sister approve of what your father wanted to do with his art?"

"She doesn't give a shit about that—she just likes to fight."

203

"With everybody?"

"No . . . mostly with herself."

"That's too bad."

"It certainly makes it difficult to win."

The traffic was heavy. They hit almost every light on Madison Avenue. As the cab started and stopped, Andrew heard Peter run through the arenas Wendy had done battle in.

"You left the day she nearly blew herself up, didn't you?" The way Peter said it made Andrew feel like a coward. "After that she tried transcendental meditation, but that wasn't rough enough, so she was rolfed . . . and then there was the Guru Maharaj Ji. That was in seventy-one. In Amsterdam. She went to Europe too. She lost some weight in that one, but I guess that's what put her over the edge. . . . She had a nervous breakdown . . . came back and was O.K. until she got into EST. . . . Have you heard about it?"

"No."

"A guy named Erhard started it. He preaches spiritual fascism . . . I think it'll be very big. . . . But EST didn't work out for Wendy either."

"What's she into now?"

"Nothing . . . same as everyone . . . herself. That's why she's in trouble. She never likes the self she finds, but at least at the beginning of her cures she has the illusion that she is going to find a Wendy she can live with. She's not like us—she has no faith."

"And what do we have faith in?" Andrew asked.

"Romance . . . you told me that. You said the ongoing theme of Western art was feeling . . . expressing feelings and emotions. You said the world's in love with love. Do you remember?"

"We were at the Frick, weren't we?"

They sat in silence for a few blocks, oblivious to the snarling traffic and the exhaust around them, remembering the pictures they saw that day and the things they had said to each other.

Peter lit a cigar and offered one to Andrew. "They're not Havanas."

Andrew took one anyway. "I've thought a lot about that idea, about our faith in romance. You still think it's true, Peter?"

"True, but sort of sad. . . . I think the Egyptians had a better idea."

"What do you mean?"

"Well, you know, they were obsessed with eternity, just the way

204

we're obsessed with romance . . . or sex or feeling or whatever you want to call it. They lived and made art with eternity in mind. Eternity is really just as impossible to believe in or to describe as feelings, as love, but at least if you put your faith in eternity, in a perfect vision of heaven, you won't be disappointed until you are dead."

Peter had put the unfinished painting of himself and Wendy on the top floor of the house along with his father's paintings. As Andrew followed Peter up the stairs, he was amazed at how little the house had changed. Unlike Peter, it seemed unaffected by his absence. Boxes were still in the halls, and rooms were still filled with things unused and unwanted. Peter called over his shoulder, "Nothing's changed . . . we still can't decide whether we want to move in or out."

But one part of the house had changed. Remembering the dazzling power of the Lerners he had seen at the top of the stairs, Andrew braced himself as he stepped into the room, but it was not the paintings that caught him off guard. The room that had been so spotless when he had left was now littered with garbage. Old food wrappers, empty wine bottles were scattered across the floor. The windows on either end of the room were wide open. A breeze blew a piece of yellowed newspaper up against a Lerner so fresh and green it looked as if it had just been painted. The windowsills were water-marked. The room looked as if a rodent had gotten into it.

Peter pointed to a stained mattress and a dirty quilt in front of the largest of the pictures in the room. "Wendy sleeps up here quite often."

Then Peter pointed to Andrew's painting. It hung on the far wall. Andrew bit his lip as he looked at this work he could not finish, on this mystery he had not yet solved. In spite of the fact that the figures were faceless, the painting stood up to the Lerners that surrounded it. Lerner's colors still reached out for him, but Andrew did not find it so dizzying to stand before the Lerners this time. His work, his painting, braced him. He always had that to hold on to.

As he studied the faceless figures Andrew heard her moan. Wendy was sprawled face down against the wall. She had gotten lost amongst the many-colored ideas that filled the room. The dress she was wearing was dark blue. It had the same quality to it as the gray one Andrew had painted her in. She looked the same. She was still fat. Her hair was still dirty.

Wendy had not changed. It was as if he had never run away.

"Wake up, Wendy, we have company . . . an old friend's come to visit." Peter called out sarcastically.

Wendy moaned again, and Andrew told himself he had no reason to feel guilty, responsible for what he was seeing.

As Peter walked toward the body he said, "She's playing dead."

When Peter saw the empty prescription bottle of Demerol in her hand, the smile fell from his face and the flush Andrew remembered returned to his cheek.

Her body twitched once, then it was still. Her breathing was shallow and irregular. Peter ran downstairs to call an ambulance. Andrew held her wrist. He could feel a pulse. She was cool to the touch, and her skin was faintly blue. He put his head to her breast. He could hear a heartbeat, but it was faint. He slapped her face, hoping to bring her around. But she was too far gone for that. He brushed her hair away from her face and held her head in his lap. It was odd to be so close to this face he could not paint, to this figure he had run from years before. Wendy was just as he had left her that day almost four years ago. Peter had painted himself, but she was as unfinished as ever. And now he was no longer frightened of her but for her.

While Andrew watched helplessly, her breathing grew softer still, until it seemed to have stopped altogether. He put his fingers to her lips. He felt no breath. He listened for her heart. He heard nothing. Was she dead? Were they too late? For a moment Andrew was paralyzed. But the figure compelled him to act. Ignorant and untrained in these things, Andrew opened her mouth and put his lips to hers, force-feeding her with his own breath, his own life.

Desperate, frustrated by his limitations, Andrew struggled with her. Her mouth was cold. He could taste what had poisoned her. He was too late. He was doing it wrong. He began to weep. He was ready to give up. But then he felt her chest rise. She began to breathe. Andrew did not hear Peter's steps on the stairs or the sirens scream. He was absorbed by the unfinished figure he had saved and by the impossible idea that he, too, might have a second chance.

XXIV

It was really no worse than waking up from other nightmares. Her head hurt. Her body ached. She felt foolish and frustrated, but, worst of all, frightened. She knew how to do it now—if there was to be a next time, it would be the last. She should have locked the door or been braver and used a gun, or a razor like Daddy, or a . . . As Wendy pushed her fist into her closed eye she envisioned herself leaping in front of trains, out windows and planes. As the pressure on her eye turned the reds and purples of her subconscious dark, she saw a hundred different types of death, then she fell asleep again.

Simon Pyne's friend, Dr. Fine, made sure Wendy had a good room at Payne Whitney, and the police were discreet. He had helped Simon out with Lerner. He was familiar with the family history. The explanations he offered for her attempted suicide were all quite sound —she feels guilty; she doesn't like herself; she wants attention; she resents her father—but who doesn't? Psychiatrists comfort those who have picked up the knife, but they tell them little they don't know themselves. Life by its very nature is self-destructive. Destroying things is almost as pleasurable as creating them, and certainly it is easier.

To Wendy suicide was a last act of faith in the cosmos, in powers beyond her, powers she sensed, that she sometimes even perceived but could not identify or understand. But she was strong—the animal in her survived. This final prayer for darkness was not answered.

Though she was conscious, though she accepted water and food, though she urinated twice and defecated once, Wendy had still not opened her eyes or spoken. The sun traded places with the moon twice, and Wendy had not acknowledged either day. She listened to Simon, Dr. Fine, and Peter talking to and about her, but she said nothing.

Peter held her hand and talked to her softly for more than three hours. When he began to cry and said, "Wendy, we'll go away together . . . we're both in trouble. You choose the place . . . I'll come," she was almost ready to speak. The idea of taking someone with her appealed to Wendy, but before she could decide what her first words should be, Peter grew impatient and threw down her hand. "I don't know whether you want too much, or I don't want enough." He slammed the door. She listened carefully as Simon followed Dr. Fine out of the room. There was just one person with her now. She heard someone walk to her bed and straighten her blankets. It was the nurse. She heard the lights click off, the door close, and as the crepe sole squeak of the nurse's step disappeared down the corridor, Wendy opened her eyes.

It was late afternoon. Wendy recognized the view. Her window looked out on the East River. She could not focus clearly, but she knew she was on the fourth floor. That's where they put the suicides. The last time she was at Payne Whitney she had been on the second floor. Wendy knew it would be too hard to do it up there. People had succeeded, but the odds were against it. She would wait until her eyes accustomed themselves to the light, and then she would sneak out. Wendy was sure she could slip out of the building. Patients did it all the time. She looked at the Fifty-ninth Street bridge. No, it was too risky—she would walk to the subway station at Hunter College. She wouldn't even have to wait for a train. The third rail was always charged.

As Wendy watched the blur of a barge struggle against the current, her eyes slowly began to focus clearly. She was able to identify the twisted wrecks that made up its cargo. She could read the lettering on the dark green hull of the tug that helped it toward the sea. And then she saw him. She wasn't alone. The end of his cigar glowed red in the shadows of the corner of the room.

He crumpled up the drawing he had made of the girl who would not see and tossed it into a wastepaper basket with the two dozen tulips he had brought but which had wilted without her having seen them. Andrew had been waiting for this moment. He had thought of a thousand different things to say, but after listening and watching for so long, he realized that it wasn't so much what was said as how and when it was said. "How are you?"

"Tired."

Andrew yawned and sat on the edge of her bed. "Me too."

208

"What are you tired of?"

Andrew flicked his ash. "Of being myself . . . and you?"

"That should be obvious."

"Of being yourself? . . . Are you like me?"

"No . . . I'm tired of not being myself."

"Well, we should be a great help to each other then . . . but, you know, your problem seems far easier to solve than mine."

"How do you suggest I start?"

"Well, since you were never friends with me while you weren't yourself, then it only seems logical that we would be bosom friends if you were to act yourself." Andrew knew he was both taking a chance with her and taking advantage of her, but the thrill he felt when the lifeless face cracked into a smile, when she cocked her head and looked at him out of the corner of her eye, made him reckless.

"All right, we're friends . . . but tell me, what do friends do?" she asked.

"They believe in each other and, because they believe, they try to help."

"But what if you didn't understand something I believe in . . . would you still help?"

Andrew knew what she was going to ask, but he had to say, "Yes."

"What if I believe that it was best that I kill myself. Would you help me?"

"I would if I knew you had tried everything else."

"And what does everything else include—shock treatment, chemotherapy—how about a lobotomy? They didn't try that one on Daddy."

Andrew was losing her. "I would help you if I knew you tried to kill it, if I knew that you'd tried, and that he wouldn't stay dead, if I knew there was no other way for you . . . then I would help."

Andrew could see her cheeks color and her eyes glisten in the darkening room as the thought unfolded in her mind. Was she angry? Had he gone too far? Too fast?

It was a moment before Wendy realized that Andrew was talking about her father.

Wendy didn't understand how Andrew knew what she only suspected. "I know how to kill a man, but how do you kill a spirit?"

"Embrace it."

"It?"

" 'It' is an interesting pronoun . . . in fact, it's more than interesting, 'it' is a mystery . . . they did it . . . it was good . . . it was ugly . . . it wasn't big enough . . . it was too big . . . I touched it . . . he made me do it . . . I did it to him . . . he did it to me . . . I loved it . . . I can't do it now . . . I need it . . . we made it. I wonder why it is we're so reluctant to name our fixation."

They talked about Lerner for more than an hour. Wendy had never been so honest about the hatred, as well as the physical attraction, she had felt for her father. She told Andrew how she would quite literally burrow beneath the covers of her parents' bed, nuzzle her face against her father's neck, and kick her mother away. Wendy laughed when she told of all the different ways she had tried to get her father's attention. Then she cried when she told Andrew about a five year old's afternoon in the railway flat on Twenty-eighth Street Lerner had lived in. Mrs. G had had to go to the doctor, leaving her father to take care of her. He was working on a celadon green painting. When he mixed too much brown in the color, he called her a bitch, said it was her fault, and told her to shut up. When she started to cry, he locked her in the bathroom, turned up the radio, and didn't let her out until his wife got home.

Andrew recognized the painting. It hung in the Tate Gallery in London.

The more Wendy talked, the more they both realized that this "it" she had to face and embrace was the painting—that was where his spirit was.

Wendy's nose was running. Andrew handed her his pink silk handkerchief. Wendy wiped, then blew, then looked at the mess she had made. "I'm sorry."

"That's what it's for."

"You know, I knew what was happening . . . that's the crazy thing. When I started sleeping up there with . . . his paintings, I knew what was going to happen. I would look into them and I could just imagine what sort of mood Daddy was in when he was painting each of them. I was able to see what he was wearing. I'd go so far into them, go so far with the color, that it was as if he were right there talking to me . . . whispering in colors instead of words, but I'd hear it just the same. That big blue one reminded me of Daddy when he was happy and strong, when he would hold me up over his head with one hand and tell me I was his rabbit, when he'd come out of the studio

210

laughing and take us away from Mama and do . . . do whatever we asked—like he was one of us. Do you know, one day we spent the whole afternoon on the roof eating peanuts and dropping water balloons on the people who walked below."

But other paintings whispered different messages. Wendy told him how the violet painting near the window would hiss, "Jump, jump, you have no place, no right here with us."

Andrew never understood how truly inseparable art and life were until he listened to Wendy that night. It was just as the bell chimed to tell visitors to leave their friends to their medicated dreams that Wendy saw a concrete way to kill "it," the spirit that would not let her live.

"I'll do it with the paintings . . . if I take care of them, I'll be free." Andrew shuddered. Did she mean to destroy them? But he didn't understand.

"Those pictures must have been special to Daddy or he wouldn't have put them all up there together." Andrew nodded dumbly. "I really will take care of them. . . . I'll learn to live with them. . . . I'll start a museum. Oh, maybe not in New York, that might be too complicated, but at Harvard. He taught there. They'd want the paintings. It would be a special place, a place that would show the paintings just the way he would have liked them to be shown. He was terribly picky about that. It's really the only way for me . . . the only way I can get at it is through the paintings."

What Peter had said was more than true. Andrew believed in her. She had not lost her gift. The nurse had to ask him twice to leave. As he stepped out the door, Wendy called out, "You will help me?"

"Of course." And as Andrew walked down the corridor past others who were dangerous to themselves, who did not know how to dream safely, he heard her call out, "Promise?"

XXV

As Simon stood at the foot of Wendy's hospital bed and watched her methodically rip up the release for the fifty-seven Lerners in her house, he knew he had made a serious mistake asking her to sign a formal agreement. He never should have asked for the paintings, he should have just taken them. Possession is always nine-tenths of the law. But he thought that after trying to kill herself, she would have been more reasonable about turning the paintings over to him. Hospitals and doctors and the medication they provided had always made Lerner easier to deal with, but Wendy was different.

Wendy threw the shredded release onto the floor. Simon grunted as he bent over to pick up the pieces. "And what does this mean?"

"It means just what I said. The paintings in the house are mine. I don't care what you do with the others, but these are mine. I need them . . . for the museum I am going to start."

"But we've already been through all that. You know nothing about starting a museum."

"I'll learn."

"Wendy, if you remember, when we probated the will, I gave you your chance to contest your father's wishes."

"Daddy wanted Peter and me to have everything in the house."

"But the paintings were not part of the contents of the house. I explained that to you several times. The paintings were all left to the Steven Lerner Foundation for the Arts. That point cannot be altered." Simon knew that the wording of Lerner's will had been very ambiguous about whether the paintings in the house were to go to the children or to the foundation.

Wendy saw through him. "You're lying."

Simon tried to fight the blush he could feel rising across his face. "I am not. This is ridiculous. It's too late. It's done. You signed away your rights to the paintings that day."

212

"I know how to fix things, too. You wait and see. I need those paintings, and I'll have them."

"Wendy, though I would hate to be forced to do such a thing, if you attempt to steal the paintings from us . . ."

"Steal from you . . . he was my father . . . you're the thief."

Simon wished he hadn't used the word "steal." He was quite red-faced by now. "Listen to me, Wendy. I would not like to, but to ensure the safety of the paintings and to carry out your father's wishes, I will go to court and . . ." Simon gestured to the bars on her window. "And I think Dr. Fine and I will have little trouble proving that you are not fit to care for your father's art, no more fit than you are, perhaps, to care for yourself."

Wendy understood the threat. She raised her hand to hit him, then stopped. "That's just what he wants me to do," she thought. For a moment Simon felt he had won. Then she reached for the phone. "I can go to court too. In fact, that's just what I'm going to do. And I'm not just going to claim the paintings in the house. I want half of all of them now."

"You can't."

"You told me yourself the day we read the will that there was a law that says Peter and I could claim half the paintings. Andrew Crowley's already talked to a lawyer for me. In fact, I'm going to call my lawyer right now and tell him I want out of here."

Simon was sure Wendy was lying, and she was. "Who's your lawyer?"

For a moment Wendy almost lost control. Should she make up a name or tell him it was none of his business or throw the phone at him? Her lip trembled. Simon leaned forward to press his attack. "You don't know your lawyer's name?" Simon had always been able to tell when her father was lying.

Simon was about to tell her she was a sick girl who would be in even more trouble if she didn't listen to him. But then Wendy blurted out, "Harrington, Dupont, and Blaine."

It was the firm that Lerner had brought in at the last moment to prepare the papers for the foundation. It meant far more to Simon than to Wendy. It was a moment before Wendy even remembered where she had heard this series of names that filled Simon with second thoughts. Wendy got the number from the operator, and Simon picked up his briefcase.

"Wendy, I do not want to fight you, but I have to do what I . . . what your father . . . wanted. I hope you don't do anything you'll regret. I know you've been under a great strain. Perhaps we should talk about this another time."

Simon left as Wendy was dialing the number for Harrington, Dupont, and Blaine. He listened at the door. He couldn't believe it. She was really going through with it. He felt sick. As Simon walked to the elevator, he thought to himself, "What does she think she's doing? . . . She doesn't know anything . . . she has no right."

Simon heard Wendy speak into the phone. He listened long enough to hear her identify herself as Lerner's daughter and ask for Mr. Blaine. But he didn't know that she had hung up as soon as she had dialed the number, that she was talking to herself . . . to no one. If he had waited longer and heard her drop the phone and begin to cry, it all might have turned out differently, but Simon was in a hurry.

All Simon could think of were those paintings in the top of the house. Barclay wanted them. He was already impatient to fix the sale with Count Pinella in Torino. Now Wendy wanted half of everything. She couldn't touch the hundred that they had already sold, but he and Barclay had taken others from the six hundred plus paintings that were left after the first sale. They had no formal agreement for that. There were already twelve in Rome and four with that man in Toronto and seven in South America. So many had been taken out of the country or sold. Something had to be done. For a moment Simon thought of having Wendy declared insane, but it had already gone too far for that. He would not be pressured into anything so rash and so obvious. If they hadn't been so impatient, if Simon had had just a few more months with the father alive, this situation never could have happened. No, he would wait. She might change her mind. She might do it again and succeed. He must be careful.

Simon could feel his blood pressure rising. He popped one of the nitro pills his doctor gave him for his heart into his mouth, rolled it under his tongue, and waited for relief. The elevator doors opened. There was Andrew.

It was odd how Andrew appeared at these moments of crises in Simon's life. Andrew could no longer be ignored. He was too close to Peter and now, it seemed, to Wendy. Simon wondered if Andrew had really gone to the lawyer for her. In the beginning he had

214

thought Andrew had come to the hospital as a favor to Peter. He could understand the attraction there, but he did not understand what was going on beneath the surface of this fancifully colored artist. He did not realize what forces were at work.

"Hello, Simon." Regardless of what others said or felt, Andrew exhibited friendly indifference to those who did not personally get in his way. Taking on others' battles or opinions required too much energy. Andrew hardly looked up at Simon. He was too busy counting the bright red anemones he had picked up for Wendy. It didn't look like a dozen.

Simon let the elevator leave without him. "Andrew, do you have a moment for me?" He could not approach Andrew the way he had other artists. He had learned that when he had tried to entice Andrew to show at Winston. He had offered Andrew far more than he received from the Noser Gallery, but Andrew had always said no. Andrew liked money, but he was not overly impressed or intimidated by it. He was different from Lerner in that way. No, to get Andrew's support he would have to appeal to Andrew as an artist, not as a man. "I want to thank you for all you've done for us. You saved Wendy's life."

"I was there . . . she lived . . . I don't know if I saved her."

"You're being modest. But there is something else that has to do with Wendy and Peter that I'm terribly, terribly worried about. Their father's art . . . she talked to you about the paintings in the house." Simon said it so it was half statement, half question.

"Yes."

Simon winced slightly. He wanted desperately to know what Wendy had said, whether Andrew had actually talked to the lawyers, what they had said, what Andrew thought. But Simon knew that he would be told more if he did not ask. "I appreciate the sentiment of what Wendy proposes to do with her father's paintings, but Steven Lerner had very specific ideas about what he wanted done with his art after he died. He left very exact instructions about what was to be done with the paintings. Now, as his friend and the man he entrusted to carry out these wishes, I have a responsibility to do what he wanted . . . not necessarily what is sweet or easy or seems to make sense to me, but what he wanted . . . as an artist. You can understand that."

Andrew understood it completely. He nodded and Simon went on.

215

"I'm sure you have specific feelings about what should be done with your work when you die. And certainly no one has the right to interfere with your wishes. We give artists so little. Certainly we should give them the right to will their art to whomever and whatever purpose they desire. No one has a right to tamper with an artist's work while he's alive, and certainly death shouldn't change that. That's why I got so furious when Greenburg had Tony Smith's sculptures stripped. It wasn't his right to say they'd look better without that peeling paint on them. He had no right to speak for him, and neither I nor Wendy have any right to speak for Lerner."

Simon had chosen his words well. In spite of all that Andrew had said and promised Wendy that week, he felt something else pulling on him. It was his own hand, his ability to take his own breath away by the way he could turn a line into a nose or a stroke of blue into an eye. This tug on his conscience was more immediate than the girl at the end of the hall.

Simon said more, but he didn't have to. Andrew had already made up his mind. He could not help Wendy. Regardless of what he thought of Lerner, he could not interfere with his art. It was not just an intellectual decision, passion was involved. As Andrew marched down the hall, he forgot about Wendy and the flowers he was carrying. That part of Andrew that pursued ideas, not people, who was moved by an image at a given moment because it had a greater integrity than the people and things in it, because its truth could not be tarnished by time—that Andrew Crowley who was governed by a rarer instinct than the one to survive, the instinct to create—that part of Andrew told him to run from Wendy and her struggle for her father's art. Leaving had always been Andrew's way of making a stand.

But when Andrew opened the door and Wendy collapsed in his arms, sobbing, "You can't let them take this from me . . . you can't . . . you promised . . ." Andrew could not say no. He could not resist the life he saw in her.

In a moment or two Wendy stopped crying. They sat on the bed. She held his hand tightly and told him what had transpired between her and Simon. Andrew promised to get her out of Payne Whitney and help her gain control of the paintings. He was listening to her, not to that voice within him.

Andrew felt oddly lighthearted as he walked home that evening.

216

It was warm and breezy. He couldn't wait for summer. He was not surprised by the threat Simon made over the paintings. People who don't make art but surround themselves with it put an odd value to it. Andrew guessed that the Lerners he saw in the top of the house would be worth at least two million dollars, but he was positive that it was not just the money that was motivating Simon. Possessing art —controlling who sees it—gives the owner a peculiar sense of power. People go to incredible lengths to gain and maintain control of "their" art.

Andrew knew stories of men and women divorcing, marrying, and murdering for art. Armies had been marched more than once not to gain control of natural resources or routes to the sea, but to seize ideas sculpted in metal and stone, visions on paper. Andrew wondered if it was the quality of life or the quality of the art that made people willing to make such sacrifices for it.

A ball flew over the fence of the playground on Sixty-eighth Street. It bounced twice. It was a welcome distraction. Andrew was tired of thinking such serious thoughts. He kicked it back to the other side. Whistling his own song, he thought of the ballet tickets he was going to get for Friday night.

It was his first real date. The evening was full of promise. Their seats were perfect. Wendy was out of the hospital. They had seen the lawyer from Harrington, Dupont, and Blaine and what he said was encouraging. The fact that Pyne was not a lawyer and had no legal right to draw up the will which Steven Lerner had signed made their case much stronger. Harrington, Dupont, and Blaine would file petition in the surrogate court against the will so that she could claim half the paintings. It all seemed quite straightforward.

The orchestra tuned up. The lights dimmed. A chord was struck, then Wendy gasped, "Jesus Christ."

"What's wrong?"

Wendy pointed to a middle-aged couple at the other end of the row. They owned the townhouse across the street from hers. "Jesus, I'm fucked."

"Why?"

"I helped rob their house."

"When?"

"A long time ago."

The crowd was beginning to quiet down.

"Who did you help?"

"This black guy from Harlem named Coco. I'll tell you about it during the intermission."

As the curtain rose, the evening that was to crown this perfect day began to go sour. It was not a mysterious black man named Coco or a robber or a crime that distressed Andrew. It was the fact that he had told Wendy nothing in the last few weeks. He had heard dozens of her horror stories, but he had kept his own nightmares a secret. He had not lied. He had answered the questions she had asked, but his silence, his not offering, opening himself up to her on his own, was somehow worse than lying.

Andrew took her hand now and whispered urgently, "I've stolen from people my whole life . . . don't ever trust me."

They did not see the curtain go down. Wendy led him outside. They sat on the steps of the Metropolitan Opera House, and for the next three hours Andrew told her his story. He had sealed himself so tightly he found it hard to open up. He went forward, then backward, then forward in time, yanking his memory first one way then the other as if he were a car caught in the mud.

Andrew told her about getting fucked in the back of an empty truck trailer; about paintings he had painted that had told a truth so specific and so peculiar to one moment in time, they were almost a lie; about putting so much Ex-Lax in a pan of brownies he baked for a sixth-grade teacher that she had to go to the hospital; about the year he was so busy getting his paintings ready for his first one-man show that he didn't bother to do anything about his roommate who was becoming a junkie; about the friend's death; about forgetting to go to the funeral; about Peter.

Wendy listened silently as she taught herself to light and smoke Andrew's cigars.

The story had no beginning or end. When the crowd began to pour out of the theater, Wendy reached out and ran her fingers through Andrew's hair and told him, "The past does not exist." Then she threw the cigar over her shoulder, pulled him up, and accomplished a rather top-heavy pirouette. Andrew did the same. Their dance had begun. They slid down the railings, used strangers to balance themselves, and fell down when they tried to lift each other up.

Wendy was startled by her expansiveness. Just as Andrew had

never opened up to another person, she had never been so comfortable about using her body, herself.

People laughed at their antics and made cruel comments about the fat girl and the fag. But unlike the thousands of watchers that surrounded them, men and women who held onto each other because they were afraid to leap or to fall, Andrew and Wendy were beyond caring.

They continued their performance until Wendy broke the heel of her left shoe. To make things even, Andrew threw his right into the fountain and the two limped home laughing.

Andrew and Wendy were not finished confessing. From that night on every time they talked, every time they looked into each other, something was told. They were both amazed and frightened by the other's ability not to judge. It was not unusual for them to say goodnight, crawl into bed alone, look into the darkness, into all they were getting themselves involved in, and suddenly panic. But then they would remind themselves of the other's sexuality, and they would feel safe, immune from each other.

XXVI

There was something childlike about Maggie Lawrence. It was the way she wanted things. She didn't like to wait and she never examined the long-range effects of what she had to do to get what she wanted.

She and Simon had reached an understanding shortly after Lerner's death. But it was not the sort of settlement that allowed him to dismiss her. Part of the agreement was that Maggie Lawrence be remembered not just as Lerner's girlfriend or mistress, but as his companion, confidante, and inspiration. She had written several articles on her years with Lerner (she had only had him for a year and a half, but she stretched the years. In her last piece she had implied that they had been "in touch" for a decade). Simon read and edited everything she wrote about Lerner before it was published. He got her on committees and invited to parties. Simon even made sure that Stan Rothkoph included a photograph of Lerner with Maggie in the book he wrote on Lerner in 1971.

Maggie had not planned to see Simon that Friday. It was Lee Krasner, Jackson Pollack's widow, that pushed Maggie on Simon. Lee had been shopping on Madison Avenue. Seeing the older woman buying four of what she could hardly afford one of was bad enough for Maggie, but when Lee ignored her it was too much.

Simon had just received a request from Wendy's lawyers to see all the sale and consignment contracts that the foundation had made with Winston. He was in no mood to talk to Maggie. He pushed the letter from Harrington, Dupont, and Blaine to the side of his desk. He would not and could not answer it now. "Maggie, I'm terribly busy. I thought we settled this a long time ago. . . . I gave you what you wanted."

"I want more."

"So do all of us. You know, the art market in the seventies isn't

220

anything like we expected it to be back then. We were all caught short—the museums, the Japanese, even the Germans. No one can afford to extend themselves any more, no one's buying. The only ones who have any money are the Arabs, and they're too anti-Semitic to have good taste." Simon didn't laugh at his joke. It was true. He and Winston were not doing as well as they had when he had joined them. It had nothing to do with Simon or the way the gallery was doing business. Winston was doing better than Marlborough or Pace or Castelli or any of the other big galleries, but the gold rush years for art were over. "Maggie, you wouldn't believe how tight things are right now for us."

"You're right. I wouldn't."

Simon glanced at the letter from Harrington, Dupont, and Blaine and thought to himself, "If she only knew." But then Simon had an idea. Why not tell her? It had worked with Lerner . . . she had always been able to push him to the edge, get him so anxious and excited and paranoid that Simon could come in after her, pen in hand, and get him to sign anything.

Maggie lit a cigarette, took a puff, then put it out. "Simon, I can't go on living like this."

"Well, maybe you won't have to."

"What do you mean?"

"If you help me—the way you used to—things might get better for all of us."

"What do you want me to do?"

"Talk to Wendy."

"About what?"

"About her father. She's confused about him."

Maggie didn't understand. Wendy had always hated her. But that was just the point. Simon told her what to say and how to say it. Maggie liked having a part to play again.

"Hello, Wendy. I know I should have called, but we've never really been able to talk and I was afraid that you would say no. But now that some time's passed, maybe we can." Maggie said it all in one breath. Simon knew it was the only way she could get in the door. It worked.

They had caught Wendy off-guard. "Yeah, I guess we can talk. I don't have much time, though."

221

"Oh, it won't take long." Maggie was already looking around the living room. "It's sort of nice the way nothing's changed." Maggie ran her hand along the mantel, then looked at the dirt on her fingers. "Are you here by yourself?"

"No, Peter lives here too. And Dora, the housekeeper. She's on vacation." Wendy had just spent the morning cleaning up.

Maggie gestured around the room and sighed, "It's just the way I remember it."

"I never knew you were here."

"Oh, your father brought me here lots of times. When the family was on vacation, he'd come back to New York to see me." Maggie showed her teeth in a smile. "God, I'm so glad you've grown up and know about men and that, well, that we can talk like this. He was quite a man, your father. We used to light a fire and sit on the floor." Maggie sighed and pointed to a threadbare spot on the rug.

Wendy tried to think of when her father could have brought Maggie into the house. Wendy didn't ever remember her father making a fire for her.

Maggie changed the subject before Wendy could ask any questions. She had confused Wendy. Now she would put her off-balance. "And tell me, what have you been up to? . . . Have a beau?"

"No."

"They're hard to find these days . . . real men, that is. It's seems everyone's gay. Your brother . . . certainly made quite a splash with that story of his. Of course, we knew he had to have something, the way Andrew Crowley picked up on him. I saw them at Le Jardin just the other night. Have you been there?"

"No."

"Very gay . . . but lots of fun. . . . Dancing is wonderful exercise." Maggie turned sideways to show off the forty-three-year-old twenty-two-inch waist.

"Maggie, what do you want?"

It wasn't quite time to hit Wendy with it. Maggie pretended she hadn't heard the question. She hurried over to a photograph of the Lerner family taken nearly fifteen years before. "Look at you . . . you were adorable . . . you and your father were so thin. You know, dear, you really should try to reduce. You could be really a very . . . very attractive girl."

222

It was like a bad dream. "Is this what you came here to tell me?"

"No, I came here to ask you to help me with an article I'm writing. I thought it would be wonderful for us each to give our recollections of your father . . . call it 'The Women in His Life' or something like that. . . . What do you think?"

It had been the most repulsive suggestion Simon could think of.

"I think you'd better leave."

"Dear, you can say whatever you want to about him. I mean, you obviously have some mixed feelings about him, dear, or you wouldn't be trying to make up for the way you feel by starting this museum I've been hearing about."

"Leave me alone."

"I'm just trying to help. You ought to listen. Everybody knows you don't have a leg to stand on . . . legally. In fact, somebody just the other day—now give me a minute and I'll remember—oh, the name's not important, but they're very reliable, and they said Barclay's going to sue you. He can be very tough, you know. Court costs are expensive. He could break you. You could lose everything."

Wendy was trying to control herself. Before she would have hit Maggie or screamed, but she didn't want to let herself go. Wendy whispered to herself, "She'll be gone . . . it will be over soon," as she herded Maggie toward the door.

"Maggie, you're really going to have to get out of here. I don't want to see or talk to you ever again."

"Well, I can understand your being bitter. I know the things he used to say about you. It was terrible. I told him so. I said you should never make jokes at your daughter's expense. I told him your weight was just a stage, but he was embarrassed by things like that. I guess that was why he couldn't like you more, because you two were so much alike."

Maggie closed the door herself. She took one last look at Wendy standing in the hallway and thought to herself, "It's true—they are just alike." Wendy's eyes had that same glaze she remembered in Lerner's. Wendy was paralyzed. It had worked. She was ready for Simon.

Wendy did not move. She stared at the closed door thinking of all the terrible things she would like to do to her father, to Maggie, and to Simon. The list of those she wanted to get back at grew and grew.

Wendy knew it was just a matter of time before the list turned into a circle and she would finish it with herself, putting her name next to her father's.

Wendy had two more unexpected visitors that day.

It had seemed like a wonderful idea when Andrew woke up. He had dreamed about the sea, about the sort of summer on the beach he had never known. At first, he just thought of his desire in terms of a weekend. There were lots of places they could stay. Tessa had a house in Southampton, and Sidney had rented a place on Fire Island. But Andrew wanted to go to some place where both would be comfortable, and as he lay alone in his bed the weekend blossomed into a summer.

By ten o'clock Andrew had called three realtors and located the kind of house he wanted—big and shingled, with its own beach. It was in East Hampton. It took more than four hours to convince the realtor that he would take it without seeing it and that he could afford it. Bob Cross had rented a house down the road, so that no matter what happened Andrew knew that he wouldn't be too lonely.

The rental was further complicated because Andrew wanted it ready by Friday if possible, and Sunday at the latest. Andrew's lawyer took care of the lease, and Bob Cross, who told him it was "a wonderful idea," arranged for cleaners to come in over the weekend and open up the house.

But as soon as Andrew had finalized all the arrangements and hung up the phone, he realized he had not made the most crucial call of all. He told himself, "Of course she'll want to come . . . why wouldn't she? It's beautiful out there—it will be good for her to get out of the house, away from the paintings and the lawyers." But as Andrew stepped into the shower, he began to have his doubts. "What if she doesn't want to come, or, worse, thinks she has to because I've already rented the place." Andrew turned up the hot water. "I'll tell her I made the arrangements to rent it while I was still in Europe. . . . But I still have to ask her, and how do I do it without making it seem that I want or expect something . . . anything. It has to seem natural."

Andrew started to dial her number four times. He never made it past the third digit. He told himself it would be easier if he just happened to stop by to offer her a casual invitation that she could take him up on anytime.

224

By the time Andrew reached Wendy's street his doubts had multiplied to the point where he was seriously considering calling up his lawyer and cancelling the rental. Then he saw Simon standing at her door, briefcase in hand, his Mont Blanc fountain pen bulging in his breast pocket.

Maggie had told Simon how she had left Wendy. She should be ready by now. He would let himself in and surprise her. Simon was just reaching for the key he had had made for the house while Wendy was still in the hospital when Andrew said, "Hello."

Simon jumped, fumbled out, "You surprised me," then began to pump Andrew's hand enthusiastically. "Doesn't seem to be anyone home." He would walk away with Andrew then circle back on his own. "Who did you want to see?"

"Wendy . . . Peter . . . both. . . . Either one would do." Andrew didn't want the purpose of his visit to be known either. Andrew reached to ring the doorbell. Simon caught his hand. "I told you, no one's home."

"Might as well try." Andrew rang twice. Simon was more than relieved when no one answered the door. It must have worked. Simon knew she was inside. Lerner had always tried to hide and not answered the door when he was ready to give in.

Simon was right. Wendy was ready to give in. She had not moved. The bell meant nothing. Andrew and Simon walked down the steps. Wendy was about to tell herself there was no one for her, but then Andrew stopped and looked up at an open window.

"Maybe she was taking a bath." Andrew cupped his hands around his mouth and called up, "Wendy . . . anybody home?"

His voice broke the spell, and a different Wendy from the one Maggie had left or that Simon expected to find answered.

A different Wendy from the one Simon, Andrew or Wendy herself knew opened the door and greeted them. She did not shout or cry. Her lip did not tremble. She did not throw herself on Andrew and pass on to him all the ugly awful things that had been said to her, because . . . she knew she could.

Wendy ran down the steps and kissed Andrew on the cheek. "Where are you going?"

"No place. . . . I mean, I came by. I didn't think you were in."

"Well, here I am."

"How are you?"

"Fine."

Simon didn't understand what was happening. "I didn't realize you were expecting company. I'll call later, Wendy."

"If it's about the paintings, Simon, call my lawyer."

After a few dozen words and three or four smiles from Andrew, what had happened to her that morning no longer seemed important to Wendy.

Andrew offered to make eggs Benedict for lunch. He broke eight before he got four to poach properly. Wendy was glad her hollandaise didn't curdle. Peter arrived just as they were setting the table. There was really only enough for two, but they stretched what there was for three. They were all hungry.

Andrew and Peter felt more at ease with each other than they had that day when they found Wendy, but there was still a tension between the two of them. At first Andrew thought that Peter was jealous of his spending so much time with Wendy, but he quickly realized that his own ego was telling him that. Peter was not jealous, but he was watching them. And Andrew was not sure if he wanted to know what Peter saw.

By eleven o'clock they had drunk several bottles of wine, finished dinner, gone to see *Cries and Whispers,* and Andrew still had not invited her. Andrew walked them home. On the way Peter went into a tobacco shop to buy a pack of cigarettes. They were alone. Andrew had his chance to ask her then, but he had fantasized about her visit, about the summer, so much that it was now so important to him that he didn't dare ask her for fear she might refuse.

Peter rejoined them and put a match to the cigarette in his mouth. Andrew stepped away so he could face them both. "How would you like to come out to East Hampton Monday. I've got this house, and I thought we might have a lot of fun." Who he wanted, who this "we" was, was unclear. Andrew would like to have done it differently, but he didn't know how.

Wendy still wasn't sure if Andrew really wanted her. "Well . . . I guess. . . ."

Peter answered for her, "Love to."

XXVII

As soon as Simon left Wendy, he knew what he had to do. He was sure she would break, but he could not wait for her to do it on her own and he would have to go too far, risk too much, to push her himself. He called Barclay at his villa in Cap Ferrat. Barclay didn't think the situation was as serious as Simon did, but then he hadn't seen the look in Wendy's eye when she had told Simon to "talk to my lawyer." Barclay agreed to give Luccio "whatever it takes," and Simon knew that the more vulnerable Luccio perceived their situation to be, the more he would take.

Simon had Elderstein stay late at his office that night so that the papers could be signed the next day when Simon and Luccio had lunch. Luccio thought they were meeting to pick the first recipients of the Lerner Foundation grants to "mature and deserving artists."

Luccio was surprised at how many painters were too proud to admit that they hadn't made it. He had expected more applications. He rather looked forward to studying the slides of their work and making the arbitrary decision that had been made about his talent so many times over the years.

Luccio's sales had slipped since Lerner's death. But Simon arranged things so that Luccio lived better than he had before. The gallery Luccio was with didn't like his latest work. But Luccio didn't worry. He knew his time would come. They had lunch at Simon's house. As soon as Simon spoke of "formalizing" the understanding they had with Barclay, Luccio knew that it was his day.

Simon's plan was simple. He handed Luccio a contract back-dated to May of 1969. It consigned the remainder of the estate, the more than six hundred paintings that were left after the outright sale of that first hundred, to Winston Gallery. It was a deliberately vague contract. It carefully did not specify exactly how many paintings were in the estate. Winston Gallery had the exclusive right to sell

Lerners for the next ten years. They were to obtain a fifty percent commission on sales to individuals, a forty percent commission on discounted sales to other galleries. There were no guaranteed checks on prices. Minimums were set at a very low theoretical figure which Simon's old friend, Richard Fence, had computed the night before. The contract included a letter from Fence also back-dated to 1969, describing the weeks of research and the careful slide-by-slide analysis of the Lerners that had led him to these absurdly low figures.

Simon had been up late arranging all this. Luccio stared at the consignment contract as Simon listed the terms between bites of his veal chop. When Simon finished, Luccio smiled at him. Simon was tired. He was glad he would not have to go through an elaborate charade with Luccio. "It's what we've been doing with Winston for years. All this contract does is just . . ."

"Just what?"

"It just . . . makes it more—"

Luccio interrupted him a second time. "Legal?"

The veal was tougher than Simon liked it. "Formal is a better word, I think. A handshake is a binding legal agreement, you know. Anyway, while you're deciding what you think of the contract, I want to tell you that Barclay was very impressed by two of the paintings in your last show."

It was a small show, badly advertised, at the tail end of the season, and it hadn't been reviewed. It was a disaster, but Luccio accepted compliments when and where he got them. "I'm glad Barclay liked them."

"When I told him of your dissatisfaction with the way your gallery has been treating you, he asked me to talk to you and see if you would be interested in showing at Winston Gallery."

Simon had a contract for Luccio Cortesi, the painter, to sign, as well as one for Luccio Cortesi, the executor, to put his name to. One was dated correctly, one wasn't. Luccio would have an income of $85,000 a year. The contract was for eight years. It guaranteed him six shows in New York and two in Europe. The Winston Gallery would take only a fifteen percent commission on all his sales.

But the unwritten guarantees to which Luccio could hold Barclay and his gallery were the most important part of the deal. There would be reviews and articles; the right collectors would buy his work. Luccio was quite realistic about his talent. But, more impor-

228

tantly, he understood that the art biz was now show biz. He knew that talent was not necessarily the most important factor in the formula for fame. Winston Gallery had the ingredient Luccio lacked.

Luccio signed his contract, then he signed the back-dated consignment contract. Simon had champagne on ice to celebrate.

The cork was bad on the first bottle of Dom Perignon. Simon apologized and opened another.

Luccio was happy. The idea that Lerner would indirectly suffer for his success made Luccio's vision of his debut at Winston all the more delicious.

Simon was not happy. He did not like courts and lawyers. They didn't understand the subtleties of art dealing. But it was comforting to know that no matter what happened, no matter what was said, Wendy couldn't prove a thing. Simon believed that he and the paintings were safe.

XXVIII

The house Andrew had rented was protected from the sea by two large dunes. They made the house special. There were very few dunes like them left in that part of the world. Most had been blown or washed away. This pair had survived only because of the life that had taken root in them. The beach grass that held them together rippled in the wind, a reminder of how precarious their existence was.

These mounds of sand blotted out the houses on either side of Andrew's. The only view they allowed was a triangle of surf, sea, and sky. It was easy to forget there was anything except this widening wedge of blue. New York, the Lerners, Simon Pyne, Barclay, the lawyers—all the factors that had sent them there—seemed as remote and unreal as the boats and planes that by day would disappear in the sun's glare and by night vanish in the darkness as they moved above and below the horizon.

The house made no sense. It was perfect for them. It had started out as a four-room farmhouse, but over the next hundred years it had grown wings, sun rooms, porches, and balconies. There were four staircases, halls that connected halls, windows that opened to other rooms instead of to the outdoors, closets so shallow all they could hold was a mirror, and all the floors angled toward the sea.

The house had had many owners, and their tastes were reflected by what they had tacked onto it. Some of the additions had been quite grand; others were more eccentric than elegant. The rococo living room, heavy with mahogany, gilt, and velvet, opened up onto a decidedly Deco dining room with a beach scene complete with speedboats and aquaplanes stenciled on its walls.

But you had to step inside to see all this madness. From the outside, from the road or from the beach, the house looked ungainly, but quite in keeping with the architecture of that part of Long Island. Its walls and roof were covered with shingles of white cedar that were a soft gray most of the time but turned silver on especially hot days and tarnished to a dull pewter whenever it rained.

Peter and Wendy originally said they were going to stay at Andrew's for a week, but one week stretched into two, and two turned into three, and by the fourth of July they stopped talking about going home and it was understood that they were staying for the summer. They slept at opposite ends of the house. Peter insisted on the Duchampsian bedroom with a white porcelain bathtub protruding incongruously from the wall across from his bed. Wendy opted for what had been a child's room, with a bed constructed and painted to look like a boat dancing on the waves. Andrew stationed himself in the master bedroom. It was a rather drab space except for the French doors that opened onto a balcony that was nestled exactly in the middle of those breasts of sand that shone white and soft beneath their green veil.

Peter moved with Andrew and Wendy as they roamed the house. He led their twice-daily pilgrimages to the beach, walked behind them when they shopped in town. He sat across from them at dinner and danced close when they went to discotheques at night, but he was careful never to come between them. Late at night when they went out driving in the long white Mercedes convertible Wendy had helped Andrew choose, Peter would sit in the back seat. He would look at Andrew and Wendy, listen to their laughter, toss his head back, look up at the stars that spiraled out from the Milky Way and wonder where they were going.

Though Peter was living with them, he was on the outside of what was taking place between Wendy and Andrew. Peter was more alone than any of them knew. He made it easy for Andrew and Wendy to be close. He was a voice to listen to when their own sounded foreign. He saved conversations that became becalmed, that suddenly left Andrew and Wendy staring at each other like ships dead in the water, waiting for wind. When they were tense or uncomfortable or impatient, they could direct that energy on him. Peter helped them to be gentle with each other.

A routine that bordered on ritual quickly developed in that house by the sea. Andrew would wake up very early and paint by himself until the others got out of bed. He ate very little, and Peter ate almost nothing. They sat around a marble-topped kitchen table, drank coffee, and nibbled at bits and pieces of conversation. That was their breakfast. Wendy found it far more satisying than the half a Sara Lee coffee cake and quart of milk that usually began her day. Andrew would paint for another hour or two. Peter and Wendy would read. Then they would go to the beach or to town, depending on the weather, come home, take a nap, go back to the beach regardless of the weather. Then they would make dinner.

They were lazy days, but Peter found them exhausting to watch and to listen to. With actions and words, Andrew and Wendy were constantly probing and exploring each other. They did not talk casually. Conversation was a rite, a constant act of confession and absolution. They took turns diving into each other, each time surfacing breathless, chilled, and slightly frightened, but happy that they hadn't touched bottom, that it was deeper than they had even imagined.

The routine was broken on their second Saturday at the beach. Andrew got out of bed and looked out his window. The sky was colorless and the ocean was flat. The only relief was a white sail. It reminded Andrew of a story Wendy had told him, and he decided to surprise her.

The sun came out, and a breeze picked up by the time the sailboat arrived. It was a Hobie Cat. The man from the boat yard pulled the bright red catamaran onto the beach. Then Andrew called Wendy outside.

"Do you like it?"

Wendy nodded, giggled, and wiped away a tear.

"The guy said you could take them right out through the surf." Andrew sat on the canvas that was stretched between the two hulls. "You sit here." He bounced up and down. "If it doesn't work, we can always use it as a trampoline."

Wendy pointed to the sail. "Or a rather large weather vane."

"I don't know how to sail."

"I'll teach you."

"I have to warn you. I get seasick."

"I'll nurse you."

"Will you hold my head when I vomit?"

Wendy laughed again, picked up the rope tied to the bow, and began to pull it toward the sea. "The tide's right—it won't be hard to get it out."

Andrew helped her. The first wave hit them at the knees. Neither

232

was dressed for the water. It had been chilly that morning. Wendy was wearing blue jeans and a sweater. Andrew had on his summer uniform. White suit, white hat, pink shirt, and shoes. The boat bobbed up. Another wave caught them. His hat blew off and skidded down the beach. Andrew looked back. Peter stood between the dunes. Andrew wasn't going to invite him on this ride. Wendy didn't know that. When she saw Andrew looking at her brother, she turned, waved, and shouted, "Come on . . . come on." She repeated the invitation, trying to hide her resignation. Peter watched them struggling in the water. Another wave broke on them.

"Hurry up," Andrew shouted.

"You'll do better on your own."

"We need a navigator."

Peter took a few steps toward the beach. "But I believe the world's flat."

"We need someone to keep us from falling off the edge."

Peter laughed, ran across the sand, and pushed on the stern of the catamaran while Andrew and Wendy pulled. When they got out beyond the break, they scrambled on board. Wendy took the tiller, pulled in the sheet, and the twin hulls cut toward the horizon. The sun was quite bright by now. Peter leaned back and turned his face to the sun. "Where are we heading?"

Looking quite serious, Andrew pulled off his jacket and threw it overboard. He united his bow tie, held it in his teeth, tossed his shirt into the sea, and did the same with his shoes and socks. Then, carefully retying his tie around his neck, Andrew announced dramatically, "West of west and east of all you ever imagined as east."

Following Andrew's example, Peter threw his shirt and sneakers into the Atlantic. "Where's that?"

Wendy turned the rudder. The boat came about with a snap. "Somewhere near Atlantic City."

The sun grew brighter and brighter. The water threw its glare up at them. The heat rising off the sea distorted the shore. Peter lay on his back by the mast, his eyes closed, dangling one hand in the water. Andrew sat by Wendy. The sailboat zigzagged and circled back and forth in front of the house all afternoon. The course of the conversation was just as erratic.

Peter joined in now and then, but it was really their conversation.

They talked about Watergate, the Rolling Stones, UFOs, the Great Pyramid, how they hated people who didn't grate their own Parmesan cheese, and whether or not a dream about your teeth falling out (Andrew and Wendy had both had one in the last week) really means you're worried about being sexually inadequate. Andrew and Wendy decided it was a ridiculous theory. Peter tried to think how long it had been since he had gone to the dentist.

Each time the subject changed, Peter would lick the sweat off his lip. He heard the boom swing overhead. He felt the wind first on one side of his face and then on the other. He listened to Andrew and Wendy scramble for ropes under bottoms and thighs, but he kept his eyes closed. The sun was too bright.

Peter didn't look when Andrew spotted a porpoise or when a motorboat cut them off or when Wendy retold a story an old lady on the beach had told her.

"The mother mouse was taking her baby mouse from their nest to the bread box—which to you and me might not seem like much of a journey, but to a mouse is quite an expedition. Halfway across the kitchen floor out jumps the cat. But rather than run the mother mouse steps forward and clears her throat and barks, 'Bow wow,' so convincingly that the cat runs away. And do you know what happens then?"

Andrew and Peter said, "No."

"Well, then she turns to her baby and says, 'That, my dear, is the value of knowing a foreign language.' "

Andrew laughed. Peter sat up. It was a wonderful story, but what was better than the story was the way Wendy had told it. Her voice had the same tone, the same inflection that she had used years ago when they had played "Let's Pretend" up in the attic. The sister Peter had known had come back to life.

Still giggling, Andrew leaned against Wendy. "God, Wendy, I . . . I . . . ." Realizing the pressure he was putting on her, Andrew sat up and finished the sentence in a less revealing way than he had originally intended. "I can't believe that we weren't friends once."

Already awkward with themselves, they laughed nervously as they listened to each other's negative first impressions.

"You seemed like such a queen."

"Those dresses of yours made you look like a small outbuilding."

Every few words the boat would toss them together, forearm

would touch side, foot nudge foot, but startled by their warmth they'd pull away as if they'd been shocked. They couldn't enjoy being close.

They could confess everything but what they felt for each other. They were speaking in code. Peter wondered why it had to be that way, why it had to be so hard. Without warning he stood up and leapt into the sea. He took two deep strokes under water to cool himself off before he surfaced.

"What are you doing?" Wendy shouted.

Peter rolled over and began to backstroke towards shore. "Trying not to drown." As he watched the twin red hulls of their boat dart back and forth across the water, Peter forced himself to admit how much closer they were, even at that moment, than he had ever been with anyone. Then Peter turned over and kicked furiously toward the dunes.

Andrew and Wendy stayed out until the wind began to die. They pulled the boat up on the beach and walked to the house. Peter was not there. He didn't come back for dinner. Their words and feelings jibed as awkwardly as they had on their sail. Andrew yawned. Wendy said it was time to go to bed. Then they heard the big Mercedes screech to a halt. A girl giggled. Doors opened and slammed shut.

"Do you really have a tub in your bedroom?"

"Of course."

The girl stepped into the dining room and posed against the exaggerated ripple of the speedboat's wake. "Hello . . . your little brother's going to give me a milk bath."

She had short dark curly hair and wore a T-shirt with "Blaze" sequined across her pert breasts. She was in her late twenties.

Peter didn't come in to say hello. They saw his shadow lurch up the stairs. He dropped his trousers down from the second-floor landing. "First a milk bath and then I'm going to shampoo your hair in heavy cream." Peter was very drunk. "Come, my darling, we must hurry. My feet are getting cold." A naked leg dangled over the landing.

"Is he really only seventeen?" the girl asked.

Wendy nodded. The girl ran upstairs. They heard a shriek. Another pair of trousers flew down the stairs.

Andrew and Wendy didn't speak. They listened to the water running in Peter's bedroom. Each was fantasizing about what they thought was going on upstairs. The ease and abandon which they saw in Peter's actions mocked them and made them feel awkward. Yet their anxiety confirmed a feeling that had been growing in them all day.

Andrew stood up and offered his hand. They walked on the beach. They walked and they walked and they walked and they walked, serious and silent, back and forth in front of the house. Then simultaneously they began to laugh. It felt good. They collapsed on the sand giggling until their stomachs hurt. Wendy sputtered out, "They must be done by now."

They walked back to the house. Wendy stopped to pick up her sandals and stumbled against Andrew as she tried to put them on. They fell again.

Her eyes seemed all pupil. The face that he had not been able to paint was more fragile than he had remembered it. Her lips were parted. He felt her breath on his cheek. Andrew shut his eyes. He was ready to make the leap.

Then they heard him. They pushed each other away and sat up. Peter was standing naked on the topmost balcony of the house. He was watching.

Certain he was laughing at them, they stood up, brushed the sand off themselves, and hurried indoors. They did not know that the girl had left, that Peter was crying, that he was watching them to learn. They were right in thinking that he was making a judgment, but they did not know he had already made a decision about them. Peter was the one on trial now.

Every few days Peter would bring home a new girl. Once he brought home two. They all left by morning and never came back. Peter had no trouble attracting more. Andrew and Wendy never bothered to ask why they left. They assumed Peter didn't want them, that he found it exciting to discard people like toilet paper. They didn't understand.

Peter left them on their own more and more each day. He would organize games and outings, get them very drunk and stoned, and then disappear for hours. The house was big. It was easy to disappear. More than once Andrew had the feeling that Peter was leaving them on purpose, that he was playing the part of Cupid. But Wendy and Andrew found it impossible to believe that anyone who treated

236

women the way Peter did could be so romantic, so kind. The thought of him laughing at them fed their promiscuous fantasies. They thought they knew about Peter's one-night stands.

Andrew put it off as long as he could. But by the end of July he had run out of excuses. He had seen Bob Cross several times in town, but no one except Peter's one-nighters had visited the house. Andrew decided to invite Sidney, Sidney's boyfriend, Bob, Bob's wife and children, Tessa and whoever she wanted, and a dozen other people who were "dying" to see him to come to lunch on the same day. He thought it would be easier to get it over with all at once.

Everyone was nervous, hosts and guests alike, on the day of the luncheon. They all knew it was a test. The morning of the party Andrew lay in bed, pillows piled over his head, pretending he was asleep, hoping that when he finally got the courage to get out of bed he'd look out the windows and see gray skies or, better yet, rain. He wanted to have an excuse so that he'd be able to call up everyone he'd invited and say how sorry he was and why don't they come the next week. He wanted to spend the day alone with Wendy. But the day didn't oblige. Skies were clear, and there was a sea breeze to take the heat off the sun's light.

Andrew went to his bathroom, discovered he was out of toothpaste, put on his robe, and went to get some. He took four steps down the back stairs and peered over the railing. The caterers were just unpacking the food. Wendy was telling the couple they'd hired to help serve where the silverware and the glass and the liquor were kept. Peter was making a punch. The floor around him was littered with empty juice cans, wedges of orange, lemon, and lime. There were blueberries and strawberries and a smooched banana under his heel. Peter emptied several bottles of clear liquor into the punch bowl. Andrew couldn't read the labels. He didn't have his glasses on. David Bowie was crooning out of the stereo about spiders from Mars, and Peter, mimicking the society matrons they heard in the streets of East Hampton, announced, "I told the girls at the club I'd never have those tacky people in my house again, but . . . it is for a good cause."

Andrew laughed. It was going to be an interesting day.

Andrew picked up the tube from Peter's bathroom. He hurried back to his sink, loaded his brush, bared his teeth at his reflection, and raised toothbrush to mouth. Andrew's nose twitched. He pulled his head back. Something was wrong. Squinting at the tube, he discovered that he had been about to use athlete's foot ointment. On that note, Andrew threw his toothbrush in the garbage, put on his glasses, and examined his feet to see if he could make use of the ointment. He couldn't.

He stepped into the shower, thinking of all the things that could go wrong, and got out before he was really ready because the water had leaked through to the floor below once that summer, and he didn't need a flood today. He wrapped a blue towel around his middle, lathered his face, picked up his razor, and touched it to the end of his sideburn. He removed two strips of hair and was halfway through a third when he heard a knock on his door. Before he could answer, Wendy burst in on him. His razor caught the corner of his lip.

"Sidney's on the phone and says he wondered if he could bring a few extras."

"What's a few?"

"He didn't say."

Andrew dabbed at the nick with a piece of toilet paper. It wouldn't stop bleeding. "Tell him it's O.K. . . . . Tell everybody everything's O.K."

Wendy left. Andrew closed the door and tightened the towel. Though they often sunbathed and swam nude, there was an odd degree of modesty, almost prudery, indoors.

Andrew was just starting in on the other side of his face when the door flew open. It was Wendy. The razor cut again. "Bob called and he wants to bring some Frenchman. I told him it was O.K.," she announced breathlessly.

"Fuck."

"I can call him back and tell him not to."

"No, I meant fuck, I cut myself."

"We have a problem."

"What?"

"We don't have enough lobster salad for that many people. What are we going to do?"

"Save the lobsters and give them McDonald's."

"This is serious."

"I love their French fries."

Stretching his upper lip, Andrew began to shave his mustache.

238

Wendy did not answer. He guessed she was angry. He shouldn't joke about the luncheon, especially after she had been so responsible about organizing it. Andrew started to apologize. "Wendy, I'm sorry. I know you're trying . . ." But then he heard her giggle. Andrew looked at her in the mirror. She was mimicking him as he made all those faces shavers make. She was copying the way he contorted his face, moving an imaginary razor across her chin. In an instant Wendy had changed. Suddenly she was an eleven-year-old imp. Andrew turned, fascinated by this unfinished girl in his life, the half-stranger he was living with. Then the towel around his middle fell. He was sure she had pulled on it. Blushing, he chased her out of his bathroom.

Andrew had thought Tessa would arrive with Sidney. But Tessa came an hour early, alone. Wendy was in the shower. Andrew was collecting the unfinished work that was scattered around the living room. There were things he was not ready to show.

"Hello, stranger."

Andrew slipped a stack of drawings under the couch. "Hello." Now that she was there, Andrew was glad he had invited Tessa. They shook hands.

Tessa collapsed in an overstuffed chair and casually hooked a thin leg up over its arm. "Did you miss me?"

"Of course."

"Of course you're lying. But I've missed you." Andrew had forgotten how striking she was. She had on a white gauzy dress that criss-crossed her breasts and tied around her waist She didn't have any underwear on. He could see the darkness of her nipple and her crotch. His eyes were focusing on details that had not interested him before.

"I meant to call." The night he had gone to the ballet with Wendy he had been expected at Tessa's house for dinner.

"It was better I didn't see you then."

"Why?" Andrew lay back on the couch.

Tessa smiled anxiously. "Because now I'm divorced, and I can do this and you won't think I'm just teasing." Tessa got up and in one well-practiced motion sat down next to Andrew, took his head in her hands, brushed his lips once with hers, then kissed him open on the mouth and slid her legs up over his.

Andrew took her kisses. He felt her tongue touch his. It was not

239

so different from a man's. She pressed her sex against his. Andrew
lay still.

Tessa stood up and adjusted her skirt. "I didn't really think it
would work." She was lying.

Andrew thought of Wendy imitating him shaving. It was the
childlike, unfinished quality about Wendy that attracted him. He
knew too much about Tessa, too much of why and how she wanted
him. There was no mystery.

"We know each other too well."

"That happens in time with anyone."

They watched as Wendy hurried across the terrace. She was carrying a large tray. She dropped a cracker. When she stopped and tried
to pick it up, she dropped two more. "God, Wendy looks like she's
lost thirty pounds."

Andrew hadn't noticed, but now that Tessa mentioned it, he saw
that Wendy was much thinner. He hadn't realized how long her legs
were or how much of a waist she had.

"You've worked wonders . . . I always knew you had it in you.
. . . I'd better see if I can help Wendy."

Andrew studied the two women as they arranged the food on
white tables that were scattered across the terrace. He watched their
summer dresses swirl up on their tanned thighs. Then he sat down
and began to draw. It was odd how much easier it was to draw Tessa
than Wendy. By this point in the summer he had done many more
drawings of Wendy than he had ever made of Tessa. He drew their
dresses so that Tessa's vanished against the white of the beach and
Wendy's disappeared in the blue of the sea. He finished the drawing
in ten minutes, but he thought it was very good. It wasn't until he
propped it up against the couch and stepped back to look at it that
he saw that he had made Wendy as thin as he had drawn Tessa.

The guests came for Andrew, and Wendy was waiting to see what
he would give them. Andrew might not have been able to resist
playing his old role if Peter had not been there. There was an awkward moment when they first arrived, then Peter dropped his drink
in his lap and laughed. "You'll have to excuse me, I'm not very
coordinated. It wasn't till this summer that I learned to masturbate
with my left hand." He continued to spin them all afternoon, telling
stories some of which he had made up, some of which had happened,
and all of which he swore were true. Peter played with the children

240

and with the adults. He drew them close then pushed them away, always laughing at himself and with himself, smiling over a private joke. Peter kissed men and women. Andrew knew the part Peter was playing. He wondered how he had had the energy to take on the role for so long himself.

Andrew and Wendy sat on the edge of the group and watched. They didn't eat their lobster salad—there was just enough to go around. Andrew was feeling so confident at the end of lunch that he asked Bob and Sidney to look at his work. He wondered how the summer might have affected that. Sidney was silent until he had looked at everything, then he hugged Andrew. "They've never been more right, more finished. You've finally figured out what it is you want, and you have the technique to get it."

Bob stared at the drawing Andrew had made that afternoon. "You know, the wonderful feeling I get from these new works is that you're finally able to really enjoy the simple pleasures—like these women in their dresses—the everyday mysteries of life."

The second compliment meant far more to Andrew. But some people didn't like what they saw. Andrew heard the slim-hipped Frenchman whisper, "He's so dead." The idea made Andrew laugh and sent him outside to look for Wendy.

The visitors left in twos and threes. Peter convinced the hangers-on they had to try a truck stop he knew about. By the time the sun had set, the plates had been cleared and the guests had left.

It had been a long day. Andrew and Wendy were tired. But they weren't sleepy. It was the sort of fatigue that comes from having to stay in one position for too long. Like travelers arriving after a long journey, they needed to stretch themselves.

Andrew and Wendy listened to the sea. They watched dark swells rise and roll toward them, then suddenly break white on the sand. They heard waves that began beyond the horizon, that had traveled thousands of miles, sound their relief.

They undressed and walked down to the beach, let two waves break without them, then stepped into the froth and foam. The ocean smelled strong. It made Andrew think of whales' tails and dolphins' backs, of all the creatures that made their home in the sea. Diving beneath each wave just as it was about to crash on them, they swam out beyond the break. As they kicked and stroked, the dark water's tiny sea creatures swirled and sparkled around their naked bodies.

As soon as they stopped swimming, swells began to lift and push them back toward shore. The moon had waned so small that it was just a smile in the sky. The same basic and enduring forces as those that moved the waves pulled these two swimmers toward each other and the shore. Calf touched thigh. Hand reached around back. Limbs intertwined. Her breasts flattened against his chest and her nipples rose. They kissed once, lips so soft and giving, mouths and bodies so warm against the cold dark around them that they forgot where he began and she ended.

They separated and swam quickly back to shore, knowing that no one, not even themselves, could stop them that night. They didn't bother to put their clothes back on. As they walked up to the house, no questions were asked, no words were needed.

Wendy took his hand. They climbed the stairs of the house leaving their wet footprints behind. They were more worried about failing each other than about being disappointed themselves. Andrew's fears were quite obvious. He had never made love to a woman. He had tried once in college: it—or, more accurately, he—hadn't worked. He winced at the vision of that anonymous woman holding his limp sex as if it were a dead animal.

Wendy, too, made a last-minute analysis of her history, of all the passion she had spent in vain. But she didn't focus on any specific ugly or disappointing moment with a man. She thought of an unpleasant discovery she had made about life on her own one afternoon when she had put together a puzzle of blue note paper and learned why her mother had killed herself.

Wendy couldn't remember all of the suicide note, but she did recall one line. "I never wanted to take that from you, and I can't live knowing you think it's my fault you lost your power. . . ." Wendy knew of her father's impotence. As they stepped into the shower, Wendy vowed never to do that. If nothing else, she would make sure she kept that alive in Andrew. That would be her gift.

The ocean had left them sensitive. The warm water and soap felt good. Goose bumps rose around her breasts and down the small of his back as they toweled each other. Neither of them remembered actually getting into bed.

They took turns touching, careful not to frighten or startle the other with their kisses and licks. They ran their fingers over each other's tanned forms, not as if they were touching a creature like

242

themselves, but as if they were caressing some talisman, an idol they had fashioned in their own image. Their faces filled with awe as first Andrew, then Wendy, then Andrew, then Wendy, trembled, grew damp, and throbbed to the other's touch. It was a primitive rite of creation. Their pleasure stemming as much from the sensation of bringing their partner to life as from the feeling of another body moving against their own.

Wendy guided him into her. He filled her more completely than she had expected. He understood her rhythm. She did not have to prod him. He did not have to hold back. Again and again and again and again each plunge was so complete that they would have been satisfied with that, but without any conscious effort they pushed and helped each other go further and further and further until there was nothing, no Andrew, no Wendy, no yesterday, no today, only feeling. And then, with a gasp and a moan, they let go.

Slowly Andrew and Wendy became aware of each other and the realities that supported them, the bed, the wall, the light in the bathroom. Wendy brushed her lips across his cheek, kissed him, and pressed her face against the softness of his neck. Andrew whispered in wonder, "It was like falling, but into someone instead of nothing."

XXIX

"I don't believe it." Harold Barclay shook a manicured finger at the Sony TV he had propped in front of the Picasso he had shown the governor's wife that morning. The TV antenna made Picasso's cross-eyed woman look even more extraterrestrial.

"It is incredible how obvious they were about it . . . they were stupid to get caught." Simon was impatient to begin the meeting, but he did not want to seem anxious.

"Of course they were stupid, but what's more amazing is that the investigation's gone this far . . . that they're pushing it." Barclay was transfixed by the Watergate hearings on the TV. He had stayed an extra day in New York just to see the rest of John Ehrlichman's testimony.

Simon rustled his papers, hoping Barclay would take the hint and turn off the TV. "Mitchell, Ehrlichman, Nixon—they all knew what was going on . . . Nixon's such an egomaniac he'd do anything to keep control. He wanted too much too fast—that was where he went wrong."

"Yes, they're all guilty, Nixon more than any of them, but they'll never touch him. They wouldn't. They couldn't." Barclay smiled as Senator Ervin needled Ehrlichman. "They'll never convict any of the principals." Simon eyed Barclay uneasily. "Principal." It was the word Barclay used to describe Simon's position at Winston. "It will all blow over. Ervin must know that. You wonder why he keeps on . . . this won't really change anything." Barclay stood up and turned down the sound on the TV. "So, first Wendy Lerner won't release our paintings from her house, and now she wants to take them out of our storerooms as well."

Simon was amazed with the confidence with which Barclay pronounced the word "our." "That's right, she intends to sue, to claim half of all the paintings, remove Luccio and myself as the executors, and void all contracts we made with Winston Gallery."

"That's ridiculous. She's crazier than we thought."

"Yes, but she's more convincing than I expected. The attorney general's looking into the case. I heard he's even considering joining their suit in behalf of future beneficiaries . . . claiming we wasted the assets of the estate."

"I know, I've heard all that. But I think the governor will speak in our behalf to the attorney general. He owns four of those Lerners himself. His brother David has two. I think he will be able to explain the subtleties of art marketing to them."

"The situation is still serious."

"Anytime an international firm sues an individual it's serious. We'll initiate a countersuit against all her claims. What she is doing is illegal. She has no right to the paintings. I've a lawyer working on it right now. There'll be other suits too . . . we'll frighten her to death."

Simon understood the tack Barclay was taking. That had been his first reaction, but he was not sure now. "You know, it might be simpler . . . safer . . . to offer a compromise—cash and some paintings. We could give her what we wanted. She doesn't have any idea what we have. We could give her some of the weaker pictures . . . those copies of earlier successes Lerner tried to knock off at the end. . . . I don't think she'd know the difference. We could probably make it work for us in terms of taxes too."

"Why should we give up what's ours . . . we have papers." A bit of Barclay's German accent slipped through. "Did you check on the judge who will be deciding if she has a case?"

"Yes, we're lucky there . . . he knows nothing about art . . . very middle class. He should be very impressed by the figures we can give him."

"Yes, I was hoping he would be the sort who'd believe we were lucky to get whatever we could for pictures that don't look like anything."

Simon winced at the thought that he would have to use that approach, that he would have to degrade the Lerners to save them. "I think if we're careful about public opinion it won't go to court. We can't let anyone write an article that makes it seem like we're stealing from orphans. We have to seem like the injured party. We should make Wendy out not just to be mentally unbalanced, but to be a ruthless and irresponsible rich girl who out of sheer greed wants to deprive artists who have struggled their whole lives."

"I'll let you take care of the PR. How many grants has the foundation awarded?"

"Three."

"We must have at least ten more before the fall season opens."

"But who?"

"It doesn't matter, except make sure at least three or four of them are black."

"Yes, that is a good idea," Simon agreed.

"Maybe we should go all the way and hire a real public relations man. I know Jack Lloyd at Dillman Quayle. They're the best in the country. He would know how to arrange things so that our side gets written up in the proper light."

"God, it would have been so simple if Lerner didn't have any children. A wife would have been so much easier to deal with. Can't Dr. Fine do anything to change her mind? He was good with her father."

"She won't talk to him. She calls him a spiritual assassin."

"Does she have someone advising her?" Barclay asked.

"Besides the lawyers . . . only Andrew Crowley. She and her brother have been at his beach house all summer."

"That must be an interesting arrangement. I don't suppose we could get at her through him."

No, Crowley never did make much sense."

"He paints well," Simon said aloud.

"Yes, but he makes too much money . . . painters always get themselves in trouble when they get rich."

Simon thought of Lerner. It was true.

Though Harold Barclay and Simon Pyne were the same age, the thin tanned little man looked fifteen years younger than Simon. Barclay knew it wasn't time to worry yet. Barclay, the immigrant Jew, survivor of world wars, man who had been on the last plane out of three countries, each time able to pick up treasures others had had to leave behind, this Harold Barclay knew the odds were in his favor. "You Americans have such wonderful expressions. 'You can't fight City Hall.' That is my favorite, but I know very few of you who really understand what it means."

Barclay's confidence, his arrogance were contagious. "Harold, I

246

don't want you to think I'm unnecessarily alarmed about this action the Lerner girl's taking. I'm not. I just want to make sure we're prepared. I think she'll burn herself out. I guess it's Crowley who's keeping her from freaking out. But this summer won't last forever . . . he'll probably go back to Europe in the fall."

"Of course." Barclay wasn't listening. He was watching the fall of an empire. He was staring at the scene on the TV screen, studying it carefully and with more genuine interest than he had ever exhibited in examining art.

Simon shuffled his papers. "One last thing. . . . Luccio wants his opening in the second week of November."

"Fine." Barclay didn't care.

"And I think it might be a good idea if you were there."

"Impossible. . . . I didn't even come to half of Lerner's openings." Barclay had lived a life of calculated risks, not for the money and the power that his hit-and-run business techniques brought him, but for time. Harold Barclay was a true egotist. His time was the most precious thing he knew of. Luccio would not get that from him.

"Yes, Harold, but Lerner is dead and Luccio is an important new artist to us."

"Perhaps." In a minute Barclay was lost in the hearings. His taut face was stretched in disbelief at what he was seeing being done to Nixon's lieutenants. Watergate defied all the laws of power; it broke all the maxims Barclay had lived by, that had made him and a thousand like him rich after the war. He looked at the Watergate hearings as a freak phenomenon. He could not believe they would change anything.

XXX

Watergate meant many things to many people. During the summer and fall of 1973 the spirit of inquest was in the air. There seemed nothing more noble, nothing more constructive, than the act of confession. The feeling was contagious. It spread into worlds having little to do with elected office. It even manifested itself in interpersonal relationships. Truth became a weapon. A blade without a handle, it cut indiscriminately. But that was only right, since we were all guilty.

The first in the art world to come to Wendy and volunteer what he knew about the fate of her father's paintings was Arthur Gillman, president and director of the Case Gallery, the second most important gallery in New York. The fall season hadn't even begun and rumors about unusual sales and lawsuits and large amounts of money made and lost were already being told among the vacationing art traders of Baghdad on the Hudson.

Arthur Gillman had met Wendy once. She had been with her father. He guessed she was seventeen or eighteen years old at the time. He had thought he had seen her in town at the beginning of the summer. When he heard she was staying at Andrew Crowley's, he had thought of calling several times, but he had put it off, telling himself he'd speak to her the next time he saw her in East Hampton. Arthur Gillman looked for Wendy each time he went to town, but he never saw the brooding fat girl he remembered.

Gillman stood in the front of the supermarket and watched a tall girl with a high waist and unbelievably long honey-tanned legs unloading her grocery cart. She had the sort of padded fleshiness just verging on voluptuousness that had been the rage when he was young, but now would be called plump. He looked down the aisle at his breastless and bottomless wife and daughter, who were scurrying around the supermarket in their tennis shorts and platform

248

shoes like whippets on stilts.

He looked back to the unknown blond girl. She dropped a can of tuna fish. As she bent forward to pick it up, he studied the way the curve of her bottom was balanced by that of her breast. He wondered if she knew how attractive she was. For a moment he thought of telling her himself. But then he decided that it was her slight gawkiness, her ignorance of her sex appeal that made her so attractive. Her unawareness of her presence made it all the more powerful.

Arthur went back to reading his *New York Times*. They were after Agnew now. What next? Arthur was following the article to page four when his wife grabbed his elbow and pointed to the electric doors of the supermarket. "Isn't that Andrew Crowley?"

"Yes, it is." It wasn't until Andrew kissed the big blond girl and took the bag of groceries from her that Arthur realized who he had been admiring. "Do you know who that girl is with him?"

"No, but I thought he was gay."

"He is."

"Well, he certainly didn't kiss her like a fag." It was not the sort of thing a man would notice.

"That girl is Wendy Lerner . . . my God, but she's beautiful."

"I'd hardly call her beautiful." Wendy's beauty wasn't yet the type a woman would notice.

"Well, she is . . . I can't believe it's the same person."

The fact that Arthur found Wendy attractive made him even more eager to talk to her. He caught up with them as they were loading the groceries into the car. "You're Wendy Lerner, aren't you?"

"Yes."

"I met you once with your father. You probably don't remember."

"I remember."

"I'm Arthur Gillman."

Andrew turned around. "Hello, Arthur . . . how are you?"

"Fine. Listen, do you two have a minute . . . I mean, are you rushing off somewhere right now?"

"No . . . are we?" Andrew turned to Wendy, hoping she'd make up an excuse.

She couldn't think of one. "No."

"Good. Then you can come to my house. There's something I want to show you. I've been meaning to call you, but you know how hectic things get in August. Please, I can't explain, but it would mean something special to me if you'd come."

The "something" he had to show her was a square Lerner in his living room called "Firstborn." It was a very early Lerner, pregnant with all the subtleties he would fully master in a few years. It foretold of the celebration of color that was to come. "Your father told me he painted it the night before you were born." The painting and the daughter both so full of promise made it easy for Arthur Gillman to say what he wanted to.

"Please know that I'm not trying to pry into your affairs. If you don't want me to speak on the subject, tell me and I'll stop . . . happy that at least I was able to show you this." He gestured to the painting. "I've heard of your distress about your father's paintings. I thought that out of respect for your father and out of a genuine empathy for the position you seem to be in, I should tell you what I know."

Gillman spoke softly, more to himself than to Andrew or Wendy. There are many reasons one could give for Gillman's decision to speak. Barclay and Pyne had many enemies. Gillman was jealous of Barclay's power, his gallery would benefit from any bad publicity Winston Gallery would receive, he would like to handle the Lerner estate himself—and they would all be partly true. But they were not the thoughts, the feelings that were moving him to speak that afternoon.

"I deal art to make money. I buy for one, sell for two, three, four, sometimes five. My father did the same with diamonds, my grandfather did the same with coal. But there are different ways of being a good businessman. Pressure can turn into . . . well, I think you know what I mean. When I met your father, his contract with Winston had just expired. He told me he needed $500,000 in cash. I wanted some of his paintings. We met, we talked, and we arranged that he would exchange eighteen paintings of assorted sizes for a half million dollars. I thought it was a good deal . . . so did he, I think. But on the day I was to pay him, he arrived at my office in tears and told me, 'I'm sorry, I talked to Simon Pyne. I can't, I just can't.' I don't know what Pyne said, but I understand your father signed a much less advantageous contract with Winston a few days later."

Wendy and Andrew knew the figures of the last contract Lerner had signed with Barclay. After a moment of mental arithmetic, they realized that Gillman had offered Lerner twice as much as he had accepted from Winston.

250

"Why do you think he did it?" Wendy asked.

"Because he was frightened. . . . And that's what I'm telling you —don't be frightened."

But what Arthur Gillman went on to say was quite frightening. "I was in Capri for a few days this summer. It was a business trip. I was trying to buy a Matisse. I was at a dinner and I sat next to Count Pinelli's wife. She was very drunk and is a stupid woman anyway. But she said something very interesting. . . . She asked me if I'd seen her husband's new Lerners. I said, 'No,' and she said, 'The house is full of them, twelve or thirteen of them, at least.' I asked when he had bought them and she said, 'Oh, he didn't really buy them; he's just keeping them for Harold Barclay. We get two for practically nothing just for promising to sell them back to Harold whenever he wants them. Harold really doesn't like art. I don't think.' " Gillman dropped his Italian accent and looked up at Wendy and Andrew. "You see what's happening?" They didn't.

"He's parking the pictures out of the country. Selling them cheaply to friends or to galleries he owns, but legally having nothing to do with Winston Gallery. Either way Barclay takes his commission and pays the rest to the foundation. That leaves him free to resell the Lerners at their real value. He doesn't have to split the lion's share of the profit with anyone. He makes a killing."

"And you think Simon helps him do this just because he works for Winston . . . because Barclay pays him?" Andrew asked.

Gillman looked up at the Lerner. "No . . . I don't think Pyne would go along with this sort of thing unless he was getting more out of it than money. I'm not sure even Barclay really knows what Pyne is after."

Wendy's summer had been so wonderful, she had received so much more than she had imagined, that she had almost forgotten how vicious the forces were with which she would have to struggle when she returned to New York.

Andrew and Wendy had dinner with the Gillmans. There were two other couples. Mrs. Gillman, her daughter, and the other women were pleasant, but they were the sort of tanned, tough little women who had always intimidated Wendy. She had never fit into their uniform. They had snickered at her at Bloomingdales and had caught her coming out of bakeries. But that night, as Wendy sat at the table by the pool, her face glowing in the candlelight, something far more surprising and really far more frightening than anything Gillman warned them of occurred. It was Wendy who held the men's attention. It was she they watched. Andrew sat by her side, laughed, and kissed her neck when Wendy recited a poem from her childhood.

Uncle Jim and Auntie Mabel fainted at the breakfast table,
Listen, children, heed this warning, never do it in the morning.

They envied what Wendy had.

XXXI

For the first time in her life Wendy knew where she was going. The lease on the beach house ran out the day after Labor Day. Wendy locked the front door. Andrew put their bags in the Mercedes. As they drove out the driveway, Peter looked back, waved to the house, and called, "Good-bye."

"Did it wave back?" Wendy asked as she put her arm around Andrew's shoulder.

"No, it winked and gave us a message."

"What?"

Peter looked at the long red nails playing in Andrew's white hair. "To take care."

They dropped Peter off at the Lerner house on Eighty-eighth Street and turned down Fifth Avenue, first making the lights, slipping through just as green turned yellow, accelerating as yellow turned red, then breaking through the red and running them all. The top down, the radio blaring, the whole world a soft blur of good and bad, Wendy sat close to Andrew, touching and kissing. Still in the heat of summer they raced downtown to his studio.

Wendy didn't ever return home to collect the things she had left behind. Her old clothes would not fit anyway. Andrew announced they would both have new fall wardrobes. His first day back in town Andrew purged his closet of clothes that he said were too "trendy" and he thought were too gay.

He gave them to a charity thrift shop. The old women who sorted through the satin and sequined costumery couldn't quite believe Andrew was giving away so much. "Why some of these things haven't ever been worn. Are you sure you are ready to part with them?"

"Positive."

She held up a velvet cape. "Were you on stage?"

Andrew winked. "Yes . . . but I've retired."

The new clothes Andrew bought and had made for himself were hardly conservative, but they were less eccentric than his old uniform. His need to outrage had been tempered.

Wendy gained at least five times the flash Andrew had given up. Andrew helped her into outfits she never could have imagined herself in six months before—clothes that clung, clothes that let you see the shape she was taking on—capes, jumpsuits, diaphanous dresses of crêpe de chine and chiffon whose lack of practicality made them all the more beautiful. Andrew chose clothes for Wendy that were not unlike the ones he had just given away.

Andrew was happy. He sat in front of his easel feeling the warmth of the midday sun on his face as he blended a red to match Wendy's lips. The painting he was working on wasn't of Wendy, but now that they were living together he found himself defining things, thinking of things in terms of her. The painting was of a shadow. But when you first looked at it, your eye read it as a picture of the terrace in the front of the beach house they had lived in that summer. It wasn't until your eye had gorged itself on the yellow and coral roses weaving their blossoms on a lattice, on the soft gray of the shingles, on the cushioned white chairs and umbrellaed table, on the dunes flecked with the pale green of the beach grass and the blue of the sea so like that of the sky it was impossible to tell where the horizon was—it wasn't until the eye had reveled in all these things that you noticed what it was that held them together. It took several minutes before you could focus on what it was that made these things special, what colored them more subtly than you knew they could ever be, what made them as vivid and as heady and as impossible as a childhood memory. It was the shadow that stretched across the terrace, that cut a chair in half, that ran smooth over gravel and then rose up against the house. This faint darkness turned the yellow roses orange and the coral buds red. It was a shadow so enlarged and distorted by the sun that it was hard to recognize as a person. The darkness it cast made a mystery of this otherwise lovely but predictable setting.

There was one final surprise in the painting. You had to look into the shadow that angled up the house for a long time before you realized that there was something caught in it. It was a pair of eyeglasses that had fallen from some window or balcony in your imagination. Andrew had painted them so it seemed they would

254

never hit ground. They were suspended in the darkness. You were sure the figure would have time to step forward, reveal itself, and catch the glasses before they shattered.

Andrew had been able to use all his favorite colors in the painting. He loaded his brush so heavily with the red he had just prepared that it dribbled across his lap. Andrew smeared the paint off his trousers but was so eager to put brush back to canvas that he forgot to wipe his hand. As Andrew continued to work he absentmindedly touched his lip, his neck, his nose, his ear. He was marking himself, coloring himself with the red of Wendy's lips, smudging his face as if she were there smothering him with lipsticked kisses.

It was more than an hour before Andrew caught sight of his reflection in the mirror at the other end of the room. He laughed for more than five minutes as much at the joy he was having painting as at the joke he had played on himself. Work had never been such fun. Intellectually he had always enjoyed it, but there had been something terribly serious, almost desperate, about painting. Since Wendy had moved in, he had been able to take pleasure from the actual act of putting paint on canvas.

Andrew rubbed his face with a rag and looked at the work propped around the room. There were paintings he had finished before and after he had gotten involved with Wendy. His work was evolving. It would continue to do that, to grow, as long as he was alive. Wendy's influence had made no radical change in his style. Yet somehow the act of painting was different for him.

There was more red on Andrew than he had realized. He tried turpentine, but that hurt his skin. He decided to let the paint wear off. Andrew wadded up the rag and tossed it like a basketball into the wastepaper basket by the kitchen door. It was then Andrew thought of the watch he had given Peter or, more accurately, of the inscription on its back, "To love the game beyond the prize." Suddenly and happily Andrew realized what it was that had changed. He was now able to enjoy the game of painting. He no longer saw the finished painting as the prize. He didn't have to create something to believe in. He had Wendy.

The thought made Andrew look up. Wendy wasn't home. She was uptown talking to lawyers, but even though she wasn't there, even though he couldn't see her or hear her voice, he could feel her presence. Andrew had lived in this loft on Prince Street for seven years, but Wendy made it new. It wasn't just the way she had rearranged the furniture. It wasn't her "fuck me" pumps that had been kicked off in front of the fireplace or the scarf dangling over the back of a chair or the pastel underpants on the bathroom floor or the torn pantyhose in the garbage. Wendy was like the shadow he had just painted. She transformed familiar things. She altered his needs and wants not by actions or words he could point to, but just by being there.

Andrew did not understand Wendy's power, and he did not try to explain it to others. He was sure they would not understand. He knew Wendy had become attractive, that her body pulled men, but this force was beyond that. There was an alchemy to the curve of her breast, the giggle in her laugh, and the depth of her eye—a magic that was for him alone.

To comprehend how miraculous it was, how it could alter people and things that had seemed so unchangeable, you had to know the darkness behind her, you had to have felt the body that was now so warm when it was cold. You had to understand how close she had come to being consumed by herself.

Wendy spent the afternoon at Harrington, Dupont, and Blaine sitting in Mr. Blaine's office. The walls were decorated with Wyeth reproductions. Wendy asked many questions, but was given very few answers. Mr. Blaine said that they had a man checking into just how many Lerners were parked in Europe. Wendy wanted to help. She wanted to feel she was doing something to speed up her claim for her father's work, but Mr. Blaine said, "It's out of your hands now. We will present Judge Potkin with the most convincing assortment of pretrial evidence we can. Until the trial is over, all communication with Pyne and Barclay and Luccio or anyone else associated with the case will be through us. It's a waiting game for you."

"Well, when do you think we'll know something? I mean, when is it going to come to trial?"

"A few weeks . . . a few months. . . . Cases like this can drag on for years. I hope that I didn't give you the impression that this would be resolved quickly."

Wendy couldn't believe it. She had told herself it would just be a few weeks. Everything else was going so well it wouldn't be fair for her father's paintings to hold up her life any more than they already had. "Why should it take so long for the judge to decide? . . . It's simple. We know what the paintings are worth and we know what Pyne sold them for . . . . They'll sell them all if we wait."

"Yes, I know, but there's never been a case like this . . . . It will set a precedent . . . make a ruling on a business, an interest, not shared in by most of the public. The art world has made its own rules, set its own standards. This case will change that . . . . But it won't happen overnight."

"Well, can't you talk to the judge . . . I mean, explain how they ripped my father off?"

"I have, but you have to understand that the man knows nothing about modern art. He never even heard of your father until this case. He promised to research it, and I gave him several books. But I can't push him any more."

For the first time in months Wendy felt that she might fail. "But you still think we'll get the paintings, don't you?"

"Of course." Mr. Blaine tried to sound more confident than he really was. He believed the Lerner girl had a little less than a fifty-fifty chance to gain control of the paintings. But the odds were good enough for him. If they won, Harrington, Dupont and Blaine would get fifteen percent of her claim, which would make the case more than worthwhile. There was also a degree of drama, a quality of good versus evil, that intrigued him. The sort of publicity it would generate would be good for the firm. But it was in the area of publicity that they had had their only real setbacks. Mr. Harrington, Mr. Dupont, and Mr. Blaine had called friends at the *Times* and other newspapers and magazines and asked them to write up Wendy's side of the case. But those articles seemed to get buried between Bonwit Teller ads and reports on tidal waves in Java. The one major article on the case that had appeared was in defense of Winston Gallery and the Lerner Foundation. It included interviews with three black painters, one Puerto Rican sculptor, and a conceptual artist from Russia who had stowed away on a freighter to escape the anti-art and anti-Semitic attitudes of Moscow. All the men were in their fifties, all were waiting for their grants, and all gave moving accounts of how the Lerner girl's claim had disrupted their lives and their art.

Mr. Blaine was already late for a four o'clock appointment. As he showed Wendy to the door, he said, "Please be patient. We'll win. Give me enough time, and I can win any case." When a lawyer is talking, time means money. It was the wrong thing to say to Wendy.

Both Wendy and Mr. Blaine would have felt more optimistic if they had known that at that moment Judge Potkin had just hung up the black robes of the court, hiked up his green double-knit slacks, and sat down with his daughter's modern art textbook. She was a junior at the state university at Stony Brook in Long Island. He did not trust the shelf full of books that Mr. Blaine and Mr. Pyne had sent him.

Judge Potkin glanced at the Lerners in the books he had been sent. He'd even walked over to the Museum of Modern Art one day during lunch to look at a Lerner. They were the sort of paintings his wife would say were pretty, but they didn't mean much to him. From what he understood of the case so far, he believed that what the executors and Winston Gallery had done was not honorable, but it was not against the law.

Potkin didn't have any personal feelings about the case until he looked through his daughter's book. There was a picture of Lerner taken in 1949 in his studio on Twenty-eighth Street. Judge Potkin had grown up only a few blocks from there. He could tell it was summer. He could see the strips of flypaper hanging from the ceiling of Lerner's railroad flat. Lerner didn't look like a painter. He reminded the judge of a Hungarian bricklayer who lived down the hall from his family, a well-muscled man who would take off his clothes every time he got drunk.

Judge Potkin became quite nostalgic that afternoon. The memory of those hot summers made him turn on the air conditioner. He read an article about the Winston Gallery in a November 1970 issue of *Time*. When he saw a picture of Harold Barclay smiling from behind his desk, the judge was reminded of the boy who sat next to him his first year at NYU law school. The man in his memory was named Arnold Apple. He had just the same way of smiling that Barclay did. Arnold Apple had stolen his notes the night before his final exam.

The judge in Potkin objected to the thought. He had never been able to prove that Apple was the person who stole his notes, but Potkin, the man who sweated over his books only a few blocks from where Lerner had struggled, knew who was guilty.

The elevator was broken. Wendy stubbed her toe running up the stairs. She was hot and tired and it seemed that she'd never be able to prove her right to her father's art, that she'd never be able to lose

258

the ghost of her father's genius. The court case would drag on for years, and even if she won, she'd be defeated by time. In the end her father would win. She could get fat again . . . she could lose Andrew . . . it was all too easy to imagine. Old fears, old doubts rumbled in her. Wendy felt helpless as she searched for her keys. She would never get her life and herself under control. She couldn't find her key. She was ready to kick at the door, but when she looked up, she saw that it was already open.

Andrew didn't hear her step in. He was concentrating very hard, trying to give a purple tint to the shadow in the painting. This darkness a person can throw on life, this darkness that can change the color of a rose and make a mystery of a common object, was a far more complex thing to render than the metaphors of glass and water that had filled his earlier works.

Andrew was squatting on the top of the high stool. Shoulders hunched, eyes only a few inches from the canvas, he held his brush like a wand and in one long graceful motion swept it over the shadow, touching it so lightly that his brush seemed to leave no pigment—only a suggestion of the color purple.

When Wendy looked at Andrew, she forgot about her sore toe and her fears. The fact that her father's art was beyond her control didn't matter. She was not helpless. Andrew was proof of her power. She did not know how she had transformed him. She did not understand what had grown between them any more than she understood his magic with a brush. But when she kissed him and wrapped herself around him and drew him in, she could feel her effect on him. She would never know a victory so sweet as the one she had won over his innate fears. Wendy needed to assert herself on nothing else only because her effect on Andrew was always so unpredictably satisfying.

Andrew looked like an elf the way he was perched in front of the canvas. "Is my frog prince ready to be transformed?" Wendy called out.

Andrew turned around, smiled, leaped off the stool, and hopped toward her, froglike. "Yes . . . it's been terribly lonely on that lily pad."

Wendy touched the red splotches of paint on his face. "What's this?"

"Part of my curse," Andrew croaked.

Wendy bent over him. Her mouth was like a flower. Her lips

opened and he tasted the sweetness of her bloom. He cupped her breast with his hand and felt her nipple rise in his palm. Wendy slipped to the floor and pulled him close. Their hands burrowed into each other's clothes, and they petted those places where the soul lies just beneath the surface of the skin.

In a moment they were lost, adrift, with no desire to be found. Their love would never disappoint them by explaining itself. It was a mystery they could touch and taste.

Andrew worked. Wendy waited. And while Wendy waited for Judge Potkin to take action, others in the art world came forward and told her what they knew about Winston Gallery, Simon, Luccio, and her father's art. There was talk of Swiss bank accounts with secret seven-figure payments to her father hidden in them, payments Barclay hoped to avoid having to turn over to her. There were hints of blackmail and stories about Barclay obtaining art for the Nazis. A well-known collector insisted that Simon Pyne had invented the Steven Lerner Foundation, that her father had never wanted his art to be sold, and a Soho painter swore that Luccio had told him that he and Pyne had each made a half million dollars from the sales.

Wendy still wanted to start the museum, to control the paintings that continued to speak for her father. She talked to several universities who were interested in giving land for such a collection. She met with architects. She even interviewed several people for a curatorial post in this imaginary depository for her father's art.

But the more stories Wendy heard about the manipulation of her father's work both while he was alive and after he died, the more insistent she was on obtaining the whole truth, on winning everything. She would not accept a compromise. The legal battle—the fight with Barclay and Pyne and Cortesi—was becoming more important than the paintings. She was able to point to these men who called themselves her father's friends and say, "You are the reason my father gave me so little. I suffered for what you did to him."

It seemed to Wendy that whoever won in court would have the last word about her father. What the victors said would be called truth, what they did deemed right.

In the third week of October the New York State attorney general's office entered the case charging Barclay and his gallery, Simon Pyne, and Luccio Cortesi with "fraud" and "wasting the assets of the estate" and "of disregarding the future beneficiaries of the foundation and the preservation and proper exhibition of the paintings of one of America's foremost artists." Judge Potkin and a growing number of people in and interested in art were impressed by the forces that had joined Wendy. Just the words "attorney general" made the sale of the Lerners seem more criminal. It became harder for PR whiz Jack Lloyd to keep articles that asked awkward questions from appearing in the press. After all the publicity about the Euphronios krater, the New York papers were eager for more art scandals.

Andrew and Wendy went to a Halloween party dressed as Peter Pan and Wendy. Wendy was able to laugh when an old friend of Andrew's told her she should have come in a lawsuit, then asked if Simon Pyne had come with them dressed as Captain Hook. Sometime after midnight Andrew leaped off the stair railing trying to show Wendy how to fly and sprained his ankle.

On November 3 Mr. Blaine called. Wendy was sitting for Andrew. He was doing a drawing of her left hand. She reached for the phone with her right. Andrew kept drawing. Mr. Blaine had just given Wendy her weekly briefing on the progress of the case. She was surprised to hear his voice. "Wendy, I was wondering if you could stop by my office this afternoon. I know it's short notice, but something's come up."

"Potkin's made a decision about the trial!"

Andrew looked up.

"No, nothing like that."

"What is it?"

Andrew could hear the disappointment in Wendy's voice.

"It's quite complicated. I'd rather not explain it over the phone."

"I can't come up now . . . I'm lending someone a hand." Andrew laughed at her joke.

"We got a letter from Barclay and Pyne. It's a compromise . . . an offer for an out-of-court settlement. It says that if you remove your suit the foundation will give you seventy-five paintings of assorted sizes, some but not all of which will be chosen from the fifty-seven already in your house on Eighty-eighth Street."

"Who does the choosing?"

"You and Pyne. It's quite specific about that, and the paintings are to be used only in your museum in which Pyne must be allowed to have a role in the organization and management. You will receive $50,000 in cash, and—now this is an interesting point—they will split any cost you incur in the establishment of the museum if you use your influence to get the attorney general to remove his suit."

Wendy did not answer. Andrew saw her left hand flex into a fist.

"Do you want to know what I think?" the lawyer asked.

"No."

"Well, do you know what you want to do?"

"Yes."

"What's that?"

"Finish what I began." Wendy hung up. Her hand relaxed. Though Andrew had heard only half the conversation, he knew what had happened. Wendy's nostrils were flared. Her cheeks flushed. She had scored her first point in the fight. Her ability to refuse the compromise thrilled her.

"You said no."

Wendy never asked how Andrew was always able to guess what she was thinking. "Yes."

"What did they offer?"

"Seventy-five paintings, some cash, and they said they'd help with the museum providing I let Pyne in on it and get the attorney general to withdraw his suit."

Andrew would have settled for that and gotten on with the business of life. He was impressed by her certainty, by her strength. Her decision surprised him, but it shouldn't have. He had a whole life outside the case. He had a greater arena to test himself in. A judgment was pending each time he picked up a pencil. "What do you want?" Andrew asked.

"Everything I can get."

Andrew looked up at her. It was like staring over the edge of a cliff. He could not resist the urge to jump. Wendy said it with such force, with such power, that Andrew had to put down his pen and make love to her.

It was no accident that two days later Judge Potkin decided there was enough "evidence of self-dealing" to issue an injunction forbidding the Winston Gallery or the Lerner Foundation to sell or transport any of the paintings in the Lerner estate without court approval. Simon had friends who were judges. He had helped one raise the capital to withdraw quietly from a real estate deal that was being

262

investigated. Simon's friend was a much more important judge than Potkin. He had not been effective in influencing Potkin, but he could at least let Simon have advance warning of what was happening.

It was also no coincidence that as soon as Barclay learned of Judge Potkin's action, before he knew if Wendy would accept the compromise Simon had proposed, he called Christina Hansen into his office. She could be trusted, she worked hard, she had two children, and she very much wanted a divorce but couldn't afford it.

Christina sat down on the straight-backed chair next to Barclay's desk. Steno pad in her hand, she thought he wanted her to take dictation. But he wanted more than that. "How are you, Christina?" Barclay asked.

She touched the cheek her husband had slapped the night before and smiled. "Fine, I guess."

"Very good . . . now then, what I have to say is really quite simple. How would you like to become registrar of the Winston Gallery?"

Christine thought of Barbara Stein, the fortyish woman with bad legs who was registrar. "You want me to work with Barbara?"

"No, you will be on your own. Barbara is leaving. She just doesn't seem to be willing . . . or able . . . to take the responsibilities I need in my registrar."

"I see."

"If you take the job, you will have more power and more responsibility than a registrar usually has. The movement of all paintings, all art in and out of this gallery—sales, loans, transferrals—you will authorize and direct them all. You've worked with me for several years, I've always been more than pleased with what you've done. I know you can do the job. But do you want it? Oh, and before you answer, I guess I should tell you that because of the added responsibilities that I will demand of you or whoever I hire as registrar, the salary will be $30,000 a year . . . plus, of course, the usual medical and insurance benefits that come from working at Winston."

It was $10,000 more than Barbara Stein was being paid, $12,000 more than Christina's present salary. She didn't understand why Barclay wanted her to take over. Barbara had always impressed her as being overly exact about her work. But the promotion would allow her to get a divorce, to start fresh. "Yes . . . of course, I'd love the job."

Barclay smiled. "Good. I thought you would accept."

263

Barclay had a contract for her to sign right in his desk. It looked just like her old contract, but it was much more involved. It specified that she was the only person who could legally authorize shipment of art. Barclay himself would have to have her signature before any work of art could leave the gallery. Christina was too excited to read any part of the agreement she was signing except the line that specified her salary.

As soon as Christina had left, Simon stepped into Barclay's office. "She seems like a good choice."

"I think she'll do the job." Simon picked up a slide off Simon's desk. He held it up to the light. It was a very mediocre Miro. "I heard an interesting rumor this morning."

"What?"

"I was told the only reason Potkin issued the injunction was to appease the attorney general. He's still leaning toward a decision in our favor."

Barclay smiled confidently. "We hold all the cards."

Christina moved into her own office that morning. The first thing she did was call her sister in Westchester and tell her about the promotion. Then she went to work. She was eager to show Barclay that he had been right to put so much trust in her. That afternoon she arranged and approved shipment of seven Lerners to Rome. A week later she sent eleven to a gallery in Zurich in which Barclay was a silent partner. He asked her to back-date both sales. She didn't ask why. About a week after that, she heard about the injunction on the Lerners. Lawyers were working on her divorce. The paintings weren't her responsibility. Barclay told her the sales had all been arranged over the summer before the injunction. She wanted to believe him. Every two or three weeks a few more Lerners left New York. All sales and shipments were dated prior to Judge Potkin's injunction.

Wendy learned about the injunction on the same day Christina Hansen was promoted. Mr. Blaine told her the judge's decision was a very good sign. "Potkin would never have done it if he weren't impressed by our pretrial evidence." They thought the paintings still in New York were safe. Wendy was encouraged. They didn't know about the responsibilities of the new registrar at the Winston Gallery or the eleven Lerners that were already on their way to the airport to be flown to Rome.

264

Andrew and Wendy wanted to celebrate the judge's decision. They tried to organize a last-minute dinner party for that night. But everyone they called was busy. Before Wendy, the men and women Andrew called would have cancelled anything to come to his loft for dinner. They preferred the Andrew of their memory.

Wendy ran out to Woolworth's and bought two dozen party hats. But the wild dinner for twenty turned into a quiet supper for three. Peter was free. The hats were pointed and had little elastic straps that went under the chin. Peter's was pink, Andrew's gold, and Wendy's silver.

Andrew and Wendy asked him questions about the story he had just sold to *Esquire* and about a play he wanted to write. They tried to make him feel at home. But Peter felt as if he were sitting at a table with foreigners, people who spoke another language. Andrew's and Wendy's was a language of looks and caresses across the table. Even the everyday words they used had a meaning Peter did not understand. They laughed at each other's stories before the punch line. They left sentences unfinished—not because they were tired or unsure of what they were saying, but because they could see the other knew what they meant.

They played off each other's words and thoughts and feelings so closely, so flawlessly, it was as if they had rehearsed their lines. They juggled the conversation, tossing back and forth ideas as if they were colored balls, first a few words about D. H. Lawrence's *Women in Love,* then three sentences about the Chinese rug they were getting for the bedroom, then talk of a trip to Haiti after Christmas that Peter *had* to join them on, then a moment of speculation about Sidney's attempts to organize a retrospective of Andrew's work at the Metropolitan, and on and on and on, never stopping, never dropping an idea, never missing or ignoring what each added to the act. They made it look so easy, so happy and carefree. Smiling and wearing those silly party hats, they reminded Peter of performers in the circus.

By dessert Peter had decided that these two people who sat across the table from him, who were so obviously in love, were more like a high-wire act than jugglers. It was the way they balanced themselves—coming close but never crowding or jostling the other's feelings. They lived high above the rest of the world, like trapeze artists, performing for each other without a net. Andrew and Wendy laughed and tumbled and always caught each other.

The three of them drank almost a whole bottle of brandy after dinner. Drunk and feeling slightly queasy, Wendy announced that someone was tilting the world and that she was going to lie down until they stopped. She went to bed. Andrew found another bottle of brandy, and he and Peter stayed up and talked. Alone, they spoke the same language.

Andrew hadn't realized how much he wanted to talk about what Wendy meant to him until he and Peter drifted into the subject. Peter was the only person who knew enough about both of them to understand. Peter listened to Andrew speak for more than an hour. Andrew's expressions, his inflection, the paintings and drawings he referred to told him more of what Andrew was feeling than the words he used.

Peter finished his brandy. "You're very lucky."

"More than lucky. I somehow feel saved." Peter thought of his vision of them on the trapeze. Then Andrew went on, "I can't remember how I did it . . . how I existed without her."

Peter looked at his drunken friend. Andrew and Wendy were happy. They had saved each other, but Peter found it impossible to believe that they wouldn't get tired. They would drop or hurt or disappoint each other—not out of any particular sentiment, but because of emotional fatigue. Their passion would become a burden, a call so insistent they would not be able to resist it, but at the same time a call they could not help but resent for its inexplicable power over them. Andrew and Wendy were racing on parallel lines, moving so close, so quickly that Peter was sure that the energy they drew out of each other, the power that propelled them, would eventually blind them. He could see them losing control of their brilliance, colliding, crippling each other without knowing how or why.

Without warning, Peter presented Andrew with his vision of the truth. "I think you should leave."

"What . . . where do you think we should go?"

"I know you're going to think I'm crazy, but I think you should leave Wendy . . . separate yourselves."

"Haven't you been listening to what I've been saying? I've never been so happy . . . our relationship is unbelievable."

"That's just it. Leave it now while it is whole, while it's still perfect. While you're close. Don't you see you can't get any closer

266

without losing something—without both of you losing something—part of yourselves?"

"You don't understand. I don't want to drift. I've done it for too long. I want somebody . . . I want this part of my life resolved."

"What you want is impossible."

Andrew was angry and drunk. "Well, I'm not going to settle for the sleazy little life you have. What do you think you're getting out of fucking around the way you do. I did it once, not with women, but promiscuity is the same. Everyone gets fucked in the end. You're the one in danger."

Peter stood up. He was dizzy. He steadied himself on the arm of his chair. "We're all in danger. Maybe it's better not to see it coming. I might not be so alone then. Maybe that's what's wrong with me. Maybe it would be easier if I were blind."

Andrew thought of the warning he had seen in that first drawing he had made of Peter. The memory made him angry. He was angry at Peter for what he had said, and he was angry at himself for not being able to convey what he felt about his relationship with Wendy. Andrew told himself it was the liquor, that Peter was jealous, as he lurched into the bedroom.

Wendy had begun undressing as soon as she entered the room. There was a trail of clothes to the bed. A shoe, a shirt, a skirt, another shoe, underpants. She had collapsed on top of the bed, too tired and too tipsy to crawl under the covers. Her legs were outstretched as if she were running. Her torso was turned up and her head thrown back. One hand at her breast, the other tucked under a pillow. Her golden hair framed her face and lent its luster to her skin. Her body commanded the shadows to play across it, adding new mystery to those places Andrew had touched and nuzzled so many times.

There are few men who have looked into the heart of as many things as Andrew Crowley. He could draw ideas, render hopes and fears. He knew how to color feelings and shade the past. Andrew was a man of vivid dreams, but he had never seen anything as beautiful as Wendy was at that moment.

He would show Peter he was wrong. He would prove that what they had could endure. Andrew ran to the corner of the loft where he worked and picked up a large sheet of paper, thumbtacks, brushes, and paints. He tacked the paper to the wall next to the bed and moved a lamp close. He didn't want to wake her up, but he wanted to work as close to her as he could. The corner of the paper was inches from her breast.

In that light, drunk and dizzy with Peter's challenge, Andrew had to paint by feel. His brushes flashed and slithered across the paper. Blues melted into greens becoming eyes. Heated by the memory of her warmth, Andrew painted her flesh with pinks and reds.

Laughing, Andrew made her larger than life. He stretched her limbs beyond the twenty-four by thirty-six-inch white rectangle he had tacked to the wall. He got more paint. He worked until her toe touched the ceiling and her arms reached out so far that her hand caressed her own breast. Wendy awoke with a smile as the bristles of his brush tickled her nipple. They giggled at Andrew's madness all night.

Andrew lay on his back. Wendy scratched his stomach. He felt like a large pet. It was a comfortable feeling. They didn't want to fall asleep. Andrew watched carefully as the first light of day illuminated the painting on the wall. "I never really sensed how similar dawn and dusk are. The light's the same. We just see the sun differently at the end of the day."

"Why?" Wendy asked.

"Because we're tired."

Wendy sat up and stopped scratching him. "You sound sad."

"Not sad . . . just thoughtful."

Wendy ran her fingers through his white dyed hair. "Well, I have a thought."

"About what?"

"About your coiffure."

Andrew pulled a few strands of hair down in front of his eyes. He guessed his roots were showing. "Needs a bleach."

"Why not let it grow out?"

XXXII

Most of us mark time, keep a mental log of our lives with memories of vacations and birthdays and Christmases, successes and failures, injuries and accidents. It is a comfort to be able to pin events to the past. Time becomes less abstract and frightening when you view it in terms of the big snow two Januarys ago or the fall you went to college or the first Christmas after you were married or divorced, the late spring in which you found love, the early summer in which you lost it.

But Andrew and Wendy weren't allowed this small pleasure of life. They had continued to live together ever since they had come back from the beach, but now in April of 1976, when they looked back over the last three years, on their life together, they thought of their first autumn together in terms of Potkin's injunction on the paintings, and the winter of '74 was filled with memories of pretrial evidence and testimony. Wendy and the attorney general's office had their facts and figures. Winston Gallery and the Steven Lerner Foundation had theirs. Spring was blustery with more evidence and testimony. June brought a new set of lawyers into the case for Wendy. She replaced Harrington, Dupont, and Blaine with Fishback, Stein, and Koch. September delivered another offer of an out-of-court settlement from Barclay and Simon. They, too, had new legal counsel.

The actual trial hadn't begun until January of 1975. February was the month Simon was supposed to appear in court, but he had a stroke instead. In March, Elderstein, the original lawyer for the foundation, shocked the art world and Potkin when he announced, "Fraud? As a lawyer and a reasonably intelligent man, the only fraud I can see in this case is that this stuff is being palmed off as art. I know it. You know it. The art dealers know it. But we're afraid to admit it. I think we were lucky to get as much as we did."

269

June was hot. Both sides replaced their legal counsel once again, and Wendy received still another compromise offer. She said "no." Over the summer of 1975, three successful dealers were called as expert witnesses to testify in Wendy's behalf as to the importance and marketability of the Lerner estate. The most impressive was Joe Riker. He had just made headlines with the sale of a Pollack to the French government. The price was over $2 million, the highest ever paid for the work of an American artist. Riker used the words "plunder," "rape," and "betrayal" when he referred to Barclay's, Simon's, and Luccio's actions. Riker estimated that the seven hundred plus paintings were worth at least $19 million at the time of Lerner's death, and by 1975 were worth $40 million. Their value would continue to escalate. He showed Judge Potkin slides of several Lerner masterpieces that he predicted would be worth a million dollars each in a few years.

The lawyers for the Winston Gallery and the foundation attacked Riker and his figures. They were quite convincing, citing their experts and pointing to low prices paid for nonestate Lerners that had been sold at other galleries. Barclay had arranged the sales with this very moment in mind. The lawyers for the Winston Gallery said that Riker's testimony was irresponsible, and Potkin was beginning to believe them until he discovered that in 1967 Barclay had tried to hire Riker to run his New York gallery.

Almost two years to the day after Wendy moved into Andrew's loft, Luccio testified. He wept and told the court, "I loved this man like a brother." He insisted that the foundation had "gotten a damned good deal." His tears disappeared when Judge Potkin queried him on his relationship with Winston Gallery. Luccio announced dramatically, "How can you say I signed these things to advance myself? I am an artist, not a politician! I have never had an exhibition there. In fact, I have not had an exhibition since this all began." Simon had convinced Luccio that it would be better for him to make his debut at Winston after the publicity had died down. There had been articles on the scandal in *Esquire, Time, Newsweek,* and *New York* magazine.

The case was being compared to the Rothko scandal. The legal battle over the Lerners received more attention in the press only because the principals involved were so much more colorful. The Rothko girl wasn't at all like Wendy. Even as a teen-ager, Kate had been able to keep herself from being tainted; the pressure of her father's genius hadn't pushed her to the edge.

Just before Christmas Wendy's counsel alerted Judge Potkin that the seventy-one-year-old Pyne, supposedly enfeebled by a stroke and too ill to testify, was arriving at Winston Gallery at nine five mornings a week. Pyne appeared in court during an ice storm in January. He also wept. But his tears were far more effective than Luccio's. He talked of Lerner and his art with a dignity and affection that neither Wendy's lawyers nor the attorney general's staff could rattle. When asked about conflict of interest, Pyne shot back, "I was involved with Winston Gallery while Lerner was alive. It was no secret. I was his accountant. I was their accountant. He knew and obviously approved. I see nothing wrong with my being administrator of his foundation as well as secretary-treasurer of the Winston Gallery."

Potkin was impressed by Pyne and by Lerner when Pyne announced, "Helping other painters, giving other men a chance, fighting commercialism was more important to Lerner than his art."

Simon confided to the courtroom, "Sarah and Wendy Lerner disliked and resented Steven and his work. They were the forces he struggled against when he was alive, and now that he can't defend himself, his daughter wants to complete her revenge on him." Simon's ugly accusation made Judge Potkin wonder what his own daughter thought of him. She had graduated from college and hadn't yet found a job. Did she secretly resent him for what he had accomplished?

On Ground Hog Day Potkin and the courtroom listened to Alfred Dutton, director of Winston Gallery, say, "I don't remember," thirty or forty times. The monotony of his testimony was relieved only by "I'm not sure," or "I'll have to check the records."

Washington's Birthday brought Christina Hansen and the Winston stock book into court. The book contained the names of all the paintings in the gallery, together with the essential data on each—ownership, dates acquired, sold, and loaned—all typed out on paste-on slips, but the slips of information on hundreds of the Lerners were missing. Christina told the court that the slips had been copied but removed so that a salesperson wouldn't accidentally break the injunction against sale. The sale dates on the slips that were still in the book had been whited out and typed over so it appeared that the sales and shipments had all taken place before the injunction. When Judge

Potkin asked for the missing slips, Christina answered uneasily that they had been lost. In fact, everything Judge Potkin asked for seemed to have been misplaced. Insurance evaluations, original invoices, as well as price lists from old Lerner exhibitions were missing. Christina Hansen became the Rosemary Woods of the art world.

On March 15, after hearing new stories of secret shipments of Lerners leaving the country in twenty-and thirty-picture lots, Wendy's lawyers and the attorney general's office petitioned Judge Potkin to impound the paintings still in the Winston Gallery. March 15 was Andrew's birthday. He was thirty-five. It is a turning point in the lives of most men. Wendy was so upset when the judge postponed a decision on the impoundment that Andrew's birthday party had to be called off.

The case overshadowed Andrew and Wendy's lives. It wouldn't have been so hard if they could have seen that they were making clear-cut progress toward regaining the paintings, but they couldn't. They still had interesting, exciting, and romantic times, but they did not chart their lives by them. The feeling that they were waiting for a decision, for the resolution of this unknown that had brought them together, began to affect the way that they looked at each other and at life. It was more and more difficult to forget the lawyers and the paintings and the trial. It was harder and harder to have fun. When they did chance upon unexpected relief, they seized it so tightly that it died. They were impatient and resentful.

It was only fitting that Harold Barclay take the stand on the last day of the trial. He was the most important art dealer in the world. Of all the characters involved in this case, he was the most enigmatic. In one article he was called the "Onassis of art." It was an accurate analogy. Like Onassis, he was the only person who knew what really went on in his empire. His power, his money, his friendship were all impressive and mysterious.

Andrew didn't want to go to court. When he told Wendy how he felt that morning, she protested, "But it's the last day."

"You know it's going to drag on. It will be months before Potkin makes a decision. Even when the trial's over, there'll still be appeals. This thing will be with us for . . ." Andrew was going to say "forever," but then he decided to temper his prediction. "It will be with us for the rest of our lives."

"How can you say that to me?" Wendy began to cry.

"I say it because two paintings that I want to be in my exhibition aren't finished. I can read the reviews of Barclay's performance tomorrow morning in the paper. I am sure he'll be convincing. My being there isn't going to change a thing. I don't want to go."

"I've never asked you before."

"What difference does that make?" Andrew thought of all the nights he had listened to her account of what had happened in court, of all the times they'd left town to try to get away from it all only to have her run to the phone as soon as they'd arrived, call the lawyer, and burst into tears about a set-back or something that had been said about her.

"Do you think I want to go?" Wendy asked with her eyes brimming with tears.

Andrew looked at his easel, at his work. He wanted to answer "yes." He wanted to tell Wendy, "Yes, you do want to go because you don't have anything better to do." The desire made him feel guilty.

"Do you think I need to wear a tie?"

Wendy did everything she could think of to persuade Peter to come with them, but he refused. He ended the conversation with an imitation of the Big Daddy of Tennessee Williams' *Cat on a Hot Tin Roof* shouting, "Mendacity . . . I smell mendacity."

Wendy hung up the phone, turned to Andrew, and announced, "He's drunk . . . drunk or stoned or crazy."

"Crazy like a fox!" Andrew had told her Peter wouldn't go. The three of them never went out together anymore. But Andrew and Peter had reached an understanding over the years. They met two or three times a week, drank and talked of anything and everything except Wendy and the trial.

Andrew and Wendy sat behind her lawyers. It reminded Andrew of a school athletic event. He felt foolish. He slipped down into his seat and pulled his hat down over his eyes. The bailiff made him take it off.

Barclay arrived in court looking tanned and refreshed. He carried two attaché cases filled with fresh Xeroxes of the records Winston personnel had misplaced for the past two and a half years. In his pin-stripe gray suit and blue shirt with white collar and cuffs, he looked like a very prosperous banker.

Most of the questions Wendy's new lawyer, Al Miller, or Judge

273

Potkin asked Barclay had already been answered, but it was interesting to see him in action. A defense of the actions of the Winston Gallery had just been printed in one of those glossy art magazines. It would have drawn more sympathy from other art merchants if its stand had not been so absolute, if Barclay had not been so self-righteous about his innocence. The only difference between Barclay and many of the men who testified against him—the dealers and the curators and the collectors, the men who called him "a disgrace," "a thief," and "a shylock"—was that they were afraid to do what he did.

People whispered that Barclay was deluding himself, that he was making the same mistake that Nixon had made. They said that he was foolish to be so confident, to think himself above the law. Some said he was senile. But Barclay had hedged his bets more carefully than anyone realized. Harold Barclay, né Harold Berkowitz, was a survivor. He had lived on the run. Like so many of the educated and cultured and resourceful Eastern Europeans who moved from country to country before, during, and after World War II, Barclay was always prepared for the worst. He was ready to pack up his bags in the night and steal away before the knock on the door in the morning.

Luccio had been frantic in court, Simon earnest, and Barclay, who hated publicity, appeared frightfully English, putting up a very good show as he fenced with Wendy's lawyers.

When asked about the power structure of the Winston galleries, he stated, "As you Americans say, I am the boss. But I have no official position at any of my galleries other than as consultant. I am not a legal officer in any of the companies." All the defendants in the case had developed their own special hatred for Wendy Lerner. Barclay seemed to be speaking to her when he said, "I have no idea of the gross income of my businesses, but I will tell you that all the profits—all cash—is put into irrevocable trusts in Switzerland in my children's names."

Wendy leaned forward and asked Al Miller what that meant. The lawyer whispered back, "It means he has no attachable property or money."

"What does that mean?"

"We can sue, but we won't get anything from him."

Barclay smiled as Potkin mispronounced the French names of a dozen different Barclay-controlled companies and galleries in Liechtenstein. When asked for specifics about these firms, Barclay answered, "I would give them if I could, but I assure you that most of these companies don't exist anymore." It was easy for Potkin to see why Barclay would sell Lerners he handled on consignment to firms he controlled. He could negotiate a low price, give the foundation a low percentage, then resell them on the open market and keep all the profit for himself. But Potkin didn't understand why Barclay would sell paintings to himself for three times what he paid for them, then sell them again to himself at a loss, each time without any exchange of money. Barclay put it in a word Potkin could understand: "taxes."

After lunch Miller brought up the subject of the irregularities in the Winston Gallery's bookkeeping. "A member of the attorney general's staff did some investigating in Liechtenstein and Paris and Rome—"

Barclay interrupted him with a smile. "Oh, yes. I know who you mean. Mr. Kallop. He took the registrar of my gallery out to lunch. She told me he was very fond of the fauves."

The spectators laughed. Wendy glared at Andrew when he joined them. But Miller continued to harass Barclay with these inconsistencies in the records of his gallery. First Barclay made excuses. "The foundation needed money. Being more than sympathetic with its goals, I hurried sales. I wanted to help get it on its feet." He blamed errors on the stupidity of his accountant, sales people, and his registrar. The German in Barclay revealed itself when, finally pushed too far, he announced, "I could not believe it either. . . . I have never concerned myself with details like this." He gestured to the stock book, "If I have so stupid people working for me, it is not my fault. It can happen to anyone."

Barclay performed well, but there were a few figures he could not argue with. Winston Gallery Liechtenstein had bought one hundred Lerners outright for $1,995,000 in 1969. In the first year, they sold twenty-five to individuals, grossing almost $2.5 million. In the spring of 1976, there were only eleven left in New York. The other sixty-four had supposedly been sold in large lots to foreign dealers and collectors. Winston made an additonal $1.2 million from these sales.

The foundation had received $1.5 million from the consignment sale of 124 Lerners. They had all been sold and shipped out of the country. It was impossible to know where they were or who really owned them. It was rumored that the 124 included all the master-

275

pieces except for those disputed paintings in the Lerner house on Eighty-eighth Street.

When Judge Potkin adjourned, everyone involved knew that the trial had really just begun. Whoever lost would appeal. Suits were still pending. Other criminal charges were being considered. More questions had been raised than answered. The only thing that was clear was that Harold Barclay had made a great deal of money and that men and women often put a peculiar value on art.

As Wendy and Andrew left the courtroom, Al Miller pointed to a conservatively dressed man who was sitting in the back of the room checking the notes he had made during the trial. "He's the one we have to worry about."

"Who's he?" asked Wendy.

"The man from Internal Revenue."

Andrew and Wendy left the courtroom with the same thought throbbing in their heads. *It isn't fair!*

When they passed a pair of foreign journalists in the hall, Andrew heard an English accent whisper, "My God! That be him! What happened to the white hair and all the nonsense?"

A French tongue clacked back, "Him! . . . She's the one who has changed. She is very beautiful now, but she was a pig not three years ago!" The unfairness of it all doubled in Andrew's mind. He studied his own and Wendy's reflection in the elevator door. He had followed Wendy's advice. He had stopped bleaching and had let his hair grow out. It was mostly gray—salt and pepper, she called it. The colors of his clothes had faded too. He had almost not worn the dark green corduroy suit he had on because it seemed so flashy. Andrew tried to tell himself that the change in the color of his hair was what made the wrinkles around his eyes stand out, but Andrew had drawn himself too many times to believe that. He knew the blush had fallen from his cheek.

And Wendy . . . she was so thin now that she had to drink Weight On. Halston said that she looked fantastic. There had been pictures of her in the previous month's *Vogue.* She was beautiful, almost too beautiful. Her beauty, her power to attract, almost overshadowed her person. He found her so irresistible that he did not know what he really thought of her actions and words.

Andrew stepped out of the elevator feeling that a crime had been committed.

276

The *New York Times* had assigned Brett Morrison to the trial. There was a rumor that he was going to write a book about it. In reviewing Andrew's last show, the young critic had said, "Andrew Crowley is the only living painter capable of picking up Picasso's challenge. He is a school of art in and of himself." Morrison was just getting into a cab when he saw Andrew and Wendy. He waved, "Which way are you two going?"

"Downtown . . . Soho," Andrew answered.

"Come on. I'll drop you".

As soon as the cab started moving, Morrison began to congratulate Andrew. "I think it's fantastic and about time . . . you must be very happy".

It was a minute before Andrew could remember what there was to be happy about. "Oh, you mean the show".

Morrison was surprised at how indifferent Andrew sounded. "It's quite an honor. No other living American painter has been given a retrospective like the one they are planning for you at the Metropolitan Museum."

"It makes me feel old . . . as if I should oblige them and die."

Morrison laughed. "Sidney told me that the old guard put up quite a stink, but that's to be expected. More importantly, he said the new paintings were fantastic . . . incredible . . . better than anything you've ever done."

"Really?" Andrew was surprised at how uncertain he felt about his work at that moment. "We'll be hanging them sometime next week. You'll have to come by and take a look at them."

The ride downtown can take a long time when the traffic is bad. Listening to Morrison talk to Andrew about his art allowed the feelings of unfairness to multiply in Wendy. Morrison had hardly said hello to her. She told herself that she was angry because they were excluding her from the conversations, because they weren't expressing concern about her struggle, but what she really felt was unfair was that Andrew had his painting and this retrospective to turn to. He could take refuge from the trial in his art. He had an escape.

It would be too simple to say that Wendy was jealous of his work, that she resented the honor and acclaim that this retrospective at the Metropolitan would bring him. She did not hold Andrew responsible for this vast unfairness in which she was emeshed. It was life that was unfair, but it was Andrew who took her arm as they got out on the corner of West Broadway and Houston Street.

The thought was so hot in Wendy that she used those words. "It isn't fair, God damn it!"

"I know." Wendy thought he was going to apologize. "I know. I had the same feeling in court. Why us? . . . Why me? I don't want to be part of it. I used to be good at staying out of things."

It was definitely not an apology. The unpredictability of Andrew that used to delight her now added to her rage. "You still stay out of it." Wendy began to run toward the door.

"What's that supposed to mean?" Andrew hurried after her.

"All you care about is your work . . . your retrospective. I understand. My father was a painter, too."

The elevator was broken again. Andrew tried to catch up with Wendy as she ran the stairs. They knew something was wrong. It wasn't fair that this couple who had saved each other should now be screaming in a stairwell. They deserved more of an answer than each other's echo. This man and woman who had raced side by side on emotion for so long were bumping each other. They were out of control.

"God damn it! Stop and talk to me," Andrew insisted.

"Talk to yourself! You do it anyway."

"Stop it!"

"You stop it!"

Wendy ran through the door. He followed. "God damn it, we're going to talk about this." Andrew reached out, grabbed her arm, and jerked her around. He was going to shake her and make her tell him what was wrong, but neither really wanted to look into what lay behind the argument. Neither wanted to think about what was so unfair, so unjust. The dilemma was so vast, so beyond any of the wounds that they had already inadvertently inflicted on each other. It was reflected in everyone and everything they saw.

Wendy was startled at how hard he gripped her. Her head snapped as he yanked her to him. They were both ready to shout, but the pressure of their bodies was too much. He grew hard against her. Her breast heaved as she tried to catch her breath to scream. They kissed so hard their teeth scraped, their lips became puffy. They kissed again and again, not daring to separate their mouths, not wanting to hear a shout or a scream.

278

They yanked at each other's clothes. Buttons flew and seams ripped. They made love on the polyurethaned hardwood floor half-way between the kitchen and the bathroom door.

Gasping, they struggled for life.

Fight then fuck. It is a very American way of settling things, but Andrew and Wendy had never fallen into it before. They were right not to talk. Words would have failed them, and they would have said things they didn't mean. The sex was good. It always was.

They lay there for a very long time. Neither wanted to get up. They were afraid. The sun had gone down and the room was dark. Finally Andrew got up to go to the bathroom. Wendy went to the kitchen for a drink of water. On the way to the john Andrew tripped over a chair. He stumbled and reached out to the wall to keep from falling. His hand slipped and knocked a picture off its hook. He tried to catch it, but couldn't. The glass shattered as it hit the sharp edge of the metal table, then crashed to the floor.

"Ah, fuck!" It was one of his drawings that had fallen.

"What happened?" Wendy turned on the light.

"God damn it! I broke that drawing I did of you."

Except for the still unfinished double portrait of Wendy and Peter, it was the first image of her he had ever made. It was one of his favorite drawings. Her face was pale. Her eyes were closed. When you looked at it, you whispered for fear you would wake her. He had sketched it while Wendy was still at Payne Whitney, but you didn't know that when you looked at it. All you saw was a girl sleeping in bed. Andrew turned the frame over. The paper was torn, ripped across her face. The drawing was ruined.

"You can have it fixed. Sidney will know someone," Wendy suggested.

"No, you can't. There are some things you can't fix." Andrew cut his hand as he brushed the bits of glass off the torn image of his lover.

"Watch yourself!" Wendy had never liked the drawing. Her face was fat. It reminded her of the old days.

"Who cares?"

Wendy was going to say, "I do," but then she looked at him. He was still naked, she was still damp from him, but their passion together was forgotten. Andrew's eyes were on the drawing. His attention was directed toward the work of his own hand. Wendy did not understand that Andrew's art reflected what he saw and felt for her. "You know, sometimes I think the only reason you got involved with me was because of your work . . . because you thought it might help you." A tear spilled out of her eye.

"Loving you is the only action I have taken without my work in mind."

"You're the most selfish man in the world."

"How can you say I'm selfish after what I've done for you?"

"You did it for you, not for me."

"How do you know that?" Andrew demanded.

"Because you have everything, and I have nothing." Wendy wept.

Bewildered, naked, and angry, they faced each other. "You have . . . " Andrew was going to say, "me," but then, hurt and frightened, he told himself, "She knows that. That's just what she means. I am not enough . . . I am nothing."

Andrew dropped the drawing and put his clothes back on. When he started toward the door, Wendy stopped crying and called out, "Where are you going?"

There was no answer.

"Wait for me!" she cried.

He was gone.

As soon as Andrew stepped out on the street, he realized how much had changed. He had lived in Soho for almost ten years. When he had moved in, it had been a world of trucks and warehouses. Artists lived illegally in barren spaces. There was nothing to distract you. There was nothing there except your work. You had to leave Soho and go to the Village or to Little Italy or to Chinatown for the necessities of life.

Artists still lived there, but the sidewalks were crowded with tourists on Saturday and Sunday. The people who moved in had baby carriages and looked as if they should be living in suburbia. There were big galleries. Bars and restaurants all crowded with people who called themselves "creative," who had majored in art or art history, who had come there because they had heard that that was where it was happening. They didn't know that it had happened, that it was over.

Andrew was always running into people who said that they knew him. He was always being invited and glad-handed by men and women whose names he didn't remember. He ignored them, but that night he found himself curiously glad to be embraced by these boring

280

strangers. It warmed him to hear them say, "Where have you been? What have you been doing? . . . Haven't seen you around. . . . We missed you." He went to a bar, then to a party, then to another party. He was offered amyl nitrite, Quaaludes, and cocaine, but they were too exciting. Andrew wanted to be dull. He drank vodka without ice or mixer. He drank it because it was colorless, tasteless, and dumb.

Andrew's eyes focused on someone even more beaten, lonely, and depressed than he. She looked to be about thirty, maybe even younger. The dances of her girlhood had come back in style. She jitterbugged with a sort of relaxed recklessness that is exhibited only by professional hoofers and well-practiced drunks. A Puerto Rican boy tossed her between his legs, twirled her around, then flipped her over his back. When this squealing blur of bosom and legs slowed down, when the music stopped, you realized that she was approaching fifty. It was Maggie Lawrence.

Simon and Barclay still took care of her. She was designing jewelry now. Maggie was just coming off a brief affair with a young Swiss painter. He had left her as soon as he had met all of her connections. Maggie turned away from Andrew, not wanting to have her evening spoiled by a snub from him. But she was just the sort of person Andrew wanted to talk to. He pushed away those who wanted to be seen chatting with a living legend, a man whose work would fill a whole wing of the Metropolitan in a few weeks.

"Maggie, how are you?" Andrew kissed her cheek. He didn't think about it, but when he saw the way it startled her, her smile exploding de Kooning-like on a face unnaturally taut from too many lifts, when he felt her hand touch his shoulder, Andrew thought of Wendy, of how outraged and angry she would have been if she had seen the gesture. The idea amused him. "May I get you a drink, Maggie?" She asked for her vodka the same way he was drinking it. She had picked up the habit from Lerner.

"How are you, Andrew?"

"Trying to grow old gracefully."

"Ready for your exhibition?"

"I'm always ready."

"Excited?"

"I'm always excited."

They were both very drunk, and purely by chance reality blurred the way they wanted it to. Maggie squeezed the thigh of genius. It was like old times. "What happened to your hair?"

"It's the new me."

"I liked it all white." She ran her fingers through his hair.
"So did I."

"Why don't you let me fix it up for you?"

"When?"

"Whenever you're ready."

"I told you. I'm always ready."

"I have something at my house that ought to do the trick."

After they were in the cab and they had kissed and rubbed each
other at two red lights, the reality of what he was doing hit Andrew.
Nothing . . . no one could hurt Wendy more. This unfairness would
make up for the greater injustice that was taking place in and around
him.

Wendy was the only woman Andrew had ever slept with. As he
stepped into Maggie's apartment, part of Andrew wanted the sexual
encounter he knew he was headed for to be wonderfully exciting and
satisfying so that Wendy would lose her hold on him, so that he
would not feel so powerless. But part of Andrew still believed in
Wendy. That part wanted it to be terrible. That Andrew hoped that
he wouldn't be able to get it up, hoped that he would leave frightened
into believing, not daring to doubt.

Andrew thought he was acting on his own, that he was asserting
his will, breaking free of her spell. But it was Wendy who was pulling
him into Maggie's apartment. It was she who had drawn him into
this.

Maggie threw her coat on the floor and turned on the music. She
had all the latest disco tunes. As she cha-cha'd down the hall, she
called out, "I've got some peroxide in my studio." Maggie had been
married to a reasonably successful color field painter who had died
in a car crash in the mid-sixties. She had gone out with painters
before and after Lerner. The walls of her apartment were covered
with photographs of her standing in the studios and next to the work
of these men. There was a picture of her throwing a pillow at Lerner.
It had been taken at Stan Rothkoph's house. There were paintings
and drawings by these men. Maggie had served the arts for more
than two decades. Andrew was surprised not to see a Lerner hanging
among the rest of these trophies.

282

He followed her into the studio. She had already changed her clothes. She was wearing a pink Chinese silk bathrobe. She held up her bottle of peroxide. "Come on. Take your shirt off." Andrew took off his shirt. She pointed to his pants. "You don't want to get any of this on your trousers." If she hadn't pushed him so hard, Andrew wouldn't have hesitated.

There were fifteen or twenty canvases rolled up and stacked against the bookcase in the corner. "What are these?" Andrew asked.

"Some dreadful things by a young Swiss painter. He was sweet, but I had to get rid of him. Love is no substitute for talent. . . . At least I think he has no talent. See for yourself."

Andrew unrolled one onto the floor. "God! They're worse than awful!"

"The only reason I'm saving them is because Emmerick took him on."

"You're joking!"

Andrew stepped on the canvas as he unfurled two more. "Real Clemsville. . . . It looks like Noland ran out of masking tape." The paintings were horizontal stripes of color that blurred as they approached the edge of the canvas.

Maggie laughed. It was good to have a man around. Lerner had been terribly funny when he mocked other men's work.

"Let me look at one more. Then we'll get down to business," Andrew announced. Maggie winked at him. Andrew's hands slipped behind the bookcase. The canvas he touched was larger than the others. It was heavy and covered with dust. "My God, he used enough paint on this one!" Before Maggie could stop him Andrew unrolled the canvas.

Instead of some young man's foolish and inarticulate attempts to use color abstractly, a deep dark brown Lerner yawned before then. It was the painting that had been missing, the masterpiece that Lerner wouldn't sell, that had disappeared from his studio the day of his death.

The fact that the painting had not been looked at for so long made it more powerful. It was like a wild animal waking after a long sleep, its organic brown rippling and vibrating across the room.

Maggie was stunned. Then she blurted out, "He wanted me to have it. I never took anything from him. It was Pyne and Barclay, and Luccio. They were the ones who did it. I only wanted him. . . . I kept this just so that I would have something to remember him by."

Maggie was frightened. She told everything she knew—not because she wanted the truth finally to come out, but because she hoped she would stumble onto some story, some excuse that would save her. Maggie volunteered answers to questions Andrew wouldn't even have known to ask. He had no idea how incriminating the painting was until she told him. Maggie didn't cry or carry on as one might have imagined. People who are truly beaten don't have the energy for dramatic shows of emotion or remorse. Barclay and Pyne gave her the painting; they took care of her because of what she knew about their business practices, because of what Lerner had told her. The truth was uglier than any of the rumors Andrew and Wendy had heard. With Dr. Fine's help, Simon and Barclay had tortured Lerner. They had forced him to follow their wishes, but not by threatening him openly; if they had done that he would have had something real, something he could see and touch to fight against and maybe he wouldn't have died as he did. Barclay and Pyne were far subtler, far more insidious than that. They blackmailed Lerner with his own doubts. Through innuendo and allusion they stripped Lerner of all his confidence in himself as a painter and as a man.

As Andrew looked at Maggie, her bathrobe open, her white bosom overflowing a black push-up bra like the topping on a sundae, the peroxide bottle she had teased him with still in her hands, he knew who had helped them destroy Lerner's confidence in himself as a man. After hearing all Wendy's stories of rejection and abuse, Andrew had hated her father. He had hated Lerner for the trial, the struggle that was pulling them apart. But now it was all too easy to see what had happened to Lerner. Andrew sensed his own vulnerability.

For over an hour Maggie spewed out her dirt. Every few minutes she repeated her plea, "I didn't know until it was too late. . . . I never thought it would go as far as it did." She began to cry at the end of her confession—not because she felt guilty or because she was afraid legal charges would be brought against her, but because she knew that neither she nor Andrew believed she was innocent.

Andrew rolled up the canvas and walked out of the apartment while Maggie practiced her lines. "I was tricked . . . I didn't know what I was doing." Andrew walked out onto the street thinking the end was in sight. He wanted to believe that this eight-by-twelve-foot rectangle of canvas that he was carrying would wash away their fears, that when he unrolled it before Wendy and the world, they would forget the words they had used on each other. Andrew believed he had the power to heal the past. It would remove the questions, the unknown that threatened them. The deadlock would be broken; the trial would be over.

It was five o'clock in the morning by the time Andrew got back to the loft. Wendy was still up. He could see the bedroom light from the street. There was a sea breeze; the air was clean for a change. The world didn't seem nearly so unfair.

Barclay was in a hurry. He had a ten o'clock plane to catch, and he was angry. As Simon's maid cleared away their breakfast dishes, Barclay folded up the papers they had signed.

"Are you still upset about the trial?" Simon asked.

"I never was upset."

"You seem preoccupied."

Barclay looked at his watch. "I have a plane to catch, and I'm having difficulty with one of the Lerners."

"What's wrong?"

"God, these idiots I have working for me. I sold a Lerner about a year ago to a German museum. It was all right, but not a great painting. Anyway, in all the confusion we've had around the gallery, they shipped the wrong Lerner to the museum. The director received it, opened it, and paid me. Quite quickly, I might add, and, of course, because it wasn't the Lerner he bought. It was one of the Lerners we were saving—"Autumn Call"—you remember the painting. It's a masterpiece worth ten times what this man paid for it. God, I would sue him if things weren't so complicated. And what is so frustrating is that he knows that. That's the only reason he's doing it. He's practically stealing it from us."

Simon changed the subject. He felt like talking.

"It's a good thing Luccio won't have to appear in court again . . . he'd never hold up. He called me in the middle of the night. Apparently he went to a dinner party and three of the guests left when he walked into the room." Pyne laughed nervously. "He thought it had something to do with the trial." None of the defendants was as welcome as he had used to be. "Luccio's gone over the edge. He told me Lerner's haunting him . . . swears he sees Lerner late at night, hears him pounding on his door."

"From the way he acted when we decided to bury Lerner at his house, it doesn't surprise me. He was always a silly, superstitious man." Barclay looked at his watch again.

"You know, there are some new painters I think we should look at. It would be the best thing for the gallery to show some new faces . . . bring in some new talent." De Kalb, Holland, four other major painters and two estates had already left the Winston Gallery. "There's a man in Brooklyn, a very good realistic painter . . . that's what the people want now, the discipline of identifiable image. The fellow's good. Perhaps his work's a little sterile, but with help, who knows?"

Barclay smirked. "You never quit."

"There's no reason to," Simon answered defiantly. Barclay looked at his watch again. "What are your thoughts about the direction of the gallery?" Simon asked.

"I think it might not be a bad time to pull out of the art game."

The idea so startled Simon that he spilled his coffee in his lap. "Don't worry, it was just an idea," Barclay reassured him.

A few minutes later Barclay's limousine pulled silently away from Simon's house. Barclay was not planning to return to New York for some time. He was flying to Venezuela. There were some oil deals he was interested in. He liked South America. They understood the way he did business.

With its narrow windows and smooth stone façade, Simon's house looked like a fortress to Wendy and Andrew as they walked toward it carrying that lost Lerner. Simon was rearranging the paintings in his living room. He always found it reassuring to handle art of which he was confident. Barclay's comment had unnerved him.

The doorbell rang. Simon opened the door. He knew what had happened as soon as he saw the painting.

"Do we have to unroll it?" Andrew wanted Simon to fight or argue. He wanted an excuse to hit him.

"It never should have been rolled up in the first place . . . cracks the paint." Simon pointed down the hall. "Why don't we talk about this in the library?" Simon told his maid and his wife not to disturb him. When they sat down, Pyne turned to them and announced, "I suppose you think this painting explains everything." His voice was calm, but his face was white and sweating.

"The painting and what Maggie told Andrew explains most of it." Andrew had told her how and why he had ended up at Maggie's house. Wendy did not shout or accuse him. She just stared into the darkness of that lost Lerner and whispered hoarsely, "It doesn't matter now."

Simon took out a handkerchief and wiped his face. "Maggie doesn't know everything."

"She knows how you tortured Lerner," Andrew said.

"Tortured him . . . he was a miserable man before I ever met him. I did what I thought was best for his work. I tried to keep him working." Simon stared at Andrew. "You can't help an artist with his work, but you can do things to force him to face the canvas . . . to keep struggling."

"You did it for yourself," Wendy shouted.

"I did it for the art. That was where my loyalty lay."

"You did it for the money."

"Your father liked money more than I."

"If he cared so much about money, why did he save all his paintings? Why did he want to start a foundation?"

Simon laughed. "Your father did it because he needed praise, because he wanted to be remembered as one of the greatest artists of civilization even more than he wanted to be rich. He never wanted to help struggling artists. He didn't care about anyone else's work but his own. The foundation was a trick . . . but not a trick I thought up. It was your father's idea so he could save the masterpieces, keep them all together and sell the rest. Under the auspices of a foundation he wouldn't have to pay taxes and we could build a museum. But not some college gallery like you wanted . . . Lerner wanted a shrine, a place where his paintings would be shown just the way he wanted them to be, lighted just the way he wanted them to be. He would share space with no one . . . but you made that impossible, Wendy. We should have talked about this long ago." Simon looked sick, but he sounded relieved. He loosened his tie. "If you'll excuse me for just a moment . . . I think I need a drink of water." Simon stared at Wendy, his eyes half shut with fear and anger. Then he turned to Andrew. "I'll be right back; there's more you don't know, Crowley."

Andrew and Wendy sat in silence before the moody Lerner above

Simon's mantel. The somber painting dominated the room, black framed by gray, its dark heart as impenetrable as its maker's passion. Was Simon lying? What he had said about Lerner's plan to build a monument to himself, a structure that would ensure that he wouldn't be forgotten, was true to the spirit of the man. They wondered when they would find a truth that would answer their questions.

Both of them wanted this drama to turn into a "good guys versus bad guys" scenario, into a detective story with clear motives and a simple conclusion. After waiting nearly thirty minutes, Wendy shouted, "Jesus Christ, where is Simon? I bet he's trying to get away."

Wendy began to search the house, and Andrew rushed outside. He didn't see Simon on the street. He asked the doorman on the corner if he'd seen Pyne leave. He couldn't remember.

As Andrew ran back inside, he thought to himself, "My God, he could be at the airport by now. . . . He's going to beat us."

Andrew found Wendy standing in the doorway of the powder room. Trousers down around his ankles, slumped forward, his head pressed against the wall, Simon sat on the toilet. His nitro pills were scattered on the floor. He was dead from a heart attack.

The police came, but Andrew and Wendy didn't try to tell them about the missing painting or what it meant. The crime was too complicated, too vague to explain.

It was two o'clock in the afternoon by the time Andrew and Wendy left Simon's house. They hadn't eaten yet and were very hungry. They bought sandwiches, beer, and potato salad at a delicatessen and walked into the park, each carrying an end of the rolled-up Lerner. Their burden linked them. People had to walk around them. No one would have believed that what they held could cost so much. It reassured them that they were able to laugh when a little boy peddled his tricycle beneath the rolled-up canvas.

Their lawyer told them the painting did not change a thing. If Wendy had won the case, Simon would have died slowly. The painting killed him, but it deprived her of revenge. When confronted with her confession, Maggie announced, "Andrew took advantage of me . . . then tricked me. He twisted everything I said. I don't know where he got the painting." The picture proved nothing. It went to the restorer instead of to court.

XXXIII

The last painting Andrew wanted to include in his retrospective still wasn't finished at the time of Pyne's death. In the days that followed he was surprised at how well he was able to work. The painting showed a pair of overstuffed chairs. There was an open bottle of nail polish on a table by one chair, a drink and a smoking cigar set by the other. The cushions were crushed. It was called "Empty Places." It was a painting about where two people had been.

As Andrew worked on the painting, the ease with which he was applying the paint bothered him. There was too little struggle involved. The transfer of his feelings onto the canvas was too trouble-free to be real. He could see nothing wrong with the picture—it was turning out just as he had envisioned it—but the feeling that something was missing continued to grow. Wendy told him it was fantastic. Sidney said it made him think of Auden. Andrew believed them. He had never painted smoke so accurately. There was a drama to the fold of the crushed cushions. It read correctly.

Even as Andrew carried it into the Metropolitan the morning they were going to hang his show, he was uneasy. Sidney had organized the retrospective. There were several people there to help hang the paintings and adjust the lights. Sidney had asked Bob Cross to come and give his advice. The plan was to arrange the paintings in chronological order. The hanging and the lighting of the canvases went quickly at first. The paintings held their own no matter where the lights were placed, but the more recent paintings were more of a problem, at least to Andrew's eye. Andrew bickered with Bob Cross about how much light should be on the shadow painting. They took a break just before they were ready to hang the last painting Andrew had made, "Empty Places."

Bob lit a cigar. Andrew cleaned his teeth with his gold toothpick. Sidney took off his glasses and rubbed his eyes. "There's so much color in them that they strain your eye. It's wonderful how they exhaust you."

Bob put "Empty Places" on a hook. Andrew stood back and watched. It was too high. Sidney lowered it. It was too low. Sidney raised it. The lights were too bright. The lights were too soft. Andrew didn't like what he saw. He began to shout commands. He turned to the man adjusting the lights. "The glare spoils the whole thing. What the fuck are you doing?"

Sidney guessed it was the strain of getting ready for the show. "Andrew, we'll do it however you want it done."

"I just want it done right. You're lighting it as if it were a jewelry store window."

When Andrew heard the door behind him open and close, he thought it was one of Sidney's assistants or a maintenance man or a lost tourist trying to find the Lehmann wing. Andrew shouted as he turned around, "Who the fuck let you in here? Can't you read the goddamn sign? These halls are closed."

"You invited me." It was Brett Morrison.

Andrew shook his head. His words rang in his ears. His tone of voice shocked him. It was as if he had just awakened from a bad dream. "Of course, I invited you . . . I'm sorry . . . I don't know what's wrong."

"You're just tired," Sidney volunteered.

"The trial, this show, then Pyne dying the way he did. It's a terrible strain," Bob reassured him.

But it wasn't any of those things. It was this last painting, "Empty Places," that made him lash out at his friends, that was what had him on edge. It was wrong, and the awful thing was Andrew knew there was nothing he could do to fix the painting. A change in color or tone or composition wouldn't help. It was beyond that.

Brett Morrison tried to make a joke of the way Andrew had shouted at him. "My God, that was the most convincing Steven Lerner imitation I've ever seen. I was working at the Modern when Lerner had his show there. He had the staff in there past midnight adjusting the lights the night before the opening. He made two people cry."

"Your eyes look a bit wet," Bob quipped.

"It's my contact lenses."

The men laughed. The reference meant nothing to them, but it did

290

to Andrew. Wendy had told him stories about her father staring into his work for hours at a time, then turning and lashing out at anyone who happened to be near. She had told him how at the end her father would look into his darkening canvases and weep.

As Andrew stared into his most recent painting, he knew what Lerner felt. Andrew's canvases had not grown dark and brooding. They were as light and colorful as ever, but they had changed. They were copies, mere likenesses of objects and memories. Andrew did not get the same feeling from them. He didn't have adequate words to express what his paintings lacked. They looked like his old pictures. He was sure Sidney or Bob could not tell the difference, but an essence, a tension was lacking. His passion had become misplaced.

Bob pointed to "Empty Places." "Let's try just one light."

"No, it's fine the way it is," Andrew muttered.

"Are you sure?"

"Positive." Andrew turned to Sidney. "Just one thing. Could I add another painting to the exhibition?"

"Of course." Andrew was behaving peculiarly. Sidney wondered if he was sick. There was an odd flu going around. "What one were you thinking of?"

"It doesn't have a name."

As soon as Andrew left the museum he called Peter. "Do you still have that painting I started of you and Wendy?"

"Of course."

"I want to finish it."

"Why now?" Andrew had not mentioned the painting for years.

"Because I know what I was trying to say then." Andrew realized that the shift in his powers had begun years ago.

"When do you need it?"

"Right now." Andrew wanted to paint the truth of what had happened to him, of how the life had slipped from his work, before he had time to rationalize it or excuse what he had just seen in his art.

"Could I watch you finish it?"

"You saw the beginning, you might as well see the end."

"What do you mean?"

"You'll see."

They did not talk. The painting was finished except for the faces of the boy and the girl in it. Andrew worked silently and efficiently in a craftsmanlike way. He completed their faces in less than an hour.

Andrew made them twins. The boy looked a bit more like Peter. The girl's coloring was closer to Wendy's. But it was the same face. They pulled on you in the same way. He painted their features lightly. They were identifiable as the Lerner children, but there was a distinctly anonymous quality to them. They could have been anyone.

"What are you saying?" Peter asked.

Andrew put down his brush. "That it would have happened anyway."

"What do you mean?"

"That I was tired, that I was ready to be eclipsed by someone."

"Is that what my sister's done to you?"

"She didn't do it. I wanted it done. I wanted to believe in something outside of me and my art."

"Do you believe in Wendy?"

"As much as I believe in myself. . . . I should have listened to you that night. You warned me. You knew what was happening."

"I knew nothing," Peter declared.

"What do you mean?"

"I was a virgin."

"What about all those girls that summer?" Andrew asked in disbelief.

Peter laughed. "I never could go through with it. . . . I knew nothing . . . I know nothing."

"You're still a virgin?"

Peter laughed again. "Emotionally."

"Stay that way."

"I'm lonely."

"I know."

XXXIV

Simon's house was searched after his death. They found boxes of letters and private papers that had been left behind by both of her parents. None of it affected the case. Wendy sorted through the notes and photographs and lists, the bits and pieces of her parents' past that Simon had felt were worth saving. It made her feel as if she were accomplishing something.

Wendy had expected the job to be more painful. But the old photographs—those that were painfully posed to make their lives look like scenes from "Father Knows Best," as well as those that captured the confusion and hurt in her family—had faded and lost their edge. She no longer saw herself as the object or the cause of angry letters and separations. She was able to marvel at the sincerity of the notes her father had written to himself in his schoolboy scrawl —personal reminders that he pinned to the walls of his studio— "Never make same painting twice" or "Sleeping too late" or "Paintings must stand up to life, not to art." Wendy was able to laugh at Lerner's recipes for special colors—Sex Flesh Red: two Skippy peanut butter jars (regular size) of ochre, one cup of beet juice, and two tablespoons of alazarin red.

But at the bottom of a Bon Ami carton, beneath the list of ideas for paintings that he may never have made, phrases like "Sun on side of face while following blue of Yankees going around the bases three times" scratched in red crayon on the back of an old paper bag, Wendy found two slips of pink paper that made her stop. She read them twice, folded them neatly, and put them in her pocket. Then she picked up all this humanizing trash that she had spread around her and threw it in the garbage.

Wendy understood what was said on those two pink forms, but she didn't know what it meant. She let the truth ferment inside her and took a taxi uptown to return a pair of trousers that were too tight

293

in the waist for Andrew. She reread the names that were typed in the spaces for "Mother" and "Father" on one the certificates— Jennifer Ann Wells and James Jones. She wondered if "Jones" was his real name. Then she asked the cab driver if he knew what "phenylpyruvic oligophrenia" was. He said he didn't know, but he'd bet it was hereditary. She shuffled the two certificates back and forth— the one that told her the names of Miss Wells and Mr. Jones and the one that spelled out phenylpyruvic oligophrenia, the disease that had contributed to the death of Lerner's two-month-old daughter on December 22, 1952.

Wendy wasn't sure what it meant that she was adopted, that any bond between herself and her father that she might fear was only in her head.

She returned Andrew's trousers. She didn't like the color, but it was all they had in his size. As she walked down Madison Avenue, she tried to direct her attention away from the uncertainty that was welling up within her. She concentrated on the sound of her footsteps on the pavement, on the mannikins in the store windows, on the faces that passed her. Then she saw a couple that was familiar. It was a moment before she recognized Kate Rothko and her new husband. Wendy couldn't remember his name. She wondered if Kate knew what she was getting herself into. She had the urge to call out to them —to warn them . . . but of what?

The opening of "Andrew Crowley: An American Eye" was a great success. It was the biggest art event in years. "The Metropolitan's Bicentennial," people joked. The paintings that lined the walls of the twentieth-century wing were called "brilliant" and "timeless." Andrew was charged with "genius." He made one change in the way the paintings were hung. The picture of Peter and Wendy was placed so that it was both the first and the last Crowley you saw when you entered and when you left the exhibition.

Andrew enjoyed the opening and the praise much more than he thought he would be able to. Wendy looked beautiful. They had talked a great deal since Pyne had died. He explained the double portrait to her. She told him everything would be all right, and not to worry.

Wendy had planned to tell Andrew about her discovery that night. Her new-found birth certificate would be her present to him. It

294

would help them to start fresh, allow them to escape Lerner's legacy. But as she watched Andrew move through the dinner-jacketed and jeweled crowd, smiling, drink in one hand, cigar in the other, addressing everyone, examining everything except his paintings, she was suddenly reminded of that man she would always call "Father." There was no point in telling Andrew. As she ripped up her birth certificate, she knew it was just a matter of time.

The thought made her cry. Not wanting to make things any worse, she walked out of the hall. She knew now what that puzzle of blue note paper her mother left behind really meant. Her father had blamed her mother for what he thought had happened to the power in his art, not his sex

As Wendy wandered through the galleries of the museum, past Breughel, Eakins, and Gauguin, the pink shreds of paper that identified her fell through her fingers. She didn't bother to pick them up. They would be swept away in the morning.

She looked at a jade Chinese sculpture attributed to a man she'd never heard of. She glanced at a Renaissance bust by a sculptor whose name she had forgotten and marveled at an alabaster cat made by an Egyptian whose work had outlived his name. Wendy realized it was always just a matter of time. The thought was a small comfort.

XXXV

Andrew and Wendy rented the house behind the dunes in East Hampton again that summer. It was Wendy's idea to go back. The house was larger, more empty than they remembered it.

On July 8 Andrew had to be in New York to check the proofs on a series of his etchings that would be coming out in the fall. The city was still recovering from the tall ships and the big birthday. It was a terrible day. The proofs were sloppy. He told the printer to "fuck himself." He wanted to leave town before the Friday afternoon traffic for Long Island, but the new BMW he had just bought broke down on Third Avenue. He left it in the middle of the street, gave the finger to the cars honking their horns behind him, and called the BMW dealer he had just bought his car from. He told the man he was going to sue him for every penny he was worth. The dealer agreed to tow the car and fix it for free. Andrew said he was still going to sue.

The planes were all booked, and there wasn't another train to East Hampton for an hour and a half. It was too long to wait in Penn Station and not long enough to do something constructive, and so Andrew went downtown to the loft.

Andrew was sorting through the mail that had piled up when the doorbell rang. Everyone knew he was away for the summer. He wondered who it could be.

"Hello." Andrew peered out the peephole at the distorted image of a little red-haired man wearing a robin's egg blue double-knit leisure suit. The fish-eye lens of the peephole made his nose and mouth look very large.

"Is Wendy Lerner in?" the red-haired little man asked.

"No."

"Oh. Well, I've come by several times. When do you expect her?"

"In the fall." Andrew always liked to use that word instead of "autumn."

296

"It's rather important . . . who are you?" the man asked.

"Andrew Crowley."

"I could talk to you," the stranger suggested.

"About what?"

"Her father."

Andrew opened the door. "You knew Steven Lerner?"

"My name is Kelly . . . Steven Kelly. I'm a reporter."

"Any questions about the case will have to be put to the lawyers."

"Oh, this doesn't have to do with the paintings—not directly, at least."

Andrew was ready to tell him to leave. "What does it have to do with?"

"His death."

"The facts of the suicide are all on record. Wendy Lerner couldn't tell you anything more about it."

"Oh, really?"

"Listen, we're not interested . . ."

"Simon Pyne was interested." Kelly snapped.

They had had weirdos come to their door before. Men and women had arrived at all hours of the day and night whispering secret stories about Lerner or Pyne or Barclay or Luccio. You never knew which were true.

"It was an unusual case . . . the tendons in both arms were severed, cut right through." Mr. Kelly made a sawing gesture at the crook of each arm.

"I know how Lerner killed himself," Andrew insisted.

Kelly smiled at him. "Do you know anything about anatomy?"

"A little."

"Well, then, you should know a muscle cannot be flexed if the tendons are cut. If Lerner cut the tendon in his right arm and thereby made it immovable, how could he possibly cut through the tendon in his left arm . . . cut the way he was? He wouldn't have been able to grip the knife."

"Why wasn't this brought out when Lerner died?" Andrew demanded.

Andrew's mind was full of visions of blood and hands gripping a knife, but they weren't Lerner's hands. "How do you know this?"

"I told you I'm a reporter." Kelly opened his wallet and showed Andrew a press card with his picture on it. "That's me . . . I don't work for them anymore. I'm a free-lancer."

"Why are you telling me this?" Andrew demanded. Kelly shrugged his shoulders. "You're saying someone else slashed his arms . . . who?"

"I thought you and Miss Lerner might know."

"What are you going to do with this story?"

"I haven't decided." The reporter smiled. It was an ambiguous grin.

Andrew didn't know if this was an attempt at blackmail, or confession, or if the man was simply mad. Andrew didn't know what Mr. Kelly's motivation was, but he was sure he didn't want to know any more. Andrew didn't need any more unanswered questions in his life. He thought of calling the police, of threatening Kelly, of calling his lawyer, of offering the little man a bribe. Andrew didn't care what he had to do or say. He just wanted Kelly to leave.

"Well, you're really talking to the wrong person. I mean, Wendy and I are friends, but that's all. . . . I'm gay." Andrew smiled and leaned toward Kelly. The reporter stepped away nervously. "Wendy would love you to write it up. She likes that sort of publicity. I mean, look at the trial. It cost her a fortune, but it's still going on. This is just the sort of information the attorney general's looking for. I could give him your phone number." Andrew reached for a pen.

"I don't think you understand what I'm saying."

"You're telling me Lerner was murdered. . . . Wendy suspected it for a long time."

"I'll tell them what you said."

"Who?"

Kelly left without answering.

Andrew bolted the door, ran to the window and looked down the street. He watched Kelly disappear around the corner. He and what he had suggested were question marks in Andrew's mind.

Andrew sat down and tried to forget about Kelly. He told himself that the man was crazy, that he wasn't really a reporter, that he was an impersonator Barclay had sent just to upset Wendy. Another compromise offer would undoubtedly follow. In his last attempt for an out-of-court settlement Barclay had offered $1.5 million and 200 paintings.

Andrew poured himself a glass of Scotch and began rummaging through his drawers. He found the last of an old bag of grass, rolled himself a joint, inhaled deeply and began to think about murder. It was not such an impossible idea. There were many people who had a reason, who would have benefited. Barclay, Luccio, Pyne, Elderstein—all were greedy for more money and more power. They were jealous of what Lerner had taken from life. They all had reasons and opportunities. They had proven they were capable of breaking the law. It could have been one of them alone or all of them together. Andrew remembered that Pyne had called everyone at the time of Lerner's death, frantic to track down Luccio. It could have been Maggie or. . . . Andrew substituted different death scenes as if he were writing the end of a screenplay.

Maggie had told Andrew that the door had been open when she arrived. It could have been a burglar. The week before a man had been murdered in the Village. All the robber got was $2.85. Lerner's gold watch was missing and a small painting had still not been found.

The possibilities were endless. Andrew wondered why they hadn't thought of murder before. But when his mind fell upon the last, and in a way the most likely of his list of suspects, Andrew threw the glass against the wall and ran out the door.

Wendy had hated Lerner more strongly and with more reason than any of them. She had told Andrew that she had taken LSD that night. Andrew thought of all the sixties bad-trip stories. Of people tripping and freaking out on LSD, and jumping out windows because they thought they could fly or drilling holes in their best friend's head so they could see his thoughts. It was all possible.

The idea was a Pandora's box. As Andrew stood in the middle of Houston Street looking for a cab, he wished he knew something that would allow him to forget what he had learned. There were parts of his past that he would like to erase, the experiences and pieces of information that interfered with his vision for the future. For a moment Andrew actually thought of throwing himself in front of that tractor trailer truck that roared toward him.

But only life could answer his questions.

Andrew missed his train. There was a faster one leaving fifteen minutes later. Bay Shore . . . Islip . . . Great River . . . with each stop Andrew proposed then rejected a new way of coping with the question of murder. He would speak to the lawyers. They would have the body exhumed. There could be another investigation. They could use lie detectors. But as the train bounced him closer to East Hampton and to Wendy, the more pointless he realized all these ideas were. Proving that Lerner was murdered or discovering who killed him would not change anything. Enough damage had been done in the name of truth.

Andrew took a cab from the station. On the way to the beach he tried to think of what he could or should say. His stomach knotted as he stepped inside. He called. She didn't answer. He walked out onto the terrace. The tide was out. Wendy was on the beach, holding her skirt up with one hand, wading in the shallows.

For one long moment Andrew thought about leaving her. She looked up and waved. Never had Andrew had so many doubts about anyone. Never had he been so frightened. He had never had to rely so much on faith.

Wendy kissed him and took his hand. "How was your day?" she asked.

"Terrible."

"Wasn't there anything nice about it?"

"I decided that I'd like to marry you."

Andrew and Wendy spent their days lying on the beach. There were moments Andrew regretted the decision he had made, when he wondered what would happen if that little red-haired man wrote his story. But when he felt doubt closing in on him, when he felt in danger, Andrew would jump up, run, and dive into the sea, and swim very fast and hard out through the breakers. He swam with a sense of purpose, as if he were trying to save someone. In a few minutes he would return to Wendy, empty-handed and breathless, but no longer frightened of her or his need. Then she would rub him with coconut oil, and they would begin the process all over again. Andrew told Wendy that was how to get the best tan.

A week later there was an electrical storm that knocked down all the power lines. The ice cream in the refrigerator melted, but Andrew and Wendy liked not having a phone, cooking their meals over a fire, and using candles. In the morning the phone still didn't work. A telephone pole, two orange crates, and a light bulb had been tossed up on their beach. Andrew took two quick therapeutic dives by himself, then they had one long swim together. The tides were running higher than usual. There was a rip. The ocean was full of seaweed. It was hard to make it back to shore. It was just frightening enough to make it exciting.

300

Breathless, they collapsed on their towels and each other and let the sun dry them. They slept for more than an hour. Wendy woke up first. She heard rustling. It wasn't a beach sound. She didn't recognize it. Andrew's head was on her stomach. Keeping her eyes closed, she put her hands over his face. "Do you hear it?"

"Umm humm."

"What is it?"

"I don't know."

"Guess," she whispered.

"Your wings."

They opened their eyes. Someone had left their morning paper on the beach. The wind tossed the pages of the *Times* around them playfully. Andrew saw it first. He scrambled to his feet and chased after the front page as it skittered down the beach.

"What is it?" Wendy called as she ran after him.

It landed in the water. Andrew dove in after it. He had to hold it carefully or it would rip.

Wendy saw her father's face, then read the headline. "Gallery ordered to return paintings; penalty put at $16 million." It was in the center of the front page in type just as large as that allotted to the hijack victims being held for ransom in Entebbe. There was a photograph of Lerner as large as the one of Jimmy Carter, but Lerner wasn't smiling. It was an odd picture. Lerner was looking down as if he were ashamed or didn't want to be recognized.

Judge Potkin found Elderstein, Cortesi, and the "late Simon Pyne" guilty of conflict of interest. The three of them were to pay $10 million in fines. Barclay was found in contempt of court for violating the injunction. All the Lerners he owned and held on consignment were to be given back to the foundation. The court would appoint a new set of executors. Barclay's share of the fine was $6 million. The figure would vary, depending on how many of the Lerners he was able to retrieve.

Wendy and Andrew knew what a long, arduous, and perhaps impossible job it would be to track down the paintings. Simon was dead, Luccio was mad, Elderstein was eighty, and Barclay had "no attachable property." The only person who might go to jail was Christina Hansen, the registrar of the Winston Gallery. The reporter estimated the legal fees for both sides at $1 million. The figure was closer to $5 million.

It was a long article. It took up almost a fifth of the front page. It was continued on page 50, column 4, but Andrew and Wendy never found that page.

They read the article in silence. When they were finished, Andrew squinted at Wendy and announced, "You won."

"Did we?"

XXXVI

Peter picked up his *New York Times* at a newsstand. He read the cover story and the two full pages of related articles about the history of the Winston Gallery, the repercussions in the art world, and some of the transcripts from the trial. He read them all twice, but he still did not understand what had been gained.

In June Judge Potkin had finally impounded the Lerners in Winston warehouses. Those paintings, along with the fifty-seven that had been in the top of Peter's house, were now in an immense West Side warehouse waiting for new executors to be appointed. After several phone calls Peter was able to make arrangements to look at the paintings. He wanted to see what this battle was all about—he wanted to look at these paintings that had absorbed so much of so many people's lives.

The skies were clear at the beach, but they were overcast in town. As Peter walked through Central Park on his way to the warehouse, he saw an old man wearing a dirty raincoat and high black basketball sneakers staring up at an unexceptional gray sky through binoculars. The old man called to several of the people who walked ahead of Peter on the path, but none of them responded.

"You know what?" the little old man shouted.

"What?" Peter asked seriously.

The man was so startled to have someone answer that it took him a moment to give Peter his message. Holding up a tattered almanac, he shouted, "There's an eclipse going on right now, but we can't see it . . . there are too many clouds."

Peter laughed and went on his way. But what the old man said reminded Peter of something Andrew had said. "I wanted to be eclipsed." It was the right word. It was what happened to his father, too. As Peter walked across the park he thought to himself, "There must have been some way Andrew and my father have avoided giving up so much of themselves." Peter wanted to know why it is that we, who understand that the darkness is only temporary, that the moon will pass and the sun will warm us again, why can't we have such faith in ourselves, in our emotions and powers. Why do we have to sacrifice so much? Why does life become a blood rite?

Judge Potkin had put Professor Davies, the head of the NYU graduate art history program in charge of cataloguing the Lerners that remained in New York. His assistant met Peter and started to show him around the warehouse. She was a graduate student, full of herself and other people's ideas. She didn't like the way Peter was looking at his father's art. He was either too close or too far away. His comments were too specific or too vague. She left Peter alone when he told her, "You know, my father used to say you can kill a painting by looking at it the wrong way."

Peter wandered among his father's colors all afternoon. He felt the power of his father's art. He felt it more clearly when he looked at some paintings than others, but he could make no generalizations or judgments. He wasn't able to answer any of the questions that he had asked himself as he walked across the park.

There was one painting that pulled Peter back to it again and again. It was dark, dark green rimmed in black, a flow of redbrown moved across one corner of the canvas. At five o'clock when the assistant came to tell him to leave, Peter was still standing in front of that painting. "What's this one called? I've never seen it in any of the books." Peter asked her.

"It's untitled. It was the last painting your father did. They found it when they . . . when he died." The assistant blushed.

"I see." His father's own blood was in that red.

The girl walked to the painting and turned it upside down.

"What are you doing?"

"You were looking at it the wrong way."

"How do you know?"

"This is the way Professor Davies said it was meant to hang. It reads best this way," the girl insisted.

Peter twisted his head around so that he could look at the painting as he had first seen it. The light was failing. It was then, just as he was ready to leave, that he saw it. Something was written faintly across the darkening canvas. Peter had to twist his head even more to read it. The girl told him it was time to leave. She stepped toward the light switch. His father had left a message. It read, "I am a man." Peter had his answer.